NAZARETH
CHILD

A DEL SHANNON
NOVEL

NAZARETH CHILD

DARRELL JAMES

MIDNIGHT INK
WOODBURY, MINNESOTA

First Edition
First Printing, 2011

Book design by Donna Burch
Cover design by Ellen Lawson
Cover illustration: background © iStockphoto.com/Roberto A. Sanchez; black bird © iStockphoto.com/Pawel Gaul; woman © iStockphoto.com/knape

Midnight Ink, an imprint of Llewellyn Worldwide Ltd.

Library of Congress Cataloging-in-Publication Data

James, Darrell, 1946–
    Nazareth child : a Del Shannon novel / Darrell James. — 1st ed.
        p.   cm.
    ISBN 978-0-7387-2369-3
    1. Women private investigators—Fiction. 2. Missing persons—Investigation—Fiction. 3. Absentee mothers—Fiction. 4. Healers—Fiction. 5. Kentucky—Fiction. I. Title.
    PS3610.A429N39 2011
    813'.6—dc22
                                        2011009139

Midnight Ink
Llewellyn Worldwide Ltd.
2143 Wooddale Drive
Woodbury, MN 55125-2989
www.midnightinkbooks.com

Printed in the United States of America

DEDICATION

For Diana, the Goddess of my universe.

PROLOGUE

Nazareth Church, Kentucky, August 1981

By now, the church had emptied out and the followers had climbed the hill to the cemetery, doing as they'd been instructed by the young healer, Silas Rule. Gone to gather in communion and pray over their dearly departed, pay homage to God, and ask forgiveness for their loved ones' sins. Forgiveness for their own. From inside the open doorway, Ella Shannon could see her husband, Roy, up there on the hill with the others—figures silhouetted in the glow of lantern light—his head bent in supplication. A brutal August heat had entered the valley, bringing with it a stifling nighttime humidity. The church without windows—and only the open door to peer through—felt claustrophobic, and Ella had begun to question the wisdom of what she was about to do.

"You stayed," a soft voice said to her.

Ella involuntarily shifted on her feet, but remained fixed in place, her back to the sanctuary. His sudden presence in the darkness

1

behind her sent an unexpected shiver of excitement through her, touching off sparks in dark and dangerous places down low. Unwanted—but irresistible—images of impending betrayal played before her, numbing her with yearning and guilt.

"I . . . I wasn't sure I would stay," she said, her voice hesitant. "All day long and all through tonight's services, I prayed for guidance."

"You have spoken to God about this?" Silas asked, his deep voice echoing in the open space.

Ella nodded but remained fixed, her eyes still on the gathering up on the hill. She was unable to face the young healer, afraid of what she might see in his eyes, afraid of what he might see in hers. Though her back was still to him, she held a clear mental picture of him—he was powerfully magnetic, with straight, jet-black hair tied behind into a loose tail. He had a strong jaw and sinewy build. There was about Silas a powerful energy—even at the age of twenty-four—that drew both men and women to him. The deep gray eyes seemed to penetrate. Then, there were the hands—big hands—fabled to carry with them the power of God's own touch.

Ella felt stirrings that were both mystifying and unmistakable. They brought with them a warning deep within, cautioning her that she was there alone in the dark with a man who was not her husband. Now, her voice trembling, she confessed. "I lied to Roy. I told him I wasn't well. I urged him to go on to the cemetery without me. He thinks I'm home in bed."

"If you feel guilty in the eyes of God, girl, go to him. You know you can leave at any time."

Ella lowered her gaze. She clasped her hands together to still the trembling. "I didn't know what else to do. Roy, he blames himself for not being able to conceive me a child."

"And so you are barren?" the preacher asked.

Ella felt her face flush with shame. She nodded. "I've tried to reason with him, tell him that *you* are our only hope. But, he doesn't believe you are what they say you are."

"And you?" Silas inquired gently. "What is it *you* believe?"

It was not so much what Ella actually believed, she realized, as what she desperately *wanted* to believe. They had been to every doctor in central Kentucky, she and Roy, even to a specialist in Lexington. All had come to the same conclusion—there was no reason why either of them couldn't produce a child.

They had tried everything. So what was left for them to do?

The wondrous acts performed by the healer since he was a boy were the fuel of legend. Stories spread from fence-line to pillow—nodded agreements in the light of day, whispered confidences in the dark of night. *The ecstasy* came first—they all agreed—a soft, warm fire that consumed you. Then, the brilliant flash of light that left many temporarily blinded and *all* filled with a deep sense of peace.

Supplicants came from far and wide—all of them there to experience "the touch." The blind were made to see, so it had been said. The crippled were given to stand and walk. For herself, Ella had but one thought—if there was any truth to it all—she must have the healer replace the emptiness in her womb with the miracle of new life.

Still unable to look at him, she said, "I think Roy's jealous. He doesn't want another man to touch me in any way."

"So you've come to me against your husband's counsel?"

Ella nodded.

"Hoping that I might heal your womb and make you whole?"

"Yes."

Several seconds passed in silence, and Ella began to wonder if Silas had gone. Then, she felt him there, suddenly behind her, placing his hands on her arms on either side.

His sudden touch caused her to stiffen. "I'm sorry! I shouldn't have come!" Ella said, and moved to pull away.

The hands drew her back.

"I shouldn't have lied to my husband. I should join the others on the hill." Once again she moved to go, but the hands held her.

"Stay!" Silas said.

"Please, it's wrong of me to ..." Her protests trailed off as the large hands moved to her shoulders and began to knead the tender flesh at the curve of her neck. She could feel something wrongfully and wonderfully intimate in the touch. Still, she reminded herself that they were the hands of a healer—no different, really, than those of a physician.

As the healer's hands slowly worked, she could feel her body beginning to relax, her knees growing weak, and she had to tell herself ... *hold on*. Something, twisted and hard, had knotted itself inside her chest. Something she tried to swallow down, but could not dislodge. With each soothing stroke, the knot grew larger. Then, in one rending rush, it expelled itself in words. "I've wanted! ... a baby! ... so much!"

"Shush-shush-shush!" Silas silenced her. His lips had moved in close to her ear. "God speaks to you, girl. Remain still and listen."

As if in a trance, Ella heard the muted chorus of prayers drifting down from the cemetery. She could see her husband there and, at the same time, could feel Silas's breath warm against the side of her face. Tears welled up and pooled in her eyes. *Don't fight it,* she told herself. *This is the moment God has promised you. Let* Him *work* His *ways.*

Ella closed her eyes and tried to calm her breathing. Tears streamed down her cheeks. She could taste the briny wetness on her lips.

"I begged God for this moment," Ella said. "I begged Him, please, don't let the healer send me away."

"And God has heard your cries, girl," Silas said, one large hand tipping her face toward the night sky. "You see *Him* there now? *His* watchful eye?"

Ella opened her eyes to see that the moon had now appeared, a large glimmering crescent, on the horizon above the cemetery.

"He has felt your insides grow cold," Silas continued, "and *He* places *His* hands upon you now to warm them."

The hands—Silas's hands—slipped around her waist and drew her tightly against him. Ella felt the air suck out of her as waves of need—oh, God!—washed through her. A muted whimper escaped her lips.

"There! You see, Ella?" he said. "It's all inside you. Always has been. You have all the womanly spark you need to produce the seed of life."

"Please!" Ella cried. The heat inside the church was suffocating. "I . . . I can't . . ." Her protests came out in quick breathy gasps as— *God! Oh, God!*—she felt her own young body beginning to move.

"But you did," Silas whispered. His one hand kept her pinned tightly against him, while the other made a slow intimate descent downward along the front of her dress. His voice had taken on a low, seductive quality. "You are here, sweet Ella."

This time, she cried aloud. "Oh, God!"

5

"There. You see?"

Breathless, she asked, "Will I ... will I ever be with child?"

"That depends, Ella," Silas whispered, drawing her tighter against him. "How strong is your faith?"

"Stro ... strong ..." Ella managed to say. "It's strong!"

"Then give yourself over to God!" he commanded. And then, in a softer, more soothing tone, "Give yourself over to me."

The hands that pressed against her were beautiful and divine, ugly and crude—relentless in their purpose. Ella felt herself being swept away on a wave of warmth, the likes of which she'd never known. She knew, on some fading conscious level, that this power seemed somehow different from what she had expected, but she rode with it, reminding herself of the *mysterious ways* in which God was said to work.

As if hearing that very thought inside her head, Silas whispered, "The miracle is in the touch, Ella!" The hand slipped lower down her dress and lower still, stopping close to the womanly place that only her husband had ever touched.

"No! Don't!" Ella said, grabbing suddenly at the hand to fight it back.

"Don't deny the will of God," Silas warned, as his hand resolutely held fast.

"*Please!*" Ella said, her protest weakening, the words coming out with less and less conviction.

Then Silas provided the final argument. "It will be a girl," he whispered. "God has revealed this to me."

Ella's protests ceased. She hesitated, only a second more, then moved her hand down to undo one of the buttons of her dress, giving access to the hand, which immediately slipped inside. She let her head fall back against Silas's shoulder. *A girl!* she thought, a fever-dream overtaking her. She would name her daughter *Del,* Ella told herself. *Del!* The name struck a musical note inside her ear.

Ella lifted her eyes to the hillside. She could see her husband, Roy, a shadowy figure among figures beneath the moon. This was a man she dearly loved and respected. Was she doing it all for him? *She could tell herself that.* For their marriage? For their unborn child? But what about the white-hot miracle fire that was spreading through her loins, the gathering insistence of her hips, moving in synchronous rhythm with the hand? The response from her body was too lascivious and selfish to be called *divine.*

With a long, guttural moan, Ella gave herself over to the healer's work—work that she knew had only just begun. She pushed feelings of guilt down, farther down, out of reach, and fixed her mind on the child that was yet to be. *A daughter—Del.*

What would she be like? Would she be pretty? Would she learn to dance?

The moon in the sky seemed to wink a reply—it had already come to an answer.

ONE
Somewhere near Benson,
Arizona, thirty years later…

THIS NIGHT, SHE HAD come for the fugitive Ruben Vazquez. The tiny house trailer, which sat at the river's edge at the end of a long gravel drive, seemed a fitting end to the chase. Inside could be heard the whistling shush of desert wind through the cottonwood trees, the nails-on-chalkboard screech of limbs against aluminum siding, the steady *drip-drip-drip* of the kitchen faucet. All of it—the sounds—served to mark time.

Del Shannon sat alone in the dark, her back to the wall, facing the door. The waiting was always the hard part, but that was behind her now. Somewhere off, a dog had begun to bark. An owl, roosting in the tree outside, suddenly shrieked a hellish lament and flapped off into the night. Footsteps could be heard crunching down the loose gravel drive. Now boot-scuffs coming onto the metal porch…

Ruben had arrived.

He came in the way she'd imagined—drunk and stumbling in the dark. She could see his outline framed in the doorway, a dark silhouette against the dim porch light outside. She saw him reach for the light switch, toggle it, and get nothing.

Del waited, then said, "Ruben!"

"Sancia?" Ruben inquired into darkness. "Is that you? Why you sitting in the dark?"

The fugitive had been on the loose for three months from the Arizona state prison complex in Florence. *America's Most Wanted*, detailing the man and offering a $25,000 reward, had warned that he would be armed and dangerous. The show's host, John Walsh, urged the viewing public, "If you see this man, do not approach him, but call our tip line at…"

Even Sancia Vega, the fugitive's girlfriend, knowing all too well Ruben's temperament, had been eager to flee the cramped trailer to get out from under the abusive little man. She had gathered her bag without hesitation and spun her tires on the highway, beating a hasty retreat for her sister's house in Douglas.

Del gave no response to Ruben's query. Instead, she let silence and the continuing drip of the kitchen faucet worry the fugitive's thoughts. A second passed, then Ruben took a tentative step inside.

It would be going through his mind, this fugitive from justice, that there was maybe something wrong with the voice—different from his girlfriend Sancia's. Del waited until he was fully inside the room, then flicked her flashlight on and stuck the beam squarely in Ruben's face. She saw his expression go wide, watched him take a step backward and stumble against the coffee table.

"Sancia's gone, Ruben," Del said. "She said to tell you she'll see you in twenty-five years to life."

Ruben straightened. He was shielding his eyes, trying to peer past the beam. "Is that right? You a frien' of Sancia?"

"My name is Del Shannon. I've come to take you back to ASPC Florence."

"How'd you find me?"

"Fugitives are like swallows, Ruben. They always return to the nest."

"You're not a cop," Ruben said, an inquisitive tone to his voice. "They come through the door with a SWAT team. You must be a bounty hunter, or maybe some kind of private police."

"It doesn't matter," Del said. "Either way, you're going back with me."

Del could see him considering, reasoning the situation in his mind. Ruben gave it a moment more, then said, "Okay, but you sound like you could be pretty. First, let me see you."

From darkness, Del tossed a string of shackles. They hit the floor in front of Ruben—the sound of chains on linoleum—skidding to rest at his feet.

"Put those on and I'll give you a look," she said.

With the seven-day-old taste of freedom still in his mouth, Ruben glanced at the chains on the floor. Del could see his mind working, considering. After a moment he said, "What if I don't want to see you so bad?"

"Then I'll put a bullet in you and take you back across the hood of my Jeep."

Ruben's eyes narrowed in the beam of light. "You could be bluffing."

"Ruben," Del said, pacing her words for emphasis, "before you misjudge my commitment, there's something you should know about me."

"What's that?"

Del moved the flashlight back to let the beam of light slide down the length of the barrel, the nine-millimeter Baby Eagle trained on Ruben's middle.

She said, "I never bluff."

By ten o'clock that evening, Ruben Vazquez was in the hands of Cochise County authorities. By morning, Del Shannon was back in the office and ready for her next assignment.

———

"YOU see the news last night?"

Randall Willingham had come out of his glass-enclosed office, carrying a file folder, and into the open bullpen area, where Del was rummaging through clutter on her desk. She'd arrived sometime after him. It was seven-thirty a.m., the business not yet officially open for the day. Patti, the receptionist, wouldn't arrive until nine, and Rudy Lawson and James "Willard" Hoffman, his other two field investigators, were both out on assignments. Just the two of them there. Randall watched Del sift through a mountain of Post-it notes and scraps of paper where she'd left messages to herself.

"I was tired," Del said distractedly, still sorting through the clutter. "I got a room in Benson and got some sleep."

"*Breaking news,* what they were calling it," Randall continued.

"That right?"

"Mentioned your name."

"Uh-huh," she said, still involved with whatever it was she was searching for.

Randall said, "I've got a missing persons ... real estate developer ... probably turn up in Cabo on the beach with his mistress ... not much of a challenge ... you want it?"

"Whatever," Del said.

Randall watched her sifting the debris. When his patience finally ran out, he said, "Christ, girl! What the hell are you looking for?"

"My messages, Randall. My goddamn messages!"

"I guess you mean this message?" Randall fished inside his shirt pocket and came out with a yellow Post-it. He held it up between two fingers.

"You had it all along? Why'd you let me fuss if you knew what I was looking for?"

"Maybe I was hoping you'd clear off some of that clutter while you were at it."

"When'd you take it?" she asked, crossing to snatch the note from him.

"Last night, around seven. I tried your cell phone, but you didn't answer."

"I was a little busy. Did the caller say anything?"

"Just to tell you he called. You know I don't get involved in your personal stuff."

"Yeah, right," she grumbled, returning to her desk.

Randall watched her slide fluidly into the chair. *My ... she was adorable, this kid.*

———

RANDALL'S first impression of Del—this was two years ago—was that she was maybe a dancer from one of the clubs. She was slender in tight-fitting jeans and sandals, a halter top snugged down to a flat, bare midriff. She had a small gold ring pierced into her navel and a tiny, yellow crescent moon tattooed on the outside of her left wrist.

She had attitude, this girl.

What threw him, though, was the hair. It was cropped short like a boy's. A blonde sprig of it had fallen across her eyes—that day she walked out of the elevator and into his office. "I want this job," she announced, dropping a folded newspaper in front of him, his own classified ad circled in red.

Randall—owner of Desert Sands Covert in Tucson—turned the paper so he could see the words he'd composed. "It says I'm looking for a field investigator. I haven't run the one for a receptionist yet."

"That's right. That's the job I want."

Randall looked her over. She was just shy of being skinny, but he liked her directness, the way she looked right at him as she waited for a response. He leaned back and propped one foot up on his desk.

"Got any experience?"

"No. But I've got my own equipment. Cuffs, vest. I'm licensed to carry, and I'm bondable."

"You've been gettin' ready, have you?"

The young woman said nothing.

"You understand what we do here?" It was more of a statement than a question.

"Your yellow-pages ad says, 'Missing Persons.'"

"Tell me what else it says."

She studied him for a moment. "It's the 'Missing Persons' part I'm interested in."

"Sweetheart, it's not a menu. It says we also do investigative infiltrations, hostage and fugitive recovery. Finding the missing person is one thing. Recovery, well, that can be a whole other story. It's not a job for the uninitiated."

"You mean it's not a job for a girl," she countered, staring him down.

Randall gave her a frown. It was all he needed this early in the morning—a lecture in EEO requirements. He said, "Just what is it you're looking for?"

"Your job ad says entry level. I'm willing to learn."

Randall studied her more closely. There was something else going on with this girl, something she wasn't telling him. He could see it in the pain she carried behind her eyes, pain she thought she was covering up. He knew he should tell her, *Go home, child! Come back when you've put a little more meat on your bones . . .*

But, then, she did have a point. A really good undercover investigator was hard to find. The work took a special talent for inventiveness and guile. You had to be tough and intuitive, with an innate knack for being able to handle yourself in different situations. You might need to mix in on the street one night, then pull an appearance at the Governor's Ball the next.

Rudy and Willard seemed to have this talent and had done well. But their caseload had become more than they could handle, which had led him to run the ad.

After seventeen years in the business, on top of twenty-two years in Naval intelligence, Randall was getting too old to be doing field work himself. So he'd decided to look for someone at the entry level—someone young and willing to take risks, someone he could train.

Randall knew he'd probably regret it, but the lost-girl look in her eyes was getting to him. He dropped his foot off the desk and leaned in on his elbows. "All right. I'm not saying this is a commitment. But take the first folder on top." He gestured to a stack of case folders on the cabinet next to her. "The guy's name is Carl Ray Ellis. He abandoned his wife and five kids. The wife has given us a retainer to find him. I want you to study the file, then come back tomorrow and tell me how you'd go about gettin' him."

"A deadbeat dad?" she asked, disappointment in her voice.

"What? You were expecting a kidnapped heiress? I haven't hired you yet, sweetheart. I just want to get a feel for how you think. That's all."

The young woman examined him a moment, distrustful, then took down the folder and thumbed through it idly. "All right," she said. "Anything else?"

Randall looked her over. "You might want to consider the way you're dressed."

She gave him a long look, nodded, then spun out the door and into the hall.

Randall watched her through the glass double-doors as she waited for the elevator to arrive. When it did, he gave it a twenty-count, then rose and crossed to the window. A minute later she appeared below, dodged traffic to cross the street, and climbed into a red Jeep Wrangler parked at the curb, mounting it like it was a horse tied to the rail.

Four hours later she was back—Christ!—emerging from the elevator pushing Carl Ray Ellis ahead of her. They were both looking a little roughed up, like the two of them had taken a fall from a horse together. Carl Ray—a tall, suit-rumpled used car salesman—was cuffed and looking embarrassed.

That had been Del Shannon's first day on the job.

———

THIS morning, she was wearing boots and jeans, with a crisp white blouse tucked in at the waist. The little moon—tattooed on her wrist—barely showed beneath her watchband. The abandoned-child look that had gotten to him that first day had been replaced by an air of confidence. She was twenty-nine-going-on-beautiful now, and after two years on his staff, she was rapidly becoming one of the best field investigators in the business.

Randall watched as she punched the numbers into the phone, biting her lip and scratching the moon tattoo on her wrist as she waited for someone to answer.

Into the phone, Del said, "Mr. Patterson? I'm Del Shannon... Yes, I did leave a message."

Randall moved to the window and looked out, giving her the illusion of privacy. On the street below, pedestrians were passing on the sidewalk—county employees heading into the Pima County Superior Court building across the street, and professionals filling the law offices nearby—the Tucson, workaday world. He heard Del say, "...I'm calling about your wife, Georgia."

Randall was hoping, along with her, that this would be the call. The one that said, *"Why, yes, I had a daughter named Del. Oh, my God, I don't believe it's my baby!"*

He wasn't holding his breath.

The irony was that she had become incredibly good at finding people. But the one person she'd never been able to find was the mother she'd never known. Internet searches, exhaustive phone calls ... how long had she been searching? Growing up, never knowing her mother, spending all her free time following dead-end leads. And Roy Shannon, her father, refusing to tell her anything about her mother, the bitter bastard too deep in the bottle to give a shit. Randall felt a sympathetic pang just listening to her now.

He heard the receiver drop back into its cradle and turned as Del rocked back in her chair.

"Any luck, sweetheart?" He had to ask, already knowing the answer from the look on her face.

Del shook her head. "Mrs. Georgia Patterson ... turns out to be eighty-four years old. She wasn't born a Shannon, was never married to a Shannon, never sat next to one on a bus."

Randall counted to three, knowing what was coming next. *One ... two ...*

"Je-sus, shit!" Del said on cue, slamming her fist down hard on the desk.

Randall had come to learn that she could hold onto her anger for a long time. The price she paid was a take-no-prisoners attitude towards everyone, including him. But he'd quickly discovered that beneath her tough exterior was a deep yearning for acceptance and affection, little of which she got from her father, Roy.

But since the first day she'd shown up and—let's face it—won him over for the job, the two of them had bonded like father and daughter. He'd discovered that once you gained her trust, you had an ally for life. He and Del treasured a mutual respect that allowed for her fits of temper. Usually, she cooled off quickly after her explosions, and sometimes, though rarely, she even apologized afterward. This time she was sitting thoughtfully, drumming her fingers on the desk.

Randall gave her time to let her blood pressure settle. After a minute, he got up, crossed to the coffee pot, poured a cup, and handed it to her.

"Maybe you should pay a visit to the cemetery, talk to Louise," he said, after she'd taken a sip. "It used to make you feel better."

"Thanks for the fatherly advice," Del said. "But I don't have time for it."

Randall moved to one of the other desks, tossing the file folder he still carried on top. He took a seat and propped his feet up. He'd been holding off saying what he was really thinking, but decided to jump in anyway.

"Del, maybe this thing with your mother … maybe it's something you should just forget about. It's obvious that …"

"That, what?" Del exploded. "Obvious that she abandoned me? That my father is so bitter and filled with poison that he won't even tell me her goddamn name? Is that what's obvious!"

"I was going to say, it's obvious that it's having a bad effect on you. I don't like to see you unhappy is all."

Her eyes were drawn to his, and the clamp in her jaw loosened a little. "Look, I appreciate your concern, Randall, you know I do. It's just … well … I can't help believing that if my mother is alive, then there's a reason why she isn't here in my life. A good reason. I just want to know what that reason is, and then I can move on."

Randall wanted to say, "*C'mon, kiddo, mothers give up their children every day. It's nothing new.*" But he didn't. Instead, he said, "Okay, honey, have it your way. I guess I just hope when you do find her, it'll be all you hoped it to be."

An awkward silence lay between them now. After a moment, he recovered the file folder from the desk. "So, the missing real estate developer... you want it?"

Del rose and came to take the file. She parked one cheek on the corner of his desk, sipping the coffee as she thumbed the report. "All right," she said, "I guess I could use an easy one for a change."

"Your daddy going to be okay with you going out again so soon?"

"He'll just have to live with it, won't he."

"Well, just call me if you need anything, okay?"

"I will," Del said, setting her cup aside before she slid off the desk and headed for the door.

Randall watched her go—out past the reception area, through the glass doors, and into the hall. He watched as she punched the button to hurry the elevator—impatient, high-strung, and so damned young.

"She will..." Randall told himself. "Like that time with Carl Ray."

TWO

FALCONET TOOK A FLIGHT from Newark to Cincinnati, found himself in Kentucky where the airport was, then drove a rental car back north, twelve miles, across the Ohio River to the city. He hated being reassigned, hated that it was to yet another location, hated reporting in to someone who considered himself better than he was. And he truly hated having to sit around this little lobby outside the office waiting to be called, like he was applying for a job.

But most of all, Falconet hated having to deal with other agencies within the Department of Justice, like these tight-ass FBI guys. He was ATFE—Alcohol, Tobacco, Firearms, and now Explosives—the latter having been added to the title right after 9/11. As though things that went *boom* hadn't been a part of it all along.

Falconet turned his thoughts to the events of the past month. His last assignment had nearly cost him his life. He'd spent nine days in the hospital, followed by five weeks convalescing at home.

While he wasn't one for sitting around the house, he had to admit, the break had given him time to think about his job.

There was the travel … you could get tired of that pretty quick. There were the places you wound up living undercover … all kinds of fucking places. A week here, a month there, sleeping alone all that time … or so he told his wife, Jolana.

Then there was his daughter, Stacy, back in Cliffside Park, New Jersey. She was turning fourteen, and already the little hard-ons were lining up outside the house. Who would meet the little pricks at the door? Jolana? She was too busy banging some other dude to give a damn.

So, he'd been thinking … maybe it was time to consider another line of work. Something, anything. He could find a gig where he could just go home at night and at least sleep in his own bed and eat food from his own refrigerator. He was tired … or maybe he was just fed up. Either way, he wasn't real happy to be here.

"Agent Falconet, you can go in now."

He rose, feeling the residual pain in his side—the scar where the bullet had ripped away muscle and nerve—and gingerly crossed to the wide double doors to let himself inside.

"Sir?" Falconet said, from the entrance, closing the door behind him.

They were eighteen floors up in the Federal Building, and the man behind the desk was George Wallace Racine, Agent-in-Charge. Racine's attention was currently occupied with a folder he had spread open in his lap. "Have a seat," he said, gesturing to a chair without looking up.

Falconet crossed inside and was now aware of another person in the room—a black man, elegantly dressed in a Cavalli suit. He had been standing off to the side behind the door near the book-shelf, thumbing the pages of a law book. Now he folded it shut and came forward.

"Frank, I'm Special Agent Darius Lemon," the man said, offering his hand.

His speech was mannered; his movements poised; his eyes watchful. He was maybe fifteen years older than Falconet, putting him in his early-to-mid-fifties, and reminded Falconet of Morgan Freeman, the actor.

Seeing the man made Falconet conscious of his own appearance—a worn leather jacket over a T-shirt and jeans. He had combed his hair, more or less, slicking his black waves back with his fingers while they were still damp from the shower, letting the ends curl upward at the back of his neck. And maybe he should have reminded himself to shave. But then, hell, he was who he was. Frank Falconet—Irish-Italian and proud of it—the son of a Dublin lassie and a Milano stonemason whose immigrant grandfather had shortened the family name from Falconetti when he first stepped off the boat.

Falconet gave Darius a nod, then slumped into one of the seats across the desk from Racine. Darius took the seat next to him.

"You're with ATF," Racine said, lifting his eyes to look at him now. "How long have you been with the department?"

"Fifteen years and some," Falconet said.

"Any field experience?"

"Is there any other kind?"

Racine gave him a dead-eyed look that said, *Don't mess with me, Junior.*

Falconet relented and added, "I've worked undercover for most of the past twelve years."

"Most recent assignment?"

"Miami waterfront, special task force ... Look, it must say that in my file. Am I in some kind of trouble?"

Racine turned his gaze to Darius Lemon. "You know, it's the first thing they all ask when they come into this office. Why is that?" Racine turned back to Falconet. "Actually, you're being assigned to the Bureau on loan."

Translation, I've just been given a shit job, Falconet thought bitterly. Go to work for the FBI and what you got were a bunch of college boys in Ray-Bans who didn't smoke, drink, or fuck. He said, "I thought I was on disability leave."

"You look pretty healthy to me," Racine said. "The doctors have written up your release. Are you telling me you're not fit for duty?"

"No, it's just ... well ... I thought I'd have more time at home, more time to ..." Falconet gestured with his hands. He didn't bother to explain.

Racine studied him for a moment, then pushed the file folder aside. Rising from his swivel chair, he turned to the large window behind him and stood there, peering out. He was tall and solid, dressed in a dark suit and burgundy tie. His hair was thick and graying. From the back, his shoulders suggested a once powerful build. *Probably played football in college*, Falconet thought.

Racine motioned him over, and Falconet rose and crossed to stand beside him. Darius Lemon followed.

"Tell me, what's wrong with this picture?" Racine said, gesturing beyond the window. There was a breathtaking view of the Ohio

River where it snaked past the city. There were riverfront condos, a stadium, a sports arena, and bridges—a number of them—crossing to the other side, where rising green hills took over.

"I give up," Falconet said. He'd seen trees before. "There's a problem?"

"My point exactly," Racine said. "That's Kentucky over there, the Bluegrass State. Thoroughbreds ... rolling hills ... some beautiful women there. What could possibly be wrong with Kentucky?"

Falconet watched the tugs working the barges along the river, probing the scene for something that didn't fit.

"You ever hear of a man named Silas Rule?" Racine asked.

Falconet shook his head.

"He's this ... I guess you could say ... religious leader. A healer." Racine shot Falconet a wry look. "Lives in a town called Nazareth Church. Well, not so much a town really, as a spot on the map. Darius here has had it under surveillance for awhile now, and he can tell you more about it."

Taking the cue, Darius stepped closer. "Place ... community—I don't know, whatever you care to call it. This leader, Silas Rule, is something of an enigma. He began speaking in tongues at the age of five, doing faith healing by the age of ten. Does that laying-on-of-hands thing. He's about fifty-four years old now."

"Silas Rule ..." Falconet said, trying the name on for size.

Darius nodded. "Good old Silas conducts traveling revivals throughout a three-state area, and he lives off contributions to his cause."

Falconet turned to Racine. "What I'm hearing is, he's a *showman*, a charismatic."

Racine said, "I think you're getting the picture. People meet this healer just once, and suddenly they're moved by God to turn over everything they own, hoping he can cure whatever ails them."

"So? People do worse," Falconet said, shrugging. "We can't arrest every guy who's got a pitch."

Racine gave him a stern look.

"I'm just sayin'," Falconet said. "Having a following, maybe it's not a crime."

"The thing is, we've had complaints, Frank," Darius interjected. "People sell off all their worldly possessions and move to Nazareth Church. You can see how family and friends might become concerned."

Falconet turned his gaze out beyond the blue-green hills to the horizon south. He'd just returned from an assignment, living in a one-room shithole near the docks for more than six months— his wife, Jolana, cold and distant when he returned, divorce papers awaiting his signature. He could see where this was headed. "So, you want to put a guy down there to investigate?"

Darius said, "Actually, we sent a guy down to Biden, the closest nearby town, just to observe. Special Agent Daniel Cole."

"And?"

"And we haven't heard from Danny in more than six weeks."

Falconet turned his gaze on the older man.

"It was poor judgment on the Bureau's part," Racine added. "These Nazareth Church people, they can be extremely clannish, suspicious, maybe even outwardly hostile to outsiders. Special Agent Cole had previously endured a very difficult personal tragedy."

"So, you put him down there knowing he was strung out?"

"He'd had more than six months to recover, Frank," Darius said. "On the one hand, we didn't expect the assignment to come with a great deal of risk. On the other, the Bureau psychologist said it was time, even best, for Danny to finally get back to work. We honestly thought he'd gotten past his grief. Perhaps we were wrong. But it's just one of the reasons why the landscape of this thing is so ambiguous. Danny may have come to harm. Or he may have just dropped his clothes alongside the tracks and walked off. We don't know."

"Either way," Racine said, "we need to dig into this clan and find out what they're all about."

"But you wouldn't mind finding Daniel Cole inside Nazareth Church eating cookies. Makes it easier than admitting your mistake." Falconet locked eyes with Racine, waiting for some reaction.

Racine held his gaze with the dead-level calm of a man who was accustomed to confrontation. Then, he retrieved a manila envelope from his drawer and tossed it across the desk.

Falconet fielded it and hefted it one time. "Homework?"

"There's a house in Nazareth Church," Racine said. "The recorded owner of the property lives in Tucson, Arizona. We want to get you into that house, undercover, inside the community."

Falconet could feel his skepticism showing. "Right. You want an Irish-Italian guy from *Brooklyn* to move to Mayberry R.F.D. and blend with the locals? You gotta be fucking kidding me. I'd stick out like a meatball in a bowl of Rice Krispies. What's the rest of it?"

"He's smart," Racine said, sharing a look with Darius. "I can see why you asked for him." A sly smile appeared at the corner of Racine's mouth.

"What?"

It was Darius who responded. He said, "I'm sorry, Frank, did we neglect to tell you? We want you to get married."

———

FALCONET took the elevator down to the parking garage and climbed behind the wheel of his rental car. Sitting there, he scanned the reports and the other items in the envelope and learned that the abandoned house was owned by one Roy Shannon. And that he had a twenty-nine-year-old daughter, Del, employed by a Randall Willingham of Desert Sands Covert, a specialized investigative agency. *Give me a break*, Falconet thought.

Then he came to the photo.

It was a clipping copied from a Tucson newspaper, showing this Del Shannon escorting a guy in a rumpled suit through the halls of the courthouse. The caption read: *Local Female Returns Deadbeat Dad to Justice.* The lens captured the two in a narrow hallway—the deadbeat in cuffs; Del Shannon, in tight jeans, boots, and aviator sunglasses. The photocopy was grainy. Still, the image of this young woman—the *idea* of her—gave Falconet a stir. He abandoned the reports in favor of studying the woman and concentrating on the way the jeans clung to the curve of her hips. He let out a low whistle.

The shit job had just gotten more interesting.

THREE

THE LADY INVESTIGATOR HAD made the local newspapers again. This time with a photo showing Del Shannon handing Ruben Vazquez off to deputies at the entrance to the Cochise County Sheriff's office.

Falconet sat in the driver's seat with the newspaper spread open across the steering wheel. It was Wednesday afternoon, and the flight had just brought them in from Cincinnati.

"'They Can Run But Not Hide,'" Falconet recited aloud, shaking his head in disbelief. "She's like some kind of rock star, this girl."

Darius briefly glanced at the photo across the top of his reading glasses. "Aren't you the lucky man?" he grinned.

They were in the car, windows rolled up, air conditioning running. *Jesus! Tucson, Arizona,* the temperature a hundred and three degrees in the shade. It was ten times hotter, Falconet believed, sitting here in the sun. Darius was in the passenger seat, sketchpad and charcoal in hand, sketching desert landscapes from the scene before

28

them. He had his suit coat off, and had thrown it across the back seat. His tie was loosened against the heat.

Falconet was in jeans, his black T-shirt soaked with sweat below the armpits and down the middle of his back. Across the road from them, back amid scrub mesquite and palo verde trees, sat a sand-colored, territorial-style house with a flat roof. The paint and stucco were chipped and peeling, and untended flower beds ran the length of the house along either side of the front porch. A few straggly perennials were dried and lifeless.

They had called ahead from the airport and a man had answered, but when they'd asked for Roy Shannon, the man had hung up. Then, they'd tried the direct approach and gone to the house, where a Hispanic woman answered through a crack in the door and told them, "Nobody home."

"I just spoke to the man of the house less than thirty minutes ago," Falconet told her. He could hear someone rummaging in the background.

"He's not feeling so good."

Falconet surveyed the yard, the burnt-out patch of grass, the two cars pulled off the side of the drive. He said, "Who do the cars belong to?"

"The Impala," the woman said. "It belong to *el papi loco*, the man of the house. The Tercel, she is mine."

"But Roy Shannon does live here." It was more of a statement than a question.

The woman didn't answer.

"What about Del Shannon, Mr. Shannon's daughter?" Darius said. "Is she here?"

"No," the woman said through the crack, "Just sometimes, when she's not someplace else."

It was like pulling teeth.

Falconet said, "Do you know when she'll be back?"

The woman shrugged. "Today. Tomorrow. How should I know? I'm only the part-time daddy-sitter. Like today, when Missy is gone."

So they returned to the car to wait.

"Why do you do that?" Falconet asked Darius, watching the black-and-white rendering of the desert landscape take form.

"It calms me. Besides, there's beauty out there. Don't you see it?"

Falconet tried, but didn't see. The trees were scrawny, the plants had thorns, the grass was burnt to shit by the sun. "I just don't see why it's got to be so fucking hot."

Darius looked up from his sketchpad. "You nervous about meeting her?"

"Nervous? Not unless you're telling me she's gained fifty pounds since the photo. I wonder, though, if she might be a dyke. You see the short hair?"

Darius gave him an all-knowing, paternal smile and continued sketching. Falconet turned his gaze back toward the house.

On the flight out, Falconet had learned that Darius was raised in El Segundo, California. He'd gone to college at Cal State Long Beach and had received his Masters in Law Enforcement at UCLA. He had a younger brother, a cop with the LAPD, named Julius. Darius liked art and theater and classical music and wine with his dinner.

It was a world away from Brooklyn, where Falconet had grown up drinking beer, eating his meals over the sink, and getting blow jobs in the front seat of his Chevy—not necessarily in that order.

He'd finished at community college. And Billy Joel was there, at least in voice, when he married Jolana a year later.

Darius was FBI; Falconet was ATF. Now, fate and the Department of Justice had brought the two of them together in the front seat of their rented four-wheel oven. The sun seemed to have gotten hotter.

"How long you figure we'll have to wait?" Falconet asked.

Darius continued to sketch. "I don't know. What time is happy hour at the Hilton?"

"Fucking now, as far as I'm concerned."

Darius made a couple of quick freehand strokes. "Be brave. Let's give it another hour. What do you say?"

Be brave. Falconet turned his gaze on the older man, watching him calmly apply charcoal to the landscape. *Look who's talking*, he thought, *the man who doesn't sweat*.

———

IT was past four in the afternoon when a Jeep Wrangler with a good-looking blonde behind the wheel passed them on the road and turned into the driveway. Falconet nudged Darius, who had dozed off behind his glasses. Darius straightened in his seat, and the two men watched as she parked the Wrangler in front of the door and slid out.

She wore boots and jeans and a billowy white blouse. She seemed to pose there a moment, looking off, her hip jutting, before crossing around the back to gather her things. It reminded Falconet of a billboard advertisement—*You've come a long way, baby!* He nodded approval.

"Now that is one attractive young wife you have there," Darius said.

"She could let the hair grow out," Falconet murmured, but he liked what he saw. There was no doubt about that.

"Yes, but put her in an evening gown and it doesn't matter, you see what I mean?"

Falconet could see it. She was basically classy enough to go either way. "You ready?" he asked, evening gowns aside.

"Let's give her a few minutes to settle in."

"Maybe slip into something more comfortable," Falconet added.

They were guys, years and worlds apart, but on the same page when it came to women. And happy, now, both of them, that they hadn't taken office jobs.

Falconet checked his hair in the mirror, and Darius checked the crease in his slacks.

Then both sat back to wait some more.

———

DEL was already feeling strung out as she came in through the front door. There was a thrill to chasing and being chased. A high like no other. But in downtimes, between the adrenaline-fired rushes, there came a kind of postpartum depression that could last for days. Cops knew the feeling. Maybe soldiers did, too. The assignment to find the missing real-estate developer had turned out to be a bust. As Randall had predicted, the lowlife had turned up, without incident, a state away, with a second wife and two kids. It had been far too long since she'd had her last fix of excitement.

What she wanted, more than anything, was to slip into a hot bath and let the warmth of it relax the knot that had gathered like a fist at the base of her neck. She wanted time to think, or maybe not think, as she decided. But that wouldn't happen, she knew. Not with Roy Shannon in the house.

Del dropped her work duffle near the door, unclipped the holster from her belt, and laid the Baby Eagle, along with her watch, on a console table in the hall. She glanced at the mail that lay there and considered opening it, but just then Engracia Lopez appeared in the hallway.

"Shhhh!" she said, a finger to her lips. "He's asleep. *Madre mía*, whatever you do, don't wake him."

"Has he been a problem?" Del asked, dreading the answer.

"Only when he drinks," the housekeeper said. "Which is always. He keeps calling me a 'wetback whore,' like I just swam across the Rio Grande this very day. Does that make any sense? I don't know even how to swim."

"He doesn't know what he's saying when he gets like that, Engracia. You can't take it personal."

"I think he knows exactly. He keeps asking me to take off my blouse."

"I'm sorry. Look, can you stay for dinner? I'll order something in."

Engracia waved the idea off and turned back into the house. "I'm going home to soak my feet."

She was gathering her things by the time Del entered the living area. Her father lay stretched in a recliner, his eyes closed, his breathing heavy. He had a glass still clutched in his hand, an inch of bourbon left over.

Bitter old fool, Del thought, blaming his absent wife for his woes in life, and using alcohol to blur the memories. He was fifty-six years old, but looked seventy. Lately, it seemed his mind wasn't altogether clear.

Del crossed to her father's recliner. She relieved him of the glass and started toward the kitchen.

From the chair, Roy Shannon opened one eye and said, "You finally decide to come draggin' home? I heard you caught up to that Vazquez guy four days ago."

Del set the glass on the TV stand. She didn't want to tell her father that she often avoided coming home. She said to him, "I had another case to look into."

"Humph!" Roy scoffed. "And what else were you doin'?"

Del didn't respond.

He gave her a sharp look. "That my drink?"

"I think you've had enough, Roy. Why don't you give it a rest for a while."

He rocked out of his chair and went off into the kitchen to pour another.

Del took a long deep breath, held it momentarily, then blew it out.

Engracia, holding her large canvas tote bag, was turning to go. Del said, "I really appreciate your help." Then, as a second thought, said, "Hey, Engracia, how long has that car been sitting across the road?"

The question halted the daddy-sitter in the hallway. "Oh, *sí*. Two men, they come to see your father. Or maybe I think they come to see you. They are with the police."

"Police?"

It brought to Del's mind the thing with Shawn Willis, a drug pusher who'd failed to appear on a $10,000 bond. Randall had sent her to bring him back, but Willis had resisted. And Del had ended up laying fourteen inches of retractable steel club against his head.

She'd delivered him in a daze to Tucson authorities and soon received notice of an improper arrest hearing from the lawyers. There was nothing improper about it, but the notice had come last week announcing a hearing scheduled ten days from now.

Del nodded, and Engracia Lopez made her way to the front door and out into the heat.

———

THE knock came as Del was unpacking her bags and came again as she reached the door. There were two of them. One, a Caucasian guy, was in his late thirties—rugged build, wavy hair, dark complexion. Italian maybe. *Not bad.* The other was an older African-American gentleman, elegant and poised in his tan suit and tie. He was carrying a briefcase and led the introductions.

"Ms. Shannon? I'm Special Agent Darius Lemon," he said, "and this is…"

"Frank Falconet," the other one interjected, giving her a smile and showing his teeth.

"My housekeeper said you were cops. You look and sound more like Feds," Del answered, giving each a once-over.

The older one withdrew credentials, handed them to her, and waited as she looked them over and handed them back.

"FBI?"

"Yes, ma'am, I am. Agent Falconet is with the Bureau of Alcohol, Tobacco and Firearms, on loan to us."

"ATF?" Del said.

The older man nodded.

"And 'E,'" Falconet added. "You know … explosives."

"Who the hell is it now!" Roy Shannon suddenly called from inside the house. "Tell 'em we already found religion and didn't like what we found!"

"They're not from the church, Roy," Del shot back.

"Well, we don't need the Sunday paper either."

"That's my father," Del explained to the men at the door.

"I think I've already had the pleasure on the phone," Darius said.

Del opened the door wide for them. "Is this about the arrest complaint?"

The two men gave each other a questioning look. "Arrest complaint?"

"No?" Del said. "Then it must be about the bodies buried in the backyard. Come on in."

She led them in and down the hall to the living room, where her father was back in his recliner.

"Roy, these two gentlemen are with the Justice Department."

"What do they want?" Roy said.

"I'm sure we'll find out. Just be nice, okay? I'm sorry," Del said, gesturing to the sofa. "Have a seat."

When they were settled, Del said, "Can I get either of you a drink? Maybe some ice water? You've been sitting in the sun."

"Ice water would be nice," Darius said, looking to Falconet. Both nodded their agreement. *Water would be great.*

Del nodded and went off into the kitchen. She knew that the two Bureau guys would be glancing around the room now. She pictured the Italian—a good-looking hunk—leaning back, holding onto his machismo, trying to appear cool. The black man—

educated, polite—would be sitting properly, looking for ways to make conversation. He'd comment on the Indian pottery, the feathered dream catcher that hung on the wall. He'd ask about the kachinas—Indian figures that stood lined in rows along the bookshelves.

Yes, interesting, he'd be saying, as Roy eyed the two of them and swigged his drink. The one named Falconet would look off in solitary disinterest. Darius would test the sofa and comment on how functional leather could be, that brown was a good choice in color. And he'd remain perched on the edge of his seat, pretending to be engaged in whatever her drunken father might have to say.

Del finished with the drinks and returned to find Roy drawing on his drink, saying, "You still haven't found Jimmy Hoffa? Christ, I can tell you right where he's at."

Darius was nodding politely. "Yes, sir, well, we appreciate any help we can get from the public."

"Roy has this theory," Del said, handing them their water, "that Jimmy Hoffa is living in Argentina and still controlling the unions through a puppet regime. Here's got a theory on just about everything these days."

"You don't see these guys turning up anything, do you?" Roy Shannon knocked back another drink.

Del took the chair across from them. The Bureau guys tipped their glasses as if they'd just been rescued from hell.

"So," she said when they'd finished, "what can we do for you two?"

Darius got right to it.

"This concerns both of you … Del … Mr. Shannon. The Bureau has been monitoring a religious community for some time.

There's nothing too serious at this point, but it's a group we want to keep an eye on anyway."

He clicked open his briefcase and brought out a photo and handed it to her. It was of a small town nestled in a valley between steep rocky cliffs. It had been taken from an elevated distance. She could make out a tiny church, a series of outbuildings, barracks perhaps, and houses scattered about.

"Not much to it," Del said.

"No. It's a small community. Not a town really," Darius said, keeping his eye on Roy Shannon, who seemed to be watching him. "It's in Kentucky. You don't recognize it?"

Roy Shannon abruptly dropped the footrest on the recliner and rose without comment to go off into the kitchen.

"No, why should I?" Del said.

Falconet said, "It's called Nazareth Church. Maybe Mr. Shannon recognizes—"

BAM!

A loud noise from the kitchen interrupted them, the sound of a whiskey bottle being slammed down hard against the counter. Roy Shannon reappeared in the doorway, his glass no fuller than before. "What are you two asking? She's got enough to do right here."

Del looked from her father to the two agents and back again. "Wait! Did I miss something? You want me to go to Kentucky?"

"There you go. Just run off, like your no-good mother!" Roy Shannon spat, wheeling back into the kitchen.

Darius turned his attention back to her. "Del, Frank here is an undercover operative. It's what he does. We were hoping to get him inside Nazareth Church, but we need your cooperation and your father's to make it happen."

Del shook her head. "I don't understand. What makes you think we can help?"

Roy Shannon appeared again, this time his glass full, the bottle in his other hand. "Why don't you two just take your business and go! We got nothing to offer! Can't you see that?"

Darius turned his attention to Del, "You don't know, do you?"

"Know what?" She was looking from the agents to her father and back.

Roy Shannon clutched the whiskey bottle tighter, looking for the briefest moment like he might fling it at something or someone. "You couldn't just leave it alone! Well, goddamn it—if you're gonna tell her, then tell her! But it's my property and you're not welcome to it."

"Property? What property?" Del said.

Roy Shannon stormed off down the hall. A second later, they heard the front door open, then slam shut. Another second and they heard him start his car, followed by the sound of gravel spewing in the driveway.

"Why is it," Del said, "that I'm the only one who doesn't seem to understand what this conversation is about? What...goddamn!... property?"

———

DARIUS Lemon studied the woman across the sofa from him. She sat with her right hand covering the small moon tattoo that he had noticed earlier. From time to time, she would scratch at the skin there, as though it bothered her. It seemed like a self-conscious gesture, the kind of thing you learned to spot when you were in law enforcement.

He said, "Del, whatever just happened here, we're sorry. It wasn't our intention to bring discord into your home."

"I just … I don't understand where all this is coming from."

"You really didn't know, huh?" Falconet said.

Now she stood. Darius followed her with his eyes as she paced away from them, then back. "You're telling me," she said, "that Roy Shannon … my father … owns a house, in … in this … this place … Nazareth *whatever*?" She was showing him his own photo. "My father! *My* Roy Shannon!"

Darius gave a glance at Falconet, who shrugged.

"I don't understand!" Del said. "How long? When?"

"All we know is that Powell County records show the property as a nine-hundred-square-foot house in Nazareth Church, deeded to Roy Shannon." Darius nodded toward the empty recliner. "*That* Roy Shannon, and it has been for the past thirty-four years. But I must say I'm surprised you don't know about it."

"And why is that!"

"Well … because," Darius said. "Our information suggests you were born there."

Darius saw the young woman's face cave in, as though she had just taken a punch from a professional fighter. She slumped back against the arm of the chair, her mouth open, but nothing coming out.

"I … I was born in … *this* house? You're telling me … I was born … *there*?"

Darius said nothing.

"Who lives there now?"

"Well, we have no idea. From our surveillance, we believe it could be vacant, but it's something we have to confirm."

"Does my mother still live there?"

"Your mother?" Darius asked, giving her a sideways, inquisitive look.

"You said I was born there, right? She could still be living there, couldn't she?"

The young woman's eyes were searching his, looking for answers he didn't have. He shook his head, "I really can't say, Del. Truly. It's the kind of questions we were hoping you or your father would answer."

"Right! Roy Shannon? Like the way he's answered all my fucking questions all my life?"

Darius gestured with open hands as if to say, *What do you want us to say?*

"Del—" Falconet began to say.

"Well that's just great!" she said, cutting him off and throwing her hands in the air in one last show of defiance. "You guys are fucking something else, you know it? I can't listen to this shit! I'm sorry! Let yourselves out when I'm gone." And like her father before her, she strode angrily down the hall and was gone.

When the front door had slammed shut for the second time since they arrived, Falconet said, "What the hell just happened here?"

Darius said, "Judging from the taste of shoe leather in my mouth ... I'd say we just put our feet in there. Too bad you didn't get a chance to propose. I'd have loved to have seen the look on that pretty little face ..."

"So, what do we do now?" Falconet asked.

Darius rose, gathering his briefcase. He said, "We give it a day or two to let things settle down, then try again. Maybe we'll catch them in a better mood."

FOUR

Del squeezed the trigger—*pop-pop-pop-pop-pop!* The Baby Eagle jerked. Brass Parabellum shell casings ejected to the floor. Downrange, beneath powerful lighting, a half-figure target silhouette took a hit ... then another ... and another ... and another.

The nine-millimeter slugs tore through the paper, fifteen rounds eating the heart from it and leaving a ragged hole you could put your fist through.

In seconds, the weapon ran empty, the slide locked open, and smoke curled from the chamber. Del ejected the magazine, slapped another in place, and squeezed the trigger.

Pop-pop-pop-pop!

Her father. Shit! Right there in her brain. What a fucking piece of work he was. All these years hiding her history from her and refusing to tell her basic facts about her life, things every human being had a right to know. Then finding out from total strangers—a pair of fucking drop-ins!—that he'd been sitting on family property in Kentucky all these years.

Pop-pop-pop!

Never knowing who or where her mother was...

Pop-pop-pop-pop!

Lying to her...

Pop-pop-pop-pop-pop! The slide locked open once more.

But why? Answer her that!

Her father would have her believe that it was because her mother didn't love her. That she had run off and left the two of them to fend for themselves. Randall would have her believe that mothers did that sort of thing all the time. *Shit happens!*

But they didn't know what she knew.

Del wanted to tell her defiant father—and Randall—*you're wrong!* She wanted to tell them both that the mother she was looking for would welcome seeing her daughter again. That the mother *she* was looking for was a loving mother, one who would be in her life right now, if she *could* be.

She wanted to say to them, *Do you know how I know?*

Del moved the gun to her left hand and let the fingers of her right hand trace the moon tattoo on the back of her wrist. It was itching again, something it seemed to do whenever she thought about her mother.

Randall didn't know the moon's significance; neither did her father. It was her little secret...hers and her mother's, dead or alive, wherever she might be.

The only keepsake she had of this mystery woman, the only physical evidence she had to prove that her mother had really existed—a tiny yellow moon, hand-embroidered on a pair of infants' terry cloth pajamas. They had been *her* pajamas—Del's—she was sure of it.

She'd been about seven years old at the time, exploring for every-day secrets in the garage. She found the wadded-up pajamas down inside a ragbag, stuffed in near the bottom beneath other used shop rags.

The tiny moon was slightly askew on the lapel and slightly imperfect in its craftsmanship, as if, out of some sentimentality, it been hand-sewn on there after the pajamas' purchase. That day had been a turning point for Del. The moon she believed was evidence, proof positive, of a once loving and caring mother—a tiny symbol from which she could draw hope.

She had clipped the hand-stitched moon from the pajama-rag and carried the swatch of cloth around with her throughout most of her childhood. She took it with her to school, kept it close when she was out to play, and stowed it in her *secret place* whenever she was at home beneath her father's watchful eye. By the time she hit her teens—tough years—the tiny piece of pajama had become so threadbare it simply fell away in tatters.

Refusing to let go of its meaning for her, Del had a yellow moon icon tattooed on her wrist beneath her watchband, where it might escape her father's attention. *Go figure.* The man had never looked closely enough to see his daughter as a living, breathing human being, much less notice the tiny moon.

Del now guessed that the idea of the moon and its symbolic message of hope was something of a melodramatic notion for a woman her age. But it was one that had kept her going throughout the years, and she wasn't about to give it up now.

Del moved the gun back to her right hand, letting it dangle arm's length, and lowered her head. It was hard to think. The shooting range was dark but for the floodlights in the target area, thirty yards out.

"I thought that might be you," a big bass voice called to her.

Del looked up to see the range's owner, the huge bear of a man named Scotty. She slipped the protective earmuffs off, letting them ride about her neck. "I'm sorry, Scotty. I didn't know you were here."

"It's all right. I told you, anytime, sweetheart," Scotty said. "Trouble at home again?"

"Don't ask. I've got nothing to say about it," she said grimly.

Scotty nodded, then turned his gaze downrange toward the target. "Nice grouping."

Del nodded.

Scotty gave it a minute, then opened his arms to her. "Hug it out?"

Del shook her head. "Not tonight, Scotty."

He nodded. "Well, just lock up when you go, okay?"

It was Del's turn to nod.

She watched him move off down the hallway and disappear. Besides being the biggest guy she knew, he was the biggest hearted. And he had never come on to her, not once. It made her wonder about him. Del waited until she heard the door out front close, then expelled the magazine from the gun and slapped another in place. Picking an imaginary spot between the eyes, she unloaded fifteen more rounds and watched the face disappear.

———

AS therapy went, the shooting range this night hadn't worked. What Del wanted to do now was to drive, giving herself time alone to think. But then there was Stonewall Jackson's, a country-western bar, coming up on the right. It was Ladies' Night, the lot filled with cars. There was neon flirting with her and music calling from beyond the entrance.

Once inside on a seat at the bar, Del ordered a shot and a draft. Around her was the usual walla-walla, the clink of bottles, the chink of glasses. Sad country music from the jukebox was exactly what she didn't need—Bob Carlisle was pouring his heart out about daddy's little girl. *Right! Maybe in the land of tooth fairies and Santa Claus, where fathers gave a shit*, Del thought.

Fuck!

Del downed her first shot and chased it with the beer. Louise, she thought, was the closest thing to a mother she'd ever known, and Randall, if he were here, would tell her, "*Get your ass off the barstool, girl, and go visit her.*"

How long had it been since she and Louise had last talked?

Sipping the beer, Del thought of the time they'd first met. She was only thirteen that summer, rebellious and angry with her father. She'd fallen in with Angel Padilla and his cousin, Jimmy Samone, who came up from Douglas each summer for the break. They were older than her. They'd taught her how to smoke and sometimes get high, and how to shoplift, too. The three of them would team up to roll drunks outside the bars.

And what about Daddy himself, Mr. Roy Shannon? Where was he all that time? The best he'd had to contribute to her résumé was, "You're just like your mother!"

Her mother.

As Roy told it, her mother had run off when Del was just ten months old, and soon afterward, in his bitterness, he had turned to drink. Del, in hers, had turned to running the streets with friends and getting into whatever trouble that would bring.

46

Later that same summer, she and Angel and Jimmy, still running together, had jacked the lock on the back door of a liquor store, the three of them taking off with as many bottles of alcohol as they could carry. They were picked up hours later by police in a stairwell less than two blocks away, arrested, and later tried. Still minors, they drew two years' probation each and were sent back to the streets.

For Del, the incident might have signaled her long and steady downward spiral, were it not for Louise.

"You smoke?" Louise had said at her first probation meeting. She was broad and matronly, dressed in a bright floral print. Her flaming red hair was teased big, and she wore jewelry—rings and bracelets and the like—things Del had never owned. She smelled nice, too. It had made Del feel self-conscious, sitting there, skinny and ragged and braless beneath an undershirt, her denim jacket hanging open. For some reason, she wished she had washed her hair.

Louise was waiting for an answer.

Del shrugged.

"Come on. Take a walk with me."

They took the elevator down to a courtyard. Louise lit cigarettes for both of them, and Del kept eyeing the gold-plated lighter.

"You like it?" Louise asked, seizing upon her interest.

"It's nice," Del admitted, trying to look disinterested.

"Then take it," Louise offered, holding it out to her.

"Naw, I don't think—"

"Go on. The doctor tells me I should quit anyway."

Del took the lighter and turned it in her hand. Sunlight jumped off the precious metal. "Thanks," she said quietly. It was the first gift she'd ever received from an adult.

They puffed together in silence.

47

"You still see Angel and Jimmy?" Louise asked after a time.

The question caught Del off guard. This officer of the court seemed to know way more than she should. Del didn't answer.

Louise nodded. "You know, Del, when it comes to friends, it's okay for you to be the one who does the choosing."

Still, Del didn't answer.

"You back in the classroom?"

"Yes."

"How's it feel?"

Del shrugged. "It's okay."

They drew on their cigarettes for a time, the probation matron not saying anything. Finally, she said, "Tell me something, Del. How are things between you and your father?"

Del shot Louise a glance. "Okay, I guess."

"Don't shit me, honey. I've seen a lot of young girls come through here."

"He doesn't hit me, if that's what you're thinking," Del could feel Louise's eyes fixed on her. "What! God, you don't think he molests me? Jesus, that's sick!"

"All right," Louise said, her voice calm.

"Look, he's just … I've been living with him all my life, that's all. My mother's been gone since I was a baby. He's never gotten over it."

"Do you ever see your mother?"

Del shook her head.

"Ever think about her?"

Del didn't say anything.

Louise waited.

"I go through my dad's personal things sometimes when he ain't around," Del admitted suddenly. "He's got this foot locker he keeps in his closet, but it's just full of old pay stubs, receipts and stuff." Del grew quiet. She dropped the cigarette to the ground and smudged it out. "I did find a picture of this woman in his sock drawer once. She was wearing a flowered dress and had her hair pulled back in a ponytail. When I went back to look at it again, it was gone. My dad had either moved it or gotten rid of it."

"You think the picture was that of your mother?"

Del shrugged. "Probably. But I don't get why it's such a big deal. Why won't he tell me about her?"

Now it was Louise's turn to kill her cigarette. She took a last drag and crushed the butt beneath her heel.

"You're still young, Del, but I think you'll learn that by the time you reach a certain age, almost every adult has something in their past they'd rather not talk about."

"But where does that leave me? I don't even know who I am!" Del bit her lip, her pain evident to the older woman.

Louise gave her a compassionate look and squeezed her shoulder. "All I can tell you is, don't worry, honey. In the end, all secrets are revealed."

In the end, all secrets are revealed.

It was the closest thing to motherly advice Del had ever heard. And in the weeks and years to come, Del would hear other catchphrases from Louise, slogans to live her life by. Concepts like *positive pathways* and *defining moments*.

Meeting with Louise had had its effect. It was the beginning of something new for Del. But the transformation of Del Shannon didn't occur overnight. She continued hanging out with Angel and Jimmy and the other kids on the street. And, in her double life, she continued to meet with Louise.

Through the winter and into the spring, she became close to Angel—she was fourteen now, filling out and feeling the onset of desire. They'd taken to cruising the strip, the three of them, with Jimmy driving his '72 Monte Carlo, his wrist casually draped over the wheel.

In the back seat, Del and Angel were busily feeling each other up. Del liked the feelings Angel aroused in her, and she'd begun to think of him as her man, imagining the two of them living in their own place together, far away from her father and his cold indifference. She started to tell herself she was in love—probably forever.

They had driven out Speedway Boulevard, where the streetlights ran out, and then headed farther up Gates Pass to the overlook, where the city skyline was laid out before them. There was a twelve-pack on the floorboards, Tex-Mex on the radio, Jimmy drumming his fingers in time with the music, Angel with his hand in Del's blouse, and Del feeling sensations she'd never felt before.

The twelve-pack dwindled and the music seemed to come from a far-off place. There was a buzzing in the air. Angel reached over and began working her jeans down, and she grew hot with excitement. His touch set off fireworks in her head.

She'd heard stories about what it was like—*first-time* stories proudly shared in girl's restrooms and beside gym lockers. She had prepared herself for this moment. She was ready for it.

What she was not ready for was Jimmy.

Before she knew it, Jimmy had slithered across the seat to join them in the back. She shot a look at Angel, but he made no protest.

"Stop it! Bastards! Get off!" she yelled, fighting them both.

In the end she'd won, leaving Jimmy with a bloody lip and Angel with his bruised manhood. It was—Del later recognized from Louise's words—a *defining moment*.

After that night, Del stopped hanging out with Angel and Jimmy. She migrated away from the street and started paying more attention to her schoolwork. That fall, she had gotten the tiny moon icon tattooed on her wrist. And without realizing it, she had begun looking forward to her visits with Louise.

Over the next two years, Del and Louise became friends, or at least mentor and protégé. And at the end of her probation period, the two continued to meet. They talked about life and love and spiritual connections to the universe—something Del liked to imagine was true. And they talked about responsibility and how it was up to each person in life to find their purpose.

Now, Del watched the bartender moving quickly behind the bar, mixing drinks, uncapping bottles, wiping his hands on his beer-soaked apron. She listened to the latest sad country song by Faith Hill coming from the speakers overhead, and watched the mindless meanderings of the Saturday-night bar crowd.

Del knew that she had finally found her purpose in life. She only wished Louise were alive today to see it.

———

BY ten-thirty, Del had ordered her third shot and was working on her second beer when the tall, lanky cowboy slid onto the stool next to her. She had seen him watching her from the other end of the bar, but hadn't noticed him step down and come around to join her.

"This seat taken?" He had a nice enough voice, and he was polite, the way he held his cowboy hat in his hand.

"Looks like," Del said and downed part of the whiskey.

The cowboy motioned the bartender to bring him a beer. He told her, doing all the talking, that his name was Allen May, up from Douglas and in town for the rodeo. He told her about riding bulls and how you could get pretty broken up sometimes. He showed her his scars. He told her that the job was—making it sound impressive—to stay on one for a full eight seconds. (Del said, over her beer, "That all?") And he told her how it was he came to own some horses and a few head of cattle, but mostly ostrich these days.

"Actually, it's my daddy Buck May's ostrich ranch," he said, "but I guess it'll be mine some day."

Del said, "Yeah, unless you find out he's leaving it all to some bastard brother you didn't know you had. Or how 'bout this? You find out you were left on the doorstep by gypsies, huh?"

"What?"

Del waved it off. "Never mind. I'm just having a bad day. Maybe you'd be better off chatting up one of these other fine ladies at the bar. I'm sure they'd be more fun."

"Yeah, but none of them would be as pretty."

And, so, when the cowboy asked would she like another round, Del said, "Why not?"

And when he moved his hand to rest it high upon her thigh, she didn't object.

And, later, in the far-off corner of the parking lot, when he pulled her across him on the front seat of his pickup truck, her jeans around one ankle, she didn't whisper sweet nothings in his ear. But rather, she rode the cowboy's motion, staying on for the full eight seconds, until the buzzer blew and the dismount came, leaving her weak and feeling like she wanted to cry.

Afterward, they sat in darkness, the neon signs of the bar out there across the sea of cars and trucks—Del with her back to the passenger door, her feet in Allen May's lap, sharing a cigarette.

"So how'd you find out about this property?"

Del considered the Bureau guys, thought of Falconet and the older, more distinguished gentleman, Darius Lemon. She wondered if they were still sitting politely in her living room, waiting for her return, or if they'd tucked their tails between their legs and gone back to whatever regional office they worked out of. She wanted to say to Allen May, *I had to hear it from the fucking FBI, can you believe it?* Scream it, if she thought it would make herself feel better. But she didn't. Professional that she was, she said, "It doesn't matter. All that matters is he has it."

"And you didn't know?"

"Nope."

"Well, so, now you do."

Del relieved Allen of the cigarette. "You know, he's owned that property since before I was born. It's likely I was conceived there, but I still don't know shit from Shinola about how I got from there to here."

The cowboy was being patient. Del took a hit off the cigarette and blew smoke off toward the windshield. Out across the parking lot, at the side entrance beneath neon beer signs, patrons came and went. After a moment, she continued. "We have this Bible at home that has all the front pages torn out. You know, the ones where you record family names and such. I don't know who my mother is or who my relatives are. I've got a birth certificate with a mother's name on it I've been trying to trace. It's probably a fake. And what I really don't understand is why my fucking father has gone to such great lengths to keep it all from me."

"Maybe you should go check this place out. The house, I mean. Maybe it'll tell you something."

Del took another drag on the cigarette. "No," she said, "the property's not mine. It belongs to my father and he'd never approve it."

Allen said, "Sweetheart, you're a big girl."

"I can't leave him, he's not well. He needs me here."

"You know what I think?" Allen said, taking the cigarette from her. "I think you're afraid ... afraid you might actually find some of the answers to those secrets you're so fired up about."

"You being a smartass?"

"I'm just trying to help," Allen said, taking his own drag on the cigarette.

Del shifted her feet to the floorboard and slid across the seat next to him. She lifted his arm and slid beneath it. "If you really want to help, Doctor Cowboy, take me back to your hotel room and let me spend the night. I'm not ready to face my father just yet."

Allen used two large calloused fingers to turn her face to his. "Tell me something. You find a guy to sleep with every time you have a fight with your old man?"

"Now you *are* being a smartass."

Allen said, "No, ma'am. I'm just making a note to keep myself handy."

FIVE

The call came at seven-thirty that morning on Del's cell phone. It was an excited Engracia Lopez.

"*Tu padre! Your father!*"

Del glanced at the sheets next to her where Allen May lay, stretched naked. His body was white except for the rancher's tan on his face, neck, and hands. Something she hadn't noticed in the dark the night before. They had lain in bed, talking and touching, until the early morning hours, drinking from the bottle of Jim Beam that Allen had taken from his duffle. Now she was feeling the hangover. She brought her feet off the bed, to sit up, saying, "Slow down, Engracia."

"Just come home, Missy, please!"

———

DEL arrived home to a patrol car sitting in the driveway. Two uniformed officers rose from the sofa as she entered the room. Engracia was sitting on the edge of Roy Shannon's recliner, her brown face twisted in pain. She dabbed tears from her eyes with a lace hanky.

"What's going on?" Del said.

"Oh, Missy!" Engracia cried.

"I'm sorry ma'am," one of the two officers said. He was a big man with kind eyes. His hair was buzzed to a flattop. He had his service cap clutched in front of him. "I'm afraid this is about your father."

"Roy?"

The kind-eyed patrolman gave a brief glance to his partner, a female, her uniform crisply starched, then turned his eyes back to her.

"At three-seventeen this morning, one of our units responded to a 911 report of an accident. The car, registered to Roy Shannon, went off the road at a high rate of speed and impacted the highway bridge abutment. The single male occupant was pronounced dead at the scene."

"My father?"

"Ma'am, we believe so, but he was missing his wallet and ID."

There was a long period of time where no one said anything. Or maybe it was just a moment.

Del stared at her father's recliner, where Engracia sat crying softly. She tried to imagine it without him in it. They'd been together all her life, and as hard has things had been between them at times—God!—the idea of him not being there…

"Ma'am?" the female officer was saying. "Ma'am, we'll need you make positive identification."

"I don't…" It was taking time to register.

Del turned to look at her housekeeper. Engracia's eyes were wide and pleading.

"I'm so sorry, Missy!"

Del wanted to cry, but couldn't. Wanted to scream, but couldn't find the voice for it. "He'd been drinking," was all she could think to say.

"Yes, ma'am, we believe so. The autopsy will confirm." He hesitated, then added, "Ma'am . . . there were no skid marks on the road."

It took a second for Del to realize what the good cop was trying to tell her. She said, "At least . . . not ones you could see."

———

THE funeral took place three days later. The service was simple, but to the purpose of sending Roy Shannon on his way. The pastor said his piece and the casket was lowered into the ground. The man of secrets was taking his secrets to the grave.

Randall was there, looking sad. Rudy and Willard, Randall's two other field investigators, were there also. They had more of an anxious *How long's this gonna take?* look on their faces. Engracia was crying softly in the background, mumbling prayers to herself in Spanish.

One by one, they patted Del's shoulder and squeezed her hand and drifted away as the service came to an end. Del looked off across the cemetery grounds, and located the stone at the head of Louise Lassiter's grave, up the rise some thirty yards away. She was feeling the loss of Louise at this moment, more so, perhaps, than that of her father. Feeling alone in the world and wondering what it would feel like to come home to an empty house.

There were flowers atop the casket, a wreath standing near the grave. *Remarkable,* Del thought, the only mourners who had come were her boss, her co-workers, and the housekeeper she had hired, all come to comfort her. *Who would comfort Roy Shannon,* she wondered?

Del remained graveside until the last of the mourners had left. Off by themselves, near the drive leading in, were two lone figures—Frank Falconet and Darius Lemon. A pair of grim reapers, in suits and ties in the baking sun. Their black Lincoln Town Car sat parked in the grass, off to the side.

Del let the warm desert breeze wash over her. Let the quiet of the cemetery settle upon her. She listened to the voice of Louise in her head, until all the comforting advice ran out. Then she said her last goodbyes and crossed the lawn to where the two men stood reverently watching. She paused without making eye contact. "You still want me to go to Nazareth Church?"

Darius Lemon glanced at Falconet and back to Del. He said, "Yes we do."

Del turned off toward her Wrangler. But Falconet stopped her, saying, "Del…"

She turned to look at him.

"Your mother's name is Ella May Shannon. Her maiden name was Samuels."

Del considered the information for a moment. Of course, her own name, Del *Ella* Shannon. It was something to take away.

Del turned away and continued off toward her vehicle without comment, leaving Frank Falconet and Darius Lemon alone with the breeze and the measured quiet of the cemetery. There was little else to say this day. But a world of questions for tomorrow.

SIX

THE DAY AFTER THE funeral, Darius and Falconet flew into Knox-
ville, Tennessee, rented a car, and drove to Kingsport. They were
there to check out a tent revival. It would be Falconet's first expo-
sure to the man they called the healer. The highway dipped and
climbed with the mountainous terrain. More forest than he believed he'd ever seen.

"So, the man preaches the Gospel," Falconet said.

"He comes from a long line of religious teachers. His father, the
infamous Jonas Rule, took over a little mountain community in
the Red River Valley of Kentucky. Named Beatty at the time. Those
days, the valley was inhabited by whiskey runners. Legend has it
Jonas ran the scofflaws off, using nothing more than a Bible and
an ill temper. Renamed the place Nazareth Church and began his
ministries."

"Bringing *good news* to the natives?" Falconet said.

"If you want to call it that. But it was the young Silas that delivered up his people. He has the *gift*, they say, a healer's touch."

"You believe that shit?" Falconet said. He was looking out at the green hills, the densely wooded landscape.

"What I believe is that it's less about belief and more about need. There's a fine line between healing and convincing, between preaching and brainwashing. Jim Jones, David Koresh, Marshall Applewhite…"

"Applewhite, Heaven's Gate guy. Now there was a nutjob. Called himself 'Do.' You've worked on these kind of things before?"

"I was in Waco for the Branch Davidians," Darius said, nodding. "But I wasn't in charge then. What a debacle that operation turned out to be. Most people blame the FBI for inciting things. But it was your guys, no offense, the ATF, that was doing most of the inciting. Mooning the Branch Davidians and showing the world their asses. Fifty-one days the standoff lasted, after the botched assault on a weapons warrant. It simply wasn't managed properly. And why we're being careful now."

"I remember watching the whole fucking fiasco on TV," Falconet said, "and thinking, 'Man, heads are gonna roll.' You think this Silas Rule is all that bad?"

Darius gave him the paternal smile that had become his trademark. He said, "Wait 'til you see him. Then you decide."

———

DUSK was setting in when they reached the field outside of Kingsport. Cars filed in through the opening in the fence line. Worshippers, most of them looking like they'd just come from dinner at the Cracker Barrel, were making their way through the open flaps of the tent.

"It's like a fucking circus," Falconet said.

"You just wait."

They parked the car in the grass in a row with others, and followed the stream of attendees to the entrance. There they were stopped.

"You have your profile?" the usher said.

Falconet noticed others coming with sheets of paper already in hand. "Gimme a fucking break."

"I'm sure you have one for us," Darius said.

"Be sure to fill out all the blocks." The usher handed each of them a form and a stubby little pencil.

Away from the flow of foot traffic, Falconet looked the form over. "You fucking kidding me. Age, gender, race? Fuck! Personal income?"

"Consider it the price of admission."

"Prayer request? What kind of crap is this?"

"I'll let you tell me, once you've seen the show."

Back at the entrance, profiles in hand, they were welcomed inside. Falconet and Darius stepped through the tent flap to be engulfed in sound.

On a stage that had been constructed at the front of the tent, a trio of identical young blonde girls, triplets it looked to Falconet, were entertaining the audience with their nasally old-time Gospel lyrics. Eight years old, or thereabouts, they were all dolled up in blue gingham dresses, with matching blue ribbons in their hair. A stand-up bass was bumping time, a guitar keeping rhythm. An old-timer with a fiddle, awaiting his turn, now stepped in between stanzas to provide the interlude.

Falconet let his eyes adjust to the subdued lighting. He estimated more than three hundred people were crammed into the sweltering space. A huge cross hung from the highest point in the tent.

Soon the music came to a close, and the Gospel group hurried off-stage with their instruments. The tent fell to darkness. A nervous chatter played across the audience. There was a long weighty pause, then the organ struck a low steady tone and held. It built in intensity, taking time. Man-made fog began pouring from the wings. The stage took on the eeriness of a graveyard at night.

"I take it all back," Falconet said, sitting up straighter in his seat now. "It's more like a rock concert."

———

A COUPLE, Jim and Julie Estep, had come from Atlanta to witness the healer in action: Julie, in recent years seeking religion for her dull-ass life; Jim Estep, seeking to keep the peace by going along and expecting to be bored to the point of suicide before the night was out. What he had not expected was the sudden rise of emotion.

The service began with music—the rich, heavy swell of the organ; the tumultuous voices of the choir; the evocative lyrics, flowing off his own lips and rising, as Jim imagined it, on wings of angels to God's own ear. He felt suddenly small and vulnerable here in the late-August heat. The emotion leaving him choked and remorseful. The source of his remorse was still back in Atlanta.

How long had he been seeing her? Eleven months? A year? Kara! So goddamn young, so willing…

She wasn't the first.

Before her there'd been the young real-estate honey from Buck-head. Before that, the marketing assistant from Norcross and the dance instructor from the city. Before them, too many to count.

Did Julie have a clue? Did she conjure up suspicions at night the times he came home late from work, the weekends he attended insurance conventions out of town? There had been a lot of conventions.

Jim glanced at his wife sitting beside him on a metal chair. She wasn't bad looking. Not for forty-four years of age. But when had she become so uptight? Look at her, even now, stoic and tight-lipped, stern eyes locked on the cross hanging high up on the tent pole. She was praying silently to herself. *Praying for what?* Jim wondered. *For the two miscarried fetuses? Praying for God to fill the vacuum in her childless life?*

If there was praying to be done here, Jim told himself, it should be him praying she never finds out about Kara.

The choir brought its chorus to a ringing close. The organ held on a long, rich, steady note, then too broke silent. The lights were cut to darkness, leaving a weighty expectation in the still night air. The silence and the darkness held, along with the collective breath of the congregation. Held … held …

Then backlights rose in reds and greens behind a tall, straight, shadowy figure of a man. His features were obscured by a billowy scrim that was kept flowing by manufactured air from somewhere in the wings. Show-fog had settled across the stage, covering the man's feet to his knees.

At once, the organ began a long, mournful cry. A spotlight hit its mark in front of the scrim and held. Jim Estep felt a trickle of sweat run down his neck, felt a chill run up his spine. Eyes watched and waited. The congregation's collective breath held … held … held to bursting. Then …

Silas Rule stepped through the scrim and into the light. His head was lowered. One hand held a Bible; the other was a tightly fisted ball. White hair swept back to shoulder length above a billowing, floor-length black coat. Beneath it, a white shirt was buttoned to the neck. The fog seemed to gather round about him, as if drawn to him somehow. Jim Estep shifted nervously in his seat. The organ continued to hold. Then abruptly ceased.

Silence replaced the drone, and every ear waited nervously for the first sound of the healer's voice. Silas lifted his eyes—black holes against a gaunt, angular face. Jim Estep heard someone behind him whimper.

"What manner of creature consorts with devils?" Silas began. His voice was subdued but deliberate.

Jim ran his tongue across lips that had suddenly gone dry. He could hear weeping somewhere down the row.

"Liars!" Silas bellowed. His words tore through the tent like a cyclone, amplified by a microphone clipped to his lapel. There was an earthy Southern accent is his voice. "Coveters!" he continued. "Fornicators!"

Jim felt a wave of guilt wash through him.

"The rebellious!" Silas bellowed. "The proud! It is these who goeth believing their sins are shrouded in darkness."

Silas lifted the leather-bound Bible high above his head.

"But there is no place on earth free of the light! And that light is ever gaining, sayeth the Lord! Even your sins shall find you out! And God's judgment will be swift! It will be mortal! It will be … everlasting!"

A heavyset woman across the way began wailing. She rose to her feet and clambered to the center aisle. She cried out in anguished torment and tore open the bodice of her flowered dress, offering herself to heaven, then swooned and fainted dead away. Ushers arrived, lifting her by her arms and legs, and carried her bulk out into the night.

Jim noticed his hands. They were trembling.

Silas stepped forward through the layer of fog. The circle of light followed. He was now center stage, where on his right sat a large wooden box emblazoned with a hand-painted red cross. On his left was a table with a rack of vials filled with a sickly, yellowish liquid.

In a calmer, but none less forceful, tone, Silas said, "But what of God's salvation?" He once more lifted the Bible, letting the threat of it hover above the congregation. "Jeez-us tells us there is a way! Jeez-us tells us whosoever believeth in Him shall be saved."

Silas scanned the congregation.

"Look around, sinner!" Silas implored. "Does the man next to you steal from his neighbor's silo? Does the woman down the aisle have wicked congress with her neighbor's husband?"

Jim could swear the man's eyes, those fiery black holes, were looking at him. He resisted the urge to squirm deeper in his seat.

The congregation shared nervous glances. Jim felt his wife's eyes on him now, but knew, sure as hell, he'd be turned to stone if he met her gaze. He kept his eyes on Silas Rule.

"It's hard to tell, brothers and sisters. Because the sinner shields his wickedness in shadows by night. Cloaks his wickedness in a veil of hypocrisy by day."

Now Jim did squirm. A layer of sweat had broken out across his brow, and his stomach began to feel queasy.

"Jeez-us tells us," Silas continued, "in his very words, there *is* a way to know who is pure within his heart. And! Who is not."

There was a weighty pause. Jim Estep felt as though every eye in the tent was on him.

"Are you ready? Are you prepared, this very night, to wager your faith against God's judgment? Are you, brothers and sisters?"

Silas waited, giving the congregation time to consider. And Jim did consider. Was he prepared? Prepared, indeed, to wager his faith against God's judgment? He wasn't sure, but he was sure paying attention.

Suddenly, Silas was moving. He crossed the stage in three quick strides, dipped his hand inside the wooden box, and came out with a fist full of snakes.

God almighty! Jim Estep thought, trying to choke back the little-girl whimper that threatened to come out.

Clenched tightly inside Silas's huge fist the serpents coiled and wound and hissed and spat and struck at the air. Silas extended the slithering mass high overhead. Jim recoiled in his seat. His wife, Julie, grabbed his arm in both hands and held on tight. Shrieks came from all parts of the tent. A man in the back shouted, "Hallelujah!" Another called, "Amen, brother!"

Silas once again raised the Bible overhead in one hand, holding fast to the slithering mass of vipers with the other. "Mark 16:17 and 16:18," he said, quoting scripture blind. "And these signs will accompany those who believe. They will pick up snakes with their hands, and the snakes they will not bite them."

Silas crossed quickly to the table, the hand full of snakes still extended overhead. He set the Bible aside and took up one of the vials.

"And they will drink poison, and it will not harm them."

Silas downed the ill-looking liquid and tossed the vial aside. It shattered somewhere on stage, accentuating his point.

With the slithering mass of snakes still held in his upraised hand, Silas leveled his eyes on the congregation.

"How strong be *your* faith?" he bellowed.

At once, Silas hurled the snakes into the center aisle, where they hit in a stunned and tangled mass, then started to unwind. Cries emanated from the crowd. The congregation drew back, shoving and pushing, knocking over chairs, to clear a path for the uncoiling serpents.

A woman shrieked and fled down the center aisle, dragging her two young children with her. A couple next to Jim and his wife leveraged their way past, then dashed down the aisle and out. Others clung to each other, pressing back against the flaps as far away from the hissing, coiling vipers as they could get. Jim found himself backpedaling, pulling Julie with him. He held to her, waiting to see what this man, this lunatic faith healer, would do next.

What he did was take up the rack with the remaining vials and wade into the center aisle, amid the coiling snakes.

"Who chooses salvation this day?"

A man in bib overalls came forward. He reached Silas and, without hesitation, bent down and picked up one of the snakes by the middle. A gasp emitted from the crowd. The snake drew around, cocked its head. Its rattle began dancing wildly. Its forked tongue darted out and in.

Silas laid a hand on the man's shoulder.

"Let God be with you, brother."

"Hallelujah!" someone said.

"Amen, brother!" said someone else.

Silas handed the man a vial. The man downed it, then tossed the snake to the floor, where it slithered backward for several yards. A chorus of *hallelujah*s and *amen*s rang throughout the tent. In the background the organ began to drone, the choir began to sing.

"Glorrry … glory everlasting …"

At the ends of the aisles, ushers came with collection plates and began passing them along the rows. Followers dug deep inside their pockets for bills and change, whatever they could spare.

Silas moved slowly down the center aisle. "If you're hurt or hurting. Now is your time."

A large woman fell into the aisle. "Jesus! Oh, Jesus!" She rolled onto her back, spread her arms and legs and began kicking and waving wildly at the air. "Take me! Take me, Jesus!"

Silas stepped past her and made his way on down the aisle, continuing to chant. "If you're hurt or hurting, now is your time. If the spirit moves you." Suddenly, he stopped.

Silas cocked his head to one side as if receiving word from on high. "One of us here tonight is suffering a great malignancy." He turned sharply to a woman at the end of the aisle. Tears began to fill her eyes. Silas drew the woman to her feet. "God tells me he has heard your anguished cries, mother. He has felt your torment."

"How did you …?" The woman began to sob.

Silas dropped to one knee in front of her. Setting aside the rack of vials, he placed both hands on the woman's stomach, and began moving them about—searching, feeling, searching—until at last they settled low on her abdomen.

"Dear God!" the woman said. "Dear, sweet Jesus!"

Silas pressed hard against the affliction. Then pressed harder until eliciting a cry of pain. He lowered his head, squeezed his eyes shut. "You've heard her cries, Lord! Take it away! Take it away!"

The woman swooned, and was caught from behind and lifted back into her seat.

"Praise Jesus," she said. Then in a voice that swelled, "Praise Jesus!"

"Hallelujah! Hallelujah! Amen!" came the responses from the crowd.

Jim Estep felt his legs go week. He took a step to correct his balance.

Silas came to his feet, taking his rack of vials with him, and turned back down the aisle. "If you are hurt or hurting, now is your time. If the spirit moves you, don't wait."

Jim watched as one by one they came forward. A man in a wheelchair, who downed the serum, then stood and walked out of the tent. A woman presented her young son, whispering something in Silas's ear that only he could hear. Silas went to his knees, clamping one large hand over the boy's face. He invoked the power of God, then kissed the child on the forehead. The mother burst into tears, sobbing openly.

"Hallelujah! Amen!"

"If you're hurt or hurting, now is your time."

Jim felt his head go light. He could only wonder what power was being invoked or what sham was being perpetrated. He could only marvel at his own drawstring emotions. Was it guilt he was feeling? Shame? Or was it fear? The idea of trading his eternal salvation for the temporary but painful-sweet ministrations of a girl half his age? Jim wasn't sure. He had never considered himself a religious man.

"If you're hurt or hurting," Silas repeated. His voice had taken on a rhythmic, lyrical quality. "If the spirit moves you, now is your time."

In the background, the crowd continued to work itself into a frenzy. Collection plates, overflowing with donations, passed up and down the rows. The organ continued to build. The choir continued to sing. The congregation joined in.

Silas made his way down one side of the center aisle and back up the other. He touched a forehead, offered a vial, prayed on bended knees.

"If you're hurt or hurting, now is your time."

Jim could feel Julie's eyes on him, watching him, maybe imploring him. To what? Step forward? Pick up snakes? Down poison? The music droned, the choir sang. Jim could feel the spring inside him winding, his emotions tightening.

He thought of Kara, felt a deep sense of dread. The healer had moved back up the aisle and was now directly in front of them, still working the room.

"If you're hurt or hurting."

The organ droned.

Jim met his wife's gaze and a sudden wave of shame washed through him. He heard the healer say, "Now is your time." Heard the lyrical call of the choir, "Glory everlasting . . ." And when he could withstand no more, Jim stepped forward past his wife and into the center aisle.

"I'm sorry!" he blurted out. It was all he could think to say.

Silas stopped and turned to look at him, then lifted his hand to the choir. The singing stuttered to a stop. The organ fizzled, like a balloon slowly running out of air. The congregation fell silent. Only the hum of the fan that kept the scrim alive and soft weeping somewhere inside the tent could be heard.

"I've been cheating on my wife," Jim said, not believing the words were coming from his mouth.

Silas's white hair was swept back at wild angles, his black eyes were narrowed.

Jim threw a quick glance back toward his wife. "I'm sorry, Julie. God forgive me."

In the seconds that followed, Jim came to realize she'd known all along. She had guided him here under the faith that guided her. Under the belief that if she only got him here, this tent, this warm summer night, God would place His hand on Jim Estep's sorry heart and he'd become a changed man.

Well, all right, God or something had touched his soul. That much was sure. But was he really a changed man? Jim Estep wasn't sure. But turning his gaze back to the healer, to those fiery black eyes, he believed he was about to find out.

Through the amplified system, Silas said, "Brothers and sisters, there is one among us who believes he has chosen truth over treachery."

Someone cried, "Hallelujah!"

"There is one among us who is standing on the threshold of salvation."

"Praise Jesus!"

"He is a rich man," Silas said, tilting his head as if listening to the wind. "God speaks to me."

Jim shifted uncomfortably.

"But Jeez-us tells us, that it is easier for a camel to pass through the eye of a needle, than for a rich man to enter the Kingdom of God."

Silas began a slow steady pace, back and forth.

"You have your cars."

"Amen!" said the congregation.

"You have your wide-screen TVs."

"Praise God!"

"You have your big, fine house."

"Hallelujah!"

"You have money with which to lavish your whore with trinkets."

He stopped, turning his eyes on Jim again. "But do you have repentance?"

"I ... I'm sorry!" Jim said.

Like a fierce wind, Silas rushed upon him. His black eyes drilled into him, inches from his own. "Kneel, sinner!" he commanded.

Jim sunk to his knees without hesitation. He bowed before Silas, and Silas placed one large hand upon his head. Jim's limbs were shaking; his mouth was dry as talc.

"I hear your words, sinner. But how strong is your repentance?"

"Strong," Jim said, meekly.

"Say it so the angels can hear you."

"Strong!"

"Say it so the walls of heaven will shake with the force of your belief!"

"Strong! My repentance is strong!"

"Are you ready to accept Christ as your redeemer?"

"Yes! Lord, yes!"

"Are you ready to forego your worldly goods for the furtherance of God's Kingdom?"

"I'll give anything," Jim said, "anything God wants."

"God speaks, and He is telling me now, there is a place for you at Nazareth Church, a place for you at the healer's side. You and your wife."

Julie Estep dropped to her knees beside her husband and looped her arm through his. She was sobbing openly.

"Are you ready to sell your house?"

"Yes," Jim said.

"The cars?"

"Yes!"

"Tell it to the heavens."

"Everything!" Jim cried.

"Then lift your face to God and tell Him like you mean it."

Jim raised his eyes. His wife next to him lifted hers. "God forgive me!" he cried. "Dear God, forgive me!"

"Forgive us both!" Julie Estep cried.

"Hallelujah!" the congregation responded.

"Are you prepared to test your faith?"

"I am!"

"We are!"

Silas handed a vial to each of them. Jim looked at the sickly, yellowish liquid, then turned his eyes to his wife. Julie was looking at him, waiting to see his next move.

Jim lifted the vial to his lips and, in a single motion, downed the murky slurry. Julie followed in turn.

Now he waited, feeling nothing but the knot of emotion in his throat and what might be the hand of God taking hold of him and lifting him up. "Praise God!" Jim said, rising to his feet and bringing Julie with him. "Praise God!"

"God's will be done," Silas said into the microphone.

"Hallelujah!" the congregation cried.

The organ kicked in and the choir began to sing. Silas crossed the room in a run and leaped onto the riser. He took up his Bible, his back to the red and green billowing scrim.

"Bear witness, brothers!" he cried. "Bear witness, sisters!"

The organ increased in intensity. And with a departing wave of the Bible, Silas Rule, the renowned Kentucky prodigy, the man with fire in his eyes and the healing touch of God in his hands, turned and disappeared through the scrim. The spot followed him out, then cut to black. The red and green backlights spun and tilted and began to chase colorful circles across the top of the tent.

Jim Estep looked up at the cross, and the red and green light trails spiraling overhead. He held out his hands to inspect them. They were no longer shaking. Inside, to his utter dismay, his heart was calm. No guilt. No shame. All that lingered were the electrically charged particles that chased each other about the space surrounding him. They left him feeling cleansed in static purity.

Where was this Nazareth Church? he wondered. What purpose did God hold for him now?

————

DARIUS and Falconet beat a quick retreat to the car and got a jump on the leaving crowd. Heading down the hill, ahead of the pack, headlights on, Falconet took a look back across the seat at the tent and the crunch of cars bottling up at the exit.

He was thinking of the guy, the one near the front with his wife. *Holy shit! Laying it out there. Confessing his affair to his wife and to the world.* He felt sorry for the guy in a way. *But—fuck—what a yak.*

When they reached the paved road, Darius said, "So, what did you think?"

"I got to admit," Falconet said with a shake of his head. "It gets to you a little."

"Well, it's nothing to be ashamed of. He's very seductive. I wanted you to see this guy, see what you're getting into when you get to Nazareth Church. This isn't your typical Miami crime syndicate you're dealing with. This will be a different challenge for you."

"Made me think of my daughter, Stacy. What kind of father I've been. Her growing up—fuck—what seems like overnight. And me missing most of it. Always being gone."

Darius gave him the paternal smile.

They made the main highway and pointed the car north in darkness, both men quiet now. Finally, Falconet said, "Something I been wondering."

Darius turned his gaze from the road to see Falconet looking at him.

"Silas Rule, you buy he really heals those people?"

"You saw the questionnaires we filled out. What do you think?"

Falconet turned his eyes back to the road. "Like I buy the woman-cut-in-half trick."

Darius said, "Now you're getting the picture."

SEVEN

STANDING ON A TALL, wooden stool in the motor home, fifty feet behind the tent, Nigel Fontaneau laid his headset aside, straightened the whistle he kept strung about his neck, and went quickly to work shutting down the sound system and the closed-circuit monitors. He then used a soft cloth to erase the grease markings from the white board on the wall above the equipment—notes to himself, critical information fed to Silas during the revival.

... aisle nine, seat two ... occupation waitress ... prays for healing of cervical tumor ...

... aisle eleven ... seat one ...

Information pulled from the visitors' profiles.

It wasn't such a bad gig, watching the monitors and reading information into the microphone. In fact, Nigel liked to think of himself as the voice of God, delivering wisdom to the healer through discreet electronics.

... aisle twelve, seat six ... prays for son in prison ... net worth thirty thousand dollars ...

Not exactly the way it was done in the Bible. But he could pretend himself omniscient, superior to the martyrs in the tent.

Nigel finished wiping down the board; straightened the stack of profiles, the source of all wisdom; then climbed down from his stool by sitting, then rolling, onto his stomach, and finally by slipping over the edge to drop to the floor. Nigel was all of three-foot-nine with lifts.

With a final inspection of his work station, he crossed the trailer to the window, the side that looked out across the parking lot. Through parted blinds he cupped his face to the glass and peered out into the night. The last of the cars, stragglers who had dallied outside the tent to decide on a good place for a late-night breakfast, were making their way through the opening in the fence and down the gravel road. Cullen was nowhere in sight.

What had Silas told the kid? *Stay put? Help out?*

No. He hadn't told the kid anything, had he? He'd said to Nigel, making it his problem, "Keep Cullen here and out of trouble. Don't let him go anywhere."

What was he supposed to do, chain the worthless piece of shit to the steering column?

What Nigel was hoping: get prepared, hit Silas with the good news for the night. This Estep from Atlanta was perhaps the biggest fish they'd encountered to date. The man and his wife were loaded. Bring it up quick, keep Silas occupied, and pray to Jesus he didn't notice Cullen being gone.

Crossing back to the stack of questionnaires, he found the profiles labeled *Jim Estep* and *Julie Estep* and placed them aside. The remaining questionnaires he stuffed into a briefcase that he closed and slid beneath the console. Monday morning's work; he would use the questionnaires for follow-up mailings—a thank-you and a solicitation for another contribution for the glory of God and the furtherance of His work through the healer, Silas Rule, *blah, blah, blah*...

Nigel heard the side door to the motor home open and swelled with a brief moment of hope that it was Cullen returning. Then Silas stepped inside. Nigel got right to it.

"I knew you'd like these two, boss. They're good ones," he said, silently damning the little frog voice that made him sound like he was speaking through a hole in his neck. He crossed quickly to Silas, handing him the Esteps' questionnaires. "Five-bedroom home, three cars...nice ones. Owns his own insurance business. Her request, look at it here," he said, pointing with a stubby finger, "prays for husband's salvation. I'm betting net worth somewhere in the neighborhood of three, maybe four, million dollars."

Nigel was talking fast and furiously, keeping an upbeat countenance.

"That be so?" Silas said, taking the questionnaire and scanning the print. "The adulterer and his wife?"

Nigel grinned and nodded, his plan working so far. "Could be the very couple you've been waiting for. Sounds like they'll be coming to Nazareth Church?"

Silas crossed to the seating area at the front of the motor home. Still studying the questionnaire, he shrugged the long coat off his shoulders and draped it over a chair. Suddenly he paused.

"Where's my boy?"

Damn, Nigel thought. "Cullen? He's...well...he was just here."

Silas's voice became a dagger. "I thought I told you not to let him out."

Nigel squirmed back a step. "He just … I was working the head-sets. I … I … lost track of him."

Silas came charging forward. Nigel saw one big hand grab for him, collect a wad of collar at the nape of his neck, and lift. All three-foot-nine of Nigel came off the floor. His feet dangling, Silas carried him to the door and tossed him headlong into the field.

Nigel landed face-first in matted grass, feeling the dewy wet-ness of it quickly soak his clothing.

"I suggest you find *track* of him."

The door to the motor home slammed shut.

Nigel lay inside a circle of illumination cast by pole lights sur-rounding the tent. Cullen. Why was it always his job to watch after the boy? Wasn't that a father's duty? But then … oh, yeah … Cullen was the son of *Silas Rule*. Shit!

Ever since that night in South Bend, Indiana, a year ago, Silas had become a lunatic about the boy. The kid, going off that night to mix with the locals, had somehow gotten himself thrown in the county jail. A bar fight, the gist of it, brought on by Cullen's big mouth and the even bigger chip on his shoulder. Nigel had seen it before—preachers' kids. Regardless, it brought the kind of attention that Silas didn't want or need. Since then, it had somehow become Nigel's job to keep an eye on the bastard.

Nigel pulled himself to his knees and brushed at the wet grass that was plastered to his shirt. His whistle was caked with mud, and he took time to pick at it, clear the mouthpiece, then drag himself to his feet, wondering where to start.

The last of the stragglers' cars had funneled their way through the exit to join the trail of taillights on the gravel road leading out. Fog now lay like a canopy over the valley.

Where could Cullen be? They were twelve miles outside of town.

Nigel put a hand to his brow and scanned the shadows, out beyond the reach of light. One car still remained out there. Laying odds, he headed off across the field through muddied tire ruts and wet, matted grass.

The windows of the Dodge Intrepid were fogged from the inside, and there was a rhythmic rocking going on. Nigel approached the car from the driver's-side door. He first cupped his hand to the window, saw little more than two figures through the haze.

Next thing he did was knock.

"Get lost!"

It was Cullen.

A muffled female voice said. "Jesus, Cullen, get up, get off, somebody's out there."

There were grappling sounds beyond the door.

Nigel reached for the door latch and swung open the door. Cullen's bare ass looked back at him from between the girl's legs. The two jerked upright, the girl fighting with the hem of her dress to get it down.

"What the fuck, little man!" Cullen said, glaring at him across the seat. Then catching sight of Nigel, his clothes and face smeared with Tennessee soil, he began to smile. "You do a belly crawl to get here?"

"Your father says we're leaving," Nigel said, unable to take his eyes off the girl, her thighs where her legs remained parted.

"She's a cutie, ain't she? Tell you what. You stand out there, keep a lookout, and I'll let you have seconds when I'm finished."

The girl straightened in the seat. "Cullen! Fuck you! He's a midget!"

Nigel said, "If you come with me now, I'll tell Silas you just stepped out for air."

"And if I don't?"

"Then I'll tell him to come get you himself."

"You little fucker!" Cullen swiped at him and missed.

Nigel bolted and ran, keeping one eye over his shoulder.

Some yards back now, Cullen was stumbling from the car, his pants still around his ankles. He tripped and went down on all fours. Then got it together, and came after Nigel.

Nigel heard the girl say, "Cullen, you asshole, come back with the keys! How'm I supposed to get home?"

Nigel dared not look back any longer. He turned his attention forward and ran, swinging his stumpy legs as fast as they would go. And...

... *treeeet—treeeet—treeeet*...

... blew on his whistle for all it was worth. Thirty yards out he heard footfalls behind him, coming fast—boots slapping at the mud. Five more steps, six, and—slam!—Cullen caught him from behind.

For the second time in one night, Nigel felt his face meet with cool, wet grass, felt the air go out of him as Cullen's weight came down hard in the middle of his back. Next came the blows, the slaps to either side of his head. The fists of fury that pummeled his back and shoulders. Cullen astraddle him now, making him pay.

"You dying to tell Silas something?" Cullen said, a viciousness to his voice. "Then, let's give you something to tell."

Cullen came up, grabbing Nigel by the arm and began dragging him back across the soggy field. The girl was now out of the car, pulling her clothes together. She looked up as Cullen approached with Nigel in tow.

"Cullen. What are you doin'?"

They were closing fast on the girl. Cullen grabbed a handful of Nigel's collar, another handful of belt, and tossed him like so much wet sack feed to collide with the girl. The girl let out a scream as the two of them went down in the mud and wet grass, Nigel landing on top of her.

Cullen put his boot in the small of Nigel's back, the heel of it digging in and pinning him down atop the girl.

"That's it. Go for it, little man." The two squirmed beneath the crush of Cullen's boot. "It's what you really came out here for, ain't it?"

Finally, Nigel rolled free and crab-crawled his way to safety. He remained there on his back, motionless. The mud that had one time been on him was now covering the front of the girl's dress.

Cullen stood over him, grinning. "Go on," he said to Nigel, "get your next beating when you go back empty-handed."

With that, Cullen drew the stunned and whimpering girl from the ground and dragged her back inside the car. The door slammed shut behind them.

Nigel sat nursing his wounds. Finally, he got to his feet and made his way back across the field toward the tent. *Tell Silas the kid was out there in a car with a girl*, he thought. *Yeah, and brace yourself for another blow.*

EIGHT

"Take the Mountain Parkway and get off at Stanton."

It was three weeks after Roy Shannon's funeral, coming to the end of the second week in September. They were under the dome at the Holiday Inn in Winchester, Kentucky, the only ones out there this evening. Pizza boxes and empty beer cans littered the table between them. A seductive, sub-aquatic glow from the pool played across their faces. Del, Falconet, and Darius—old buddies by now it seemed.

Darius turned the map so Del and Falconet could see it, guiding it past the boxes and cans, and keeping the spot marked with his finger. He was laying out the plan for the two of them, their mission into Nazareth Church.

"Follow State Route 11 past Biden," Darius said. "About six miles up, take the gravel road. Cross the river and stay to the right where the road forks and follow the river. It'll lead you directly to Nazareth Church."

They'd been there for nearly an hour. Del was feeling a mild buzz from the alcohol. A number of times over the course of the evening,

Del would glance at Falconet to catch him studying her with something of a sly, knowing smile on his face. It made her wonder if he was flirting with her or evaluating her fitness for duty. Now there he was again, rocked back in his seat, thumbs hooked in his belt, his eyes locked on hers. What? Trying to read her?

Del turned her gaze to the map, the job at hand. It was a single page, about six hundred square miles of central Kentucky. Most of the map was a pale shade of lime, indicating large expanses of rural terrain. The spot where Darius's finger held fast was a dark, forest green.

"There's nothing there," Del said.

"It's bumfuck. I've seen the photos," Falconet said and took a swallow of beer.

"More bumfucked than this? I expected to see potato wagons parked outside the lobby."

"You think this is country?" Darius said, shaking his head. "My girl, you haven't seen anything yet. Think *Deliverance* without the music."

It was all new to Del. The mountains she knew back home rose abruptly off flat desert and seemed to sit on the landscape like hotels on a Monopoly board. She'd driven east more than three days, seeing the terrain change from ragged desert to pastoral rolling green hills. And gradually climb from the Mississippi basin into the Appalachian region. Here in central Kentucky, the farms shared the land with the mountains.

"Nazareth Church…" Darius said. "I mean, I don't want you to get your hopes up, either of you. It's jack-frame storefronts and old houses scattered about the hillsides. One here, another a half-mile up the road, some propped on stilts, others squatting like dogs along the river bottom. Its only draw is the church ... and iso-lation, if you're into that kind of thing."

Del studied the map, trying to capture a mental picture of the layout. "Where's my house?" she asked. *My house*—the words sounded strange to her ears.

"The two of you are on your own on that count," Darius said. "Once you get there you'll have to ask about the house. And while I'm thinking about it ... is that the way you're going to dress?"

Del looked up to see Darius looking at her. "Me? What's wrong with the way I dress?"

"Nothing. At least, back in Tucson. But this is Kentucky. These are Christian fundamentalists. The idea is to fit in."

"Huh-uh," Falconet interjected.

It surprised Del.

"The idea," he said, "is for her to turn this town upside down and shake it until the rats fall out. Besides, there's an old saying in undercover work. 'The best lie is the one closest to the truth.' Better that she be herself. Both of us. That way there's less chance of us making a mistake and giving ourselves away. We're just a married couple. One of us from out west, the other from back east, come to claim a house. They don't have to like us, just believe we are who we say we are."

"All right," Darius said, "I'll defer to your experience, Frank. Now, moving on ... "

Well, looky there, Del was thinking, taking a new look at the Fed from New Jersey and stifling a smile. The tough guy had come to her defense. Maybe what you get is more than what you see with this cop ... then, again, as the man said ... *The best lie is the one closest to the truth.* Del made a mental note—maybe give this hotshot another look—and turned her attention back to Darius.

"…the mail gets delivered to one large box," Darius was saying, "near the entrance of Nazareth Church. It's all sent 'In Care of Silas Rule.' How or whether the residents get it from there is anybody's guess."

Del said, "I keep picturing a fortress of some kind."

"There's a walled perimeter and a gate, but the gate usually remains open. There's a semblance of a town. Most of the houses are spread around the hillsides or along the river. There are some barracks and a couple of outbuildings beyond the church and the farmhouse where Silas lives with his son, Cullen. You could call it all a compound if you like. It's his domain, down close to the river where it makes a bend. Certain goods are delivered to the community. That's why we had Agent Cole set up with a propane route. But mostly they're self-sustained. They farm, can fruits and vegetables, weave, bake their own bread, and generally keep to themselves."

"Sounds quaint," Falconet said.

"Yes, but don't expect the people to greet you like long-lost relatives."

Del gave Darius a quick look.

Darius said, "I know what you're thinking, Del. I'm just trying to prepare you. There may be someone living in the house, maybe not. You may have kinfolks still around those parts, maybe not."

"And my mother?" Del said.

Darius removed his reading glasses, lowered his head in a reverent way, then raised his eyes to hers. "Honestly, Del, we don't know any more than you do."

Del let it ride. The truth was she didn't know how to feel about the whole thing. Let's say she showed up, and Ella May Shannon was actually living in the house. What would she say? What words would she have for the mother who was idling away in a rocker while her daughter was growing up a half-dozen states away? *Hi, Mom. Where've you been all my life?* What kind of mother does that? Maybe this whole thing, in fact, was a bad idea. Had she thought about that? What if her mother didn't want to see her? What if she were going through all this and her mother didn't care? What if she isn't even there? *What if...*

Del realized she'd been stroking the tattoo on her wrist again, and laced her fingers atop the table to keep her hand still.

Falconet had been watching. He had that same sly, analytical smile on his face. Without taking his eyes from hers, he said to Darius, "What else can you tell us?"

"Let's talk a little about the topography," Darius said, smoothing the map in front of them. "It's mostly mountainous with deep forest and high rock outcroppings. You'll see a wide, green valley where the town is constructed. You'll see some corn and bean fields beyond the compound. Some tomato patches. There's orchards on the hillside and a cemetery. Then there's the river basin. There's a gorge cut by the river, with sheer rock facings." Darius used his finger to point. "Up here, at the mouth of the gorge, there's a dam built by the Army Corps of Engineers. Stay away from the area just below the dam. The river flattens there, and the land is riddled with natural springs and runoff. It's snake-infested swamp, I'm told, and pocked with sinkholes."

"You paint such a rosy picture," Del said.

"I tell you these things for your own good," Darius said. "Watch yourselves."

Del had been picturing a town, streets lined with little white houses, picket fences, and well-tended window boxes. Now she was saying, "Are there any stores? What about supplies?"

"There are what pass for services. But realize, it's communal living for the most part. They grow the food they eat, sew the clothing they wear, and share in the goods equally, like a family. You may have to depend on Biden, the nearest town, for many of your supplies."

"You're telling me there's no pizza delivery," Falconet said. "That's it, I'm out of here." He mimed a motion toward the exit.

"I suggest you initially stock up," Darius said, ignoring the theatrics. "Maybe the day will come when you can share in their bounty. That would suggest you're being accepted and aid in your ability to investigate."

"Lovely."

"I don't plan to be here that long," Falconet said. "Get in, get the job done, get out."

"Well, that brings me to the last item on the agenda," Darius said. "What is the job? Why are we here?" Shuffling through some papers, he produced a small photo and handed it across the table.

Falconet glanced at it and passed it on to Del. The photo was of a clean-cut young man in his mid-twenties. He had dark hair and an innocent expression.

"That is Special Agent Daniel Cole," Darius said. "It's now been nearly nine weeks since the department last heard from him."

"That's a long time," Del said.

"Yes it is," Darius said. "And, honestly, we don't know whether to consider foul play or not. He could be dead. He could be inside Nazareth Church, somewhere, doing exactly what we sent him to do. We won't know until you've had a chance to investigate. For all we know, he could have just gone off somewhere."

"Without saying anything?"

Del watched eye signals pass between Falconet and Darius.

Darius said, "The thing is, Del, Daniel had recently gone through a pretty significant tragedy in his life. His son was run over and killed while playing on a Big Wheel in the driveway of their home."

"My God! Did they get the guy that did it?"

Falconet and Darius shared another look.

Falconet said, "It was Danny, backed over his own kid."

Del felt the hair on her arms prickle. She looked off toward the turquoise blue of the swimming pool, the underwater lights, changing shape and winking with the soft undulations of the water. *My God!*

There was a long silence around the table.

Finally, Darius said, "Look, here's the thing. Finding Daniel Cole is a priority, absolutely. But the Bureau is also convinced this healer is, at best, a con artist. At worst a major threat. We're gambling that the two of you living there will give us some insight into him. We need to know: should we be going in with force or let him preach his message in peace? All we know at this time is that there's too many indicators that point to this guy being something more than what he shows the willing public. In the meantime, Del, if it can help you reunite with your birth mother, well, God bless. Just remember, you're a newly married couple, come to claim the house that Del has inherited from her father. Got it?"

Del and Falconet sat looking at their hands, nothing more to add.

Darius rose and began collecting his paperwork. "All right, the two of you will be heading out in the morning. I'll be moving down to Biden day after tomorrow to get closer. There's a motel called The Palms. God only knows why. I'll keep our people in Cincinnati up to date. Meanwhile, watch out for each other. Okay?"

Del said, "So, is that it?"

"Oh, yeah, except for this," Darius said. He withdrew a pair of felt-covered ring boxes from his pocket and set them on the table between them. Then he tucked his papers under his arm and strolled away.

Del and Falconet sat looking at the boxes, neither in a hurry to reach for them. Finally, it was Falconet who opened one to reveal a man's gold wedding band inside. He then opened the second box and turned it in place for Del to see. Inside was a modest diamond engagement ring, marquis cut, and a narrow gold band.

"He's serious, isn't he?" Del said.

"What do you say, lady, will you marry me?"

"Really, how can I refuse? It's all so romantic."

Del removed the bands and slipped them on. She splayed her fingers in front of her, turning her hand side to side to let aquamarine light dance across the facets. It gave her a funny feeling, one she wasn't sure how to take. She said, "Not exactly how I imagined my wedding set."

Falconet slid his ring in place and tossed the box back onto the table. "But, I guess it makes us official."

"And with that, a sign for me to go."

Falconet said, "Or stay and have another drink."

Del gave him a look to see if he was coming on to her, but there was nothing in his eyes this time, nothing in his expression.

She said, "It's not every day a girl gets married. I think I'll just go get all girly and soak in the tub. Besides, it might be the last time we see indoor plumbing for a while."

Falconet shot her a look. "Are you shittin' me? Outhouses?"

"Don't worry, Frank," Del said. "You're a tough guy. I'm sure you can handle it."

NINE

THE LAST THING SPECIAL Agent Daniel Cole remembered of the real world was coming out of the diner in Biden. Thinking at the time how ridiculous he felt in his uniformed work shirt—*his disguise*—the little patch on the pocket reading *Valley Propane.* Then...

This place.

It was damp and cold at night, stifling hot during the day. Four walls of concrete, underground. His only source of daylight came from above, through a one-foot-square opening crossed with metal bars. He could see the end of a drainpipe there, emptying in. It was a cistern, he believed, and dry for now. But beyond the opening dense gray clouds were forming on the horizon.

Daniel prayed for drought.

It was the kid, Cullen, the evangelist's son, who had brought him here, tied and gagged. First coming to him with his hand out. Telling him that he'd seen him come with the propane tanks and that he'd heard he'd been asking questions. That he had information he thought might be of interest. Information about Nazareth Church, what goes on there and ... bam! Hitting him with something heavy when his back was turned. He had woken up in this hole with a group of them looking down at him. Daniel touched his scalp, remembering the spot where the lump had been. The swelling was gone now.

They'd been holding him for ... how long? He wasn't sure. They'd provided him with food and water and a lard pail in which to defecate. The smell was suffocating. He had a thin, woven mat to sleep on. The place remained in dark shadow during the day and fell to pitch blackness at night. The hours were long between occasions of human contact. They would come at night—three of them usually. Men, bringing with them bright spotlights to shine through the hole and wake him. Grill him with questions, like: What was he doing in Biden? Why was he inquiring of them around town? Were there others working with him?

Sometimes they would leave the light shining throughout the night, preventing his return to sleep. And they would allow him to go hungry and thirsty for long periods of time before bringing him food or water.

Had he told them anything?

He couldn't remember.

What he'd learned in his two weeks living at the Travelodge in Biden was very little. Except that the hill people here were clannish as all hell. His first day in town, men loading a farm truck outside the feed store had stopped loading—stopped, with feed bags still in their hands—to watch him drive past.

Then later, casually asking the motel clerk, an older woman, about "that place up the road, Nazareth Church." Even then, the woman had let her eyes remain on him for the longest time before informing him he'd be staying in number nine. Nothing more.

He had made only two trips to Nazareth Church, driving in past the tall wooden cross to make his propane deliveries. He was met at the gate both times, where he had off-loaded tanks of gas. He was then turned around, back through the gate, learning nothing of the people inside, their ways. Never seeing or catching a glimpse of their fabled leader—the healer, Silas Rule.

Daniel thought of his motel room in Biden and wondered what had become of his things. There were his clothes and a toothbrush, which he wished he had now. There was the new pair of binoculars he'd bought with his own money, the per diem advanced by the department. There was his laptop with a running report of his activities. Had the kid Cullen retrieved it? Did his captors now have it? Had they read it? And what of the rental car? Was it still in the slot outside room nine? Or was it at the bottom of the swamp that some said lay upriver, beyond the gates of Nazareth Church? Daniel tried to remember his training.

It was hard, the idea of remembering. Things were becoming muddled with time. Thoughts and memories had a way of getting mixed up with one another. They'd kept him sleep-deprived, confused, and afraid, for sure. And had given him time to think. An excess of time. Time to contrive fears, construct demons, imagine various scenarios.

Scenarios where ...

Daniel shook it off.

It was late morning and they had not yet brought him breakfast. From where he sat, hunkered down in the corner, his back to the block wall, he could see nothing but sky and the now continuous churn of gray storm clouds passing overhead. If he stood on tiptoe, close to the drain, he could see the eaves of an attached building. If he jumped to chin himself on the bars, press his face close to the steel grate, he could see off across an open yard to a complex of buildings. The nearest two were long barracks-style buildings. Occasionally someone would cross the yard.

How long would it be before the FBI would come charging in to pull him out? Maybe never, Daniel considered. The Bureau couldn't afford another Waco fiasco—teams of agents laying siege to the compound the way they'd done with the Branch Davidians, attracting fleets of news vans and the attention of the world. Would they send another agent to follow up? Had they even begun to miss him, or were the higher-ups, Racine and others, busy in board rooms discussing more important world agendas. Perhaps he was simply lost and forgotten.

This assignment. Christ! What was he doing here?

It was supposed to provide breathing room. That's the way Lindsey, his wife, had described it. It would give them time to heal.

The way Racine had put it made it sound like a vacation. "Spend a few weeks in the mountains, take in the scenery, report back what you see of Nazareth Church and the man named Silas Rule." He was only supposed to observe. So simple even a rookie agent like himself could handle it.

Well, he wasn't feeling healed, and the assignment had been anything but a vacation. How long had he been down here in the hole now? Shit! Three, four weeks? It felt like a lifetime.

And what about Lindsey? He knew exactly how she would see his absence. *Coward*, she'd be telling her friends and family, believing him run out, like he was too weak to deal with things like a man.

Well, maybe he was.

Coward!

She'd be thinking it now, he bet, wherever the fuck she was.

And where … where was that? Where was his wife this very minute?

Daniel imagined Lindsey in bed this morning, that apartment she'd taken, unable ever to go back to their house after …

… imagined another man … a muscular guy … fucking asshole … lying next to her … God!

Don't think about it!

Okay, there had been the big blowup. Every name she could think to call him. What would you expect? There was a lot of pent-up resentment. *Naturally.* But he was taking responsibility, wasn't he? Owning up to it? Yes, it was he who had drunk too much. Yes, it was he who had started the fight over … what? Funny, he couldn't remember now.

But he remembered clearly backing out of the driveway, thinking, *Cigarettes, I need cigarettes.* And, Christ, why the fuck did he always have to get so worked up … and … not thinking of … and … *Oh, God! Brandon!*

Was he forever condemned?

They could work it out. Daniel still thought so. Brandon was his son, too. He'd suffered the loss also, goddamn it! Just as much as she had.

Yeah, but she hadn't been the one who …

Who pays the price? Who pays for the child whose lifeless body lies crushed beneath the tires of the family car? And how do you expect a mother to react in a case like this? Would she ever get over it? Would she ever stop blaming? What would living the rest of your life with her be like? Huh? *Have you thought about that, asshole?*

Goddamn it! So much fucking time to think. What's a guy got to do for food around here?

Daniel rose and crossed to the opening. "Hey! I'm fucking starving, assholes!" He leaped to catch the bars and chinned himself to the surface. "Hey! Anyone!"

There was no one in the yard.

Daniel dropped to the floor, waiting hopefully for movement at the opening. When none came, he returned to his place in the corner and squatted with his back to the wall once more.

So much time. So goddamn many scenarios.

———

WHEN they did come, it was first the usual two who slid the concrete slab covering away. Then the midget who brought the food. This morning, however, he was carrying a Bible. No sign of the food basket or fresh lard pail. Looking up through the bars, Daniel squinted against the sunlight.

"I'm hungry," he said, putting defiance into his voice. "I need water."

The midget's face appeared above the opening, the sun overhead forming a glorious halo around his disproportionate head. "You speak of food when it is your soul that lies starving," the midget said, as if reciting something he'd been instructed to say. His voice was a comic little kazoo voice.

Daniel could feel his stomach growling, but heard the words *soul* and *starving.*

The little man laid open the Bible and began to read. "What good is it for a man to gain the world, yet forfeit his soul? Or what can a man give in exchange for his soul?"

This! Daniel thought. Start with this, goddamn it!

"If anyone be ashamed ..." The midget continued reading, his delivery almost mechanical.

Daniel let himself slip backward to sit flat on the concrete floor. He was entering the next phase of his tortured imprisonment, he realized. The regular and repeated lecturing on scripture. Would they soon be waking him in the middle of the night to hold hands and pray?

"And I tell you the truth, some of you here will not face death before they see the Kingdom of God."

Daniel laid his head back against the cold concrete. He was still hungry, but the words were somehow comforting. The defiance had gone out of him, just a little, and he was listening. And this time, when the memories came, he didn't fight it.

Daniel thought of his wife. He tried to remember a time before ... thought of his son ... *poor Brandon ... poor, poor little Brandon.*

And when he heard the midget, "O unbelieving generation, how long should I put up with you? Bring the boy to me," Daniel put his face in his hands ... and cried.

TEN

MORNING CAME QUICKLY. DEL remembered dreaming: about her father Roy Shannon saying, *"You didn't get it out of me, did you? Now you'll have to wait and hear it from someone else."* Louise was there, telling her, *"That's the thing about the devil, Del. The devil knows how to wait."* Randall was there, too. *"I told you, you're just a girl."* Frank Falconet was pressed against her from behind, his hand on her hip. And the cowboy—Allen May—was stretched naked on the bed. *"Go on, girl, you know how it's done. I think you're afraid."*

And how did Falconet suddenly become part of the picture?

There was a difference, Del believed, between confidence and cocksureness. Allen May, the cowboy, was quietly centered, while Falconet, a cowboy of another kind, seemed a little too full of himself. Was she unaware of an attraction to him? Take away the New York attitude, and she had to admit … *he was pretty damned sexy*.

It was seven-thirty when Falconet came out of the elevator dressed pretty much the way she'd been used to seeing him—

leather jacket over T-shirt and jeans. His dark hair was still damp and combed back. It made her think of John Travolta in *Grease*. They came together in a brief hug.

"Is this what you call shaking them up?" she said, indicating his manner of dress.

"Fucking whatever," Falconet said, then nodding to the front desk, added, "These corncobs, right? I was supposed to get a freakin' wake-up."

"Any sign of Darius this morning?"

"No, haven't seen him."

"So, I guess this is it, then?"

"Just me and you, kid."

They loaded their bags in the Jeep and made a quick stop at a grocery store for paper goods, bottled water, a twelve-pack of Bud Light. Coffees to go. It would hold them for now, they agreed. But once they found the place and settled in, someone was going for groceries—toss a coin.

She pointed the Jeep onto the Mountain Parkway. It took them south and east, passing through towns like Westbend and Powell Valley—towns strung out alongside the highway with nothing much in the way of appeal to make you want to visit.

They were mostly quiet, the two of them, sipping their coffee and taking in the mountain scenery. Somewhere along, Falconet broke the silence. "You miss your father?"

Del gave it some thought. "Roy? I think I feel more guilt than remorse. You get numb to the conflict."

"Fucking tell me about it. My wife, Jolana, and I had this, like, combat relationship."

"You're married?"

"That's the thing," Falconet said, "I don't know. The papers, I signed 'em before I left home to come here. It's up to her and her stooge lawyer to make it happen."

"I'm sorry."

"Don't be. It's for the best. I was always off somewhere. Mostly working undercover, one assignment or another. I can't expect her to sit home wondering, right? It was too much to ask."

"Children?"

Del turned her eyes from the road to see Falconet staring off out the window. Now he turned to look at her. "One girl, Stacy. She's coming up on fourteen but thinks she's twenty-five."

"Uh-oh," Del said.

"Uh-oh is right. I can picture the little hard-ons lining up on the front stoop this very minute."

"I imagine that's what real dads do. They worry."

The conversation lagged. Then, Falconet came to the rescue. "What about you? An obvious babe. You ever been married? I mean to someone besides me?"

"You kidding? Not even close. I was always afraid to bring guys to the house. You met Roy, can you blame me? But I did date a guy for a couple of years named Jeski. We had some good times, but it didn't work out."

"I was noticing . . . how come you call your father by his first name?"

This time the silence was long.

Del kept her eyes on the snaking highway; Falconet watched the hills rolling by through the passenger-side window. They were climbing in elevation.

Finally, Del said, "Maybe I do miss him some."

———

FALCONET let his gaze move across the mountain terrain, rocky outcroppings the only thing disrupting the blanket of green. He'd been thinking of Jolana, and the new boyfriend she'd taken time to tell him about. A goddamn car salesman at the Chrysler dealer where she'd bought her Sebring. He should have seen it coming the day she traded the minivan for a convertible.

His last assignment had been the death blow to his marriage. Undercover as an arms buyer. Six months setting things up and making contacts. Then another three months winning the trust of the guy, Tamerand, an American-born Haitian, who was trafficking AKs from Russia and bringing them in by the container load through the docks. Shit!

It hadn't gone well.

Then to come home, gut-shot and hurting, to a woman he hardly knew. Nearly a year gone by, and Stacy—*fuck!*—all but exploding from her little stretch-tops by then. He'd felt awkward, his daughter hugging him from his bedside that first night in the hospital, and feeling bosom where a flat chest used to be. Not something you get used to quickly as a dad.

Falconet stole a glance at Del in the driver's seat next to him. Tight-fitting jeans and top, a level gaze behind aviator sunglasses. If the time away had driven him and Jolana apart, think what she'd be feeling now, knowing his latest assignment meant him shacking up for a time in an isolated cabin with this young and very good-looking woman. It brought a smile to his face.

"Something I've been wondering," Falconet said. "How it is you came to work in private investigation?"

"You mean, what's a nice girl like me doing in a place like this?"

"Come on, not like that. I was just wondering."

"Sorry. It's just I get that a lot." Del paused, considering where to start. "Okay, well, I was dating this guy, this cop." She paused again. "No wait, let's back up. It probably started with Louise, my probation officer."

"Hold on," Falconet said. "Your probation officer? I thought you were one of the good guys?"

"You should have seen me at twelve or thirteen."

"Thanks, that makes me feel a lot better about Stacy."

"Well, what's to tell? We were just kids on the street, always in trouble for something. One night we broke into a liquor store. We got picked up a couple blocks away, huddled in a stairwell, drinking our take. Not too smart. We each drew two years' probation."

Falconet grinned. "Big-time criminals."

"To hear Roy Shannon tell it."

"So this Louise turned it around for you?"

"You could say she did. She didn't have any kids of her own. So, I suppose she became something of a mother figure to me."

Falconet nodded, picturing it. After a moment, he said, "You ever been shot, your line of work?"

Del shook her head.

"I've been shot five times," Falconet said, a mixture of pride and disbelief in his voice. "In fact, get this: I've been on five undercover assignments in seven years, and I've been shot every time."

Del turned her eyes to look at him. "You kidding? And you still do this?"

Falconet turned his gaze back out the window. "It makes you think sometimes."

———

THEY found the state highway at Stanton, a town of reasonable size. Continued on into Biden, the place Darius had said they could buy supplies. There wasn't much to it—a bank, a grocery, an old-time-looking gas station, a feed store. The Palms Motel was at the far end of the strand.

Six miles farther outside of town, they caught the gravel road. Soon they were passing through morning sunlight and fields of wildflowers, the knobby tires of the Wrangler kicking up dust, creating a cloud that followed them.

Falconet was watching Del in profile. She had a great jawline, delicate but defiant. He was beginning to like the short hair, the way it fell across her eyes. Great eyes—green and sharp as ice. She was looking off at the fields of wildflowers, but now turned to catch him studying her. She gave him a knowing smile, then turned her gaze back out the windshield. Falconet covered, saying, "Not exactly your desert, is it?"

Del shook her head. "No, but it's pretty in a way that's different."

"So, tell me about the cop. Ruski … Jet ski … the fuck his name is … how come it didn't work out with that one?"

"Jeski," Del said, showing him a smile. "Ed. He was just this guy I came to be with, back when I was still working construction. A cop. I was twenty-six. He was forty-two. It was Ed that taught me how to handle firearms. How to a take a man down. But mostly how to handle myself in, you know, situations."

Falconet nodded.

"We'd go away for long weekends. There were times when I thought I might be in love, might want to settle down with him. I was still pretty angry with my father at that point. I sometimes fantasized about the two of us running away together somewhere. One of those beaches in Mexico, maybe. That kinda thing."

"Yeah, but you didn't answer my question. What happened?"

Her eyes came to meet his. "His *wife* is what happened."

———

THEY crossed the Red River on a steel bridge and followed the road that forked east along its north bank. Bright meadows gave way to deep, aging forest. Sharp, ragged cliffs rose on either side, boxing the landscape. The river, and the road that followed it, cut deep into the hills. Del was starting to wonder if they'd missed a turn. A mile or so farther in, she said, "I don't know, Frank, I think we passed it."

"Huh-uh," Falconet said, his gaze pointing the way beyond the bend in the road. "Look."

Ahead, looking down on them from alongside the road, stood an enormous white cross. On the horizontal beam, hand-painted lettering read *Nazareth Church*. And vertically down the leg: *God Welcomes You*. Just beyond the cross, a stacked-rock wall, ensnared with briars and brambles, ran off in both directions. A large wooden gate, standing open, gave entry into Nazareth Church. Del eased the Jeep to a halt.

"That's one big cross," Falconet said.

"You get the feeling it's watching you?"

Spreading before them was the wide, green valley that Darius had talked about. Orchards blanketed the hillside to the left. Down to the right, where the river made a wide swing, lay the compound. There was the church she had seen in the photo, a sprawling farmhouse that was all rooflines and dormers and windows and shutters. The house had a long wraparound front porch. Behind it were two military-style barracks. And there were sheds and outbuildings that might house farming equipment or be used for storage. Beyond all that, closer to the river's edge, were corn and bean fields, and rows of tomatoes.

Del said, "So how do you want to do this? I mean, we're supposed to be husband and wife. You're the married one. Tell me. How are we supposed to act?"

Falconet reached out and took Del's hand in both of his. He said, "Well, we hold hands a lot ... like this. We call each other by baby names. And bicker over every little thing."

"That it?"

"Well, and have sex five times a week."

Del withdrew her hand. She said, "Huh-uh. No way I'm using baby names." It was meant to be funny.

Falconet leaned across the seat and planted a kiss on her. What he expected was pursed lips and a wide-open, deer-in-the-headlights expression. What he got was a mouth that parted softly, and green eyes that drifted closed, then opened as he drew away.

"That was intended as a training exercise," Falconet said, the cocky smile back on his face.

Del said, "Yeah … but who was giving the lesson?" She eased the clutch out, and the engine idle pulled them through the gate and into Nazareth Church.

A cemetery sat on a rise below the orchards. The hillsides, higher up the grade, abruptly angled toward the sky. The ridges were blanketed with aging forest and snarled with undergrowth. Ragged rock formations jutted from the greenery.

Del let the Jeep coast, giving them time to take it all in.

"Its pretty isolated," she said. "You get the feeling these people want to be left alone?"

"The Bureau sent me down to Obregon a couple of years back. Mexico, right? Peaceful as all shit, but with like this overlay of menace. Same kind of thing here. Quiet, but creepy. You suppose that's really the town?"

Del followed Falconet's gaze to the small grouping of buildings lined along the main street ahead. There were what resembled storefronts with wooden porches. Some buildings had bare block façades. Some were covered with shingles, a few with corrugated tin. The street was boot-trodden hardpack; the sidewalks wooden plankboard, one step up from the ground. A store called The General advertised chewing tobacco and feed grain and the like. Further down was a wooden barber pole. There was a bakery across from it. And a one-room diner. No movie theater, no bank, no game room, no bar that Del could see.

"I'm going to withhold judgment," Del said.

Del nudged the Wrangler forward and pulled in at an angle in front of the General. She and Falconet stepped out into the street, taking time to stretch and survey the town around then.

Falconet draped one arm around Del's shoulder, getting on with appearances.

Down the way, at the bakery, a woman came onto the porch holding a broom. The first sign of life they'd witnessed. Seeing the two of them, she stopped to stare. Her housedress was brown and faded; her hair was pulled back in a bun. Del was suddenly aware of her own appearance: tight jeans, bare midriff, gold navel ring gleaming brightly in the sun, dark aviator sunglasses obscuring her eyes. Del raised her hand in greeting. The woman turned and went back inside, making no attempt at hospitality.

"Well, at least we know someone else lives here. I guess all we have to do now is find the house."

"Why don't I wait here while you ask around," Falconet said. "You know, keep an eye on things."

Del left Falconet at the Jeep and crossed onto the wooden sidewalk, removing her aviators as she entered the General.

Inside were wooden shelves with canned goods loosely displayed. Not much in the way of selection. There were racks with what looked like Goodwill clothing. A heavyset woman came out from the back. Cooking smells followed. She wore an apron over a drab work dress. She had large, heavy breasts that sagged beneath the bodice. Her jaw was swollen to one side. She said nothing, but eyed Del in a head-cocked way, as if to say, "*You lost?*"

Del said, "I'm looking for the Shannon place. Can you tell me where it is?"

The woman continued to inspect her. Finally, she turned her head and spat—Del hearing the ring of a spittoon behind the counter and realizing the swell in the old woman's jaw was chewing tobacco.

"Who's asking?" the woman said.

The remark struck a nerve. "Is that important?"

"What do you want with that old place?"

"I'm moving into it," Del said. "*We're* moving into it, me and my husband."

The woman cocked her head, now, the other way, as if studying her could only be done from a lopsided view. "Take a lot of work," she said.

"Maybe you could just tell me how to recognize the place."

The woman eyed her some more, then finally said, "You follow the main road into the draw, maybe you'll see a mailbox with a name on it, maybe you won't."

Del said, "Thanks." Thinking ... *for nothing*.

She started to leave, then on a whim said, "Ella Shannon, do you know her?"

The woman just stared at her: no response, no expression.

Del turned toward the door.

"Got a dress might fit," the woman said, "you feel like changing into somethin' decent."

"I'll keep it in mind," Del said, and banged her way out into the street.

———

FALCONET was on the far side of the street, taking things in and looking like a fish out of water. Del came off the sidewalk and crossed to join him.

"You notice," Falconet said, as she reached him, "there's no cars parked on the street? None in sight anywhere."

Del let her eyes scan the street, absorbing the eerie stillness of it. "This place already gives me the creeps. We're going to have to find the house on our own."

"Right? Shouldn't be all that hard," Falconet said. "We're inside a box."

They were turning back toward the Wrangler when their attention was drawn to the diner. The bell on the door jingled as a man exited and crossed into the street. A midget. He made it halfway across before catching sight of them from the corner of his eye. He stopped, cocked muscled little arms on his hips, and stood staring.

Del didn't bother to wave this time. Instead, she calmly slipped her aviators back over her eyes and stared back. Falconet moved closer, to where their shoulders touched, displaying unity.

The little man watched them for a moment longer, then without a word, turned across the street, headed down the sidewalk away from them, and disappeared into the barber shop.

Del looked at Falconet. "I'm betting within five minutes every one in Nazareth Church will know we're here."

Taking Del by the hand, Falconet said, "Right? Say we go find our house?"

ELEVEN

NIGEL STEPPED ONTO THE sidewalk to watch the Jeep pass on through town. Strangers heading into the draw—the young woman driving, the man turning in his seat to look back at him.

Still wearing a striped barber's cape, Virgil Aikens, one of the church deacons, came out to join him. He was followed by Harland Wilson, another deacon, who'd been next in line for a trim. Now, the three of them watched as the Wrangler disappeared into the trees beyond the last of the buildings.

"You think they've got anything to do with that federal agent Cullen came dragging in here to his daddy?" Virgil said.

Harland said, "The way a cat drags home birds they done kilt."

"It was a stupid thing," Nigel said, "by a stupid kid." Then gave the question some thought. "I doubt it. The Jeep had Arizona plates."

"You want Harland'n me go talk to 'em?"

Nigel was still watching the road leading into the draw. He craned his neck to look up at the dumb redneck standing next to

111

him, the barber cape draped around him, that ridiculous white-wall haircut, only one side complete. "No, let me talk to Silas first."

"He ain't at the house, I know for 'fact. Only Cullen, playin' Game Boy and watchin' porn while his daddy does the work of the church."

Right, the work of the church, Nigel thought. He was picturing the woman with the sunglasses, the cool manner to her.

"What do you want I should do?" Virgil said.

Nigel considered Virgil. The man was full-grown and still needed someone to tell him when to piss. "Why don't you go back inside," Nigel said, "and have your whole damned head shaved. Be done with it."

Nigel turned off up the sidewalk toward the General, leaving the deacons to ponder the idea.

———

NIGEL toyed with items on a shelf until Magda came out from the back, drying her hands on the front of her apron.

"What can I get you?"

Looking at her over the edge of the counter, he said, "The girl and the man that came through, they stop in here?"

Magda spat. "Didn't see no man."

"Then what about the girl? She say anything?"

"Said she was looking for the Shannon place."

"Shannon?"

"What she said."

Nigel studied the old woman's eyes. Nothing there but age and ignorance. "She say anything else?"

"Asked how she'd recognize the place, like she'd never seen a mailbox before." Magda paused. "You want anything? Not, I got lye boiling on the stove."

"No. But, for now, they want anything from the store, go ahead and give it to them."

Magda turned toward the back. "Already tried to give her a dress. She could use some decent clothes."

Nigel turned and left the General.

———

AT the house, Nigel made his way across the long front porch, glancing in windows where he got the chance. He was being careful, not particularly anxious to see the kid. The bruises from Kingsport had nearly healed, but the humiliation of that night had left a scar. Now he had to find the spoiled brat to ask him where Silas was.

Nigel followed the line of the porch to where it made an L and let himself in through the kitchen door at the side. There were no cooking smells, no homey atmosphere. Just two men living alone in the big old house. Moving cautiously, he entered the dining area, where sunlight struck angles on the hardwood floor. The living area, filled with old furniture, lay in shadow. The house was quiet, too quiet. It reminded Nigel of a funeral home.

Quick movement suddenly flashed at the corner of his eye.

Nigel jerked around in time to see the creature, high on hind legs, fangs bared, descend on him.

"Rawwwwww!"

Nigel stumbled backward, falling and striking his head against the corner of a lamp table, envisioning teeth and claws that would tear his flesh.

Cullen stood over him, laughing. The bearskin rug, which seconds ago Nigel had believed to be an animal come out of the woods, was draped about the kid's shoulders. The head of it was tossed back like a hood, to hang at the back of his neck.

Cullen leaned forward, hands on his knees. Beaming down at Nigel, he said, "Damn, little man, you should see your face."

Nigel got carefully to his feet, rubbing the spot where he'd struck the table, feeling a pulsing warmth there, but nothing liquid or gooey on his fingertips.

Cullen tossed the rug aside. "So what is it you want, come tiptoeing around?"

"I'm looking for Silas. There's some new people in town."

"People? So what?"

"It's a woman."

Cullen's interest was suddenly piqued.

"A woman?"

"And a man," Nigel added. "Maybe her husband."

This last bit of news deflated Cullen a bit, but he quickly recovered. "Maybe I should meet 'em?"

"No, I need to talk to Silas about them."

"Now, there you go," Cullen said, stepping closer. "It's that tone of yours gets you in trouble. You know it? Bossy little fuck, I got a mind to—"

Cullen raised the back of his hand, but Nigel was already moving out through the kitchen. He heard Cullen calling to him.

"Come on now, tell me where they're at."

Nigel didn't slow until he was out the door and well across the yard.

———

LARRY BOY Martin was the middleman. On one end of the supply chain was the Renegades, the outlaw bikers up in Dayton. Here on the other, the buyer end, there were these religious fanatics that wanted—God knew what for—twelve pounds of high-tech explosives. Larry Boy didn't want to ask. He didn't like dealing with the holy rollers. Truth was they were spookier than the bikers. All that holier-than-thou church gab, "brother" this, "sister" that. God "opening a door" for you here, "closing one" for you there, like you couldn't do shit for yourself. And the preacher, this Silas Rule. Oh, man! Wild, white hair, uncombed, looking like he just rolled out of bed this afternoon.

"As I was saying, there's twelve pounds, like we discussed, timers and detonators," Larry Boy said. "I already unloaded 'em by the back door."

The preacher glared, those flaming black eyes that reminded Larry Boy of wildfires burning in the night, riveted on him. The bare bulb above the man's head, brought dark shadows to his face.

"My connection wanted to know where all the munitions was going," Larry Boy continued. "I mean, automatic weapons one month, explosives the next. But, don't worry, I mean, I didn't tell 'em nothing. Swear to God."

"You blaspheme, Brother Martin," Silas said, "as though you have no thought for tomorrow."

"I ... I didn't mean ..." Larry Boy said. "Kinda just a figur' of speech."

Silas, behind his wooden desk, studied him like he was inspecting his soul for termites. Larry Boy avoided his gaze, letting his eyes run about the space.

They were in the basement of the preacher's church. The ceiling low, bare rafters overhead. Along the walls were exposed water pipes. There was a furnace and a water heater, scraps of lumber piled against the wall. Electric wire, ripped from some building or another, was strung loosely on the floor. In the corner was a table with racks of clear, empty vials. There were large spotlights with green and red scrims. A fog machine, like the ones Larry Boy remembered seeing at a Metallica concert once. There were floor fans, a big rustic cross lying on its side. And there was a large wooden box, the image of a red crucifix emblazoned on the front.

What Larry Boy was thinking was, *Lord, just get me out of here.* What he said was, "Uh ... we agreed, four thousand, ain't that right?"

Silas continued to stare.

"Now, I know that sounds like a lot of money," Larry Boy offered, filling the silence. He felt sweat break out beneath his armpits. "But you should see the people I gotta deal with to get the stuff."

Silas cocked his head, but said nothing.

"It's some hard types up north. Bikers, you can imagine."

Silas leaned forward over his forearms.

Just stop talking, Larry Boy told himself. *Shut your stupid mouth and wait for him to speak.* But he couldn't help himself. He said, "Personally, I don't go in for that kind of gang mentality. What I mean to say is, I got nothing against what people do, but robbing and raping ain't my kind of thing. No, sir. It's just ... well ... tell you what. Make it three. Three thousand and I'll get out of your way."

Silas continued his silent stare.

Larry Boy said, "See, there's a lot of risk, what I'm sayin'. And a man's got to make a profit, right?"

This time, Larry Boy bit his tongue to keep from talking.

"You speak of risk," Silas said, after a moment. "As though you know something of it."

"Ahhh ... what?" Larry Boy said, unsure of where this was going.

"In my ministry," Silas said, "I see people gamble far more than their time and worldly possessions for far less gain."

"I'm sure I ... what?" Larry Boy said again. The man had a confusing way of talking.

"How pure is your soul, Brother Martin?"

"Well, I'm a believer, sure enough," Larry Boy said, hesitating. "I mean, born into a Christian way of life. But, well, hell, nobody's perfect, right?"

"Yet you come to me speaking of profit and risk."

"I ... I just thought we'd agreed."

"You know what the Good Book says about profit and risk, Brother Martin?"

"I ..." Larry Boy was trying to remember his scriptures. How long had it been since he'd cracked the Bible?

"Jesus, tells us, Brother, 'What profit a man, should he gain the world but lose his soul?'"

"I'm just trying ..." Larry Boy stopped mid-sentence. He was beginning to feel like game in the crosshairs of the healer's deer rifle. He found himself thinking back, suddenly tying to evaluate his life in rights and wrongs. Rationalizing the times he beat on Mary Jo or cheated a friend at cards. He was counting lies he'd told, the times he fornicated with the whores out at the truck stop on the interstate. The hell did this man want?

Silas reached into his shirt pocket and withdrew a wad of bills. He unfolded them and laid them neatly on the corner of the table.

Larry Boy looked at them, unsure if he was supposed to reach for them or not.

"There's two thousand. You can take it and go. Or you can collect the remainder of the money, there," Silas said, gesturing toward the wooden box in the corner.

Larry Boy let his eyes run to the box with the hand-painted cross on front. He studied the wire mesh covering on top. The preacher was screwing with him, that much he knew. But he wasn't sure how or why.

"There's two thousand more in the box?" Larry Boy said.

Silas was back to staring.

Larry Boy gathered the stack of bills from the table, unable to look directly at the man. He folded the stack and stuffed it into a front pocket of his jeans. Now he looked to the box in the corner.

"All I gotta do is get it?"

"If your faith be strong," Silas said.

Larry Boy crossed the basement to the wooden box and cautiously peered inside.

His first reaction was to take a step back, catch his breath to halt the girlie sound forming in his throat. There, in the bottom of the box, was the stack of bills as Silas had promised. Surrounding it were coiled masses of snakes. Some had brilliant copper markings, others had diamond patterns up their backs. A dozen of them, maybe, hard to tell the way their scaly bodies were intertwined. Most seemed like they were sleeping. Or maybe in hibernation. *Let it be that,* Larry Boy thought.

But then one, a thickly muscled diamondback, began to move. Powerful bands of sinew tightened and coiled. Its head drew back and locked in a cocked position. Its forked tongue tasted the air as the tail began to rattle. Milky yellow eyes locked on him, watching him guardedly for any sign of movement.

Larry Boy could feel Silas watching him, observing him. He understood the idea was a matter of faith. Believe strongly enough in God, the message, and God would tell the snakes to let him be. But what about the snakes? How strong was their faith?

Larry Boy weighed his chances. Reach quickly, grab the bills, and hope he was fast enough. Try to create a diversion with the other hand, then do it. Or, how 'bout take the slow way in, inch by inch, try not to spook the mean, ugly things.

Slowly, he took hold of the steel mesh that covered the box and lifted one corner. His eyes were fixated on the bad boy in the middle. The rattling took on a sudden urgency; the sinews tightened. As if hearing the call of a friend in need, a few of the other snakes now began to move. Fluidly, they slipped and separated into long, scaly individuals. Some of them coiled and struck at the air. Larry Boy brought his free hand to his mouth and rubbed lips that had turned to parchment. It was two thousand dollars lying there, an arm's length away. All he had to do was reach for it.

"How strong is you faith, boy?" Silas called to him.

There was an instant where Larry Boy thought of just going for it. Just say *what the fuck* and grab. But then the moment passed as he saw fangs on the alpha male, bared and dripping with fluid.

Larry Boy dropped the screen and turned abruptly for the stairs. He could hear Silas laughing into his back as he took the steps three at a time. He reached the door leading out and burst through it into the light of day. If it was shame he was supposed to be feeling, well, too bad … all he felt right now was *God blessed* relief.

NIGEL didn't recognize the pickup parked at the back of the church. Didn't recognize the wooden crates, stacked near the rear door, labeled *CAUTION EXPLOSIVES* in big red letters. Nor did he recognize the man in the T-shirt and jeans who came flying from the back entrance, almost tripping over the crates. The man cut a fast path to the pickup's driver's-side door and slid in, firing the engine; he spewed gravel as he gunned the vehicle through a tight donut and pointed it toward the gate. Nigel watched until the man found the road leading out and disappeared in a cloud of dust.

Inside, the sanctuary was empty. No one in the pews. No one at the altar. The windowless place gave Nigel the creeps, like being in a large box with only the angled light from the doorway to see by. He was about to leave when he noticed the door to the basement, back behind the risers, standing open, and saw dim yellow light filtering up from below. Nigel crossed behind the curtains and made his way down the stairs.

On the bottom step, he paused. He didn't see Silas at first, but then spotted him near the corner. He had the wire mesh to the snake box raised and had his free hand extended inside. He brought the hand out clutching a wad of bills. Spotting him there on the step, Silas came toward him, to where the church's heavy steel floor safe sat tucked beneath the stairs. He worked the dial through its schedule and opened the door. Only then did he speak. "What is it?"

"I thought you should know," Nigel said, his voice froggier than usual from the recent cool nights, "there's strangers in town. A couple."

Silas tossed the wad of bills inside and closed the door, giving the dial a spin. He crossed back behind the desk and sat beneath the bare bulb. Donning reading glasses, he pulled a ledger from the lap drawer and began making notations. "What do they want?"

"The woman stopped in to the General and talked to Magda. I was wondering if you want me to check them out?"

"They'll make themselves known soon enough."

Nigel gave it a beat. Then said, "The woman was asking about the Shannon place."

Silas's eyes came up quickly. "Is that right?"

Nigel nodded.

"She say why?"

Nigel shook his head. "Just wanted to know how to find it. Do you want me to call on them?"

A dark shadow crossed Silas's eyes. "No. Let 'em get settled. Come supper, I'll pay 'em a visit myself."

Silas lowered his head again to the ledger, and Nigel took it as his cue to leave.

"Hold a minute," Silas said, stopping him.

Nigel squared himself around.

"That couple from Atlanta … the wife and the adulterer. When do we expect them?"

"Day after tomorrow," Nigel said.

Silas nodded his approval.

"Do me a kindness," Silas said, not looking up. "The old Buick, the one that used to belong to the Bakey sisters? Take a couple of the deacons and drop it for me. There's an old sawmill up Forest Road 15, the other side of the gorge. Cover it with the tarp that's in the trunk and bring the keys here to me."

"Sawmill?" Nigel said, repeating the order to make sure he heard it right.

"It's abandoned. Make sure you fill the tank first."

Nigel waited, searching the man's eyes. Then, learning nothing more of reasons from this healer, he turned back toward the stairs and exited the church.

TWELVE

Falconet's groan said it all.

The old house sat in a small clearing, some thirty feet back from the road at the end of a gravel drive. The densely wooded hillside rose steeply at the back. There were shingles missing from the roof. The once-white siding was now weathered and gray. Windows had lost their glazing. The porch railing was missing some teeth. The yard and drive were overgrown with weeds. The mailbox was lying on the ground next to its post. The name *SHANNON* was barely visible in faded, red lettering across the side.

Falconet said, "Not the fuck what I expected? You?"

Del studied the house. "I don't know what I expected."

"She's not there, you know?"

Del nodded. The truth was, she was somewhat relieved to see the house empty. What would she have done? How would she have reacted if a happy and contented Ella Shannon had appeared on the porch? Suppose she'd found her mother living here with another daughter, a half-sister to Del, and several grandchildren

123

playing at her feet? Maybe feeding one from a bottle, the other daughter looking at her like she'd just caught her stealing chickens? What then? It was a possibility she'd never considered.

Del let her eyes leave the house to scan the landscape. There were other residences loosely spotted throughout the wide valley. Some were higher up on the hillside, through the trees. Others sat below them along the river. Turning in her seat, she could see the town back there in the valley, the stores lined along the main street like matchboxes, the compound partially hidden by trees, and the church, its steeple rising against a rocky backdrop.

"There but for the grace of God?" Falconet said, more of a question than a statement.

"You tell me, Frank," Del said, turning back to the house. "So, what do you think?"

"I think it's time for me to carry you across the threshold."

Del said, "Think again. Not even as a training assignment." She cut the wheel sharply toward the house and gunned the Wrangler up the drive.

Del stepped out and waited as Falconet gathered a carton of Coke and the twelve-pack of beer from the back, and came around to join her. Together they crossed onto the porch.

The railing was loose, the second step rotted, there was a porch swing that hung cocked from one chain.

"Hang on a second," Falconet said, setting the cartons aside. Del waited as Falconet reattached the chain to the drooping end of the porch swing. "For all we know," he said, "it's the only seat in the house."

Del didn't smile. She hesitated, then knocked. When no answer came, she turned the knob and pushed open the door. It squeaked on rusted hinges.

"Anybody here?" she called. Dust hit her throat and she coughed. Del glanced at Falconet, then stepped inside.

It was dry, to her dismay, the furniture covered with dust. There was a sofa, a recliner, cheap paintings on the wall. And there were footprints in the dust on the hardwood floor. Del gestured Falconet's attention to them. Falconet nodded his understanding.

Del tried the light switch and, to her amazement, the overhead light came on. "Unbelievable."

"At least we won't be watching television by candlelight," Falconet said.

Del had to glance at him to see if he was kidding, and found him smiling back.

Now she crossed further into the room. Falconet followed. There was nothing but silence. Two doorways led off into the rest of the house, one on either side of the sofa. Falconet handed Del the Coke and beer and took the path to the right. Del went off to the left and found herself in the kitchen. There was a gas stove and a monstrous old Philco refrigerator. There she stowed the drinks. There was a sink basin that would need scrubbing. Del turned on the faucet and got water—another surprise. There were cabinets above and below the counter. A door to a pantry.

Del took time to listen. She'd never heard any place so quiet.

At the end of the kitchen, Del found herself looking back down a hallway to where Falconet stood halfway inside a doorway, his hand still on the knob. He called to her. "Babe, you got to see this."

So she was *Babe* now.

Del crossed down the hall, seeing an entrance to the bathroom on her left, and came up behind Falconet, still standing in the doorway. When she touched his shoulder, he edged aside to give her access.

Christ, the smell!

Del covered her mouth and nose with her hand and choked back the impulse to gag.

The hillside that rose at the back of the house had, at some time in the past, given way. The avalanche had struck the house near its base and continued on, taking out a lower section of the wall and ripping the window from its frame, leaving a jagged hole the size of a small car. Drifted earth lay heaped inside the room, three to four feet deep. A bureau against the same wall had narrowly escaped the blow. It was still intact but stood drawer-deep in rich black soil. The bed was partially buried, the coverlet was defiled where sodden runoff had seeped into the fabric.

"Jesus!"

"That nasty smell is coming from the dead squirrel, over there against the wall," Falconet said.

There was also a bird, a starling maybe, feet-up on the windowsill.

"What are you thinking, Frank?"

"I'm thinking I'll take the floor and you can have the sofa until we can get this place fixed up."

It was the first time sleeping arrangements had been discussed, and now Del was looking at Frank-the-gentleman, beginning to discover yet another layer to him.

Hand still to her nose, she said, "Come on, I think I'm gonna barf."

They backed their way out of the room, easing the door shut behind them. Del stood with her hands on her hips. "Well, I guess we're stuck. We've inherited a fixer-upper. How good are you with your hands?"

Del caught the mischievous look in Falconet's eyes and headed off a response. She said, "Don't say it."

All of a sudden, the guy was on the verge of becoming a comedian.

———

THE coin toss went his way. Del would start the cleaning, while Falconet made a run back into Biden for supplies. Alone in the place, she found herself wandering the house. She felt ghosts from the past moving about with her. Roy Shannon in field clothes, settling into the recliner. Her mother, an image of the pretty, pony-tailed woman from the picture in her father's drawer, knitting beneath the soft glow of lamplight. Had her mother and father really begun their married life here before she was born? She tried to imagine a bassinet in the corner. Baby clothes—her clothes—folded in a drawer. A simple little family, in a simple little house. It didn't fit with anything she'd ever imagined.

Now she thought of Roy—in the ground these past three weeks. And the mystery mother, Ella Shannon.

Del stood in the hallway, outside the bathroom. She was lost in thought, when the hair on the back of neck gave a subtle warning. She turned to catch a glimpse of a lithe figure as it suddenly burst from the pantry and dashed off toward the front entrance. Del quickly turned through the adjacent doorway, crossing fast past the end of the sofa, catching sight of the fleet figure as they converged on the exit.

A kid, she registered, *a girl*.

Del caught up with her, grabbing her arm and spinning her to a halt. One step more and this little springbok would have been out the door and gone.

"Let go!" the girl said, tugging at Del's grip. She was no more than fifteen, with long, straight black hair. She had dark, defiant eyes.

"It's okay," Del said. "I'm not mad. Really."

The girl eased her resistance a little, and Del gradually released her grip.

"It's okay," Del said again. "I didn't mean to scare you."

"Ain't scared," the girl said, sticking her chin in the air.

"No, I suppose you're not."

The girl averted her eyes.

"Those your footprints?" Del asked, indicating the tracks in the dust but giving her a smile.

The girl nodded.

"They look like Converse."

"They're All Stars," the girl said, hesitantly offering out one foot for inspection. "I got 'em at the thrift store in Clay City."

A sudden picture of herself as a teen flashed through Del's mind. Those days running the streets with Angel and Jimmy, those angry, rebellious days with her father. This girl was just like her, the way she was back then—skinny, in baggy blue jeans and T-shirt, her hair falling across her eyes.

The girl eyed her. "You wear your hair like a boy."

"Yeah, I guess I do. It's easy to take care of this way."

The girl looked at her as if she didn't comprehend.

"You know what?" Del said. "The place is pretty much of a mess. I could use some help cleaning it up. I'll pay you if you're up for it."

"You gonna live here?"

"Well, they tell me it's mine now, so I guess so."

"What about the man? He gonna live here too?"

"My husband? You saw him?"

The girl nodded.

"Yes, him too. But, right now, it's just us chicks."

The girl seemed to like that.

"My name's Del. What's yours?"

"Mariah."

"Then, come on, Mariah, let's get to it."

Mariah, as it turned out, was a wealth of knowledge. She had obviously, as was the way with kids, explored every uncharted inch of the house, making Del recall times going through her father's closet, his clothes drawers, looking for information.

After assessing the job to be done, Mariah led Del to the side of the house where a pair of doors led down into a storm cellar.

Del found a switch at the base of the stairs and a bare bulb came to life.

"I still don't believe it," Del said.

"All the houses, Nazareth Church, they're supplied by a *generraider*," Mariah said. "We call it the *co-wop*."

"Well, God bless the co-op," Del said.

"Yes, He does," Mariah said, matter-of-factly.

Del liked this girl. "Water too, I guess?"

Mariah nodded.

In the corner of the cellar were brooms, mops, and pails. They gathered their supplies and headed off up the stairs, Mariah loosening up and beginning to talk freely now, to the point you couldn't seemingly shut her up.

"They got stuff like this at the General," Mariah said. "But if you want, like, tools or lumber, you'll have to drive over to the Feed-N-Seed in Biden. You know Biden?"

Del nodded. "And I get a feeling I'm going to get to know it a lot better, from the looks of the bedroom."

By late afternoon, Del and her newfound friend had cleaned the bathtub and sinks, rearranged furniture, and chased dust into the corner, where it was collected and tossed over the front porch railing and into the yard. Now, they sat on the busted front steps, Del with a Bud Light, Mariah with a Coke.

"I like your tattoo," Mariah said.

Del glanced at the little image on her wrist. "It's there to remind me of my mother." After a moment, she said, "How long have you lived in Nazareth Church?"

"All my life." She gave Del a look, as if to say, *What else*?

"Tell me something, Mariah. How long has his house been empty?"

"I don't know ... long as I remember, I guess."

"Really? What about the hole in the wall, how long has the house been like this?"

"That just happened last year. We had terrible rains, flooded the whole valley. Hillside gave way. Gram thought it was gonna take our house with it. This place is supposed to be off-limits. But I still come here sometimes."

Del nodded. "You know a lady named Ella, by any chance?"

Mariah shook her head no. "I live up there," she said, pointing off through the trees to a house farther up the hillside and across the ridge.

"You have brothers or sisters?"

She nodded. "Ten or twelve, I guess."

"Wait," Del said, "you don't know how many?"

Mariah shrugged.

"You all live in that little house, all together?"

Mariah shook her head. "Just me'n Gram." She sipped from her Coke.

"Then what about the others? Where do they live?"

"Here and there 'round Nazareth Church. Most with relatives or other people." Mariah paused. "What's it like where you come from?"

There were other questions Del wanted to ask, but said, "It's nothing like this. It's desert. Very dry. We don't have all these woods. Instead we have cactus."

"Really?" Mariah wrinkled her nose at the idea.

"We have fabulous sunsets though, where the sky turns orange and pink and purple."

"That sounds real pretty. I've never been any further'n Biden. Well, 'cept this time, last month. Granny sent me off to stay with my aunt in Clay City. Me'n Momma weren't gettin' along. Was my aunt bought me the shoes."

"Yeah, I guess I know what it's like to have a parent mad at you. My dad and me fought all the time. I mean, *all* the time." Del turned sharply to look at the girl. "Wait, you said your mother? I thought you lived with your grandmother?"

Mariah nodded and sipped her Coke. "Yeah, I do. Momma lives in the dormitory with the other wives."

"Wives live in a dormitory?"

"Them belonging to Silas do."

Del allowed a long silence, then said, "Silas has more than one wife?"

Mariah said, "Sure." There was innocence in her voice. *Of course, why not?*

Del shook the idea off and tried to get back on track. "So, your mother sent you to Clay City to live with your aunt. Why'd you come back?"

"For the wedding."

"Yeah? Who got married?" Del took a swig of beer.

"I did."

Del choked, spraying a nose full of beer into the yard. She coughed until she could breathe again. "I'm sorry, did you say, *you* did?"

"There wun't like a ceremony or nothin'. I'm s'posed to be livin' in the dorm, too. But since Gram don't get by so good, I go to Silas when he calls."

A sick-sour feeling settled into Del's gut. "Mariah, how old are you?"

"Fifteen, next week," Mariah said. "Silas still has to give me my baptismal name. He said for my birthday."

"A new name?"

Mariah looked at her, a look that said: *What part of this don't you understand?*

"All the wives get new names."

Del told herself, *Slow down. You're in a different world, where different customs abide. Different rules apply.*

After a minute, Mariah said, "What about you? You like being married?"

"It's new to me. I lived with my father until a few weeks ago. He died. That's why I came here. This was his home once."

"But you and him weren't married?" asked Mariah.

Del felt a sudden, cautionary chill run down her spine. She turned her eyes on Mariah and searched the young girl's face. The still, dark eyes added nothing. "No. No we weren't."

"Oh," Mariah said simply and sipped her Coke.

Oh, my God! Del thought, piecing together the implications. *This girl. This place.*

"Mariah," Del began, then hesitated. "Do you come here a lot?"

Mariah looked up at her. "Is it okay?"

"Sure, honey, anytime. But … do you come here to … get away?"

Mariah shrugged. Then took another sip of Coke.

"Listen to me, sweetheart. Are you listening?"

Mariah turned her open gaze once more her way.

"If you ever need to … you know … get away," Del said, speaking slowly, giving weight to each word. "I want you to know it's okay to come here. All right? Anytime. It doesn't matter what time of day or night. You understand?"

"Okay," Mariah said simply.

For all the strife Del had gone through with her own father, nothing—none if it—was like this. She couldn't begin to conceive the mounting horror of this young girl's life. She wanted to march

Mariah down the road to the compound, the Baby Eagle in hand, find this asshole, and . . .

Just then, a powerful voice cut the rural stillness. "Mariah!"

Next to her, Del felt the girl recoil and turned to see a tall, angular figure standing at the end of the drive.

"Get home, girl!" the voice commanded.

"I gotta go," Mariah said to Del, tossing the half-empty plastic Coke bottle into the yard and rising.

Del grabbed her by the arm, halting her. "Mariah, is that who I think it is?"

"It's Silas."

The girl turned away but Del held her back. "You mean your father?"

Mariah said nothing, but for the first time Del thought she saw that still, innocent gaze falter.

"I gotta go," she said, tearing loose and running off up a path that led through the trees.

Silas remained staring back at the porch, the weight of his gaze overpowering. Del felt the urge to look away. But didn't. Instead, she put a defiant edge on her lip, one she'd cultivated throughout years of dealing with her father. She held it and waited as Silas came up the drive and crossed to within a few feet of the porch. Sitting three steps up on the elevated porch, she still had to look up to meet his gaze. Over six feet tall, she estimated. Sinewy forearms showed beneath the rolled sleeves of a work shirt. His long, prematurely white hair was finger-combed back. He stood glaring down at her. Del forced resolve and held on.

Finally, Silas said, "You come here seeking this place, but I feel it only fair to warn you, there's no comfort in Nazareth Church for nonbelievers."

"The sign on your cross says, *Welcome*."

Silas let his eyes slide past her toward the door. "You came with a man?"

"He's gone for supplies. He's my husband."

"And who might you be?"

"I might be Del Shannon," Del said, keeping her tone steady and firm. "This was my father's place. It's mine now."

Silas studied her carefully. "Of course. It's in the eyes. You take after your mother."

"What do you know about my mother?" Del put defiance in her voice.

"So that's it. That's why you're here, is it? To find your mother? Well, a shame, really." Silas's lip curled in a tight sneer. "You can return back, now, to wherever it is you come from."

"Why is that?" Del said, biting back the trembling that had come upon her lip.

"Because ... she's dead," Silas said.

The pronouncement punched the air out of her. She could only say, "I ... I don't believe you." Her voice was weak.

Silas turned off down the driveway, but stopped long enough to cast a dismissive look over his shoulder. "Believe what you want, child. But be gone by sun-up. You and your man."

Del watched him stride off down the road. She wanted to say something, wanted to *throw* something. But there was nothing heavy at hand and no words seemed to come. All she could think to say was, "Bastard!" And even that was said under her breath.

THIRTEEN

"HIS OWN DAUGHTER, FRANK! Fifteen years old!"

Falconet returned from Biden to find Del in a stew. He was in the kitchen, stowing groceries in the cupboard and listening to her through the doorway, where she was shaking out bedclothes and making herself a place to sleep on the sofa. Falconet's bed was an air mattress on the floor nearby, one he'd thought to pick up at a fish-and-game store in town. Now he gathered boxes of takeout fried chicken and bottles of cold beer and went out to join her.

"You say she lives with her grandmother?" Falconet said, handing a beer to her. He had the boxed chicken sandwiched beneath one arm.

Del finished punishing a pillow before accepting the beer. "Only because the grandmother's incapable of caring for herself. Otherwise, he keeps his women in a dormitory. Like fucking concubines."

Falconet set the takeout on the coffee table, keeping one box for himself, then sat back on the newly made bed with his beer and withdrew a cold drumstick from the box. Tearing into it with his teeth, he sipped his beer and watched Del pacing, arms crossed, her beer tucked into the crook of her arm.

"That bastard!" Del said. "They dragged her back from her aunt's house, where her grandmother had sent her for protection. He justifies having sex with his own daughter by calling it *marriage*. She was hiding out here when we arrived. Now she's got nowhere to go. He needs to be arrested and now."

"It's not that simple." Falconet tore off another bite and chased it with a slug of beer.

"The hell. I know it's a different place and there are different customs, Frank. But there's no custom that justifies incest."

"I'm just saying. I'm not sure Darius will want to move on Rule just yet."

"And why not? You said you wanted this bastard. What else do you need to haul his ass to prison?"

Falconet took time to consider, then sat forward, setting his boxed chicken and beer on the table. He put a reasonable tone in his voice. "I'll talk to Darius, but I already know what he'll say. He'll ask first, 'Will she testify?'" He paused. "Will she?"

Del said nothing.

"Next he'll ask what kind of witness will she make? Is she credible?"

"Talk to her, you'll see."

"Then he'll want to know, is it enough to prosecute?"

Del threw him an angry glance, her arms still crossed over her breasts. "Did you miss the part about incest?"

"He'd need other witnesses to come forward and corroborate."

"It's bullshit, Frank. And you know it. Just what's the bottom line?"

"The bottom line?" Falconet said, lifting his eyebrows. He could feel his own anger starting to build. "The bottom line is we have no idea yet what became of Daniel Cole. We're just getting started."

"So that's it. The mission," Del said, sarcasm in her tone.

"Well, goddamn it then, what would you do? What's your big plan?"

"I can kill the sonofabitch," Del said, her jaw tightening.

Falconet scoffed aloud.

"You weren't there!"

"Sure, put a cap in his ass, why not? Mission complete. That's real smart. Then what? Go back to looking for your mother through want ads."

His words were spoken in haste. An icy silence suddenly filled the room.

Del was staring at him, a look of disbelief. She said, "Fuck you, Frank!"

Falconet turned his eyes away. He bit his lip to keep from responding, gave himself time to calm. After several moments he turned back to her again. Del was still glaring.

"I'm sorry. That was uncalled for. But, listen, all I'm saying is there's a lot at stake here. For both of us."

Falconet met her gaze, returning the challenge in her eyes.

Del held on, then, at last, broke away. Her shoulders sagged just a bit. And now she was shaking her head in resignation. "You should have seen the brazen way he walked up to the porch. I tell you, if I'd been wearing my weapon then ..."

Del took a slug of beer, then recrossed her arms.

"I understand how you feel," Falconet said, pacing his words. "I do. But we came to do a job. Come on, sit down. Have something to eat."

Del continued to stew, then, at last, took up the boxed take-out from the table and flopped down on the far end of the sofa away from him. Falconet sipped his beer, watching her, as she approached her meal with disinterest. Outside, tree frogs and cicada were holding a symphony.

She was strong-willed, this woman. The tension had come back into her shoulders, the tightness to her jaw. Falconet let her stew a moment longer. Then said, "Del." When her eyes came around to meet him, he said, "What's *really* bothering you?"

———

SILAS stood at the window, staring out at the single porch light up in the draw. He was in his quarters, upstairs in the old farmhouse his father Jonas had built, darkness engulfing the compound below.

How long had it been since that porch light had last burned?

Twenty-eight, twenty-nine years, judging by the woman's age. She'd come out of nowhere. So damn much like her mother it stirred longing. Ella Samuels Shannon, in her budding woman-hood, a small delicate vessel, the blush of innocence in her cheeks. Roy Shannon, a child of Nazareth Church—as was he—his girl bride from Estill County. Behind the porch light, the two of them, in a time before time. The happy young couple.

But childless.

She had come to *him*, hadn't she? With the prayer to make her whole. There was no persuasion. Had come on her own to the young-man healer to receive his *touch*.

And he *had* touched her.

He was twenty-four years old at the time. Only beginning to understand the full power within his hands and within the command of his voice. But feeling it. Feeling it as he touched her silky thigh. Feeling it as he drew the hem of her flowered dress high. Feeling it as he caressed the nape of her neck with his lips, that summer night, her husband up at the cemetery where he, Silas, had commanded him to go. Unaware of his young wife's deceit, dismissing a belief in his healing touch. Alone in the church just the two of them. Power running through his hands as he cupped the dewy mound between her legs, touched guarded and tender flesh, heard the throaty, near-frightened inrush of breath. Felt quakes. And tasted tears upon her cheek.

God's power. That's where she had come from, this girl. This … Del … born to the happy couple just nine months later and now here in Nazareth Church. Grown.

God's grace? Or the devil's due?

A knock on the door brought Silas back to the present. Stepping away from the window, he composed himself, shaking off ghosts of the past, along with new and powerful longings.

"Come," he said toward the door.

———

DANIEL Cole heard the healer's voice call to him from behind the door. He took a hesitant look back at Nigel, who stood further down the hall, urging him on like a father might urge a son who was returning something he'd stolen. He was happy to be out of the hole for a while: happy for the shower, the clean clothes; happy for the warm meal, sitting down at the kitchen table for a change. There was a swell inside of him, something wanting to bubble out. What was it? Gratitude? Joy? Love, maybe?

How long had he been here in this place, in this community? It was hard to tell. A week? A month? Three months? Longer, it felt like. Time had turned elastic on him, stretching out long before him, then collapsing back into a tightly compacted moment—what he'd come to think of as the *now*.

This *now*, the healer beseeching him ... *Come.*

Daniel balanced the food tray in one hand and turned the knob with the other. He stepped inside to find Silas standing, facing the door—a towering, earthy presence, suspender straps hanging, his sleeveless undershirt soaked with perspiration.

"Your dinner, healer."

"Set it there," Silas said, indicating the table in the far corner of the room.

Daniel crossed to the table and began off-loading the tray. Self-conscious, he worked carefully, deliberately, wanting to do well for this man of God, as he organized a place setting, a plate of meat and vegetables, a wine glass and bottle.

Hunched over his task, he took quick opportunities to sneak peeks about the room. It was spacious, perhaps two or more rooms gutted and joined to make a suite. There was a large, solid four-poster bed against the wall, a small table for writing, a sofa chair in the corner. There was a Bible, as he might have expected, on the lamp stand where Silas was now rummaging, his back to him, now turning with a pipe in hand, a pouch of smoking tobacco.

Daniel averted his gaze and finished up quickly.

"To serve is to welcome God's grace," Silas said, the sound of his voice surprising Daniel.

"I … I believe that," Daniel said, turning to see Silas settling into the plush recliner, the man's dark eyes watching him closely.

"Do you?"

"Yes. I … I owe everything to God."

"Your time of redemption approaches, boy. Have you prepared yourself?"

"Yes, I think so," Daniel said, cursing inwardly the uncertainty in his voice.

"Don't think," Silas said. "Thinking is an act of pride. You must renounce pride and come to know God on a personal level. Feel his presence. You understand?"

"Yes," Daniel said, forcing more resolve into his tone this time.

Silas nodded. "Good. Before you go, do me a kindness and send Nigel to see me, would you?"

Daniel turned away without reply and let himself out through the door.

In the hallway, he put his back to the closed door and let his breath out for what seemed the first time. He'd gotten through it, passed the test. Things would be better from here on in.

Nigel was coming toward him from down the hall, asking in that strange guttural voice of his, "How'd you do?"

"Okay, I think. He wants to see you."

"You go on now," Nigel said. "You did fine."

"Do I have to sleep in the cistern again?"

"I think tonight we'll find you a place in the dorm."

Daniel smiled at the idea of a warm bed, another hot meal. *Praise God*, he thought. These people, these new friends of his, they were so very good to him.

———

SILAS crossed to the table where his dinner had been arranged. The lit pipe rode the corner of his mouth. He sat, tucking the napkin into his undershirt beneath his chin. He was uncorking the wine bottle as Nigel knocked once and came through the door, removing the cap he was wearing and holding it in front of him.

"You wanted to see me?"

Silas set his pipe in its holder on the desk and poured himself a glass of wine. He held it as he turned in his seat toward Nigel.

"You've done well with our young friend," Silas said, before taking a sip of wine. "He seems at peace."

"He's coming along," Nigel said, and waited.

"The couple from Atlanta, everything following?" Silas asked.

"I spoke to the wife this afternoon. She has your instructions."

"That's good," Silas said. "We don't get many like the Esteps, so … how should I say … *capable* … of honoring God in a financially meaningful way. It's imperative that we bring them along. Do you understand?"

Nigel nodded his understanding. He said, "The Bakey sisters' car, the Buick, we dropped it as you wanted at the sawmill beyond the ridge. The key's in your desk, over in the church."

Silas took another sip from his glass as he studied the dwarf who did his bidding.

"I don't give you enough credit, sometimes, do I, Nigel?"

"You give me a place to live."

"And yet you still take the hand of God's chosen with a certain amount of trepidation. Why is that?"

"Have I displeased you?"

Silas smiled at the little man standing before him, hat in hand, the whistle around his neck.

"Just make sure the Esteps follow through. That will please me."

"And what about the strangers, the new couple?" Nigel asked.

The question brought Silas's mind back to the girl, the image of her on the porch, the mirror image of Ella Shannon looking back at him.

"This is an important time for our kind," Silas said. "I have given them until morning to get out."

Nigel nodded. "Is there anything else?"

Silas swirled the wine in his glass, watching the way it spiraled. "Have Virgil bring Esther to me. I feel like company tonight."

"I can bring her."

Silas looked up from his glass.

"You'd rob a man of the opportunity to serve?"

"It's just—"

"It's God's will," Silas said, putting authority in his voice. "Surely this you've learned."

Nigel took a moment before responding. "No, you're right. I'll have Virgil do it."

———

VIRGIL Aikens was crossing the compound when he saw Nigel coming toward him with a wave. He waited for the man's little legs to get him there before saying, "What's Silas want now?"

Nigel, sounding winded, said, "He wants to see Esther tonight."

"Esther? Doesn't he have one of the others to keep him company?"

Nigel shrugged. "He insisted on her."

Virgil nodded, and Nigel turned back across the yard. He waited until the little man had disappeared beyond the house before turning away. He made his way across the lawn past the men's dormitory to the one that housed the women. He let himself in through the door at the west end of the building, took the stairs to the second floor, and found the door to his wife's room on the right. He hated this part, having to see her, smell her, be close enough to touch.

Virgil knocked once and entered.

Esther came out of the bathroom wearing a silky robe, hanging open. Nothing under it. Virgil could see her full breasts, the dark tangle of hair between her thighs. She stopped, discovering him there, and pulled the robe together.

"I didn't hear you come in," she said. "I was shaving my legs."

"You're getting ready?" Virgil said. "How'd you know he wanted to see you?"

Esther shrugged and crossed to the vanity. Standing before the mirror, she picked up a brush and began stroking her hair. "I just figured. He keeps track of our monthlies. It's my turn."

Virgil stepped inside and closed the door. The room was sparse. There was a bed that wasn't much more than a cot, a vanity, a closet-sized bathroom in the back. Still, it was better than his own room in the men's dorm.

Virgil watched his wife brushing her hair. On the vanity next to her, the Bible lay open to Leviticus.

"You look beautiful."

He could see his wife's reflection in the glass—creamy white skin, delicate features, the contoured outline of her beneath the silky material.

Virgil crossed to her and put his arms around her from behind. Esther stopped brushing, but allowed his hands to slip inside her robe. He filled them with her soft breasts and pressed more tightly against her. He could feel the firm curve of her backside against his groin, feel the hardening nipples against his palms. He continued to work the flesh with one hand, and let the other slide down to the union of her thighs.

"Melinda," he whispered.

"I'm Esther now," she said.

"Please!"

"You know it's forbidden."

"Who forbids, Melinda? God or Silas?"

Esther pulled away, leaving an ache in Virgil's groin. "Would you be the one to claim difference, my husband? Silas speaks for God. 'Wives be submissive, like Sarah who obeyed Abraham as her master. If so any husband may not believe, they be won over by the service of their wives.' It's what the Bible teaches, Virgil. Would you then have me defy Silas? Would you then risk your own salvation?"

Esther crossed to the bathroom door and took down a black evening dress that was hanging there. Virgil watched as she slipped the robe off her delicate shoulders and let it drop to the floor. She removed the dress from its hanger, her back still to him, and stepped into it, pulling it on. Next she slipped her feet into slingback heels.

When she was ready, Esther turned to face him.

Virgil knew what came next. He licked his lips in anticipation, desperately wanting it, yet hating himself for it at the same time.

Slowly, Esther reached for the hem of her dress and began gathering it upward, exposing herself inch by inch, until it was bunched in a roll above her breasts. Now, she spread her stance, giving him a full view of all the womanhood she possessed. A superior smile appeared on her lips.

Feeling pain and humiliation, Virgil unzipped his pants, freed himself, and began to stroke. With one hand, she held the dress bunched above her breasts. The other hand she brought to her lips, licking two fingers seductively with her tongue, then bringing them down to draw a wet trail along her thigh. Virgil followed with his eyes, letting them lock on the dark triangle of hair, the place the trail ended before her fingers withdrew.

Virgil increased his stroke and finished all too quickly in an agonizing cry, squeezing his eyes shut as he did. When he opened them again, she was still standing that way, giving him one last glimpse, before letting the dress fall back in place.

Now she crossed to the vanity and gathered a string of pearls, and brought them for him to fasten.

Virgil tucked himself away and zipped up before reaching for the clasp. His breath was still coming in gasps as he hooked the catch.

"Stay with me, just a while," Virgil pleaded.

"I can't do that."

"Why? Why not? Silas can wait."

Esther turned to face him. "The healer might wait, Virgil. God's salvation won't."

FOURTEEN

DEL SAT WITH HER legs tucked beneath her on the porch swing, the robe she was wearing pulled down to keep the morning chill off her feet. It was like a dream, waking up in Nazareth Church. A layer of fog blanketed the valley, giving it a still, peaceful melancholy. And it was quiet. A quiet like she'd never known. Still, there was a subtle anxiety about the place, a warning that lay just beneath the surface. She had not slept well the night before. Two words—Silas's words—had echoed inside her mind and were still echoing now: *She's dead.*

The night before, Falconet had tried to comfort her. But the street cop had little to give. He'd hung onto his beer throughout her tirade with a pained expression on his face, looking like he'd have given a nut to be anywhere else. They retired near midnight, Del rising before him to find a place alone on the porch. Now, with birds chirping in the trees, the light of dawn on the issue, he was at the doorway, two mugs of coffee in hand—a peace offering.

"I'll leave you alone if you want, but I thought you could use something to maybe brighten your morning." He looked half afraid to come onto the porch.

"Was I that bad?"

"Let me just say, remind me never to truly piss you off."

Del patted the space next to her, and Falconet came out to join her, handing one of the coffees to her and taking a seat.

Sparrows flitted through the low-lying bramble. A squirrel was playing across the roof, rolling acorns into the sagging gutters. They sat in silence for a time, rocking gently and sipping their coffee. It tasted good, much to her surprise. Del had to admit, she was glad to have Falconet with her.

"It's a strange place, right?" Falconet said.

Del nodded.

"The little midget. How about him for a freaking sideshow?"

Del said nothing.

They sipped for a time longer, then Falconet said, "You still thinking about going home?"

Going home. It had been the last thing she'd said to him the night before, before turning out the lights. Now she said, "I was angry then. When Silas told me my mother was dead, man, it was like he'd punched the life right out of me. It would be just the irony, too, wouldn't it? I believed him."

"And now?"

"I don't know. Maybe. Maybe not. I mean, what should I believe? Everything I've ever been told has proven to be a lie. But I committed to doing a job, so I've decided to see it through."

"Good," Falconet said with obvious relief. "What do you say we head down to the diner, have some breakfast? Get to know the locals.

Then we can drive into Biden and pick up tools and lumber to repair the wall. We'll have to think about buying a new mattress for the bed. It'll give you a place to sleep, and I can move to the sofa. The freaking floor's killing my back."

"I need to drop off some laundry."

They continued sipping their coffee, the conversation lagging. Across the valley, the morning sun had peeked through the layer of fog.

After a time, Falconet said, "I've been meaning to ask you something."

"You're going to ask about the tattoo," she said, noticing him looking at her wrist—she'd been scratching it again.

"Just wondering, right? I mean … it's a kind of odd choice of symbols … strange place to put it."

"It's a reminder," she said. "A little icon just like this one was sewn to my baby pajamas. I believe my mother put it there."

Falconet nodded. "Right? Like a remembrance."

It was Del's turn to nod. "This place, Frank … Jesus! There's a feeling about it, like there are secrets buried underground, just waiting for good rain to wash them out."

"Yeah, but it's quiet, right? Peaceful. Sometimes I think about dropping out, finding a place in the country just like this, where I can just sit on the porch and whittle."

"I can't see you doing that."

"What? You don't think I can whittle?"

Del said, "I don't think you can sit on a porch."

———

THE fog had lifted by the time they dressed and drove down into town. Del was wearing a white blouse over jeans. She sat in the passenger seat this morning, a pillowcase full of laundry in her lap, one boot on the dash. Falconet was behind the wheel. He wore jeans and a black windbreaker, open. There was life in Nazareth Church this morning. Oven-vented heat rolled from a stack on the roof above the bakery and turned vaporous. Warm bread smells filled the air. Residents were up and about, some maintaining their duties in the stores, others out in the fields. Late corn waved in the morning breeze.

Falconet pulled to a stop in front of the laundromat.

"You can wait in the Jeep if you want," Del said. "I'll put some stuff in to wash. We can pop it in the dryer when we come back by."

"You need quarters?"

"I'll take what you've got."

Falconet searched his pockets and came out with three.

Del stepped out with her laundry bag. Then, conscious of watchful eyes, she leaned back inside and gave Falconet a peck on the cheek. "For show," she said, "and maybe for being a nice guy," then made her way across the wooden sidewalk and through the front door.

Two broad women, sisters from the look of them, one slightly larger than the other, were hunched over a dryer, stuffing clothes inside. A third, a frail and sickly woman, stood folding at a table in the back.

"Morning," Del said.

All three women glanced her way. The two at the dryer straightened, crossing their arms and tightening their jaws. They dressed Del down with their eyes, taking in the boots and jeans. There was a long, awkward moment, all of them looking at her. Then one of the women addressed the frail one, saying, "Sarah, why don't you go into the storeroom, see you can find more laundry detergent."

The frail little woman averted her eyes and left through a door in the back.

Del watched the woman until she was gone, then turned with her laundry bag to one of three large washers. She hesitated. There was no coin exchanger, nowhere to put money. "I'm sorry," she said, addressing the two women, "isn't this a public laundromat?"

"We do the laundry here," the larger of the sisters said. "You see us doing it?"

"Then, what? I pay you?"

"Money's no good in Nazareth Church."

The women stared back at her, arms still crossed.

"I don't understand, so, what, I just leave the bag?"

"You have name tags?" the smaller sister asked.

"Got to have name tags sewn in," the larger sister added.

They were pissing her off, these two.

"I'll tell you what," Del said, handing the bag to the larger of the two. "I'll just leave the bag with you. Mine will be the ones without the names, okay?"

The woman hesitated, giving it a moment's more defiance, then took the bag.

"Thanks," Del said, and turned to go. In the doorway she paused with her hand on the knob. "My name's Del, by the way. Just so you know." She turned and pushed out into the street.

———

ELLA Shannon had her head inside the supply cabinet, the conversation out front muffled. But the girl's name came through loud and clear. A name she could hear and would recognize in a dust storm. *Del!* She abandoned the cabinet and crossed quickly into the front in time to see the young woman join a man in a vehicle, then drive away.

Her first instinct was to run after them. Her second was to doubt it could possibly be true.

"What did she say her name was?" Ella asked the women.

The larger of the Bakey sisters said, "They're strangers, Sarah, none of your concern."

Ella let her eyes follow the vehicle as it made its way up the street. She wanted to tell the Bakey sisters that *the girl was no stranger. That the proud young woman who just left was her daughter.* She took an involuntary step toward the door, but the Bakey sisters moved quickly to block the entrance.

"Don't you have work to do, Sarah?" the bigger one said.

Ella watched the vehicle pull to a stop at the curb farther up the street. She was here in Nazareth Church at last. *Del.* Her daughter. And there was nothing she could do about it. Ella dragged her eyes away from the couple as they crossed the sidewalk and disappeared into the diner. Then she turned her attention back to the folding table and the work at hand. She felt a flood of emotions. Should she let herself feel pride, she wondered? Or give in to the mounting dread?

———

THE diner, as they came to learn, was called "the commissary." And, like the laundromat and every other place in town, it did not accept money.

"You notice," Falconet said, "there's no menus on the table."

They sat next to each other, close, Del's hand on Falconet's thigh. She took a moment to scan the place. There was a drab and dreary absence of decor. Tables and chairs were arranged across the open space. There were booths along one wall. Patrons, maybe a dozen of them, ate their morning meals in silence. Suspicious eyes threw glances their way.

"Is it just me," she said, "or do all these people look like they need their pilot lights lit?"

"What comes from not having a good bar in town," Falconet said.

"Or even a bad one."

She was hungry, having barely touched the chicken the night before. A young man appeared, peering out through the door from the kitchen. As if on ball bearings, he spun immediately back inside, then, as quickly, returned with a pot of coffee.

"Our waiter," Falconet said, giving her a wink.

The boy was coming with the pot, saying, "Kin I pour you some?"

He was skinny, maybe nineteen, wearing an apron over a short-sleeved plaid shirt and jeans, and carried the flush of pubescent acne on his cheeks.

"Thanks," Del said, motioning toward the cup. She watched him pour with an unsteady hand.

"You got a name?" Del asked.

"I'm Lowell," the boy said. "I serve the commissary."

Del reached a hand to the young man. He took it and shook it hesitantly, his face flushing at her touch, bringing fire to his acne. Del held on, watching the kid's eyes shoot nervous glances at Falconet, then released.

"Kin ... kin I get you somethin' to eat?" he stammered.

"What have you got?"

"I kin fix what'er you want."

"Then," Del said, giving him a slight smile, "I'll have eggs over-medium and wheat toast. What about you, sweetie?" she asked of Falconet.

"Mister?" The boy said, having trouble looking directly at Falconet.

"Why don't you give me the same. Maybe throw on a slice of ham."

The boy nodded, but remained in place, staring at Del, mesmerized it seemed. She wanted to stamp her foot and say, *Now!* Instead, she said, "That'll be all, Lowell."

The boy finally broke free of whatever held him and went off into the back.

"He acts like I'm gonna beat him up," Falconet said.

"Weren't you ever nineteen?"

"Sweetheart, there's *Brooklyn nineteen*, and then there's *Kentucky nineteen*. I was never like that."

———

IN time, Lowell returned with their orders. Del watched him fuss with the coffee cups and table condiments, rearranging them to make room for the plates. After a moment, she said, "Hey, Lowell."

The kid nearly dropped a saucer.

"Let me ask you something. You've lived here a while, haven't you?"

"Yes'um. All my life, I guess."

Del nodded. "You ever know a woman named Ella?"

"No," Lowell said, studying hard on it. "Can't say I know any Ella."

One of the patrons—a fortyish, sunburned farmer with white sidewalls for a haircut—suddenly pushed back in his chair with a loud scraping sound. He'd been listening to the exchange, Del was aware, and now rose to come up behind Lowell and lay one hand on the boy's shoulder. "Don't you have something to do in back, Lowell?"

Lowell dropped his eyes. "Yes, Daddy," the boy said, and headed for the kitchen.

The man brought his eyes to stare down at Del for a moment, then shifted them to Falconet.

Falconet set his coffee down and leaned forward on his elbows.

Speaking to him and not Del, the man said, "You'll have to excuse us all, but we don't see many passers-through."

"Is that right?" Falconet said. "Well, we're not passers-through. We're planning to live here."

The man looked at him long and hard, eyes not flinching.

"You'd be the husband?"

Falconet nodded.

"Well, sir, I wouldn't really make it my plan."

"Oh?"

"This here's a close-knit town. If you're not one of us, well, it just might not work out."

"And exactly who would *us* be?" Del asked.

Now, the man shifted his gaze to her. "Believers. We're a God-fearing people."

Del held his gaze. "You sure it's God you fear?"

The man's eyes sharpened. "Woman's place is to serve. Somethin' maybe you weren't given to learn comin' from outside our gates. If I were you, I would return to wherever it was you came from."

Del said, "And what if I said I like it here?"

The man turned his eyes back to Falconet. "Better teach your woman, lest her insolence be your damnation."

"You know, I was telling her that just this morning. But you know how women can be. You mind passing the ketchup?" Falconet gestured to the row of condiments.

The man turned his eyes on the bottle, retrieved it, and let his gaze lay on Falconet long and hard before handing it to him. He then turned and walked away.

"Pass the ketchup? That's what you thought to say?" Del said.

Falconet shrugged, pounding ketchup onto his eggs and digging into them.

Del studied the man she was coming to know, stifling a smile. There were smooth sides to this cop. You just had to look beneath the rough-cut exterior to see them. It made her think of the night before, her tirade, contrasting the moments they'd shared on the porch swing earlier this morning. Del turned her gaze through the window, to the quiet street outside. And once again, let her mind go off.

———

IT was Falconet's turn to watch her, Del could feel it. He was studying her, most likely to see where her mood would run to next. After a minute, she heard him say, "You're thinking about your mother again."

Del let her gaze come around to him. "Why is it you mention the name Ella and all these people suddenly go dumb or they take on an attitude?" They were speaking privately, keeping their voices close.

"Right?" Falconet said. "You thinking she's still alive?"

"I don't know. But, even if she isn't, she lived here once. Silas confirmed that. All I want is to know the truth. Where is she? And what happened to her?"

Falconet took a sip of coffee. "You know what I think? I think we should make a stop by the cemetery. Then you should take the day and do a little investigating on your own. Start with a trip to the courthouse over in Stanton. Repairing the bedroom can wait."

"You okay with that? I mean, it will put you on the floor for another night."

Falconet shrugged. "I've slept worse. It'll give me time to mingle with the locals, maybe kick the shit out of one of them just to make me feel better."

Giving Falconet a smile, Del said, "You had me worried for a moment, Frank."

"Why's that?"

She said, "I thought you were on the verge of becoming a sweet guy."

———

THEY left the diner and drove out toward the gated entrance. The cemetery lay on the hillside above. Falconet pulled the Wrangler off the gravel and into the grass at the base of the hill, and took time to call Darius on his cell phone.

"The signal's weak," he told him into the phone, having to shout over the static in his ear, "and there's no other telephones of any kind in Nazareth Church … That's right … It's been one day and Del's already threatening to kill the preacher. I'm thinking about letting her do it, right? The piece of shit."

He covered the phone and gave Del a wink. "How's that for being a sweetheart?" Into the phone again he said, "Yeah, we're taking it easy. Not upsetting the natives too much."

Darius responded through the static, something unintelligible.

"I said, we're doing okay … Shit! … Darius? Can you hear me now? Yeah, listen …"

Static pierced his ear.

"Shit! Lost him." Falconet ended the call.

"Looks like we're in this all alone, cowboy," Del said.

Falconet looked at her. "Come on. Let's take a walk up the hill."

———

"LOOK at the two of them," Darius said. "They look like they belong together, don't they?"

He closed the flip-phone that he'd placed on speaker for Racine to hear. From the rocky plateau overlooking the gorge, the two men, in suits and ties, could see through binoculars the whole of Nazareth Church. Out there was the wide green valley, the fields of corn and beans, the compound, the town, the houses dotted about the hills, the river that snaked along the escarpment from the west. There were a handful of cows grazing in a field. Together, Darius and Racine watched as Del and Falconet slipped out of the Wrangler and made their way, hand in hand, up the hill toward the cemetery.

"Good to be young," Racine said. "They do share a certain unpolished vibrancy."

"That girl is hell-bent to find her mother."

"Isn't that why we're using her?"

Darius lowered his binoculars and looked off to where white clouds drifted through blue skies above the gorge. "Maybe that's just what troubles me. I'm afraid we are using her."

"I don't know," Racine said, still looking off through the field glasses. "From all I can gather, she knows how to handle herself." He lowered his glasses to look at Darius. "We've got a missing agent. *That's* what troubles me. Granted, he could be on a plane to Pocatello or someplace. But we absolutely have to consider the possibility that he's come to harm."

"Still," Darius said, "I question the wisdom of letting her bang freely around down there, asking questions. She gets in the way of whatever *thing* this Silas Rule is into, it could be the match that ignites a fire."

Racine nodded. "And what exactly is the *thing*?"

"Well, since you ask," Darius said, lifting Racine's field glasses for him. "Follow the river up beyond the curve in the gorge."

He waited as Racine adjusted the focus.

"About three miles up, there's a dam that supplies electric power to the county. Now bring your glasses back to the building farthest right of the compound, that big piece of equipment.

See it?" He waited while Racine realigned, then said, "That's a generator."

"Which says these people are too distrustful to let the government provide."

"Which says," Darius corrected, "that Silas Rule wants complete control over these people. Mind, spirit, and resources. It makes them dependent on him."

"All right," Racine said. "Go on."

"Take a closer look," Darius said. "Tell me what you see."

Racine scanned the valley. "I give, I don't see anything."

"That's because it's not what's there, but what isn't. No factories, no sawmills, no mines. No vehicles that he doesn't control. No one gets up and drives off to work in the city. No one hauls their goods off to market. They sew garments for their own needs, do a little farming, share in the bounty whatever it might be. No one brings home a paycheck."

The two men lowered their glasses and looked at each other.

"Totally self-sufficient," Racine said.

"Totally *dependent*," Darius added for emphasis.

Racine seemed to think about it. "So what happens to all those funds they raise at tent revivals, the mounds of contributions from religious supporters, mail campaigns?"

Darius paused, giving his response the weight that it deserved. He said, "That is the question, isn't it?"

———

"FEEL better?" Falconet said.

They were at the low wrought-iron fence that surrounded the graveyard. Falconet had his hand on Del's shoulder. She had

161

brought her hand to cover his and hold it there, something unrehearsed, Falconet believed, witnessing for the first time a measure of affection directed toward him.

"She's not here," Del said, when they'd finished scanning the inscriptions on the stones.

Falconet gave her shoulder a light squeeze.

"I'm not sure what's worse," Del said, "knowing, or not knowing."

"Well, for now, I say hope's alive, right?"

"See the two in the corner?"

"Torin and Alvey Shannon. Relatives?"

Del shrugged. "I guess. But no sign of Ella May."

Falconet nodded. "Check out the biggest stone in the graveyard," he said, pointing to an impressive marble monument. "Jonas Rule, Silas's father."

When Del didn't comment, Falconet turned to see her looking at him, something vulnerable in her eyes. She held his gaze for a time, and Falconet began to wonder if there was something going on between the two of them, something he either hadn't anticipated from her or had elected not to see. But before the thought was fully formed, she turned away and headed back down the hill toward the Jeep.

Falconet watched her go, admiring the silky, economical way she moved, as she crossed down the hill and around to the driver's-side door of the Wrangler, to pose in a cool, hip-cocked stance as she donned her aviators and scanned the valley.

Man! Falconet thought.

She was behind the wheel and cranking the engine when he caught up to her. Her earlier vulnerability had been replaced by a determined, steady-level set to her gaze.

"You going to be okay if I take the Jeep?" she said.

Falconet studied her eyes through the glasses. If he had ever had any doubts about this girl—her capacity for toughness, or her capacity to love—he believed he could forget them now. He said, "You go on, right? I'll play Columbo."

Del nodded.

There was a quiet moment where a hug would have been appropriate, Falconet considered. A kiss on the cheek the thing to do. Either would have been nice; both would have been perfect. What he got was a touch on the shoulder as she dropped the sun visor and emptied the clutch.

It was something, at least.

Falconet watched as she headed out the gate and onto the road heading for town—this girl of contradictions. And for the second time in as many minutes, Falconet thought, *Man! Oh, man!*

FIFTEEN

Nigel knocked on the door to Silas's quarters and entered to find Esther tugging her dress into place. She gathered her shoes and brushed barefoot past him on her way out the door. Silas lay reclined in bed, covered to the waist, his bony upper torso white, his muscles cabled and sinewy.

"The newcomers spent the night," Nigel said. "It looks like they're planning to stay. They had breakfast at the commissary."

Silas said nothing, his eyes fixed on something far off.

"She dropped clothes at the laundry."

Silas's eyes came around to meet his. "And Sarah?"

Nigel shook his head. "Bakeys say she was in the back, but got a look at the daughter and knows she's here."

Silas thought on it a moment, then slid out of bed and began pulling on work pants. Nigel had to avert his eyes, not wanting to look at the long, bony, Ichabod Crane legs, the pale and dimpled flesh of the man's sagging buttocks.

"There's nothing the girl could have suspected," Nigel added. "The Bakeys referred to her as Sarah. The girl would only know Ella by her given name."

"The only name she has is the one *I've* given her!"

There was vehemence in Silas's voice, and Nigel made a mental note to choose his words more carefully in the future.

Silas pulled on an undershirt and took a seat in the recliner to pull on socks and shoes. Nigel gave him a minute before saying, "So what do you want me to do?"

"I think under the circumstances, best you take Sarah back to the whiskey shack."

Nigel hesitated. "The shack? But she's not well. It's why we brought her to the dorm, so there'd be someone to look after her ... Bakeys and the other wives."

"Then look after her yourself for a time. The girl and her husband won't last. They'll be gone soon enough. Then you can return her to the dorm."

Nigel wasn't sure. The woman, in her condition, shouldn't even be standing, much less forced to work for hours folding clothes. He watched Silas as he slipped into a long-sleeved denim shirt and began buttoning it. Arrogant, self-serving. He wondered where men like him come from. He wanted to tell Silas he was the most selfish man he'd ever known. Yet, he'd been saved by this man. Not in any religious sort of way, but rescued by the healer from his carney life where he'd been shoveling shit for his food and sleeping in stock trailers to stay out of the cold.

Silas had come that time like a brushfire down the midway, spouting damnation and overturning the gaming booths. Like Jesus in the temple. Man! A Bible in one hand, a lightning bolt in the other, it had seemed to him—Nigel rushing after him, telling him that he wanted to go where he was going. Anywhere but here. That had been eighteen years ago. Now, there wasn't much Nigel didn't know about selfish. And, still, Silas was asking him to move a dying woman into a cold shack in the middle of a marsh. The man had given him a more comfortable life, sure. But shit was shit, no matter where you shoveled it.

Nigel turned to go.

"On your way out," Silas said, "tell my boy I want to talk to him."

———

TWENTY-NINE years had passed, since the night Roy stole away with her child. But Ella Shannon had always believed her daughter would someday return. And now she had. Her beautiful girl, all grown-up and looking for answers. Wanting to seek out the mother she'd never known. Wanting one chance to ask: Who am I? Where have you been all these years? And why, why did you leave me alone?

She deserved answers.

Ella pictured Del the way she had seen her: confident, determined, climbing into the vehicle.

What answers did she have? How did you begin to explain just how it all came to be? What excuses did you give? Tell her about the nights working her needlepoint and rocking her life away? Tell her about the years aching to be free and burning with hatred for the man who had caused it all? Tell her about the unbearable unfairness of it all?

Or tell her nothing.

Let her discover on her own the story of Sarah—the crazy woman, the defiant and faithless first wife of Silas, locked away in exile, while rumors of snakes and mosquitoes and a disease-infested swamp circulated among the flock. Let her hear on her own the whispered confidences of past indiscretions, of sex and betrayal. How she'd been held as Silas's prisoner—his property. How she'd been brought out of isolation and rejoined with the community only after the cancer had struck.

No matter. There was little left of her now. Soon, Nigel, maybe a couple of the deacons, would be coming for her, to lock her away again. Then what? Would Del move on, frustrated and weary of searching?

Ella let her gaze move to the wash-and-dry sisters, the Bakeys, their eyes watchful, suspicious, and resentful. She let her hands trace the material of her daughter's clothing where she had folded each freshly laundered piece with care. Observed her hands there, bony and spotted with disease.

You've gotten all you're going to get, she told herself. *One glimpse. That's it.*

———

NIGEL did come. And it was Harland, the fool's fool, who came with him. There was also a young man she hadn't seen before, someone relatively new to Nazareth Church. They pushed through the door, Harland first, throwing a glance at the sisters, who straightened from their work. Now his eyes were on her.

Ella managed weak sarcasm. "What took you so long?"

"You know to come peaceful-like, Sarah," Harland said, calling her by the name Silas had given her. Nigel stood waiting by the door. The other young man stood at his shoulder, seeming unsure of himself.

Ella took time to finish folding her daughter's shirt. Then straightened and arranged the stack before loading it into the pillowcase it had all arrived in.

"You taking me back to the whiskey shack?"

"Come on now, Sarah. You have to go," Harland said.

"Why? Because Silas says?" She hesitated and said, "She's come looking for me, you know?"

Nigel said, "She'll give up after a while."

"Can you be sure?"

Nigel and Harland said nothing. The new young man looked on.

Ella glanced at the sisters, catching what might have been a hint of sympathy before they averted their gaze to the floorboards. She crossed out the door, shrugging Harland's grip on her elbow, and climbed voluntarily into the front seat of Silas's SUV. Harland crossed around behind the wheel, while Nigel and the young man slid into the back. They drove off and down through the compound, toward the river leading into the gorge.

The SUV rode the crest of the bumpy gravel road. They passed houses along the river, and continued on past where the gravel road narrowed. The landscape to either side steepened the farther in they drove. Trees and undergrowth thickened. The SUV bounced and rocked as the roadbed became more pocked and pitted. The gorge narrowed, and the sloping hillside on their left angled into a rocky escarpment, mirroring the opposite side. The narrow river, which had remained formed and true along the right side of the vehicle, suddenly flattened and spread into a wide soggy bottom. A chilled shadow lay over the basin. Ella had made this trip only once before. This time she knew she wouldn't be coming back.

———

CULLEN knocked once on his father's door and entered. The old man at his desk, writing, looked up across narrow reading glasses.

"You wanted to see me?"

"Have a seat," Silas said, gesturing to the recliner nearby.

Cullen hesitated, but took the seat, feeling himself becoming smaller as he settled deep into the soft cushioning. Being called like this brought back childhood memories of standing before his father with food on his face—maybe something like that—getting that squirmy feeling inside as Silas unleashed his wisdom upon him. There were lectures, always lectures, that were meant to instruct and guide, but that only cut deep and felt cruel. Silas's demands for order and discipline. Ideas Cullen understood all right, but had trouble somehow mastering. All that soul-serious righteousness, it didn't come natural to him the way it did to his father. Cullen waited with sweat forming beneath his arms and a nervous, unsettled feeling in his stomach as his father finished writing. Only then did he take time for him, removing his glasses as he turned in his seat.

"How's my boy doin'?" Silas asked.

He only called him *his boy* when he'd been drinking, but Cullen didn't see an open bottle anywhere.

Cullen nodded. "Doin' all right, I guess."

"I want you to do something for me," Silas said. "I want you to start preparing for a little trip."

Cullen stared at his father. There was a kind of blank feeling behind his eyes. "A trip?"

"Pack a small bag and have it handy. We'll be leaving Nazareth Church soon."

"Leaving? You mean the flock?"

"I mean you and me, the two of us."

There was something inside Cullen, busting to get out—elation or surprise, he didn't know which. But he'd learned a long time ago to keep his emotions in check in front of Silas. He said, "Okay."

Silas rose and crossed to the nightstand, fished inside and came out with his pipe. He stuffed the bowl full, then struck a match to it and huffed it to life. The rich smell of cherry smoking tobacco hit Cullen's nose. Standing there, the pipe at the corner of his mouth, Silas studied Cullen for a time.

"You've never found yourself much in the light of God, have you, son? This life I've so carefully constructed, there's no call in it for you?"

Cullen felt the squirmy feeling coming over him again.

"God has not sought to favor you," Silas continued. "But he gave you to me, my only boy. One strong male seed in more than a dozen weaker ones. And that's why we'll leave Nazareth Church together."

"I don't understand," Cullen said. "Why we leaving? Where we going?"

"All will be revealed soon enough. For now, let's just say that God has sought to reward us for our good work. I just want you to be aware, however, to avoid any strangers that might be asking questions."

"You talking about the woman and her husband, come to town?"

Silas's gaze sharpened. "You do as I say, Cullen. Stay clear of the strangers and soon your life will take a change for the good."

Cullen nodded. "That all?"

Silas motioned him off with his pipe, and Cullen drew himself from the chair and headed for the door. He expected Silas to stop him with one final caution. But he didn't, and Cullen didn't dare look back. There were new and exciting smells on the wind. And the healer—his daddy—had spoken.

———

DANIEL Cole had heard rumors of the swamp, but it was far more vile than he'd imagined. Jagged and rotting tree stumps were surrounded by black water. Exposed, gnarled root-hands clawed the muddy banks for whatever grasp they could find. Paddies of green scum floated on the dark surface. Patches of swamp grass stood motionless in the stale, earthy air. In the murky water's edge, frogs sat partially submerged, their bulbous eyes blinking at him. Dragonflies and mosquitoes circled about. A snake, possibly poisonous, skimmed the surface and disappeared off across the swamp. Another slithered from the hollow of a stump, slid beneath the scum, and disappeared.

Across the bog, on the only patch of solid earth, and backed against the rock escarpment, sat a sway-backed structure. A place the others referred to as the "whiskey shack." It was sided and roofed with split-wood shingles. Swamp grass and cattails, sprouting from the shallows, surrounded the posts that supported a rickety wooden porch that wrapped around the side of the shack and extended over the water's edge.

Harland pulled the SUV to a stop where the edges of the marsh came to meet the road. With nowhere else to go, he killed the engine. Daniel waited until Harland and Nigel had extracted the woman, then stepped out to join them. They stood there, the swamp stretching out before them, staring at the shack.

"Let's go, Sarah," Harland said, placing a hand on the woman's elbow.

"No!" she cried and suddenly pulled away.

"Sarah," Harland cautioned, "now don't be difficult."

"I don't want to go back there! You can't!"

Harland grabbed for her as the woman backed away.

"Come on, now!" he said, grappling to get hold of her.

"Take her!" Nigel said.

Harland stepped in and swept the frail woman off her feet and threw her over his shoulder. He moved off in a fireman's carry, with Nigel following, and crossed to the water's edge, where railroad ties were laid in to form a landing and a plankboard raft was anchored.

Daniel held back.

"It's okay, boy. Come on," Nigel said. "God's healer orders, and his servants comply."

Daniel hesitated, but then did as he was told. Together, the four of them boarded the raft. Harland kept the woman across his shoulder, controlling her with his free hand. Nigel began hauling at ropes used to ferry the raft across. Soon Daniel was joining in, pulling against the ropes and feeling the raft pick up momentum across the swamp.

When the raft finally bumped to a stop against the opposite landing, Harland righted the woman on her feet.

"Don't make me carr'ya the rest the way," he said.

Daniel was suddenly stricken with how lonely the swamp was. Only the sound of the raft creaking on its ropes, water lapping at the landing, and the on-again, off-again buzzing of flies. The grip of illness was plain on the woman's face and in her eyes. Too weak to continue her fight, she nodded her compliance and stepped off the raft and onto the shore.

As a group, they crossed the short patch of land to where steps led onto the porch. Below them the black water lay still. Partially submerged and scaled with corrosion were the remains of what might have once been a still—a large metal cooking pot and coils of copper tubing. Harland and Nigel led the woman up the steps and through the door. Daniel followed, keeping his eye on the coils, the shadows that moved through them beneath the surface of the water.

The shack was one room, covered in dust. There was a bookcase with no books, a sink basin, a table, a small cot, and a commode. A single recliner sat atop a coarsely woven area rug. Firewood was stacked in the corner, a half-burned log in the fireplace. Coal oil lanterns sat on a mantle. There was no source of electricity that Daniel could see.

Daniel let his eyes run the perimeter of the room. All about the place were curious squares of white linen, displayed proudly, like treasured masterpieces, on the walls. Each linen square was expertly embroidered with rows of letters and icons, images stitched into the fabric. He crossed to them and examined one, letting his fingers run across the stitching, the thread in various colors. He

173

studied the hieroglyphic images as Harland settled the woman into a chair.

"You afraid I'm going to run off on you?" the woman said.

Harland patted the woman's shoulder. "I just want you to accept God's will for you, Sarah, that's all."

"God's will," Sarah scoffed. "What do you know about God's will? Any of you."

Daniel abandoned the wall hangings and turned his attention to the woman. He said, "Sometimes we have to find ourselves alone, become very still, in order to hear God's voice." He was thinking of his last night in the cistern.

The woman turned her eyes on him. A condescending curl wormed its way across her lips. "Did *Silas* teach you that himself? Or did he have one of his goons impart his wisdom on you?"

"That's enough, Sarah," Harland said. "We'll bring you rations time to time."

Nigel nodded them toward the door, and the three of them left the shack. Daniel was happy to be leaving.

On the raft trip back, Daniel studied the shack, sensing the loneliness of the woman inside. *Defiance,* he thought to himself. It had once been *his* stairstep to damnation.

SIXTEEN

THE COURTHOUSE IN STANTON had no record of a death certificate for Ella May Samuels Shannon. Likewise, archives at the *Bluegrass Gazette*, the local newspaper, had no obituary for her either.

"If there's anyone who would know 'bout Nazareth Church
and its residents," the woman at the records office told Del, "it
would be Jan and Joan."

Jan and Joan, it turned out, were the keepers of the Powell
County Historical Archive. The tiny shopfront was piled with
books and records, artifacts and framed photographs—a mad
collector's assortment of antiques, all with the dust and smell of
time on them. The women were both in their late fifties. Joan was
a solid woman with thick ankles and heavy black shoes and socks.
She wore a pants suit over a simple pale blue blouse. Her hair was
trimmed short, shorter than Del's. Reading glasses were strung
from a silver chain around her neck.

Her partner, Jan, was thin and waifish. She had on a long flowered dress. Her hair hung in curly strands. Her feet were some of

the smallest Del had ever seen, slipped bare into simple flats. She was cute, this little one, with only the lines around her eyes giving away her age. Jan offered Del a seat in one of the two opposing rockers that sat in the corner, where book ledgers were stacked twenty to thirty deep.

"Those are guest registers from the Piquane Hotel. They date back to the nineteen-twenties," Joan explained, taking the rocker across from her once Del had settled in.

Jan came with tea, handing a cup and saucer to her partner, and asking Del, "Would you like some?" Her tone was sweet and without a trace of ego.

"I'm more of a coffee drinker," Del said. "But, sure, I'd like some."

Jan went off and returned with two more cups. She handed one to Del and took her own to stand at her partner's side.

After they'd all had time to sip, Joan said, "So you're looking for information on Nazareth Church?"

"Actually, about someone *in* Nazareth Church. Or someone who once was. I don't know if she's still alive or not. I've been told she died. I'm just trying to confirm that and find out what happened to her. Her name is Ella May Shannon. Or she might have been known by Samuels, her maiden name. I'm not sure. Do any of those names ring a bell?"

Jan and Joan shared a look. Joan said, "We knew Ella once upon a time. She was originally from Estill County, I believe. Married Roy Shannon and moved into his parents' house up the hill. That was sometime after the elder Shannons passed."

"Wait, you actually *knew* Ella?"

Shifting on her feet, Jan said, "We lived there once, Joan and I both. But we left more than twenty years ago."

"Ella was my mother."

There was silence, then surprise registered on Joan's face. "Don't tell me you're little Del."

Del looked at her for the longest time, feeling her teacup chattering against the saucer. It seemed impossible. "You ... you know who I am?"

"If Ella was your mother," Joan said, "then I held you the day you were born, was there at Ella's side as you delivered. There are no hospitals or doctors in the valley. Babies up there are midwived into existence."

The sudden blast of new information left Del stunned. She was having difficulty finding words. All she could think to say was, "I've been searching so long."

———

THEY told the story from the beginning, starting with Roy Shannon, born and raised in Nazareth Church. He later married a girl from Estill County, young Ella May Samuels, and brought her to live in the house he'd inherited from his parents, Torin and Alvey.

"I saw their gravestones," Del said.

Joan continued, saying that life had looked promising for the young newlyweds at first. However, toward the end of their second year as husband and wife, storm clouds began to form, as Ella's attempts to become pregnant failed.

"They tried seeking the help of doctors here in town," Joan told her. "Tried mountain remedies: herbs and potions."

"They even tried burying a dead cat by the light of the moon," Jan added. "The hills are alive with folk rituals."

"But she still didn't get pregnant?" Del asked.

Joan shook her head. "By then, though, Ella was becoming pretty entrenched in the community's way of life. She got it in her head that Silas could help."

"As a healer?" Del offered.

Joan nodded. "By that time, he'd already made a name for himself across four counties. The suggestion of it, the very idea of this young healer putting his hands on his young wife, practically drove your father insane."

Jan said, "See, he'd grown up with Silas and didn't buy into his healing-touch routine. He thought of him as just a charlatan."

"You sound like you don't either."

"People believe what they want to believe," Joan said.

Del sat thinking about it, plugging pieces into the puzzle. After a minute, she said, "So, what you're going to tell me is my mother went to Silas anyway. And later became pregnant."

Joan sipped her tea then nodded. "Nine months to the day, almost. You could have set your sidereal clock by it."

Del sat staring into her cup, examining the pattern of tea sediment at the bottom. There were some weighty implications involved, depending on which side of the religious coin you cared to place your bet.

Joan said, "So now you're wondering if Silas could be your real father, right?"

Del looked up to search the woman's eyes.

"It's the same thing your father wondered when he found out Ella had gone to Silas," Joan said. There was no delight in the woman's voice.

"What happened?" Del asked.

"There were accusations, name-calling. You could hear them arguing just about any time you passed by the house. Then, one night, in the dead of winter, Roy Shannon was up and gone, and baby Del with him."

"Why?" Del asked. A bit of defiance had crept into her voice. "Why would he do that, if he thought the baby, thought I, wasn't his child?"

Joan shrugged. "To get even with Ella. To punish her. I don't know. To punish both of them, maybe, her and Silas."

"No ... I just ... I mean ... you're not telling me the man who raised me, the man I grew up with, isn't even my own flesh and blood?"

Joan's eyes turned soft, she said nothing. Jan turned her gaze to the floor.

There was a long period of silence, Del not knowing what else to say. Finally, she said, "Well, even if you buy all that, the thing I don't understand is why Ella didn't go after her daughter? Why didn't she come looking for me? A mother would do that, wouldn't she?"

"For all we know, she did," Joan said. "We didn't see Ella much after that. Jan and I took off together shortly thereafter. We haven't been back since."

"So you can't really tell me if Ella is alive or dead."

Neither responded.

Del studied both women. "Why did you leave?"

Joan glanced to her partner, and Jan brought a reassuring hand to rest on her shoulder. When Joan's eyes came back to meet her, she said, "Let's just say there's not a whole lot of room for our kind in Nazareth Church."

SEVENTEEN

By now, word of the young woman was all over town. It gave Cullen a rise. At the diner, they were saying her name was Del, a Shannon, married and moved into the abandoned house up the road. At the General, they were saying she was from Arizona, making reference to the state being next to California, like saying it was Sodom, and Arizona must then be Gomorrah, just across the state line. In the barbershop, the men were saying she was wicked. That she cropped her hair short like a boy and wore clothes that revealed her young body. Virgil Aikens referred to her as a little slut. Harland Wilson called her a godless whore.

She sounded pretty good to Cullen.

From the trees behind the Shannon house, he could see in through the window. He imagined it at night, lit up inside, and pictured her, as he'd conjured her to look, moving around with nothing on. What he wanted was a glimpse of this woman. Wanted to believe, maybe, that her husband was off somewhere and gone, doing what husbands did when they weren't humping their wives. Wanted to imagine her alone inside.

This afternoon, though, the house was shadowy and still, and there was no vehicle parked in the drive. Cullen moved out of the trees, giving a quick glance to the house up the hill where his half-sister lived with her grandmother. Mariah, tasty enough, was on the verge of filling out. But his daddy had already claimed her for his own as he had already claimed virtually all the worthwhile women in Nazareth Church, declaring them off-limits even to their own husbands. Fucking them until they got sick or too old to fuck, then throwing them out with the trash or sending them home to their men all used up. Doing it all in the name of God. And Silas's followers, the baaing sheep, going along with it to save themselves from damnation or maybe a thrashing. The sonofabitch had that kind of power. Giveth the love of God with one hand, the backhand of the Devil with the other. But this one, this Del Shannon, she wasn't like the other women of Nazareth Church, come here to kiss his daddy's ring. Huh-uh. She and her husband had come of their own accord. Silas had no claim to her.

Cullen crossed down the hill and into the narrow backyard where the collapsed hillside had punched a hole in the wall. He could go in through the front; it would most likely be unlocked. But he liked the idea of skinning in through the narrow opening. It felt more … covert … more exciting. Taking one last look around, he poked his head through the opening.

The room was filled with dirt, the bed, the mattress, partially engulfed, and—fuck!—smelled of roadkill. Cullen squeezed through the tight opening, holding his breath. He crawled on hands and knees until he could stand upright inside the room. Then waited and listened.

Hearing nothing, he eased out through the door leading into the interior of the house and followed the hallway to the kitchen. He checked cabinets here, a drawer there, liking the idea of being alone in the house. He helped himself to a beer from the refrigerator and carried it with him to the living room. Then stopped.

The girl had spent the night on the sofa; the man had made a bed on the floor. Why? There were rumpled bedclothes, a nightshirt tossed over the arm of the chair.

Then Cullen remembered the bedroom, the mattress stained with rotting soil, the putrefying stench ... and imagined the woman resigning her poor, dumb schmuck of a husband to the floor in the corner, while taking the sofa for herself. Cullen pictured it, liking the idea the woman sleeping alone; feeling in need in the middle of the night and wanting someone, maybe anyone, to join her.

Cullen sat the beer on the lamp table and picked up the nightshirt. He held it to the light of the window, imagining the woman wearing it with nothing underneath. On the floor was a travel bag. Cullen squatted over it, unzipped it, and began rummaging inside.

There were a couple of knit tops, some jeans—the woman casual or traveling light. He rummaged further and felt something cold and hard. Cullen fished the object out. A gun, a little automatic, light in his hand, but black and sinister.

Whoa.

It raised more questions. Who was this woman? This man? Should he warn Silas?

Cullen let his fingers caress the barrel, admiring the tooling, feeling excitement course through him ... remembering the last time he'd tried to please his father ... bringing the FBI agent to him, the one who'd been asking questions around Biden ... remembering the back-lashing he took ... remembering his daddy's displeasure ...

His curiosity heightened, he set the gun aside and dug further inside the bag, letting his hands do the searching. T-shirts, a sweater, then—hey now!—something thin and silky.

Cullen withdrew his hand, bringing with it a pair of panties. He strung them out in front of him, to gauge the size. It was no more than a string with the tiniest triangle of sheer fabric at the crotch. Cullen felt a rush of excitement and mentally adjusted the picture of the woman in his mind, moving her, unseen now, to a *nine*, up from the seven he'd initially allowed, and placing bets whether she might even go a *ten*.

Whoever they were and for whatever reason they had come, Cullen made up his mind—then and there—to keep it all to himself. Keep the *woman* for himself.

Giving into his urges, Cullen stretched out on the sofa, tucking the beer in at his side. He cupped the panties to his face in both hands and concentrated on the smells. He pictured Del Shannon the way he'd created her in his mind—this new woman, untouched by his father. He let his tongue come out to taste the silky fabric, let his hand drop to the front of his pants. A voyeuristic rush washed over him. And, feeling a bit like Goldilocks in someone else's home, he hoped for Baby Bear to return home ... alone.

———

183

PSYCHIC awareness brought Cullen from his sleep. He bolted upright, spilling beer, and quickly stuffed the panties into the crack between the sofa cushions.

Nigel stood in the doorway, his stubby little arms cocked on his hips.

"Goddamn it! You sneaky little shit!" Cullen cried. "Can't you knock, you come callin'?" He came quickly off the sofa, his face red, ready to beat Nigel into the cracks of the hardwood flooring, but then, seeing Harland and the agent he'd brought in standing on the porch outside, he held back.

"We've got work to do here," Nigel said. "You need to leave."

"I saw her first."

Nigel said nothing, just stood there with his arms cocked.

"All right," Cullen said, giving in.

He rescued what was left of the beer, taking the near-empty bottle with him, and crossed out past the midget, pausing to say in his ear, "You say anything 'bout this to Silas, I swear, little man..."

Harland and the new guy pushed inside as Cullen exited past them out the door. He was onto the drive and heading off, when the door to the house closed firmly behind him.

———

FALCONET spotted Del's Wrangler coming through the gate. During the course of the day, he'd been into the barbershop and over to the bakery. He'd gone down to the melon patch, where women were gathering honeydews into baskets. Now he was coming down off the hill from the orchard, where he'd been talking to a man picking apples. Or, at least, *trying* to talk to him. Having to look up at the man on his ladder, the conversation going:

"How you doing?"

Nothing.

"Nice day, huh?"

A sullen glance.

"I guess you know I'm new in town."

No reaction.

"Just trying to be neighborly."

Nothing again.

"I was just wondering. Most of you people seem like you've been here awhile."

No reaction.

"Anybody else as new as me to the place? Some other beginner to talk to?"

Falconet wanted to gag, the pansy-ass words coming out of his mouth, but was hoping the man might volunteer the whereabouts of a recent arrival, like Daniel Cole maybe. He didn't. Instead, the man had come down the ladder, moved to another tree, and climbed to pick in silence once more. It was midafternoon. The whole day had gone pretty much the same way.

Falconet stepped into the street as Del approached and pulled the Jeep alongside.

"These people," Falconet told her in frustration. "They all seem to have been struck dumb."

She was quiet, not giving him much more than the man on the ladder.

"What's the matter, you don't look so ..." He hesitated, then said, "Awww, fuck ... don't tell me?"

"No," Del said, "I still don't know about Ella May. She could still be alive or dead. Who knows?"

185

"Well, that's good, right?"

Del removed her aviators. "Get in," she said, "and I'll tell you all about it."

On the ride up the hill, Falconet learned of her visit with the two lesbian curators of the Powell County Historical Archive. She told him the story of her parents, and of her mother's indiscretion with Silas, emphasizing how it "comes as quite a fucking shock" to find out that she could possibly be the daughter of Silas Rule.

"Come on. You don't believe that?" Falconet said. "It could have gone some other way, right? I mean, the lezzies weren't right there in the room at the time. Am I right?"

Del didn't reply. Then, after a moment, said, "I don't know, Frank. I really just don't know. What about you? Any news on Daniel Cole?"

"No, nothing. This fucking Silas, right? He takes all the assets, screws all the women, then names them to his …"

Del hit the brakes hard and the Wrangler skidded to a halt in the road. She grabbed Falconet's face in both hands and planted a huge kiss on him. "You are the man, Frank," Del said, breaking away and leaning back in the seat, a smile now on her lips.

"What? Wha'd I say?"

"Don't you see? I was so caught up in the question of Silas, I didn't think of it myself. If Ella somehow became one of Silas's wives, then …"

Falconet finished the idea for her. "Then we've been asking for the wrong person."

"Exactly. Remember! Mariah said that Silas would soon give her a different name. But the two ideas just didn't click."

"So you think Ella is known here by a different name?"

"Think about it: someone like Lowell—what would he know? He's just a kid. It could have been decades since she went by her real name."

"So not only do we not know if Ella is still alive or not, we don't even know her name."

"No, Frank, we don't," Del said, dropping the Jeep into first. "But sooner or later, we're going to find out."

———

THEY arrived at the house to find the front door standing open.

Del stepped inside, then stopped, halting Frank.

"I see it," Falconet said.

The room had been tossed, their personal effects thrown wildly about. On the wall above the sofa, graffiti had been spray-painted in red:

CONDEMNED BE THE HAND THAT'S OFFERED FALSELY!

Falconet stepped past her into the room, drawing his service revolver from beneath his windbreaker.

Del put her back to the door and eased it shut. She waited as Falconet cleared the kitchen, the hall, the bathroom, and lastly the bedroom.

When he'd once again returned to the living area, Del said, "I think they're trying to tell us something, Frank."

"Or trying to learn why we're here. I'm carrying my weapon and credentials. What about you? Anything incriminating?"

"Only the Baby Eagle," Del said, pointing to the gun, lying on the floor beneath the end table. "It was tucked inside my bag."

Del crossed to the bag, now sitting open on the floor. Her clothes and personal effects had been rifled and carelessly tossed about. She spotted red silk protruding from the crack between the sofa cushions and retrieved it to dangle the thong by a finger. "Which one do you suppose was going through my panties?"

"I don't know," Falconet said. "And I don't even want to venture a guess about the wet spot on the cushion."

"Actually, it smells like beer. At best, I'd say they're suspicious of us."

Falconet said, "Yeah … at best. Promise me you'll watch yourself from here on out."

"Why, Frank," Del said, "you're starting to sound like a concerned spouse."

"I'm sounding like a guy who's been undercover before," he said, conscious of the surgical scar that ran the length of his abdomen and remembering with painful clarity his most recent assignment in Miami. "This is how it starts. The suspicions will grow, and things will get a lot tougher. Sooner or later, we'll have to go head to head with this guy."

Del took a look at her clothing scattered about the room. She thought of Mariah and of her mother—alive or dead.

"Then I say, bring it on!"

EIGHTEEN

THE DEACONS WERE STARTING to complain. The godless harlot and her faithless husband being here was "just not right." They'd settled into the community "without so much as a howdy," and besides were "askin' lots of questions."

How quickly their faith falters, Silas thought, looking at the two deacons, Virgil and Harland, who had come to see him at the church. They were standing before him, Bibles in hand, shifting nervously on their feet—emissaries for the rest of the deacon body. Outside, the world had gone dark. Dim bay lights, high above them, cast shadows on the floor. Nigel had taken a seat a couple of rows back to observe the proceedings. Silas, sitting stoic at the end of the front pew, legs crossed, let the deacons say their piece.

"Healer," Vigil Aikens said, "the girl and her husband, you're not thinking to let them stay? Please, healer, tell us you're not. They're not a part of us."

Harland said, "They've got a gun in the house, and the woman dresses like a whore. What kinda man lets his wife do that?"

"And you shoulda heard her sass me in the diner over breakfast," Virgil added. "So the girl's looking for her mother. But the man's also been asking questions, wasting God-fearin' people's time while they're trying to do God's work. The girl constantly askin' for *Ella*. What if she's not really a Shannon?"

Silas rose to his feet and crossed past them to the altar. His back to them, he said, "She's a Shannon all right. Trust me."

"Well, all right. Maybe she is one," Virgil said. "Still, what if she's connected to the authorities somehow? Or the man is?"

He was listening to them and thinking of the girl. She was troubling to him, true. Was it God's test—the girl appearing suddenly after all these years, appearing just now, as the Esteps were making their way to him with their fortune? Or were there other forces at work? Forces outside Nazareth Church? Governmental forces? Things to consider.

"They could be spies," Harland said, picking up where Virgil had left off. "What if ...?"

What if, what if, what if? Silas wanted to scream. *Glory! The weight of them!*

Silas turned sharply, letting his voice form a knife with which to stab. "Fools!"

Virgil and Harland took a step backward; Nigel, not in the direct line of fire, squirmed in his seat.

"Do you think they have the power to stop *my* will? Your maker's will?"

Silas started slow and let his momentum build. "Do I not care for you?"

"Why, yes, you do—" Virgil attempted.

"Do I not provide for your every need. Bring safeguard to your very soul? Do you not know that all that *was*, or *ever will be*, has already been written in the Book? Surely this you believe."

Silas turned his gaze toward Nigel. "How long have I been teaching you?"

Without waiting for an answer he turned back to the deacons. "How long before you understand? You have a chance to learn my salvation. But what do you do? You cry like lambs before the slaughter. The girl! And the man! Are here because you are weak! God places them before you as your enemy, but dare you stand your ground? Instead, you come to me, your faith withered and dry."

A whine registered in Virgil's voice. "We only wanna know what you want us to do."

Silas crossed to them in three long strides, and glared down from his full height.

"I tell you again, so you may hear. The day is coming. Have I not prepared you? What armies can man send against us that will thwart God's plan? You fear a girl. A girl!" he repeated for emphasis. "And this one faithless man. Are they so powerful? What would be the outcome should they discover God's will at work? You come seeking direction? Go! Out of my house! Wisdom will come to you at an hour I decide!"

Virgil and Harland backed away, then turned and hurried from the church, clutching their Bibles close.

———

NIGEL remained in the pew, waiting and watching as Silas turned his back to him and moved several steps away in thought. Of late, he had been seeing Silas building toward some end. The guns, the explosives, the car that he had instructed him and Harland to drop miles above the gorge. He understood without doubt the importance of the Esteps and their wealth. Those before them were small change. A way of sustaining the cause. But the Esteps … huh-uh … Nigel had spent too much time among the carnies not to recognize a *big fish* when he saw it. The girl and her husband, they posed a complication for Silas—whether here by coincidence or on some assignment from authorities didn't matter. Their presence at this untimely juncture would bring Silas to a decision. A hurried implementation of his plans. Plans Nigel wasn't sure included him or not. What Silas needed ultimately was to buy time. What Silas needed right now was God's trusted guidance. Risking retribution, Nigel thought to help him out.

"The Esteps …" he began.

Silas said nothing.

"… they arrive tomorrow."

Silas still didn't respond.

Nigel slipped from the pew and crossed toward him. "You could get rid of the young woman and her husband, but what if it's true that they were sent to look for the agent?"

"Then it could bring more unwanted attention at a time when I can least afford it," Silas said, finishing the thought for him.

"But as you so aptly put it, what power do they have? If they were sent here by authorities, what harm would come from them seeing their co-worker's welfare?"

"What harm indeed?"

Nigel let the question go unanswered and waited.

Silas turned and stepped onto the risers. He leaned against the podium and looked out across the sanctuary. Nodding in self-satisfaction, his eyes took on the luster of black pearls. "If the girl and the man are here to find the agent, then, yes, what harm? Perhaps, best we let them see him as he is. Best we let them bear witness."

Nigel said, "And they'll report back that the agent is safe and continuing to fulfill his assignment."

"And if they have come simply, as they say they have, then all I have to do is keep the girl away from the shack where her mother is."

"Either way it buys you time," Nigel said.

"Time," Silas said, contemplative. "All I need is a little time."

"Praise God," Nigel said.

"Yes," Silas said. "How clear His voice when you but turn your ear to Him."

Nigel remained quiet and watched as Silas stepped from the risers, crossed around without another word, and exited through the back door of the church. Now he climbed onto one of the front pews and sat back, crossing his feet at the ankles and lacing his fingers behind his head.

How great it was, Nigel once again reminded himself, *to be the voice of God.*

———

"I'D like to get a look inside those dorms first chance I get," Falconet said, coming out of the kitchen with beers and into the living area where Del was reorganizing her bag.

She took the beer he offered. "And I'd like to get a lock for the front door."

"Here's to that."

They toasted the idea, clinking bottles. Del took her beer and settled onto the sofa. Falconet slipped his shoes off and dropped to the bedding on the floor.

"Poor guy, your aching back. I'm sorry about the bedroom, Frank. No more questions for now. Tomorrow we get the stuff to fix the wall, I promise."

"It's not so bad," Falconet said. "I hear there are plenty of undercover operatives with walkers and canes." He lay back, balancing the beer on his chest.

After a time he said, "That trip today, the ladies telling you about Ella and Silas . . . it make you feel any different about her?" Falconet waited for an answer.

"Well," Del said, her eyes fixed on the bottle cupped in her lap, "she's still my mother, no matter what. But it's all like some kind of dream. You know? Those women actually knowing her and my father. Actually knowing *me*." She took a minute, still gazing into the amber bottle. "You know I grew up imagining that my father might have actually murdered my mother."

"No shit?"

"No shit. I used to stand in the backyard, staring at the grass and wondering if he might have buried her there. He kept so many secrets, Frank."

"I can see your father being pissed off," Falconet said. Del's eyes came to meet his. "I mean, this fucking guy's hands all over his young wife, fuck yeah."

"You think I belong to Silas, too, don't you?"

"I didn't say that. I mean, no … look at you … you look nothing like the bastard. You've got those beautiful green eyes."

Del let herself smile. "Silas said I had my mother's eyes."

"Then I bet she's a looker, too. You'll see when we find her."

"You honestly think she's still alive somewhere?"

"Yeah, yeah, I do," Falconet said, taking time to sip his beer. "See, I been thinking. Why else would these jerk-offs be so secretive. What's the old saying? 'People with nothing to hide, hide nothing.' That kind of thing. I don't know, call it cop's intuition."

Del said, "I think you're right."

"Yeah, right?"

"*Yeah, right*," Del said, mimicking. "Call it *women's* intuition."

NINETEEN

THE CHURCH BELL TOLLED and continued tolling. The throaty resonance rang through the gorge and echoed off the rocky escarpment. Del came upright out of a sound sleep. On the floor, Falconet raised on one elbow.

"The fuck time is it?"

Del lifted her watch from the lamp stand and examined the illuminated dial.

"It's two a.m."

There was a murky light coming through the windows. Falconet came to his feet, pulling jeans over his boxers, and went onto the porch. Del tugged her nightshirt down and followed.

Floodlights lit the valley, refracting off the fog layer that hovered in the gorge, giving a fearful glow to the night. The loud ringing continued.

"The rats are coming out of the woodwork," Falconet said. "Like freaking zombies or something."

Del leaned across the porch railing to see as much of the road leading down as possible. Porch lights were coming on, and the residents of Nazareth Church were leaving their houses—one by one—and making their way down the hill toward the sound of the bell.

Mariah appeared on the path and came out past the porch.

"What's going on, Mariah?" Del asked.

"It's Silas. He's calling the flock to come."

"Where's you grandmother?"

"She's got phlebitis. She's allowed to stay behind. But you gotta come."

"But I'm not dressed."

"There's no time. Everybody's gotta go. Hurry."

"Grab a jacket and my shoes, and let's go," Falconet said, speaking close to her. "This might be a good time to do some snooping."

———

DEL was feeling naked in her nightshirt and sandals, the denim jacket pulled on in haste. And she was chilled. The cool night air had begun to crawl up her exposed legs. The townspeople moved like zombies toward the sound of the bell. Mariah led them down the road, imploring them to hurry. At the church, the townspeople crowded through the entrance.

Falconet said, "You go. I'll catch up with you later," and slipped away without notice.

Inside, the pews had filled. Del and Mariah were crowded into the space at the back of the sanctuary, forced to stand shoulder to shoulder with the others.

Silas was at the podium, leaning over it, projecting himself into the congregation. His denim shirt sleeves were rolled up, revealing sinewy forearms. He waited, his eyes leveled on the crowd, as the doors were closed.

When silence had fallen on the room, he said, "I am your life and your death! The law is mine! Through me you shall find the truth!"

Del took time to scan the audience. There was the kid from the diner, Lowell, their server; and the tobacco-chewer from the General. She spotted the two stonewall laundry mavens, but not the sickly little woman who did the folding.

"Through the voice of the Father," Silas continued, "I offer you my wisdom."

Does he believe what he's selling? Del wondered.

Silas stepped from behind the podium and down off the riser. The front pew of followers edged space for him to advance. Silas stepped where they parted, onto the seat, then up, to rest one foot on the backrest of the pew.

"We have talked of the Day. I tell you now, it draws near."

Now, he was moving again, wading on long legs from pew to pew, parting his seated followers like the parting of the Red Sea as he made his way toward the back.

"By His hand He made heaven and earth. By my hand He will take it away. Your sins are more than you can bear. Why will you be lost?"

Silas waded to within three rows of the back. Del could see clearly the hammered-leather face, the eyes that burned with a dark light. She saw him take her in with those eyes, a brief connection, before turning to wade his way back toward the front.

Now he stopped again, astride a pew, and faced his flock.

"I tell you now. One day soon you will hear my thunders. The heavens will be pulled away to reveal His judgment. Are you prepared? Do you believe? Or must I speak in warning again?"

Silas let the weight of his words hang heavy on the air. Then, in a quieter voice, "One among you has sinned. One among you knows God's anger. One among you prepares himself this night."

At once, Daniel Cole appeared in the wing off-stage. The sudden recognition caused a chill to run up Del's back. She hugged her jacket tighter.

Daniel crossed onstage, carrying a lamb. There were tears forming in the young man's eyes. He stood the lamb on its feet before the congregation, holding it still by the wool of its nape. The lamb bleated, as if sensing its demise.

Silas strode the last few pews and stepped to the floor. He crossed onto the riser to join Daniel Cole.

Del turned to see Mariah taking it in, her eyes wide. Del realized … with thoughts that flashed on her own childhood … all this, this way of life … it would have been her way of life had her father not taken her away. *My father*, Del thought—the man she'd know as such.

Del heard the gasp of the congregation and turned in time to witness Silas with a drinking glass in one hand, a long hunting knife in the other.

The lamb let out another long and plaintive cry as, without hesitation, Silas laid the blade beneath its chin and cleanly slit its throat. He caught the glass half full of blood before the lamb dropped unceremoniously to the floor. The bleating silenced.

Now Silas tossed the knife aside.

"Let the sins of the father …"

With one bloodied thumb, he drew the sign of the cross on Daniel's forehead. The tears, which had previously puddled in the young man's eyes, now streamed shamelessly down his face.

"… be cleansed with the blood of the lamb."

"Praise God!" someone said.

He handed Daniel Cole the glass and said, "Let his blood be one with your own."

Daniel turned the glass up and drank.

The midget, and a man Del didn't recognize, appeared on stage and quietly led Daniel Cole away. It was for her, she realized. The *show* was all for her.

Now Silas was back at the podium, his eyes scanning the congregation. "You have witnessed faith, brothers and sisters. God's glory in our very midst." Now his voice swelled. "But God is not smiling on Nazareth Church on this eve of reckoning. No! There are strangers among us. Prideful, they bring arrogance to our home. They flaunt lasciviousness before our children."

Del looked over the audience. The eyes of the congregation, which had been fixed on Silas, were now throwing glances her way.

"But, I tell you, brothers and sisters, God is not unhappy with these intruders. He does not waste time on devils and demons. No! What concerns God, this eve, is complacency. What concerns God is the faithful. What concerns God are those who would claim him for their own, while allowing wickedness to walk unchallenged."

Del watched the man, listening to him weave his carefully worded message, corrupting the congregation's minds with hatred, turning them against her and her husband-partner, Frank. Falconet had warned her, things would get tough. Now Silas was seeing to it.

"I have to go," she said, close to Mariah's ear. "I'll catch you later, okay."

"You can't just go. Silas ain't finished yet," Mariah whispered.

"He is as far as I'm concerned."

Del pushed her way into the night, through a gauntlet of stiff shoulders and hard stares, leaving Mariah and the sheep of Nazareth Church to the rantings of their messianic leader.

———

FALCONET moved beyond the bath of floodlights that was trained on the town and the road leading into the draw. He stayed close to the tree line, circling wide of Silas's house, ducking in and out of shadow. He reached a long cinderblock building, a garage of sorts, where a flatbed farm truck sat parked along the wall. Inside, beyond the open barn-style doors, sat a small farm tractor and some unrigged attachments for tilling and mowing. Next to the tractor was a Cadillac Escalade SUV, then two more empty slots that could hold more vehicles if needed. In the corner was a large roll-around tool chest and a workbench with tools scattered about. Falconet stopped, taking time to listen to the night.

From the church, he could hear muffled condemnations. Silas berating his flock, enjoining them to everlasting damnation. Farther down in the compound sat the matching dormitories—two-story, military-style barracks. The windows on both levels were dark.

Falconet crossed the yard to the first dorm, and with a quick look back toward the church, let himself inside. There were doorways on either side of a long hallway, stairs at either end. Falconet moved quickly down the hardwood corridor, using a pocket flashlight from his jacket to guide the way. He checked the rooms in order. They were tiny quarters with sparse furnishings, little in the way of decoration—cots, lamp tables, lamps, vanities, mirrors, water closets. There was women's clothing in the first room, more in the next. More again after that. Falconet was starting to realize the dorms were divided between men and women.

At the end of the hall, he took the stairs two at a time to the second level. More of the same, eight rooms on either side, women's clothing in all of the rooms.

In the third room from the end of the hall, Falconet spotted something different. Where the other rooms were bare of wall decor, this room had several wall hangings. Falconet stepped inside. On the wall were several squares of white linen, each with curious rows of neatly embroidered letters and icons stitched with brightly colored thread. Falconet let his flashlight slide down a row of images. They were like hieroglyphics—alphabet letters, making no real sense, tiny icons that could be representative of anything. On the vanity, next to where he was standing, was a sewing box. Inside were the makings of these hangings—swatches of cloth, needles, and colorful spools of thread. *One room*, out of dozens, Falconet considered.

Outside, the night had grown almost too quiet. There was an impending sense that time was running out. If there was any chance of finding evidence of Daniel Cole having passed this way, it was obvious he would have to check the other building. Falconet moved to the stairway and down, and let himself out into the night. He stepped off in the direction of the second dorm, then froze. There were voices in the yard, heading his way.

Falconet quickly checked his options.

Spotting a small shed down beyond the dormitories, he moved quickly that way, keeping shadow in his path. Taking cover at the corner of the shed, he drew his service revolver from beneath his jacket and looked back across the yard. Three men approached, coming down toward the dormitories from the house. One he recognized as the midget, the other perhaps one of the deacons. Falconet got a closer look at the third man.

"The fuck," he said to himself.

Daniel Cole was laughing and talking as if the men were old friends of his. They crossed to the far barracks and stood beneath the cone light outside the door. Falconet slipped farther into darkness and watched.

"I bet you'd like a cigarette," the midget was saying, shaking one from a pack and holding it for Daniel to take. Falconet could hear their voices carrying across the yard.

"God bless you," Daniel said.

Falconet watched the young agent accept the offered flame, draw on the cigarette, and blow smoke. Watched him take time to inhale the dewy night, like he'd never tasted air so sweet.

Falconet waited.

The kid wasn't shackled. And there was certainly no sign of coercion from the others. It made matters worse, Falconet realized. Either the kid was the grand-fucking-master of undercover work and had thoroughly infiltrated the community, or there was something deeply disturbing about the scene before him.

Falconet took time to study the road leading down to the river. It ran along the water's edge and disappeared into darkness where it led into the gorge. The door to the shed, at his back, was slightly ajar. Falconet took a brief look inside.

In the murky shadows, Falconet could make out rows of what looked like weapons, lined in racks along the walls. He eased the door open a bit, hoping the hinges didn't give him away, and slipped inside. There were weapons all right. AR-14s standing on end and MAC-10s hanging by straps from nails in the framework. There were handguns, Smith & Wessons, Berettas and the like, spread out across a small table. And, on the floor, ammo boxes filled with various ammunition. There were also two compact wooden crates labeled:

CAUTION EXPLOSIVES.

Falconet used the butt of one of the Smiths to jack the lid off one of the crates.

Sifting through shredded straw, Falconet hit the mother lode— C-4 plastic explosives. And a lot of them.

What was Silas up to? He estimated the explosive power within the crate and felt a chill run down his spine. Darius would love to see this. And, oddly, so would Del. He was wishing she were here right now—a girl who hunted men for a living and could maybe appreciate the adrenaline of the moment.

Falconet returned the lid to the box using the palm of his hand to quietly press it back in place, then stepped out into the night.

At the men's dorm, Daniel Cole was finishing his cigarette, tossing the butt to the ground to step on it. Now Nigel was leading the young agent inside, a hand on the kid's shoulder, leaving the other man to wait outside the door.

Shit!

Falconet turned back inside the shed. He took a brief look around, then with no place else to sit, positioned himself above some eight to ten pounds of very high explosives and took a seat. There he waited.

TWENTY

Del followed the three men at a distance, passing down along the side of the house. She edged along the porch railing, where light spilled from the kitchen window, its yellow glow casting suspicion on shapes and shadows in the yard. She could hear muffled praises from the congregation back at the church, sharpened condemnations from their leader. There was no one inside the kitchen.

Passing beyond the glow of window light, Del continued on to the back of the house. Down at the barracks, the three men had paused outside for a smoke—one was clearly the midget, the others appeared to be Daniel Cole and one of the men who had led him on and off the stage. Del took cover at the corner of the house, where a broken downspout protruded awkwardly and a cistern lay partially open, its concrete-slab covering pushed away.

In the black hole below, Del could make out shapes. A basket? A pail? Litter scattered about. It brought to mind dark stairwells and homeless men amid the shredded remnants of their lives. Had someone been living here?

Del drew her denim jacket tighter. It was cooler down here near the river. The night breeze licked beneath her nightshirt and sent chills up her back. Across the way, the two barracks sat with their windows darkened. No sign of Falconet. Now Daniel Cole was stubbing out his cigarette with the toe of his shoe, and he and the midget were going inside. The other man, remained behind. Still no sign of Frank.

She was turning back along the side of house, coming into light cast by the kitchen window, when a voice spoke to her from the shadows. "He's down there in the shed."

It stopped Del in her tracks. She shaded her eyes and tried to see beyond the light. "Who's there?"

A figure appeared on the porch, leaning into the light from where he sat in a rocker—blond hair and boyish features looking back at her.

"You're that new woman."

"And let me guess," Del said. "You must be Cullen."

Cullen rose and came down off the porch. He wasn't as tall as she might have expected, not at all like his father. But he wasn't bad-looking either, with a risky shock of hair that hung across his brow.

"They said you were different."

"Who's they?" Del asked

"Townsfolk. But that's okay, I like different. You're not interested to know where your husband is?"

"I don't know what you're talking about," Del said.

Cullen smiled.

"What about you?" she said. "Shouldn't you be at the meeting?"

"Why? I already know what he's gonna say." Cullen waved his hands dramatically. "The End Time's coming! The End Time's coming!"

"You don't seem altogether bothered by the idea."

"Oh, I believe it's coming, all right, just not the way these people might think."

"What's that supposed to mean?"

Cullen put a finger to his lips. "It's a secret just me'n my daddy share."

"Actually, you don't seem to buy your daddy's bullshit."

"You are different, you know it," Cullen said. "Listen, while your husband's tied up, why don't I get us a bottle from the kitchen and I'll show you around. We can go down by the river."

"And tell me a secret?"

"Maybe, if you're nice."

"I'll take a rain check, thanks."

Cullen reached for her, putting one hand on her shoulder. "Come on," he said, and moved his other hand to her thigh beneath the hem of her nightshirt.

Del pushed his hand away.

"You wouldn't want me to tell Silas you were snooping around down here, would you?" Cullen brought his hand back again, this time boldly slipping it higher.

Del caught Cullen by the crotch, getting a handful and squeezing. Pain and surprise registered on the young man's face. She held on, saying, "And you wouldn't want me to tell Silas you're a panty sniffer either." It was a long shot, but something seemed to register on Cullen's face. Del gave him a last squeeze, then shoved, sending him stumbling backward over the steps, to land flat on his seat on the porch. "Aw, don't look so disappointed, Cullen. Maybe we'll hook up at the church social and I'll give you a dance."

Del left Cullen holding his privates and headed back toward the church.

The church doors were opening as she arrived, and the congregation was beginning to file out. She mingled with the crowd, found Mariah, and joined her to make their way with the others back up the road.

Del had been off in a funk since her father's death—depression being a sneaky thing. But now she was feeling it lift. Physical confrontation had brought it on, the thrill of the chase. And inside, Del could feel that old familiar adrenaline starting to flow.

————

IT was four in the morning when Falconet made it back to the house. Del was waiting for him, giving him a hug as he came through the door and saying, "I was getting worried. You okay?"

She was out of her jacket and sandals, standing before him in the nightshirt. Very sexy.

"It was close," Falconet said. "Where's Mariah?"

"She's gone back to her grandmother. Find anything?"

"They've got separate men's and women's dorms, and a freaking arsenal like you wouldn't believe. I wish you had been there. Honest to God, enough explosives to wage a hillbilly jihad. I'm going to have to talk to Darius about it."

"Yeah, well, guess who I saw?"

"Daniel Cole," Falconet said. "I saw him too. Surprisingly, he didn't look like he was under duress."

"Not if you don't count mind control. He seemed *vacant* on stage, if that's the right word. I also ran into the son, Cullen. He knows we were snooping around, but I get the feeling he won't say anything. I don't think he buys into the whole *heaven and hell* routine. He put a move on me."

"He what?"

Del helped him out of his windbreaker, helped him off with his shoulder holster and revolver, feeling a sudden urge to comfort him. She wanted to say, *Poor guy, sit down, let me rub your shoulders.* What she said was, "Don't go all macho on me, Frank. I handled it."

"Little asshole. We have any beer left?"

"I think so. I'll get you one," she said. Something closer to the way she was feeling.

Del went off to the kitchen.

When she returned, Falconet was seated on the sofa. She handed the beer to him and took a seat at the far end to face him, bringing her feet up under her gown.

Sipping, Falconet said, "The kid, Daniel . . . if you're right about the mind-control thing, it might become something of a bitch to get him out of here, short of fucking kidnapping the rookie. It was a big-ass mistake sending him here."

"Well, I don't think the Bureau totally knew what they were sending him into at the time. Now they do."

"We go to town for supplies tomorrow, I'm going to try to hook up with Darius."

They were quiet for a moment—Del aware of Falconet, his presence at the far end of the sofa. She was surprised by her feelings—a sudden onslaught of tenderness toward him. Falconet, the cock-sure Fed; Falconet, the little boy, sipping his beer and looking idly about the room. She coached herself to keep her emotions in check. But she gave Falconet one more once-over, before getting back to the topic at hand. She said, "You were right about things getting tougher, Frank. The whole show at the church tonight was staged specifically for us to see Daniel alive and well. Now Silas is turning the community against us."

"You realize, of course, shit around here may hit the fan before you find out about your mother."

Del nodded. "Or, just maybe it takes getting the shit to fly to find out what you want to know."

TWENTY-ONE

THEY LEFT ATLANTA a little after nine in the morning, catching back roads as they came out of Tennessee. There were no interstates, these parts. For the love of God, not much in the way of civilization either. Jim Estep was tired and hungry and damn sick of listening to Julie complain. It was either too hot with the windows down and the air conditioner off, or too cold with the windows up and the air conditioner on.

And he'd been thinking about Kara again.

Why were they doing this? Oh, yeah ... to save his ass from eternal damnation and ... oh, yeah ... to save his sorry marriage.

The airy weightlessness he'd felt leaving the tent that night in Kingsport had in the weeks since begun to subside. He had stood by, feeling helpless, as Julie took immediate control. She had pressed for a quick sale of the house and brought in an auctioneer to liquidate their belongings. And she'd taken control of the proceeds, grabbing the bearer bond and hiding it away somewhere he couldn't get his hands on it.

Up her twat seemed a likely place.

All in all, it had taken less than five weeks to liquidate their lifestyle. The house in Atlanta had sold for one million, two hundred thousand dollars; the insurance brokerage, with its book of clients brought another two million six. With the furniture, the jewelry, the personal effects, and two of three cars sold at auction, the net price of Jim Estep's salvation had come to a grand total of more than four million dollars. Now he and Julie were on their way to find redemption for his tainted soul in the place called Nazareth Church.

"The turnoff's supposed to be just south of Biden," Jim said, driving and puzzling over the map spread open on the steering wheel. "The sign says this is Biden. Damn it! Your damn complaining, we must have missed it!"

Julie, on the seat next to him, said nothing. Choosing instead to glare out the window at the landscape, acting pissy that he wasn't one hundred percent joyous over the move.

Jim made his way through the center of town, trying to read and navigate at the same time. "I don't understand why it's not on the map. It should be on the map."

"Oh, for God's sake, Jim, just stop and ask."

Jim crushed the map in his hands and tossed the crumpled wad into the back seat. He spotted a store named *Feed-N-Seed*, its sign also advertising farm tools and supplies. He wheeled the car off the street and into the angled parking at the front of the building, where a young blonde with short hair was loading lumber into the back of a Jeep.

Jim noticed the way her small breasts moved inside her shirt as she stretched to slide a half-sheet of plywood into the back; noticed the flash of trim, bare waistline beneath the rise of her shirt-tail as she reached for a two-by-four and slid it in on top; noticed her glance his way as she reached for another. And ... shit! Noticed Julie watching.

She, and God, were constantly on the job.

———

DEL saw the man in the white Lexus sedan checking her out. A married guy in his forties going through the whole midlife comb-over, gut-sucking, get-it-while-you-can-still-get-it-up phase. It made her think of Ed Jeski, the married man cheating on his wife with her. Was he still a Tucson cop? That brought her to Falconet, another kind of cop. Did she have a thing for guys with guns? Maybe. Or was it a thing for married men?

She finished sliding the last two-by-four into the Jeep and was checking the load when the man from the Lexus stepped out and crossed toward her.

"Hi," he said to her. He was smiling maybe a little bigger than necessary. "One nice day, isn't it?"

Del wiped her hands on her jeans and offered one for him to shake.

"You live around here?" the man asked.

Del had to think about that one. She'd been here three days and nothing about it felt like home. "Up the road."

"That's quite a load of lumber you've got there."

Del expected him to call her "missy," or "little lady." But he didn't. "What can I do for you?" she asked.

"Yeah, well," the man said, "I'm looking for the turnoff to Nazareth Church."

"That your wife?" Del said, tossing a look at the Lexus.

The man followed her gaze toward the car, then turned his eyes back to her. "Her? Why don't we just say—"

"Ask her to join us," Del said, cutting him off.

"What?"

Del tossed another nod in the direction of the car.

The man hesitated, crestfallen, but turned toward the Lexus. "Honey, she says she wants to talk to you."

The passenger door opened, and a thin, angular woman stepped out and came around to join them.

Del held her hand out for the woman. "Just so there's no misunderstanding," she said. "I'm Del Shannon."

The woman took her hand in a dainty grip and shook it lightly. "I'm Julie Estep. This is my husband, Jim."

"So you're looking for Nazareth Church?"

"You know the place?" Jim Estep said, optimism returning to his voice.

Del gave him a look and held it until the man shifted on his feet and diverted his gaze. Returning her focus on Julie, she said, "You need to head back south about six miles. It's a gravel road on the left. The only one between here and there."

Julie said, "Thank you."

"You don't mind my asking," Del said, "what brings you here?"

"We've been invited to join the healer," Julie said. "We met him at a revival in Kingsport. It's a chance to get our lives right with God. You might say it's a new beginning for us, Jim and me."

Right with God, Del thought. She wanted to say something. Wanted to tell these naïve hicks to turn their car around and thank God they missed the turnoff. She didn't. Instead, she simply nodded.

"Are you here for the healer?" Julie asked.

"Me? No. I just moved into a house in Nazareth Church. An inheritance kind of thing, long story. But I'll be sure to check on you, see how you're doing."

"You're a nice person," Julie said. "Maybe you'll attend services with us."

"Well, maybe, sometime. I've got ... you know ... a lot of stuff to do." Del patted the stack of lumber for emphasis.

The woman smiled, then nudged her husband who had gone mute. Together they made their way back toward the car.

Falconet appeared from along the sidewalk from the direction of the Palms Motel. He joined her at the back of the Wrangler as the Lexus pulled away.

"I know those yokels," he said, nodding to the departing vehicle.

"You do? From where?"

"From the revival in Kingsport. Should have fucking been there. Guy stands up, right in the middle of the sermon, and announces to the world he's been banging some other twinkie. Had some kind of fucking spiritual conversion."

"Yeah, well, if he did," Del said, "I get the feeling it didn't fully take. You get to talk to Darius?"

Falconet shook his head. "He's gone back to the office for the day. I left a message at the desk and on his cell phone. I'll have to catch him tomorrow."

Del let her gaze move to the road leading south out of town.

Falconet said, "Something bothering you?"

Del gave him a slight nod. "Pilgrims," was all she could think to say.

———

DOWN the road, Jim Estep said, "Not very friendly around here." He was feeling scolded. Everybody conspiring, it seemed, to make him a better man. They drove on, not speaking, until they reached Nazareth Church.

"My Lord," Julie said, "that's a big cross."

Jim eased the car through the gate and into the edge of town. He stopped where the gravel road split: one way continuing on past storefronts, the other curling right, down toward a church and some sort of compound. Above them, on the hillside, was a cemetery.

"Is this it?" Jim said. "I mean, I wasn't exactly expecting the Crystal Palace, but, c'mon. There's nothing here. What are we supposed to do? Where are we supposed to live?"

Julie reached out to touch Jim's hand. "Whatever it is, remember, it's God who has brought us here." She hesitated. "Jim, honey, before we begin our new lives together, there's something I feel is only appropriate I tell you."

Julie turned in the seat to face him, her back against the door.

Hearing the quiet, serious tone in his wife's voice, Jim thought, *What the hell is it now?* He said, "Yeah?" and turned his gaze off out the side window, past the cemetery to the orchards.

Julie took her time responding. "I … well … you see …"

Jim had been studying the apples still hanging from the trees. Now he turned to look at his wife. "For God's sake, just spit it out."

"Well, the thing is, darling," Julie said, wringing her hands. "There was that time you were in Chicago for three days."

"Julie, what the hell are you talking about?"

"About eight years ago. I guess I'd known for a long time about the women you'd been seeing. I mean, not any of them specifically, understand, but you know, in general."

"Julie, if you've got something to say, for God's sake come out with it."

"I had an affair, too," Julie blurted, bringing her eyes to meet his.

Jim Estep felt his bowels go soft.

"What?"

He was watching her now, scanning her face for the change that would say, *Just a joke, silly. You should see the look on your face!*

It didn't come.

"A man from our church," Julie continued. "We had dinner a couple of times. I don't know why. I guess I was just lonely. On one of those evenings, we took a long drive after. We stopped at a place overlooking Lake Lanier. It was a beautiful night."

"Who?"

"That doesn't matter. We were just …"

"It sure as hell does matter!" Jim felt his voice rising on the bile that had entered his throat.

"I wanted to tell you," Julie said, "because we're entering a new phase of our life. I've made my peace with God, but I think it's important that we start things over with nothing between us."

Christ!

Jim Estep killed the engine and turned to face his wife across the console. "Did you fuck him?"

"I just wanted to …"

"Did you?" Jim demanded. "Did you bend that skinny ass over the front of the car and let him use it?"

"It wasn't like that."

"God! I am so fucking stupid! Letting you sell the house. My business! Jesus fucking Christ! Let you talk me into this whole religious bullshit. Look at this goddamn place!"

"I didn't talk you into anything," Julie said, her voice taking on an edge of its own.

"Well, you sure picked a helluva time to tell me, that's one thing for sure. You bitch!"

"What about you?" Julie fired back. Tears were forming in her eyes. "What about all those little hussies you've been putting your dick in. Huh! What about them, you bastard!"

Just then, Jim caught movement from over his shoulder.

Three men were approaching from down the road. One was a little guy, a midget, leading the way, his biceps large and oddly out of proportion to the rest of his body. The other two looked like farm hands—maybe men who could work in coal mines, run a sawmill.

As they neared the car, the two hands split off. One moved around to Julie's side of the car, the other followed the midget to face Jim through the window. Jim touched the window button and the glass came down under power. He started to speak, but before the words could be formed, the farm hand reached through the window and took the keys from the ignition.

The midget said, "Welcome to Nazareth Church."

———

DEL and Falconet arrived back in the late afternoon—the Jeep overhung with tools and lumber, Del driving. She slowed as they passed beneath the cross and through the gate, taking time to check out the compound for the Esteps' Lexus.

"It looks like our newcomers made it," she said, spotting the classy white sedan down near the compound.

Falconet followed her gaze. "Ten to one they didn't expect Green Acres. I still don't see what it is about this asshole, that makes people want to jump on his wagon?"

"He's got this force about him, that's all I can figure. You should have seen the way he came up to me on the porch that day, the sonofabitch. I felt like I wanted to curl up in a little ball. I still feel like I should have told this couple to turn around and go home before it's too late."

"I get the feeling it was too late for these two a long fucking time ago," Falconet said. After a minute he added, "You notice how quiet this joint has been today?"

"I think they're shunning us. The only reason we haven't noticed is because we've successfully managed to avoid the place all day."

"Let them shun all they want. They weren't all that fucking friendly to begin with."

Del gave Falconet a smile, dropping the Jeep in gear. She said, "Come on, hotshot. Let's get you home."

TWENTY-TWO

DINNER WAS SET FOR three.

Jim Estep sat glaring at his wife across the table—napkins in their laps; bowls of beef stew and a plate of cornbread between them growing cold; glasses of wine, already poured, within reach. They'd been instructed to wait for the healer to join them before they began.

"I don't see why we have to wait. I'm starving."

"Behave, Jim, honey," Julie said, her hands folded primly in her lap. She was speaking in hushed tones.

Jim wasn't sure exactly how he was supposed to *behave* under the circumstances, but he was feeling like a ready keg of dynamite. The bitch and her sanguine, manipulative ways. His fuse was getting shorter.

"We've been here for four hours, and this guy finally decides to honor us with his presence? And, while I'm on it, why do we have to sleep in separate dorms?"

"I'm sure it's part of our indoctrination, Jim," Julie said. There was a patronizing tone in her voice. "It adds to the spiritual experience."

"Spiritual experience, my ass." His voice rose now. "You see what you've gotten us into. You tell me where you've put our life savings, and I'll walk out of here right now."

"Shush! They'll hear you."

"Yeah, well, maybe I want them to. And while they're listening, maybe I should tell them how you fucked your way here."

"Don't start, Jim. This is a time for forgiveness."

"Well, then you'll forgive me if I don't take this shit anymore."

Jim stood, pushing his chair back from the table. He was turning to go when the door opened and Silas stepped inside. He was taller than Jim Estep remembered, wearing freshly laundered work pants and suspenders over a faded denim shirt.

"Sit," Silas said, nodding Jim back and taking his seat at the head of the table.

Jim eased himself down obediently and retrieved his napkin.

"You'll join with me in prayer," Silas said, reaching to clasp hands with each of them.

Jim could feel Silas's leathery fingers, cold, across the back of his hand. Now Julie's soft touch as she took his free hand across the table, completing the circle.

"Father," Silas began, his eyes shut, his face lifted to the heavens, "bless this sacred reunion. Lift out your hand, Lord, and receive this couple into your grace, that they might find eternal life in You. Be with us, now, as we partake of Your bounty..."

Jim was watching through one parted eye, the preacher's face etched with humility; his wife, Julie, holding tight to Silas.

221

"… in the name of the Father and the Son and the Holy Ghost, Amen."

Eyes opened around the table, hands retreated.

Silas took up a piece of cornbread and offered the plate across to each of them. They both accepted, Jim taking a square and placing it on the table next to his stew. Silas motioned for them to eat and shoved the bread and stew into his mouth together. Jim picked up his spoon and tentatively touched at his meal. Julie dug in.

When Silas had cleared his palate with wine, he said, "I trust your travels were not too burdensome?"

"The place was a little hard to find," Jim offered.

Julie said, "We're both excited, Jim and me, to begin this new life together. We have so much to learn, so much to be thankful for."

"Your journey is a great one," Silas said. "It must not be entered into lightly."

"We've been preparing," Julie said. "As you've instructed."

Silas turned a reverent smile in Julie's direction. "We must purge ourselves of worldly bonds, that we might be received into the kingdom of God."

Jim said, "Yeah, about that. I noticed our rooms are a little sparse. Will we have access to phones, television … you know … those kinds of things?"

Silas spooned stew from the bowl and brought it to his lips. He let his black eyes explore Jim's face. "It's only natural to forget one's commitment to God when there's a lapse in spiritual guidance." He took the stew in and swallowed, saying, "The Israelites, after being brought out of bondage, you'll recall, fell back into sin while Moses was on the mount. They were weakened by doubt.

Doubt is the tool of the devil. He uses it to gain mastery over our souls. And, thus, I see the devil gathering his mastery over you."

Jim stole a glance at the ceiling, half expecting to see cameras in the room. "It's just ... I was expecting ..."

"You were expecting what? To trade your worldly purchased comforts for ones provided you?"

"We sold everything," Julie said. "Relieved ourselves of those things which stand between us and a true relationship with God. Reduced it all to a single document, as your little deacon requested."

Jim wanted to kick her under the table.

"Nigel?" Silas shook his head. "Nigel is no deacon. He's a lost soul among us, I'm afraid. But he is practiced in all matters of the church."

Jim Estep listened to the two of them, wanting to scream.

"Then, to redemption," Julie said, lifting her glass.

"To redemption," Silas repeated, touching his glass to hers.

They were both looking at Jim to see what he was going to do.

"No," he said, shaking his head. "No, I'm not buying into this."

"You don't buy your way into heaven, brother Estep," Silas said. "You earn your way in."

"Huh-uh. I'm not your brother, and it's all a scam. There's no reason to have sold our home, my business, all our belongings."

"No reason?" Silas wiped his mouth with his napkin, folded it on the table in front of him. "Is there something I've missed? Some sign from God that I've ignored? Did you not get in your car and drive to Kingsport? Was it not you seeking God's forgiveness? Did you not stand before God and his faithful and confess your earthly sins?"

"It's not what I wanted." Jim pushed his chair back, to stand on legs that threatened to buckle. "It was her." Jim pointed a finger at his wife. "It's what *she* wants."

"I witnessed the words coming from your mouth," Silas said.

"It was just the emotion of the moment. I got caught up."

"Perhaps it was your time."

Julie said, "I'm sure that's it. It was just your time, Jim, honey. Don't you see?"

"We're going home," Jim announced, spiking his napkin on the table.

"At the cost of your eternal soul?" Silas asked.

"At any cost," Jim said.

Silas moved one large hand to lay it over Julie's, staying her. He kept his eyes on Jim. "You understand, there's more than your own salvation at risk."

Jim saw Julie shift her gaze to Silas, saw her fingers move to intertwine with his.

"You're no man of God. You're just a lowly con."

"So much defiance in your soul, sinner," Silas said. "When you've had time to pray on it, perhaps you'll see things differently."

Jim turned his eyes to his wife. "I'm leaving, Julie. You can come with me now or stay. It's your choice."

"God rewards supplication. God punishes the arrogant."

"God can kiss my ass," Jim said, and turned to go.

Silas snapped his fingers.

The door opened and men quickly entered. The two sinewy farmhands from earlier took up positions on either side of the opening; the midget, the weird little stooge, came through to take his place off to one side, his disproportionate little arms crossed at his chest.

With a nod from Silas, the farmhands moved in, to take Jim from either side.

"Stop! Julie! Tell them it was a mistake! Tell them you want to go home!"

"We will care for him," Silas told her, squeezing her hand reassuringly. "Belligerence is the sinner's last stand. I have seen it many times before. Not to worry."

The men strong-armed Jim and turned him toward the door. He wrenched his head toward his wife and caught sight of her—her eyes still locked on Silas, his fingers still entwined with hers.

"Tell them! Have you thought of us, Julie? Huh? Have you? Have you thought about what this is doing to our marriage?"

Jim resisted with every step. But now the midget was coming to put his shoulder behind the effort. With a surge, the gathering gained momentum and Jim was swept toward the door.

"I'll see you burn in hell! Both of you!" His last words as they rushed him out and away.

———

FALCONET watched Del moving about, straightening and organizing. She would bend to pick up something here, reach to set it there. He was aware of urges that had been building since the day he'd first seen the grainy photocopy of her. The dumpy little house was almost feeling like home. And Del in her bare feet, being domestic...

It aroused intimate thoughts of home and marriage.

"You ever think about kids?" he said, sitting with his feet propped on the coffee table, a beer in one hand.

"You mean, as in having them?" Del continuing to move about.

"Yeah."

The answer was slow in coming. "I guess I think about it."

"When I first got married," Falconet said. "I thought I'd like to have, like, ten kids, right?"

"Let's see," Del said, stopping to count. "You're thirty-seven. Counting the one child you have now, a kid a year for some poor girl, you'd be seventy by the time Tiny Tim was finished with college."

"That's okay," Falconet said, "I came along late in life. My father was almost fifty when I was born. Older parents are wiser, more settled. It makes for a peaceful childhood."

"Well, that explains it. You're a nice guy, Frank," Del said, crossing into the back hallway, taking a change of clothing with her. He heard the bathroom door close.

Falconet imagined her behind the door, slipping out of her jeans and into her nightgown. She was really something, this girl. But full of contradictions. Hot enough one minute to spark global warming, cold enough a second later to bring on another ice age. At the cemetery, the day before, she had laid a hand on his, sending signals he had wanted to believe were intimate. Then she'd driven away without so much as a nod.

Those goddamn tight jeans, Falconet thought. *What's it take to get her out of them?*

She came out of the bathroom seconds later, surprising him again, wearing only a man's dress shirt—his. Her breasts pressed

226

against the cotton where a single button held it closed. He caught a flash of bare midriff and silky panty as she crossed to where he was sitting.

"I hope you don't mind. I didn't get my laundry back yet."

Her voice had taken on a throaty, seductive quality, making even this mundane communication sound sexy. Falconet ran his tongue across lips that had suddenly cracked and dried.

"No," he said, the words coming out course and stilted. "You … want to sit down?"

Del kneeled next to him on the sofa, then settled in with her legs beneath her. He could feel her breast through the material, pressing into his arm, feel the flare of her hip against his side. He lifted his arm to bring it around her shoulder, feeling like a nervous schoolboy on his first date.

But this was no schoolgirl.

Del took his beer from him, sipped it, then leaned across to set the bottle on the lamp table and kill the light. She remained that way, stretched across him, far longer than necessary to complete the task, and Falconet's free hand came up to pull her in.

They exploded into each other, searching hungrily in the dark—lips and tongues, hands that couldn't hold enough—breaking only long enough for Del to say, "Your place or mine?"

They made love on the floor, on the air mattress and bedding that Falconet called home. Their motions were urgent, yet tender; selfish, yet caring. Afterward, they lay naked in the dark, breathing heavily, a sheet pulled over them, Falconet's arm supporting her beneath her head.

"I had a feeling from the start," he said, "that we'd be coming to this."

"Frank the lady-killer. Had me in your crosshairs, did you?"

"Not like that. Just, you know, this kind of feeling, like we're two of a kind, right?"

"Maybe."

"You still have the capacity to surprise me though."

"Good. Let's keep it that way."

"So, if it's not, like, treasonous to the feminine mystique, tell me, when did you decide?"

"On this?"

"Yeah…this."

"I think it was fifteen minutes ago, the boner you were sporting in your pants."

"Come on."

"I don't know. I was attracted to you right away. You seem like a cool enough guy sometimes. A girl has her needs, too, you know."

"That's it, huh? I'm a good lay."

"As judged by a jury of your peers."

"Come on."

"What do you want me to say, Frank? We've been together less than a week."

"I don't know…I guess I was just starting to think of us as a pretty good team. Don't you ever think about what happens next?"

"You mean after we're finished here?"

"Yeah. I mean, where do we go from here?"

Del said nothing.

"So, you're saying you don't think about it?"

"I'm saying I came here to find my mother. I can't see any further than that."

Falconet was conscious of Del's eyes turned toward him in the semi-darkness. He waited. After a minute, she said, "All right. I guess I started realizing some real feelings for you yesterday, when we walked up to the cemetery. I could tell you were concerned about me. It made you seem more like a real person. Not just a cop here to do a job."

"So there is something more."

"I've been burned before, Frank. Let's just take it as it comes for now."

"Back to Jeski, huh?"

Falconet could sense Del searching the past for answers. She said, "Among others."

He left it at that.

TWENTY-THREE

DEL AWOKE AHEAD OF Falconet and went down into town, driven by the baking smells that were filling the valley. It was especially warm for late September. A Thursday, their fourth day in Nazareth Church. She was dressed in khaki walking shorts, work boots, and an undershirt, prepared to begin work on the back of the house. She had a red bandana tied into a cap to cover her head. There was a morning-after tingle, Falconet's caress, still playing on her skin.

Del eased the Wrangler through the center of town. There were a few residents on the street, others in the fields. Down at the compound, all was quiet, no sign of the Esteps. She pulled the Jeep to an angled stop in front of the bakery.

Through the window, Del could see an elderly little woman behind the bakery case. She spotted Del as Del slid from behind the steering wheel. The woman immediately dropped what she was doing and quickly hurried for the door. It was a race, it seemed, to see who would get there first. The fleet-footed little woman won, going immediately for the lock. Del heard the catch turn as she reached for the knob, and now saw the *Open* sign being flipped around to read *Closed*. The little woman glared at her through the glass for a moment, then went off into the back.

Del let her gaze shift down the street to the General, where the tobacco-chewing clerk was sweeping the porch. The woman spotted Del and abruptly turned inside, seeing to it that the door slammed sufficiently behind.

And so it starts, Del thought. They were systematically being driven from the pride.

Del walked the half block to the diner. There were patrons inside, a half-dozen of them, eating. Hearing the bell on the door jingle as she entered, they looked up to give her a glare. One by one, they pushed back in their chairs and brushed past her out the door, leaving their breakfasts to turn cold.

Lowell appeared that very minute, a plate of food in each hand. Seeing her, he veered away, turned this way and that, uncertain where to run.

"Lowell!"

Lowell stopped. "I'm not supposed to be talking to you," he said, his voice a whisper.

"Really? I suppose that rules out breakfast to go?"

The boy kept his eyes averted.

"And just when I thought we were becoming friends."

Lowell turned his gaze to her. There was a sad and painful look in his eyes.

"It's okay, Lowell. But someday, should you recognize that you actually own the set of balls between your legs, do yourself a favor and get them the fuck out of Nazareth Church."

Del turned and exited the diner.

———

ON the sidewalk again, Del spotted the two wash-and-dry mavens, the sisters, exiting the laundromat. Seeing her, they gave her a sharp glare and hurried off, turning between the buildings to disappear. Del approached the laundromat and went inside.

Machines were running—washers *slush-slushing*, dryers humming. Del took a quick look in the back room, but there was no sign of the frail little folding lady; no one else in the laundromat. Back in the wash room, she found her pillowcase stashed safely beneath the folding table. Inside, her clothes were freshly laundered and neatly folded. Del took the pillowcase and returned to the Wrangler.

There was a method to their madness. The plan—to cut them off from all contact, refuse them resources, and eventually they would grow weary and leave.

Del fired the engine and spun her tires backing into the street. Giving it some gas, she jammed the gear into first, and spun the tires some more.

If that's what they think, she told herself, then they've got another thing coming.

———

NIGEL sat watching the morning develop, looking from the kitchen off through the dining room window that faced north toward the main part of town. Across from him, Cullen sat with his legs propped on the table, giving Jim Estep, the convert-slave, room to mop beneath his feet. The man was a slow learner, Nigel realized, not as bright as he might have expected—the man having earned a respectable amount of wealth in his day—and he wasn't going to be one to easily convert to Silas's plan for him and his bony wife. Still, it was amazing what you could get someone to do if you kept them hungry and isolated, and indoctrinated them with self-doubt.

"I'm thinkin' I could use a beer. What about you?" Cullen said.

The two of them had come together here in the kitchen this morning, almost buddies it seemed, to begin the slow but methodical dismantling of Jim Estep's ego.

Estep stopped mopping for a moment, turning a weary look to Cullen. "I guess I'm supposed to get them for you?"

"Of course, you're supposed to," Cullen said. "Part of your penitence to God for being such an immoral prick to your wife. Didn't Silas explain that to you?"

"But beer? I mean, for the love of God, it's nine o'clock in the morning."

"And some Cheetos, too," Cullen said. "They're in the cupboard there."

Nigel watched as Estep leaned the mop against the door frame and went off toward the pantry.

Cullen said, "I don't think this boy fully appreciates the honor he's been given." Then: "Uh-oh!"

Nigel caught Cullen's gaze and followed it out through the dining room, beyond the window, to the road leading down. The red Jeep Wrangler was approaching fast.

"Get him out of here," Nigel said, slipping off the chair to the floor. "I'll see what she wants."

"How come you get to talk to her?"

"Just do it. Silas wakes up, I don't want to have to explain to him how we let her see this guy."

Cullen kicked at the linoleum but complied, catching Estep returning with the bag of Cheetos and beers. There was a wide-eyed, puzzled wonderment that had become a part of the man's demeanor. A look that had come to say, *How did this all come about? What has my life become?* Cullen relieved him of the beers and quickly turned him down the back hallway and out.

Nigel gave it two beats, then went out to meet the girl.

———

DEL skidded the Jeep to a halt near the front porch and slid out. Nigel was waiting for her.

"I want to talk to Silas," she demanded.

"He's not here."

Del let her eyes move past him. It was shadowy inside the house, no movement beyond the window.

"I'm betting his SUV's in the garage down there," she said, letting her eyes point the way toward the building where the vehicles and farm equipment were housed, its sliding door closed.

Nigel shrugged. "You have no business here. You should go back to where you came from."

"You going to call him out? Or do you want me to do it?"

"We don't call the healer," Nigel said. "He calls us."

"Is that right? Well, the next time he calls you, tell him this: if he wants me out of Nazareth Church, he's going to have to provide me some honest answers. You tell him that. It's the only way I'll leave."

Nigel continued staring down at her from the porch.

Del said, "You know, I've made a couple friends here in Nazareth Church. The new couple, Jim and Julie Estep. Maybe I'll take time to get to know them better."

She saw the midget's glare waver.

"There's no one here by that name."

"Are you sure? What if I slide the door open on the garage down there? I won't find a white Lexus?"

Nigel crossed his arms.

Del said, "You just give Silas the message. I'll be at home, working on my house."

———

NIGEL returned to the house and watched through the dining room window as the girl drove off up the road, through town, and into the draw.

Cullen appeared in the back doorway. "She gone?"

Nigel nodded and stepped away from the window. "Where's Estep?"

"I put him in the hole, put the lid on him. Figured that ought to shut him up." Cullen came fully into the room. He had both hands secreted behind his back. "His wife," he said, "I checked on her in the dorm. She's a skinny little thing, you know it? Got those wishbone legs. You know what I mean?"

Nigel shook is head.

"Kind you make a wish on before you pull 'em apart." He cut loose with laughter, as though he was the funniest man on the planet. Then seeing Nigel's face, the grim, serious look, he said, "Come on, that was funny, little man. What's the matter?"

"The woman's causing trouble. Silas isn't going to like it."

"Her? Why would he care?"

Nigel said, "There are things you don't know. Silas keeps you sheltered."

"Well, I say fuck it. Or maybe fuck *her,* I get the chance." Cullen brought his hands around from behind his back and produced the two beers. "Remember these two girls?"

Nigel looked at the beer. He'd suddenly lost his taste for it. But he took one, clinking bottles with Cullen, before sipping. The kid was attempting pleasantries. He'd take advantage of it while he could.

———

FALCONET appeared in the backyard in jeans and a T-shirt, the sleeves rolled up. Del had a shovel in her hand and had already begun to work at loamy, black soil.

"You starting without me?" he said, a feigned hurt look on his face.

She had let him sleep as long as he wanted, feeling a certain, motherly fondness for him this morning. The lovemaking had been good the night before—Del straddling him on the floor— something she had needed.

Falconet picked up a second shovel and joined in. "You know, I was thinking last night about you wanting to run away, once upon a time. Maybe you and me should finish up this assignment here and take off for one of those beaches off Baja, like you said."

"Mexico?"

"I'm thinking, yeah. We'd have fun together. The two of us. What do you say?"

Del sunk her shovel into the soil. Except for Ed Jeski, her love life had consisted of a rather lengthy string of hit-and-run encounters, usually leaving her, afterward, feeling like roadkill on the pavement of life. Now Falconet was proposing they move their relationship to the next level. So, how did she feel about the idea?

Well, he'd been right about one thing. There was a certain connection between them. But was it a lasting connection, or just a kinship born of two people who played with guns? Del wasn't sure. For all his bravado, Falconet struck her as a guy who needed to be cared for. And wasn't that the way of it? Her father had needed care. Ed Jeski, with the wife who didn't understand, he needed her comfort. Now, Falconet, the unappreciated undercover operative, a guy with an undecided marital status and a job that kept him alone half the time. They were wounded ducks, all of them. One way or the other. What did she get out of it? What need was she fulfilling?

She said, "I think you better keep digging, Frank. We've got a long way to go to reach Mexico."

———

THE yard was narrow and ran the length of the house. The retaining wall that held the hillside back was partially collapsed. Sparrows and squirrels played among the trees. There was a sweet natural innocence to the day. Falconet watched Del working with the shovel, admiring the way she moved.

"I was down to see Silas this morning," Del said.

Falconet stopped working. "And?"

"I was intercepted by his little stooge. He lied to me about the Esteps. He said he'd never heard of them. Why would he do that?"

"People who have nothing to hide…"

"Hide nothing," Del said. "They've cut off all our access to the services. I was going to bring you something back for breakfast, but the little bakery-witch locked the door on me. Same thing at the diner."

"You were bringing me breakfast?"

"Just something I felt like doing."

"See, I knew there was a domestic side to you."

"Don't get any ideas, Frank."

———

BY noon, they had cleared the drift and reset the rocks in the retaining wall. Now, the only dirt that remained was inside the house, and the job was to get it out. Del slipped through the hole and used her shovel to scoop up the dead squirrel and bird and toss them into the yard. Falconet came through and began collecting broken glass into a bucket. The busted pieces of framework, he pitched through the opening and into the yard. Together they pushed and shoveled and swept until all that remained was a dark, loamy stain on the hardwood flooring and the ragged hole in the wall where the window used to be. It was going on two o'clock.

"I hate to abandon you before the job is done, but I have to jump in the shower," Falconet said. "I have that meeting with Darius, remember?"

"What will you tell him?"

"I'll tell him about the guns, the explosives. About Mariah. And I'll tell him about Daniel Cole. See what he wants to do."

238

"You might want to have him look into the Esteps. Their background. I'd be curious."

Falconet took a last look at Del standing there leaning on her shovel, the bandana, the smudge of dirt on her cheek, nipples showing through her sweaty undershirt. He could easily picture her on a ranch somewhere, this Arizona girl, grooming horses and mucking stalls.

He said, "Listen, I've been meaning to tell you, be careful. We're beginning to push these people's buttons. It's hard to say how they'll react."

Falconet waited, expecting a glib answer.

What Del said was, "You be careful, too."

TWENTY-FOUR

NIGEL DRANK WITH CULLEN until the kid began to show his alcohol and became belligerent. Now, with his head feeling like a rock, he still had to find Silas and tell him about the woman coming to visit. Crossing the yard toward the church, he spotted the Wrangler passing back through town. This time it was the husband behind the wheel, heading for the gate.

Nigel found Silas in the basement of the church, counting the church's money. Around him and throughout the basement was the miscellaneous clutter and the road-show paraphernalia. On the table was a huge pile of bills of varying denominations. Silas continued counting, thumbing bills and stacking them until he reached an even count.

Nigel cleared his throat.

Silas ignored him, making Nigel wait as he banded the bills and added them to others that were stacked neatly inside a red metal box that sat next to him on the floor. This time Nigel didn't give him the chance to begin another count. He said, "What are you doing?"

Silas looked up, letting his eyes come across the top of his reading glasses. "The banking. What's it look like?"

Nigel waited again as Silas counted off another stack, banded it, and added it to the box. "You get the Esteps' contribution?" Nigel asked.

"Matters of money often require patience," Silas said. "The Estep woman will present it when her spirit is so moved."

Nigel watched the money build. "It's getting to be a lot. With the Esteps', maybe you should get Virgil or Harland to take it to the bank for you."

"I don't trust banks, never did."

Once again Nigel waited until Silas finished stuffing another bundle into the box, then said, "The woman came by earlier."

Silas paused and looked up.

"She was angry about the townsfolk shunning her."

Silas went back to counting. "Then it's working, isn't it?"

"She said to tell you she's not leaving until you personally tell her the truth about Ella."

"Wants me to visit, does she?"

"She was asking questions about the Esteps."

Silas stopped counting now. He laid the bills on the table and removed his glasses. "The Esteps? What would she know of them?"

Nigel nodded. "Claimed she met them in town."

"Where is the girl now?"

"She's returned to the house, saying she had work to do on it. I just saw the husband leaving town in the Jeep."

Silas studied him a moment. "Why don't you take Virgil, or maybe Harland, and go into town. Keep an eye on the man."

"And the woman?"

Silas slipped his glasses on and went back to counting. "Don't worry about her. I'll see to it."

Nigel watched Silas—the healer—his huge hands thumbing bills. "And what should I do about Estep? Someone's got to keep an eye on him."

Silas paused again midcount, a large purple vein in his forehead beginning to bulge.

"Never mind," Nigel said, holding off a scolding. "I'll handle it."

Shit! Like everything else.

———

OUTSIDE the church, Nigel spotted Cullen and Harland returning from the river. They were dressed in camouflage hunting gear and had automatic rifles—Harland with an AR-14 leaning across his shoulder, Cullen with one of the MAC-10 submachine guns hanging from its strap. There were rabbit pelts strung from their belts. Nigel caught up with them down between the dorms. "Don't you think that's a bit of an overkill?"

"You should see these little bastards run," Cullen said. "Their little cotton rears bouncin', MAC-10 … I'm telling ya … eatin' up the ground behind 'em."

"Harland," Nigel said, turning to the man, "get rid of the dead animals and get the Escalade ready."

"Wait, what's going on?" Cullen said.

"Nothing. Silas just wants us to keep an eye on the husband, see where he goes when he leaves the valley." To Harland, he said, "You going, Harland?"

Harland unhooked his rabbit pelts and handed them to Cullen, then went on up toward the garage.

Cullen said, "You mean you get to follow him around, spy on him? I want to go."

"Huh-uh, somebody's got to stay and continue to keep an eye on Estep."

"Then you do it. I'll go with Harland."

"Silas wants me to do it," Nigel said, turning away. "And don't forget to take Silas his meal around six."

Cullen was shaking his head. "Huh-uh, not this time. You get to have all the fun. I'm going with Harland, and you're stayin' here."

Cullen turned off toward the garage, and Nigel had to run to catch up. He managed to get a hand on him, meaning to turn him about. Without warning, Cullen turned on him, coming around with the rabbit pelts in a vicious arc. They caught Nigel on the side of the head, smacking him to the ground. He covered himself as Cullen began whipping him with the bloody carcasses—first one side, then the other, back and forth, across his face.

Now the kid was tossing the pelts aside to use his fists. The first blow slammed him on the left side of the face and brought stars to his eyes. The second caught his jaw in an uppercut, and Nigel felt a tooth chip. He tried to cover himself by rolling into a tight little ball. Blows rained down on him—serious blows. Nigel, still curled like an armadillo, hung on as best he could, rolling with the punches and keeping his head tucked tight. He managed to get a hand on the front of the kid's shirt and draw him close, hoping to shorten the distance between them.

Cullen continued to punch in short little jabs. The pair of pelts, still hooked to his belt, flipped and flapped and kicked at the dust. A cloud of it filled the air around them.

With his free hand, Nigel searched frantically for his whistle. Managing to get a grip on it and get it to his lips, he drew a deep breath and let blow, close to Cullen's ear.

The shrill trill was like an ice pick jammed through the kid's ear canal. With a cry, Cullen went rolling off, his palms coming to cover his ears. Nigel expected to see blood trickling between Cullen's fingers. But none did. Cullen flailed about, like a pellet-shot dog, cursing and kicking and rolling in the dirt.

Just let him stay down, Nigel was praying as Harland arrived in the SUV, his head hanging out the driver's-side window.

"You little bastard!" Cullen cried.

Harland said, "You might'a busted his eardrum."

"He'll be all right."

Nigel crossed quickly around and climbed into the passenger seat, slamming the car door with a bang. He took one last look at Cullen, still clutching his shattered ear. "Let's go," he said to Harland.

Heading out the gate, Nigel adjusted the review mirror to get a view of Cullen coming to his feet. He didn't know when or where or how, but soon, he knew, he'd have hell to pay for this.

———

DEL was missing Falconet. And the feeling surprised her. Maybe there was something to having a man around the house. Or maybe it was just this place, the quiet provoking the need to have *any-one* around. She carried the half-section of plywood to the back of the house and tested it for size at the opening. It wasn't pretty, but it would keep the critters and maybe other intruders out until she could properly rebuild the section of wall and replace the window.

Del nailed it to the siding, then took time to step back and admire her work.

"So, you're still thinking to stay?"

Del recognized the voice, deep and resonant, the touch of southern drawl. She turned to see Silas above her on the hillside. He was squatting on a tree stump, his forearms resting on his knees.

How long had he been watching?

Del was conscious of the hammer still gripped tightly in her hand, aware of soft dirt caked on her boots, the smudge drying on her cheek. She could feel sweat clinging to her brow and upper lip. The sun was in her face, and Del used her free hand now to shade her eyes.

"I see you got my message."

Silas continued to stare from his squatting position. Tree limbs, moving in the breeze, caused shadows to dance across his leathery face.

"God leads His repentant to me. But the defiant come on their own. You seek to heal some hurt in your heart? Very well."

Silas rose. He stepped down from the stump and strode casually, several steps down the hillside, to stop on the retaining wall and leer down at her.

"Where's Ella May?" Del said.

"I told you, she's dead."

"I don't believe you."

Silas stepped down off the retaining wall and closed the distance between them to within a few steps. He studied her, his black eyes searching. Del stood her ground, conscious of the hammer still grasped in her hand.

"Poor child," Silas said. "An innocent victim of Roy Shannon and his lies? Did he tell you what a whore your mother was? Tell you how worthless? How she was no good for abandoning him and her child?"

Del lifted a proud chin to him. "I know about you and her," she said. "How she came to see you."

"Is that right?" Silas said, putting mock surprise on his face. "And now you've begun to question all the other precepts that you've believed to hold as truth. I see the troubling questions in your eyes, girl. You want to know if you're mine."

Silas stepped closer, right in front of her now, looking down on her.

"Well, the answer is no. I laid my hand between your mother's milky thighs, and I healed her barren womb. But you're every bit the product of Roy Shannon's putrid seed. There's your truth. Are you happier for it?"

Del held Silas's powerful gaze, cursing the trembling that had come upon her lip. "Where's my mother now?"

"You won't leave well enough alone, will you?"

"She became one of your wives, didn't she? You made her stay. Kept her here against her will. That's why she didn't come looking for me."

"It comes down to that, does it? A question of love?" He brought a hand to her cheek and stroked it. "So much like your mother, the way she was then, it brings back memories." His voice had taken on a dreamy, far-off quality.

Del pushed the hand away, conscious of her grip tightening on the handle of the hammer.

"Where's Ella May?"

Silas brought his hand to rest on her shoulder. "I know it is hard to gain acceptance, particularly for one so young and faithless as yourself. But, I'm afraid Ella May left here years ago."

"You're a liar!"

"So much like her…" Silas continued to speak in that dreamy tone, his huge hand moved to encircle her neck. "God has brought you to me after all. I see that now. His circle of life come full before the *time*."

Del pushed at the hand, but this time it held fast.

"Get off, you sonofabitch!"

The hand began to pull her forward.

Del brought the hammer up and around. Silas ducked it, catching her wrist and wringing the hammer from her grip. She tried to pull away, but his hand remained clamped vise-like about her neck.

Slowly the grip tightened.

Del felt her windpipe closing off, felt her lungs begin to ache for air. She struggled, burning up what precious reserves she had left. Her arms became heavy, her vision began to blur. Her legs weakened. With nothing left, her knees buckled and she folded to the earth.

Now, he was on her, straddling her in the loosely scattered, black soil. He forced his weight upon her, pressing out the last remaining air from her lungs. The world moved in lazy circles, turned sepia before her eyes. The yard, the house, the woods were stretching away from her.

"God has brought you to me," she heard Silas say. His voice was far away and hollow as if coming to her from the depths of a well. His one hand remained about her throat. The hand holding her wrist came to the front of her shirt. In a single motion, it ripped the front away, exposing flesh and pride to his greedy eyes.

"God's will be done," Silas said.

"You bastard," Del managed to squeeze out.

Silas's free hand found her belt buckle and began to work. The other remained locked about her throat. The world around tilted and spun sideways.

"You fuck … ing … bas …!"

Her eyes began to close.

"Stop it!" A voice suddenly called.

Del forced open her eyes and skewed her face to see Mariah on the hillside above them. Her arm was cocked, and the rock she let fly struck the side of Silas's head with deadly aim. It brought a grunt and rocked him sideways, shifting his weight, and freeing the grip on her neck.

Del caught a sudden inrush of breath, a violent gasp, as Mariah let fly with another rock. Silas's hands came up in an effort to block the blow. Del seized the moment, rolling away from him, freeing one leg that she used to kick out. Her boot made contact and Silas fell backward in the dirt. Del quickly scrambled to safety, finding the hammer in the soil.

"I didn't see it coming the last time, you bastard! But this time I'll split your skull!"

Del staggered to her feet, raising the hammer above her.

Silas brought himself to his feet, wiping at blood that was trickling from a cut above his eye.

"Get the fuck out of here!" Del cried, wanting to finish him there, but knowing she had not enough strength to defend, much less launch an attack.

Silas turned, his stoic manner returning. "God punishes the defiant, child."

"Go to hell, you bastard!" Del yelled.

She'd had it with sermons.

TWENTY-FIVE

"So you say you saw Daniel Cole alive?" Darius said.

"Alive and well," Falconet said. "Two nights ago. Del witnessed him, too, going through some kind of hillbilly communion at the church."

"We should have seen it coming, really. Daniel was a near-textbook candidate for Stockholm syndrome. He'd already suffered a tragic shock, the first requirement for it. We supplied the isolation, sending him down here alone. Nazareth Church provided indoctrination. All that was left was a promise of a reward."

"As in, a reward in heaven," Falconet said.

Darius shrugged his brow. "It all fits."

They were on stools at the bar at the Palms Motel. Darius in tan slacks and a flowery Hawaiian shirt, a pinched, concerned look on his face. There were mugs of draft beer in front of them.

"They've got some bad-ass illegal weapons down there also," Falconet said, sipping his drink. "I've seen some stockpiles in my days with ATF, but I gotta tell ya, man, there's enough weaponry to start a small war. C-4, right?"

"What do you suppose he's up to?"

Falconet shrugged. "I don't know. It's not like they're some kind of terrorist group. Best I can tell, they never leave the place 'cept to go on one of their revivals. C-4 isn't exactly the explosive of choice when it comes to defense. Am I right? Still, they've got a shitload of it, along with some pretty odd fucking ideas."

Darius began punching numbers into a cell phone and waited for it to ring through.

"There's a young girl," Falconet continued, as Darius waited on the line. "Barely older than my daughter Stacy. Bastard's been sexually abusing her, according to Del. It's his own daughter."

"George Racine ..." Darius said into the phone, and waited, saying to Falconet, "Incest?"

Falconet nodded as Darius turned his attention back to the phone.

"George? Darius ... Yeah, back in Biden. Listen ... "

Outside, the sky was turning dark. Falconet turned his own attention back to his beer. He was thinking of Del, stuck up there at the house alone. In the past five days, he'd become aware of feelings. Feelings that he hadn't felt in a long, long time. Was she having them too? Maybe. Maybe not. They'd slept together. But, where did it go from there?

They would get to Daniel Cole and bring him out. Darius and likely a tactical team would launch a raid on the place, on weapons charges, charges of incest and rape, and the whole assignment would come to a screeching end within a matter of days. *Bada bing, bada bang.*

251

Then what?

Well, there'd be a few of days of searching through all the outbuildings, looking for further evidence. Some more time interviewing the residents of Nazareth Church. Time spent digging through church records, if there were any. Would Del remain there, or return right away to Tucson? Would he go home to Jersey, to deal with Jolana and divorce, alimony, and ill feelings? Or would he be off on another assignment?

It got complicated fast.

"Yes, sir," Darius was saying into the phone, "we'll keep it tight."

Darius flipped the cell phone closed, bringing an end to Falconet's mental interlude. "Racine says they'll begin the process of cutting warrants."

"When …?" Falconet started, then hesitated as a man crossed past them at the bar. He was dressed in duck bib overalls and wore a ball cap, looking like he'd just left his fields for a quick one. Falconet waited until the man was out the door and gone before he continued. "When do you want me to go after Cole?"

"Tonight," Darius said. "Take him by whatever means necessary. Then you and Del clear out fast. I'll get a tactical team ready and we'll come in behind you, just after midnight."

"A team? Here?"

Darius nodded.

"You mean, right here, right now?"

"They're here and there about town. In their rooms, or sightseeing. I didn't tell you so you wouldn't always be looking over your shoulder. You want another drink before you go?"

Falconet said, "No, I gotta bust outta here."

Darius was looking at him, eyebrows raised. "Don't tell me."

"What?"

The look remained.

"All right, fuck," Falconet said. "What did you expect, putting me in a one-room house with her, not even a bed between us? She's really special."

"Special," Darius mimicked, that sly paternal grin coming to his face. "Not beautiful, not sexy, not desirable?"

"She's up there alone," Falconet said. "I should get back."

"Because she's *special*," Darius said, still giving him the Morgan Freeman grin.

It's hard to explain, Falconet thought. The irrational feeling that he was having. A gut feeling that said, *Go to her … she needs you … now.*

He said, "Yeah, fuck, because she's special."

———

FROM where the Escalade was parked at the back of the self-serve car wash, Nigel could see the parking lot at the front of the Palms Motel, but not the exit from the bar around the side. Then he saw Harland out on the road, his thumbs in his overalls, his ball cap pulled low. He watched him wait for a car to pass before crossing.

Harland approached the passenger side where Nigel sat with his arm out the window. "He's inside at the bar with some Negro fella."

"They see you?"

"Well, sure. I was having a drink in the corner booth. But the man don't know me from squat."

"What did the black guy look like?"

"Like a tourist. Some wild shirt with orchids on it. But smart. You know how the educated ones look. Got that superior turn to him, like he might be a doctor, a professor, or something."

"Or an agent for the FBI?"

Harland shrugged.

At that moment, Nigel saw the husband come into view in the parking lot. He was crossing to the Wrangler where it sat in one of the lined spaces. Seconds later, he pulled away, taking the main road heading back toward Nazareth Church.

"Do we follow him?" Harland asked.

"I think I'd like to see what happens with the other one. Get in. We'll wait."

Harland crossed around and slid into the driver's seat. And they waited, seeing the sun slowly disappear behind the ridge.

"You notice anything different about Silas lately?" Nigel said after a time.

"Different? Like what?"

"Well, like sending us to drop the Bakeys' car at the abandoned sawmill."

Harland shrugged. "He can drop it where he wants, I guess."

"That doesn't cause you to question?" Nigel said. He was watching Harland's face to see if the light of recognition might blink on.

"Question what?"

Nigel shook his head and turned his gaze back to the motel parking lot.

These followers ... Nigel thought ... *where do they come from?*

———

THE shower had calmed her down, but it had done nothing to diminish her resolve. Del stood, wrapped in a towel, hair wet, her work duffle open on the dining room table in front of her. She checked the load in her weapon—Mariah watching from a place on the sofa—the little Baby Eagle, fifteen rounds in the magazine, the chamber empty for now, safety on.

"You gonna kill Silas?" Mariah said.

"I've sure considered the idea," Del said. "But no. I'm going to find my mother. He tried to tell me she was dead, then he tried to sell me on the idea that she left on her own. I don't believe any of it. He can prove me right, or prove me wrong, but I'm gonna hold this gun to his head until I get some answers."

"Ain't you scared?"

"I'm mad, is what I am."

Del dug inside the bag for a shoulder rig she sometimes used, untangled it, and slipped the gun into the holster.

"I wish I was you," Mariah said.

Del looked at her, the teenager's hands folded in her lap, her eyes downcast. She said, "Aw, honey, you don't want to be me." Del crossed to her. "Look at me . . ." She lifted Mariah's face to her. "You're a beautiful young woman. You're going to meet a nice, good-looking young boy some day. You're going to have a home and children . . ."

"Babies?"

"Yes, babies."

"What about you? Ain't you gonna have none?"

Del wasn't prepared for the question. She said, "I don't know . . . someday . . . maybe."

"I bet you'd have real pretty babies. You'n your husband." There was sincere admiration in the girl's voice, the set of her face.

255

"And so will you."

Del returned to the table and finished organizing. She drew her Kevlar vest from the bag, laid it on the table, dug out cuffs and laid them on top. Motioning to the laundry sack, sitting on the end table near the sofa, she said, "I have to get dressed. Can you hand me some clothes? The shirt, the jeans. Maybe the blue undies."

Mariah rose and began sorting out the requested items. Halfway into it, she said, "Oh, this is pretty."

"What?" Del said.

Mariah withdrew a folded square of white linen. Holding it by its corners, she let it drape into view.

"Let me see that," Del said, crossing to her. She held her towel in place with her elbows and took the cloth in her hands. "Where did this come from? How did I get it?"

Mariah shrugged. "It was in the bag. Maybe it got mixed in by mistake. It's an ABC sampler."

"A sampler?"

Mariah nodded. "You make 'em. It's how you learn your letters. And how you learn to sew."

Del examined the swatch of linen. It was neatly embroidered with rows of letters and icons, hand-stitched with variously colored thread. Every other row was made up with the letters of the alphabet—A to Z—reading forward, then backward, across the swatch. In between the rows of letters were rows of icons, like hieroglyphics, all neatly designed. She said, "There are little pictures."

Mariah took the sampler from Del, and moving the stack of laundry aside, spread it on the table. "It's kinda like a storybook too," she said. "You can tell 'bout births and deaths and other things important to you. I have one that tells about the time I went to Clay City. But it's not very good."

"Stories?" Del said, she was still in her towel, her hair still damp.

"They're kind of like secret code, you have to figure 'em," Mariah said, running her finger down a row of images. "The little emblems depict events. See these? There are two circles, intertwined. The circles are rings. Linked together like this they stand for marriage."

"So, it's a story about two people getting married?" Del said, letting her eyes scan farther along the row of icons—a sequence of hearts, a star, a series of flowers.

"And what's this?" she asked, pointing to an icon in one of the other rows.

"It's a cradle."

"But it's empty."

Mariah shrugged. "Maybe they were hopin'."

Del let her fingers continue across the rows of images, trying to do her own interpretation. There were *X*s and *O*s, more hearts, more flowers. Then in the next alternate row of icons, Del came to another cradle icon. This time her finger froze in place. Her heart lurched, then began a drumbeat ... *baboomp-baboomp-baboomp* ... as her mind raced to unravel the implications.

"Oh! My God!" she said, only vaguely aware of her own voice.

"What? What do you see?" Mariah asked.

Del adjusted the swatch for Mariah to see.

Mariah followed Del's finger, and a tiny gasp emanated from her, as her eyes fell on the second cradle icon. This image was identical to the one in the earlier row, but this time there was clearly visible, inside the cradle, the stitched image of a bundled baby. And more ...

Above the cradle hung a tiny crescent moon … *stitched in a brownish-yellow thread.*

"It's … it's just like your tattoo!" Mariah said, astonishment in her voice.

Del rolled her wrist to bring her moon tattoo into view—feeling her heart nearly bursting from her chest now. Together they compared it to the hand-stitched icon on the sampler. It was identical. Shape, color, size … *identical.* Del turned her eyes to Mariah and found her looking back at her in wide-eyed amazement.

"There's only one person who could have possibly sewn this," Del said. "My mother! But … but, I still don't understand how it got here. Who would have …?"

Mariah lifted the corner of the sampler and held it for her to see. There, in a neatly hand-stitched autograph at the bottom, was the name of the sampler's author …

"*Sarah!*" Del said, slapped with the memory of the morning at the laundromat, the larger of the two sisters saying, "*Sarah, why don't you go into the storeroom, see you can find more laundry detergent.*"

A picture of the folding lady came into focus in Del's mind. The frail and sickly woman who kept her eyes averted. One who would have had last access to her clothing and would have folded them and placed them in the bag. Her mind shot to the photograph she had once found in her father's drawer, ricocheted and landed on the brownish-yellow moon, hand-stitched on the lapel of the baby-pajama rag in the ragbag in the garage.

"Mom!" Del said.

It came out in a choked, anguished cry, as Del felt her knees suddenly buckle beneath her.

TWENTY-SIX

Men began assembling in the parking lot of the Palms Motel. First a handful, then more arrived, coming from rooms or in cars from elsewhere in town. Beneath pole lights, a matching pair of vans were brought around and lined up along the grass. A large, dark-colored box van was brought around to join them. Nigel poked Harland awake where he'd dozed off in the driver's seat of the Escalade. He straightened, turning his eyes across the road.

"Who're they?" he asked.

"They're not the Welcome Wagon," Nigel replied.

Within minutes, several more arrived. The men wore slacks and casual shirts and poplin windbreakers. A few others joined them in jeans and sweatshirts, some in golf shirts. Not from around here, Nigel could tell.

They began breaking out equipment, testing flashlights and radios. Now they traded street clothes for black jumpsuit coveralls, broke out Kevlar vests and piled them on the hoods of the cars. They traded their sweatshirts and windbreakers for slick nylon pullovers that read *F B I* in stenciled lettering across the back. They broke out guns, checked ammo. Passed communications down the line from man to man.

Now a tall black man joined them from the motel, wearing slacks and one of the FBI insignia jackets. The men gathered near the front of a parked sedan and huddled around as the man spread open maps across the hood.

"That's the Negro fella I was telling you about," Harland said. "He ain't wearin' his *Ha-wi-yen* shirt no more."

"Let's go," Nigel said. "We need to get back and warn Silas."

———

DINNERTIME, and Cullen's ears were still ringing.

This place, nothing ever to do.

He stirred the soup, letting it come to a boil.

These people. These zombie do-nothings who need Silas to tell them when to wipe their ass.

Cullen turned the burner off beneath the soup.

The deacons ... last night ... Virgil Aikens escorting his wife—his own fucking wife!—to Silas's doorstep. Leaving her there—you believe it?—and going off. Shit! Putting his mind on God and studying on salvation, while Silas puts his bone up his wife's ass and brings her to glory.

Cullen poured chicken soup into two bowls and placed them on a tray.

Silas, up there in his room.

Never outwardly brutal with him, but disparaging, making sharp comments that cut deep and left scars.

He got down a bottle of red wine and two glasses, put them on the tray with the bowls.

Jim Estep! Christ, what a joke! Walked away from everything just because he fucked around on his wife a little. And Nigel ... always sticking me with the shit jobs ... the weasely little prick! ... doing it again.

Twisting a finger inside his ear to clear the ringing, Cullen left the tray and made his way out the back door to the cistern. He dragged the concrete slab back a short way, creating a narrow opening. Then brought the ladder around to slide it into the hole.

The little freak show. Every time, taking the good jobs and leaving me to do the grunt work. Take Silas his dinner! Keep an eye on Estep! Holding Silas over me like a hammer. Always getting away with it.

Cullen peered down into the cistern and saw Jim Estep's red eyes, peering back at him.

Well, not this time. Not this fucking time!

————

JIM Estep saw the ladder slide into the hole, saw the kid, Cullen, looking down at him.

"Did you bring me something to eat? I'm hungry."

"Come on out," Cullen said. "You run one quick little errand for me, and I'll give you food."

Jim took the rungs one by one.

His life as he'd known it had evaporated, turned to nothingness, like so much dry ice on a sunny day. He hadn't seen his wife since the night before. What had they done with her? Christ! How had this all happened?

261

Jim squeezed his way out through the narrow opening and steadied himself on his feet.

"What do I have to do? I'm so hungry."

"Just come with me," Cullen said.

He allowed the kid to lead him in through the back hallway and into the kitchen, brightening as he saw the tray prepared with food and drink.

"Is that for me?" he said, reaching for it.

Cullen slapped the back of his hand.

"Huh-uh, not just yet. The tray's for Silas; he wants you to bring it to him. You take it like a good boy, then I'll feed you."

Jim Estep regarded the kid, who looked like he was fighting back a snicker, then picked up the tray.

"Where?"

"Up the stairs, second door on the right," Cullen said, gesturing out through the dining room, still with that mischievous twinkle in his eye.

Jim made his way through and into the living area, Cullen following to the foot of the stairs. There Jim hesitated.

"Go on," Cullen said, still stifling a grin. "Second door on the right."

Jim took to the stairs with the tray, found the hallway leading off to the right. He came to the second door and found it closed. He knocked and heard a voice say, "Come."

Jim balanced the tray in one hand, turned the knob with the other, and pushed the door open wide.

His wife, Julie, sat propped amid rumpled bedclothes, her back against the headboard. The straps to her silk slip were off her shoulders; her skinny white thighs were showing below the hem.

"Oh my God! Jim!"

Silas stepped into view, snapping pants at the waist and zipping them.

Jim staggered against the doorjamb. The tray clattered to the floor. "How could you do this?" He addressed his question to both of them, choking on his words.

Julie adjusted the slip strap, a feeble attempt at modesty, and stared back at him.

Silas reached for his shirt, hanging from the chairback, and slipped it on. He began working the buttons without comment.

"You fucking whore!" Jim yelled. "And you! You fucking bastard!" he said to Silas. Jim pulled himself upright, his fists involuntarily clenching and unclenching. "I gave up my home! My business! I gave up on a young woman who adored me. And for what? For what!" he cried. "Can you explain me that?"

"For your salvation," Silas said, not bothering to look at him. Now he crossed to the bed and retrieved a single document lying next to Julie on the nightstand. He examined it in plain view of Jim. It was the mysteriously absent bearer bond, worth all their life savings. Negotiable by anyone who had possession of it. Silas folded it once, then ceremoniously tucked it into the front pocket of the shirt.

The earth beneath Jim Estep erupted.

"Awwwwwwwwwww!"

His cry started as a low rumble and built to a shrill crescendo as he charged headlong into the room. Dropping his shoulder, he plowed into Silas, driving him back, the two of them crashing into the chair and over, toppling, upending.

On the bed, Julie opened her mouth wide to ...
SCREAM.

———

Downstairs, Nigel arrived in time to hear it. There was scuffling on the floorboards above. Cullen was at the foot of the steps, both hands poised on the banisters, like he was ready to launch himself upward any minute, but stuck for some reason, his feet glued to the floor.

"What's going on?" Nigel said.

"I ... I don't know. It must be—"

"You stupid shit!"

Nigel brushed Cullen aside and mounted the stairs. There was shouting now, the sound of furniture crashing, wood splintering, glass breaking.

Nigel pumped fast up the stairs, kept his legs moving down the hall. Just then there was a shot—one quick *pop!* And another scream, this one even louder.

Nigel screeched to a halt just short of the open doorway.

There was a *ga-lumping* sound, then quiet.

Nigel peered around the corner and into the room. He saw Silas with his back to the wall. Saw smoke curling from the barrel of the automatic he held extended in one hand. On the floor, Jim Estep lay in a crumpled ball. On the bed, Julie Estep sat screaming silently into a fistful of sheets.

Nigel crossed into the room and checked Estep for a pulse.

"This ain't good," he said. "There are men gathering in town. They're Feds."

Silas crossed the room in three quick strides, bringing the flat of the gun down in a vicious arc. It struck Nigel on the shoulder. His arms came up instinctively to ward off the blows that followed. When the beating diminished, the room fell silent. Silas stood over him, breathing hard from the exertion. Soulful moans were coming from the bed.

Just then, Cullen appeared in the doorway wearing a wide-eyed expression. "What's going on?"

"Get him out of here!" Silas said, throwing a look to the body on the floor. "And take his alabaster whore with him. Get them into the basement of the church."

"The basement?" Nigel asked.

"Am I not making myself clear? Raise the deacons. Close down Nazareth Church. Call my flock to me."

Silas stuffed the automatic into his pocket, pushed past them into the hall, and was gone.

Nigel looked to Cullen, not bothering to hide his contempt. The inertia of Silas's plan had collided with the onslaught of justice. Game over. The foretold endtime come.

"Get his arms," he ordered Cullen, then crossed to the bed and dragged Julie out by the hair. He shoved her harshly, sending her stumbling over her husband's body. The woman, hysterical, quickly crab-crawled into a corner, shrieking into hands that were cupped to her mouth.

Nigel crossed the room in a half-dozen quick steps and backhanded her to shut her up. Cullen laughed nervously.

"You grab a leg and help. Stupid cunt! And stop your sniveling."

Julie did as she was commanded, and together the three of them lifted, pulled, pushed, and dragged Jim Estep into the hall and down the steps.

In the yard, beyond the kitchen porch, Julie lost her grip and the sudden extra weight caused the body to slip from Nigel and Cullen's grasp. Jim Estep piled into the grass. Julie sobbed silently.

"You stupid shit!" Nigel said to Cullen, the two of them taking time to catch their breath.

"I was just—"

"Save it. I know what you were 'just.' There are Feds on the way."

Nigel lifted the whistle that hung about his neck and blew hard. He continued blowing, and within seconds Virgil appeared outside the men's dorm. He was followed closely by Harland. Seeing Nigel and the others in the yard, the two hustled to their aid.

"Glory be to God!" Virgil said, seeing Jim Estep's bloody carcass sprawled on the grass.

Harland said, "What the hell happened?"

"Pull some weapons. Silas wants the town shut down," Nigel said. "Then get everyone into the church."

The two men stood frozen in place, unable take their eyes off the corpse.

"Do it now!" Nigel shouted, surprising himself with the command in his voice.

Finally, the deacons spun into action, racing off for the shed.

"Make sure you keep them inside! Make sure!" Nigel called after them. To himself, he said, *Don't want anybody to get away.*

"What's Silas going to do?" Cullen said.

"Just get his arms," Nigel ordered, nodding Cullen toward the body.

They carried Jim Estep toward the church, Julie stumbling and sobbing along the way, Cullen continuing to drill Nigel with questions he wouldn't or couldn't answer.

When they reached the back door of the church, Silas's Escalade was backed to the entrance. The rear cargo hatch was raised, the motor was running. They met Silas coming out the door, carrying the red metal box containing the church's funds. Silas hefted it into the back of the vehicle. Opening the lid to the box, he removed from his shirt pocket a folded document, straightened it, smoothed it, and spread it atop the layers of cash. It was the Esteps' bearer bond, Nigel realized, recognizing it by its size and shape, the formalized imprint on the paper.

Silas closed it all inside the box and slammed the hatch.

"Daddy, where you going?" Cullen asked.

Nigel had never heard Cullen refer to the man by any name but Silas.

"Finish your job, boy. And when you're done, meet me at the munitions shed. You remember our conversation from the other day? Well, now is the time."

Nigel approached Silas. "What about the flock?"

"Just get everyone into the church," Silas told him. "Tell them to wait. Tell them, God's will be done. Tell them, the time is near and that I will be coming for them soon."

Nigel watched Silas slide behind the wheel, slip the Escalade into gear, and drive off. The time was near all right.

"You heard him," Nigel said. "Let's go."

They dragged Jim Estep, the three of them, into the church, crossed behind the front risers to the steps leading down into the basement. There they paused before the narrow passage, resting from the weight of the body a moment.

"You go first and shoulder it," Nigel said to Cullen.

"Fuck that!" Cullen said. "I'm tired of dragging." He grabbed the body beneath the arms, folded it forward over the feet, and gave it a shove, sending Jim Estep tumbling head over heels down the steps.

Julie Estep grabbed her stomach and vomited on the floor. Cullen danced aside to avoid the splatter.

"Aw, Christ, Cullen!" Nigel said.

"He's already dead."

"Just go on! Get down there."

At the bottom of the stairs, Cullen dragged Jim Estep to a spot in the center of the small basement and laid him unceremoniously on this back, his arms and legs splayed. Nigel led Julie to a spot against the back wall, where the furnace and water pipes converged. Across the room lay some wire, nearby the stack of lumber.

"Grab some of that wire and tie her up," Nigel said.

Cullen found an adequate length of cord. Julie began to struggle as he approached.

"No!"

Cullen shoved her against the pipes, pinning her with his body.

Nigel turned the job over to him, watching the kid as he wrapped the cord tightly around one of her wrists and began to tether it to a pipe that ran horizontally just above her head.

Julie bucked and jerked. Cullen threw his weight against her, hard, taking most the air and all of the fight out of her. Then he went to work securing her other arm.

The bare hanging bulb cast raw shadows across the room and penetrated the sheer material of Julie's slip. Cullen said, "Shit, looky there! All spread out like that. You can see her bush. Glory be! A dark one!"

"That all you think about?" Nigel snapped in disgust.

"Come on, look at her, little man. Don't tell me, all tied up, she doesn't arouse you some?"

"Some," Nigel said. He paused, seeing the way the kid's gaze was fixed on the dark triangle between Julie Estep's thighs. He said, "Go on then, you have to. Just get it done. Silas is waiting for you."

"You kidding?"

"Why not?" Nigel said. "Silas doesn't want her any more."

Cullen grinned. He stepped in close, using one foot to spread Julie's feet wide. She started to scream, but Cullen clamped a hand over her mouth.

"Go on. Squirm the way you did when my daddy fucked you."

Cullen's free hand started at the knee and slid upward, taking the hem of Julie's slip with it, kept going until it found the patch of black hair. His mouth was on her neck, his tongue licking, his teeth biting.

Nigel took one step back and leaned to gather a short piece of two-by-four from the pile.

As Cullen reached for his belt to undo it, Nigel brought the slab of wood around in a grand arc, a home-run swing that caught the kid on the back of the head. Blood splattered across Julie's face and the walls and pipes behind her. She screamed once more as the hand clamping her mouth fell away.

Nigel brought the two-by-four around a second time, sending Cullen off his feet to land face-first on the concrete floor. With Julie watching, eyes wide, he brought the two-by-four down with all his might, striking Cullen at the base of the neck, remembering that night in Kingsport, the mud in his face, the beatings, the humiliation, thinking of Silas—the bastard!—and knowing full well what it would do to him.

Then brought the wood down again … and again … and … one last time for good measure.

He looked down at the kid he hated so—a puddle of blood forming around his face—and somehow felt better. He wiped blood splatter from his arms and tossed the two-by-four clattering to the floor.

Julie had turned into a slack, whimpering mass, held upright by nothing but her bonds.

Nigel said, "Redemption can be hell."

And, leaving Julie Estep tied to the pipes, he turned up the stairs and left the church.

TWENTY-SEVEN

FALCONET ARRIVED AT THE entrance to Nazareth Church to find the huge cross lit up against the night. The floodlights were on, sending white brilliance against the shadowy darkness. There was hurried movement throughout the compound. Men were coming from the dorms, double-timing toward the gate, automatic rifles in their hands. He rolled on through, seeing one of them drop to one knee to unsling the rifle and bring it around. He gunned the Jeep hard, feeling the knobby tires tearing at the hard pack. Behind him, he heard the *stuuk-stuuk-stuuk-stuuk* of rounds unloading. He gave the Wrangler all the rein she had. Racing through town and into the draw, beyond the reach of the rifles, he watched the rearview mirror as armed guards now swung the gate closed and hefted a heavy beam in place to bar it. Others took up positions along the stone perimeter.

His thoughts were on Del.

Falconet arrived at the house, leaping from the driver's seat before the engine had completely stopped, and took the steps in one long stride, bursting through the door and into the living room. Del was already suited up: her Kevlar vest, bulky beneath a denim shirt; her weapon strapped on and hanging from the holster beneath her left arm. Mariah was on the sofa, biting her nails.

"I'm glad you're here," Del said. "What's going on out there?"

"They're breaking out the weapons and closing the …" Falconet saw the bruising around Del's throat and stopped. "What happened?"

"A little run-in with Silas. But I'm okay, thanks to my guardian angel here." She tossed her head toward Mariah.

Falconet crossed to Del and gently touched the purpling flesh, then glanced to Mariah. She was watching the two of them as though she'd never seen a man and woman interact in caring ways. Falconet gave her an approving nod, and her eyes came alight with pride.

"My mother is alive, Frank," Del told him. "And she's still in Nazareth Church. I believe I saw her in the laundromat that day I dropped off the clothes."

"You sure?"

"I'm certain." She proffered the square of stitched linen. "She left this for me as a way to tell me she's still here."

"What is it?" Falconet examined the cloth.

"Tell him," Del said to Mariah.

"It's called an ABC sampler."

"We were right about the name thing, Frank. My mother's name is now Sarah. See it there," she said, showing him the stitched autograph in the lower right hand corner. "And the moon there, above the cradle, just like the one on my baby pajamas. I believe Silas has kept her here all these years against her will."

"I've seen these things before, just like this," Falconet said. "That night in the women's dorm. There was one room with these on the walls. But there was no one in the room at the time."

Del moved to the table where her work bag still sat open, rummaged, and came out with spare magazines of ammo. "It all fits. It's the wives' dorm. I'm going after her."

Falconet crossed to her.

"Slow down." He relieved her of the magazines and tucked them into her shirt pocket. "Don't rush into it. We need to work this out together. There are men with automatic weapons down there, one of them took potshots at me. Darius gave me the go-ahead to bring Daniel out. If your mother's there, we'll get her, too, I promise. But we'll have to work together. Darius is pulling together a tactical team. As soon as we're out of harm's way, he's prepared to move in."

Del hesitated, but then nodded.

Falconet said, "Good."

Just then, the church bell began to toll. And behind it came the brain-numbing wail of the siren.

"It's Silas," Mariah said. "He wants us to come."

Del crossed to the window; Falconet followed. Leaning in over her shoulder, he cupped his hands to the glass to peer into the night. Outside, porch lights were coming on along the hillside; residents began appearing and moving toward the road.

"Actually, this just might be the break we need," Falconet said. "We can take advantage of the crowd." Falconet stepped away from the window.

"What about me?" Mariah asked. There was fear in her voice. "Silas'll kill me after what I did to him."

Falconet said, "I'm afraid you're going to have to stay here."

"No," Del said. "She stays with me. Your grandmother will be all right, Mariah. We'll send someone for her."

"All right," Falconet said. "But we just need to get moving."

Outside, the air-raid sirens seemed to intensify their call. The church bell continued to toll. Mariah climbed into the back of the Wrangler, Del behind the wheel.

Falconet slid into the passenger seat. "You ready?"

Del patted the Baby Eagle, the little gun with the nine-millimeter bore. "You're damn right I am."

———

AT the munitions shed, Silas broke open a crate of C-4 and began stuffing bricks of plastic explosives into a backpack. He added to it a handful of detonators and a timer, and loaded it into the back of the Escalade next to the metal box containing the money.

Now he had to wait.

At the door to the women's dorm, a couple of his wives could be seen exiting and making their way toward the church. That was okay. Where he was going there would be other women. Voluptuous and brown-skinned creatures eager to serve. Members of the flock were also appearing on the road in the center of town. Mariah and the dozen other daughters of Nazareth Church—his offspring—would soon join them to await God's judgment. That was okay, too. They were women, meant for service and nothing more. And when the service was through, well, it was God's way for the world. *But Cullen.*

Cullen ... Cullen ... Cullen ...

As progeny went, Silas had to admit, the boy had not turned out the way he had hoped. There was none of God's light at work in him. No gifted touch. No prophecy in his words. His mother, a sniveling woman, had gone on to meet the Maker some fifteen years ago now, leaving the boy motherless and without maternal nurturing since he was six. Nonetheless, he was the oldest and his only male child. Cullen would be leaving with him tonight.

The motor running, the driver's-side door hanging open, Silas crossed to the corner of the shed and watched the action near the entrance to the church. There was an anxious churn to the air fueled by the siren's wail, the church bell's drone.

What in God's name was keeping the boy?

———

NIGEL had begun to question his own fate. In the heat of the moment, he had seized the opportunity and beat the healer's son into a bloody, lifeless heap. Now the kid was lying back there. Was there remorse for the evil little prick? No. Just a smug and glowing sense of satisfaction.

But what now?

Nigel crossed from the church toward the dorms, spotting Silas down at the munitions shed. The Escalade was loaded and ready and sounding anxious to go with the motor running. Silas had a hand cupped to his brow, shielding the floodlights, and looking back his way toward the church. He was watching for Cullen.

It didn't take a genius to figure out that Silas was making a run for it. Planning for it with pressures mounting. Waiting, since that day in Kingsport, for the Esteps to arrive with the money. Fortuitous, it coming together in time. Now, the flock, the doting followers, were gathered in the church, awaiting guidance from on high.

Silas would dispose of them, without conscience. Eradicate the town and all in it to cover his tracks.

But what tracks? Where was Silas headed?

The Feds were on their way, so Silas couldn't simply drive off down the road. And the valley was boxed in by steep hillsides and jagged cliffs. A big man in the dark, carrying a heavy box across countless miles of snarled undergrowth? No. He would need an easier way out and transportation waiting to put distance between him and Nazareth Church.

Nigel remembered the car he and Harland had delivered to the abandoned logging camp on the other side of the gorge. Then he thought of the shack.

A whiskey runner's hideout.

Fitting pieces into the puzzle, it made sense. An outlaw would give himself an escape.

So what was it? A tunnel? A cave?

Nigel didn't know, but he was certain of one thing. Silas had a plan. Silas was planning to leave and take Cullen with him, or so he thought. The question was, where did Nigel fit into the picture? What exactly was Silas's plan for him?

Nigel crossed down past the dorms, hurrying on legs that never seemed to go anywhere.

Silas spotted him approaching. "Where's Cullen?" The first words out of his mouth.

"Cullen?" Nigel said. "Why, I thought he was here with you."

Silas glanced off toward the church where members of the flock were beginning to gather, anxious communications passing between them, furtive glances toward the armed men at the gate.

"They're getting nervous," Nigel said. "Wondering where their leader is."

"Then perhaps you should go stay with them, settle them down."

"You want me to join them?"

"Why not, you're one of the flock, aren't you?"

He looked Silas over. The man was looking off, watching anxiously for his son. Nigel had never considered himself one of the flock. Silas had given him a roof over his head and warm meals, made him part of the work, and gave him purpose. He was Silas's shepherd; that was the way he pictured himself. He was there to manage the flock, keep them moving, keep order among them 'til the *Time* came. But the *End Time* had come. Hadn't it? And now he was simply *one of them. Disposable.*

Nigel gave it a moment's thought, then pointed toward the gathering at the church. "You know, I think I see Cullen. That him helping Virgil with the flock?"

Silas squinted to sharpen his view. "I don't see him."

"There. That group milling around the entrance?"

Silas moved off in the direction of the church, taking some twenty strides, to get a better look.

"Cullen!" Silas called toward the church. The sound was drowned by the wail of the siren. "Cullen!" Silas called again.

With Silas still looking off, Nigel turned to the idling Escalade and climbed quickly onto the driver's seat, slamming the door and locking it. The sound bought Silas around, surprise and disbelief on his face. Now he was charging back toward the Escalade.

Nigel had never driven a car before, but thought now was maybe a good time to learn. He felt for the automatic seat adjustment, pressed it, and felt the seat move back. When it had hit its limit, he slid off to stand between the seat and the steering wheel. Silas closed on the Escalade, the big man striding toward him, purpose in his eyes.

Nigel dropped the shift lever into drive. There was pounding on the window, what might have been a work boot thumping against the door. There was cursing. Nigel didn't dare look at the man. Standing on one leg and hanging onto the wheel, he reached with his free foot to apply the gas. The vehicle lurched, almost toppling him. Silas was moving with it outside the window, pounding, cursing. Nigel tried again, this time holding tight and planting the accelerator to the floor. The Escalade's big engine roared. The rear tires spun, kicking out a plume of dust and gravel, then dug in. The SUV lunged off down the gravel road, Nigel balancing, hanging onto the wheel and craning to see over the dash. He glanced in the rearview mirror, seeing Silas, a silhouette in the dust cloud behind him, giving chase, almost catching him. But then, at last, the man no competition for the SUV's V8, he abandoned the effort.

Soon the big vehicle was on the river road, headed into the gorge, Nigel let out a deep breath, smiling to himself. *There, that wasn't so hard.* He was wondering to himself why the devil he hadn't tried driving before. Feeling accomplished and proud. Satisfied with what he felt was a major and successful revolt against his oppressor.

Only then did he glance over his shoulder, back toward the compound and…

Shit!

Headlights were angling from the barn. He recognized the Esteps' white Lexus nosing out, turning his way, then gathering speed fast as it raced between the dorms.

"Mother of God!" Nigel muttered to himself.

It was Silas behind the wheel.

TWENTY-EIGHT

DEL POINTED THE WRANGLER straight through the center of town, passing residents on foot making their way to the church. Falconet was in the passenger seat, both feet braced against the floorboard. Mariah was lying flat in the cargo space behind the seat. They reached the intersection beyond the General, where the road led down to the compound. At the gate in front of them, armed men turned their way at the sound of the vehicle. Del cut the Jeep left down the road and gunned the engine. There were more men in front of the church, ushering followers inside.

"They've got guns," Mariah said, peering from behind the seat.

"Keep going," Falconet said, "don't let up until we reach the dorms."

Del sped the Jeep past the church, on down past Silas's house, and slid to a stop in the gravel hardpack between the dorms. Dorm residents, stragglers, were exiting the buildings. Some, half dressed, ran to catch others to hurry quickly toward the church.

"Mariah," Del said. "I want you to wait here, inside the Jeep. Stay down and don't let anyone see you. Can you do that for me, honey?"

Mariah nodded.

"I'm headed for the men's dorm," Falconet said. "I'll meet you back you here in five minutes. Just watch yourself. And if you run into any of Silas's men, don't hesitate to use your weapon."

Del nodded.

"I'm not kidding. Put the fuckers down, you got it?"

"Don't worry," Del said, sliding out of the Jeep.

Falconet followed, and the two raced off, each toward separate dorms.

At the end doors of the barracks, Del encountered four women, wives of Silas Rule, exiting in a hurry. The first three looked at her as they passed and kept going. The forth, a smallish woman, had her head lowered as she fussed with buttons on a blouse. Del grabbed her arm and brought her abruptly around.

The woman, a stranger, stared back at her with surprise in her eyes.

"Ella Shannon?" Del said.

The woman's eyes formed a question.

"Sarah," Del said. "Sarah, where is she?"

"I … I haven't seen her lately. Maybe in her room."

Del released the woman's arm and hesitated long enough to watch her move off toward the church. Now she turned her attention to the dorm and went inside.

There were doorways on either side of a long hallway, stairs at either end. Del moved fast down the hardwood corridor, checking the rooms in order. Tiny quarters with sparse furnishings.

"Sarah! Ella! Ella Shannon! Mom!" Del called.

She finished checking the rooms on the lower level with no success, then took to the stairs, clearing them two at a time. She repeated the process along the upstairs hallway, banging into room after room, calling her mother's name as she knew it and as she'd come to know it in Nazareth Church.

"Sarah! Ella! Ella Sha—"

Del stopped at a parted doorway three rooms from the end of the hall. On the vanity sat an open sewing box, spools of colored thread visible inside. And on the walls were ABC samplers, a half-dozen of them.

There was no one there.

Del stepped inside, keeping her ears tuned to the night. She crossed to the vanity, taking in the articles there—a comb, a brush, a mirror, a sewing basket. She let her hands roam across the items. *Personal effects.* She removed one of the samplers from the wall, feeling the texture of the linen, the grain of the delicate stitching. She pictured the frail and sickly woman from the laundry. Imagined her, her mother, there, nimble fingers working with needle and thread. Del wanted to cry, but there was no time for tears. She wanted to scream, pull her weapon and begin firing. Let the Baby Eagle destroy it all, everything in sight. But there was no time for hysterics. Her mother was not in the building.

Del left the room and headed back down the hall. Her mother was alive, Del was sure of it now, somewhere in Nazareth Church. *And by God*, she affirmed, *I will find her!*

———

FALCONET found Daniel Cole in the last room down the hall on the second floor. He was in his bathrobe, sitting alone on the bed, his feet together, a Bible spread open in his lap.

"Daniel?"

The young man looked up at him blankly, then returned to reading.

"I'm Frank Falconet, Danny," Falconet said, hoping the casual form of the kid's name might coax him to reality. "I'm with the Federal Bureau of Investigation. The FBI. You remember us, don't you? Darius Lemon? George Racine?"

The young man's eyes came away from the page. "How is Darius?" he said. There was little emotion in his voice.

"Good," Falconet said. "He's good. He's been worried about you though."

Daniel turned back to his reading.

"I want to take you out of here, Danny." Falconet watched the young man's lips moving silently as his eyes followed the lines of scripture. "Will you let me do that?"

"God has plans for me," Daniel said. "I should wait."

Falconet studied the young man's face. There was a far-off, lost look in his eyes.

"Well, that's the thing, Danny. I just spoke to God, and He told me His plan was for you to go home. He said you're needed there."

The young man looked up now, meeting his gaze. "Home?"

Falconet could see the young man's mind working, searching for the concept. He would be sorting through filmy memories, conjuring half-formed images of a cheery subdivision, children in the street. Fuzzy pictures of a pretty young woman, a sandy-haired little boy, maybe trying names on them for size.

Falconet knew he had to be careful with this kid. "Yes. God said to tell you that He forgives you. That your wife forgives you. We all do. And that ... that you should go back with me now. You should go home."

Daniel turned his eyes back to the page.

Falconet gathered one of Daniel's hands. The young man's eyes came back to him as Falconet rose with it, coaxing him to his feet. The Bible spilled free of Daniel's lap, flipping closed as it hit the floor. He allowed himself to be drawn to his feet. Allowed himself to be coaxed toward the door.

"That's good," Falconet said. "Nice and easy."

Falconet led him slowly from the room, watching the young man's eyes for signs of life.

Somewhere down the hall, Daniel said, "Did *God* say anything about Brandon?"

———

DEL spotted Falconet crossing the compound with Daniel Cole and caught up to them, keeping pace.

"You didn't find her?" Falconet asked her.

"No, but she's here somewhere, Frank. One of the wives confirmed it. She must already be in the church. We've got to get in there."

"That's going to be risky. This place is ticking away, anything could happen at this point."

"I'm not leaving without her."

Falconet turned his eyes on her, assessing her resolve. Finally, he nodded. "Let's try the back entrance."

"Does God have plans for you?" Daniel asked, speaking to Del.

Del briefly studied the young man. She said, "You bet your ass He does."

They crossed off through the yard—Del setting the pace, Falconet leading Daniel by the arm. At the front of the church, the armed men were ushering the last of the residents inside. The doors were being closed and barred, and the armed men were making their way to join the others at the firing line along the walled perimeter.

Del tried the door at the back entrance—unlocked. They slipped inside and made their way down a short, narrow hallway that led directly into the sanctuary. Del forced her eyes to adjust to the semi-darkness. One spotlight above the altar was the only source of light in the windowless church. Out there, the congregation, shadowy figures, had taken seats in pews or were lined against the walls. She scanned the faces for her mother, up one row and down the other. Worshippers, some shifting anxiously, others waiting quietly, stared back at her.

"I don't see her, Frank," Del said, still scanning the congregation. "She has to be here somewhere."

Falconet's gaze had moved elsewhere. He handed Daniel off to her and crossed behind the risers, to a narrow door. There was a puddle there, a bilious yellow spew where someone had vomited. Falconet stepped around it, opened the door a crack and peered through.

"There's a basement."

Del drew Daniel with her and crossed to the door that Falconet now held open. Behind them the congregation remained unmoved, some waiting patiently with hands folded, others praying silently in their seats. Falconet found the light switch and flipped it on, bringing a garish, yellow glow to the hole below.

And, with it, the weak and sad cry of a woman.

"There's someone down there," Falconet said.

"Mom!" Del called.

She abandoned her hold on Daniel and charged down the stairs. There was hope in her heart, the swell of it holding until she hit the bottom step and saw the improbable scene in the room below.

Julie Estep, not her mother, stared back at her across the bloodied space, a pitiful and plaintive look showing through muddied mascara and spatters of blood. On the floor lay her husband. And across from him the bludgeoned body of Cullen Rule.

Falconet arrived with Daniel in tow. "What the fu …!"

There was a long moment. Each coming to terms with it.

"He did this!" Julie cried, breaking the silence. "Silas killed Jim and … " Her voice trailed off as her eyes fixed again on her husband's body.

Del crossed quickly to her.

"Give her a hand, Danny," Falconet said.

Daniel obeyed, joining Del to work the bindings loose. Julie slumped as the last of the wire was wound free. Del gathered her arm across her shoulder, and with her free hand on Julie's narrow waist, she turned her from the wall. "Come on," she said to Falconet. "Let's get them out of here." She nodded Daniel forward, and together they mounted the steps.

Falconet remained behind momentarily, his attention occupied with the heavy safe beneath the stairs.

"Frank, you coming?" Del said.

Frank looked up, nodded. Del led the way up the stairs.

———

A nervous chatter had come over the congregation. Followers, lined along the wall, shifted nervously on their feet. Now, seeing the three of them reappear with Julie Estep—her ravaged appearance—guarded whispers began running back and forth along the aisles.

"They're crammed like sardines in here," Falconet said. "The whole freakin' lot of them."

"All but Ella," Del said.

It brought Falconet's eyes around to her.

"Where could she be, Frank? Tell me. I saw her samplers in the dorm. I asked one of the women for *Sarah*, and she told me she hadn't seen her *lately*. Lately! That means she has seen her recently. Goddamn it! Isn't that what it means? Where is she?"

"She's at the whiskey shack," Daniel Cole said, a quiet matter-of-fact tone to his voice. It stopped them both. Del and Falconet turned together to look at the young man.

"What are you talking about, Danny?" Falconet asked.

"The sick woman, Sarah, we returned her to the swamp."

"What do you mean *returned*? She's sick and you took her there?" Del said, the words biting.

Tears began to puddle in Daniel's eyes.

"Easy, Del," Falconet said. "Danny, listen to me. Is Sarah there now?"

"God punishes the defiant."

"Is she there now?" Falconet repeated, emphasizing each word carefully, giving Daniel time to assimilate.

Daniel nodded.

Del looked Daniel square in the eye. "Where is it, Daniel? Where is this shack?"

"It's up the river. In the swamp."

"I'm going!" Del said, and turned quickly down the back hall-way. She reached the door—Falconet, Daniel, and Julie forced to hurry to catch up—grasped the knob and pushed. The knob turned but the door didn't budge.

"It won't open," Del said.

Falconet came forward and threw a shoulder into it.

"They've barred it from the outside. We're trapped like the rest of the fucking sardines."

"What's happening, Frank?"

Falconet seemed to give it thought. "It's starting to fit," he said. "Yeah, since that night in the munitions shed. I kept puzzling about the C-4. Why that particular choice of explosives? Why not grenades or Claymores, if it's defensive weaponry you want?"

"Because it's not defense he's interested in, is it, Frank?"

"Exactly. Shit! I should have recognized it!" Falconet said, pacing as he spoke. "There's a hydroelectric dam a couple of miles up-river. Darius mentioned it to me, but I didn't give it much thought at the time. Look at it, I mean, the whole town is here. We're all no more than a few lousy feet above river level. Silas plans to blow the dam and wipe out Nazareth Church, as ..." He stopped.

"As what, Frank?"

"As ... I don't know ... culmination of some glorious prophecy maybe. Or to cover his tracks. I mean, look around. Where exactly is their inspired leader? There's a safe beneath the stairway in the basement, the door to it was standing wide open. That's what I was studying when you called to me from the stairs. It was cleaned out."

"So he split with the money," Del said. She gave it some thought, then added, "But why all this? And why now? He could have left with the money anytime."

"He was waiting for *us*," Julie said.

The tiny voice surprised them. Del and Falconet turned to the ashen-faced woman, standing behind them in the narrow hallway.

"I turned the bearer bond over to him earlier tonight," she explained, an almost dreamlike quality to her voice. "Four million dollars. Everything from our lives. Including Jim's business." There was a far-off look in her eyes.

Daniel joined the conversation. "God has called us here. Our time of repentance. The coming."

Del and Falconet exchanged glances.

"I don't know about the *coming*," Falconet said. "But we damn sure need to be *going*. We need to get these people out of here."

Falconet crossed back into the sanctuary and stepped onto the riser.

"Listen up!" he called to the congregation. Eyes turned his way, a quiet chatter ran through the congregation. "I don't know how to tell you this, but your leader has skipped out. He won't be coming back."

Now the chatter increased.

"He's taken the church's funds and he's gone."

"He told us to wait," someone called from the congregation. "God would have us obey."

"God would have you live," Falconet continued. "It's your prophet who doesn't give a damn."

"Blasphemer!" someone shouted.

An uproar of voices filled the church—cries of outrage and condemnation.

Falconet stepped from the riser and returned to the others, drawing them back into the narrow hallway.

"I think you made the natives angry, Frank," Del said.

"Yeah. They're not going anywhere except at gunpoint." Falconet turned to Daniel. "Come on, Danny. We have to get that door open."

Falconet pressed Daniel ahead of him down the hall. Del followed, coaxing Julie along with her.

At the exit, Daniel balked. He turned to face them. "This isn't right," he said. "Silas would want us to stay."

Falconet said, "We really need to get going, Danny."

Falconet attempted to push past him to the door. Daniel moved to block his path.

"Danny, come on. We really don't have time for this."

Falconet attempted to go around him, and again Daniel blocked his way.

Falconet tried once more. This time, Daniel grabbed him, locking him in a bear hug. The two men struggled briefly, Falconet trying to free himself of the young agent's grasp. Then, at once, Daniel pushed off, pulling Falconet's service revolver from its holster. He extended the muzzle of it to Falconet's nose.

Falconet stepped back, his hands raised in a placating manner. "Okay, Danny. Take it easy. We can talk about this."

Daniel's eyes became wet and weepy. "It's the time. The time of repentance," he said. "Silas will come for us. We must make ourselves prepared."

"Danny," Del began.

"Don't!" Daniel snapped, turning the muzzle her way. "And keep your hands away from that gun." He indicated the Baby Eagle with a nod.

Del showed him the open palms of her hands. She was aware of spectators, members of the congregation, gathering behind her near the end of hallway.

"Now, we're all gonna march back into the sanctuary, find a pew among God's chosen, and wait," Danny said.

"Danny," Falconet said, trying to reason with him. "This is not right. Think about your family. Your wife … and your son … Brandon …"

"Shut up! Brandon's gone! God took him and He's calling me to join Him. He's calling you, too! All the sinners!"

"It's just words, Danny. Silas Rule … these people," Falconet said. "They prey on vulnerability."

"Liar!" Daniel cried.

"Okay, okay. Take it easy."

"Danny," Del said, a tone that was calm.

The young man's tear-filled eyes came around to look at her.

"If God wanted these people to die, he wouldn't use guns and explosives to do it. He'd send famine or plague or a swarm of locust. Wouldn't he? You've read your Bible."

The idea seemed to confuse the young man. His resolve seemed to waver. The muzzle of the gun sagged toward the floor, and there was a moment when Del believed the troubled man might sink to his knees from the weight of remorse.

"Blasphemers!" someone called from the gathering. "The whore of Babylon sent by Satan to defy God's will!"

Now others joined in a chorus of condemnations. Del caught the stiffening in Daniel's body, the sudden rise of agitation in the young agent's eyes.

"Sinners!" Del heard someone cry.

Daniel raised the gun.

In the same instant, Del went for the Baby Eagle and Falconet charged. The first round of the service revolver struck Falconet low on the thigh, collapsing his knee to send him sprawling on the floor.

And in a heartbeat, his eyes on what he'd done, Daniel placed the weapon against his own temple and pulled the trigger.

TWENTY-NINE

In the parking lot of the Palms Motel, Darius was feeling anxious. The tactical assault team was suited up and ready, but now they were forced to wait while someone, somehow, somewhere, found a federal judge to sign the warrants. Equipment lay on the ground and inside the open tailgates of the vans. The men were gathered in small groups, talking, smoking, a few of them sleeping in the grass. Darius, his radio in one hand, his cell phone in the other, flip-closed the phone and turned to the men close to him. "Well, they found the restaurant where the judge is having dinner with his wife or mistress—one of the two—and now they just have to get his signature." There were groans from some of them. Others shrugged it off and went back to chatting.

Darius let his eyes run down the road to the west. He was thinking of Falconet and of Del, not liking the feeling of uncertainty. Had they retrieved Daniel Cole by now? Were they clear of Nazareth Church?

Just then the radio squawked. John Bender, his agent assigned to watch from the promontory, spoke to him in a scratchy voice.

"Chief, we've got activity in the compound."

Darius depressed the talk button, holding the gaze of the handful of team leaders who had gathered around to listen. "Talk to me," he said into the radio.

"They've barricaded the gate, put men with automatic weapons on the wall. There's church bells and air-raid sirens going off. Can you hear them in the background?"

Darius imagined his scout holding the radio to the air for him to listen, as the sound of sirens intensified momentarily. He said to his team, "Someone's tipped them off. I was hoping we could do this the easy way."

"There's more, Chief," Bender continued on the radio. "The residents have all incarcerated themselves in the church. They came at the first sound of the bell."

Darius depressed the talk button, said, "Where's our UCs? Have you got a twenty on them?"

"They're in the church, too."

"Ten-four. Keep me advised." Darius cursed silently to himself. Now he turned to his team leaders. "Call your men and mount up. We're moving on Nazareth Church."

"What about the warrant, Chief?" one of the men inquired.

"Call it sufficient cause," Darius said.

The men nodded their assent and turned off toward the others scattered about the parking lot. There was a flurry of activity as the teams went into action.

Darius looked off up the street, to the dark and vacant storefronts. The town had all but rolled itself up and tucked itself into

293

bed—eight-thirty on a Saturday night. It was an unlikely place for warfare, he told himself. But the shit was about to hit the fan.

———

THE Lexus, moving fast, banged and bumped through potholes and tire ruts, but Silas kept the accelerator to the floor until he was right on Nigel's tail. He steered with one hand, using his free one to blast the horn. He could see only the top of Nigel's head above the seat's headrest—the Escalade driving itself, it seemed. From time to time, Nigel's eyes would come into the rearview mirror, wide and frightened, but he somehow managed to keep the Escalade floored and moving toward the shack.

They passed beyond the last of the houses squatting at the river's edge and bored deep into the gorge. The wail of the siren and the toll of the church's bell were fading in the distance. The headlights of both vehicles bounced wildly, swinging left, then right, scraping first the riverbank, then the undergrowth on the inside of the road. Silas pressed the accelerator harder. Both vehicles bucked in the ruts.

When just a few feet separated them, Silas jammed the gas pedal hard to the floor, pinning the nose of the Lexus to the rear bumper of the Escalade. He held it there, seeing the rear end of the vehicle ahead threatening to fishtail. The gorge narrowed around them. The vehicles remained pinned, fishing in the loose gravel. Ahead, the shack appeared like a tiny illusion, its reflection shimmering off the water. Soon, the raft landing came into view. The end of the road approached fast. One hundred yards … seventy-five … fifty …

Silas backed the Lexus off a bit, then gunned it hard, ramming the Escalade between the taillights. He saw the rear of the big SUV fishtail right, then whiplash left. It dipped into a rut, came out, and rocketed off the road. With its wheels spinning free, the heavy vehicle went airborne, made a clean arc, then nosedived into the murky waters, sending a tidal wash across the marsh.

Silas drew the Lexus to a stop at the water's edge, stepped out, and came around the front of the car. Standing in the crossbeams of the headlights, he could see the Escalade nosed hood-first into the swamp. Its tail end, from the rear quarter panel back, was sticking obscenely from the shallow black water. There was no movement from within, no sound in the still night air but for the distant call of the siren and the church bell back at the compound. The money, the explosives, the inflatable raft—they were all out there. Thirty, forty feet of bog to reach them.

Silas studied the distance, gauged his chances of wading out in the sucking mud. What choice did he have? Keeping his weight on solid ground, he hesitantly stepped with one foot down off the bank, testing, feeling the cold water engulf his leg. Gradually, he shifted more of his weight toward the water and felt the bottom give beneath him. More weight and his foot punched deep into the silt and held. There was still no movement from inside the Escalade. Water was now beyond the rear quarter panel, encroaching on the hatch. The vehicle was sinking.

Silas studied the distance to the vehicle once more and brought his anchor leg off the bank and into the water; the silt beneath him gave further. Stepping forward, his lead leg now plunged into the muck. Silas tried to draw his rear leg forward, but instead of retrieving it from the mud, the action drove his lead leg deeper. He tried to pull back and felt the rear leg slip again. Each effort—forward, back, forward, back—caused the mud to suck him deeper, hold him stronger. In a quick, desperate act, Silas twisted and threw his upper body to the safety of the bank. Scratching and clawing, he dragged himself free of the swamp's grip and lay panting, exhausted at the water's edge.

———

NIGEL came to with a fuzzy memory of flying. The vehicle, weightless for long seconds, had catapulted in a lazy arc across the marsh, then slammed against the water. The force had been like hitting a wall, doubly jarring when the airbag exploded and punched him in the face.

Now he was in the dark. No light coming from the dash, no light coming from above. And it was quiet, like being in a cocoon or maybe a womb, surrounded by water. He felt like closing his eyes and going back to that dream place he'd just left. Go back to that safe, liquidy birth place.

But the water had broken through and was flooding into his quiet little world through the seams around the doors. He was lying in a puddle of it, the smell of dirty carpet nearby, his face wedged beneath the dash on the passenger side. Nigel squirmed himself around and got his feet beneath him. He began climbing over seats toward the rear deck of the Escalade. He pushed his way past the metal money box, the crate of explosives, and a solid vinyl mass that might be a tarp, which were jammed against the seatback. He found the hatch, found the door latch, and felt it give. Then muscled the heavy cargo door up and over, feeling it bang against its hinges.

Nigel stood on the rear seatback amid Silas's treasures and turned his eyes toward the land.

In the roadway, in the headlights of the Esteps' Lexus near the water's edge, Silas lay soaked and covered in mud to the thighs. He was staring back at Nigel.

Now Silas gathered himself and stumbled to his feet.

Water was beginning to pour in along the sides of the Escalade's rear cargo hatch. Nigel felt the SUV shift, felt a rush of water across his feet. Soon the SUV would go under, consumed by the swamp, the vile soullessness of it.

He called to Silas. "The SUV—it's sinking! Don't leave me here!"

"First you defy me! Now you ask for my hand in salvation!" Silas's voice echoed through the swamp.

Nigel thought he saw slithery things moving beneath the dark water. "Please! Don't let me go like this!" Then remembering the red metal box, he rescued it and dragged it onto the rear bumper where Silas could see it. "You'll want the money," Nigel said. "I can bring it to you."

Nigel waited, feeling the weight of the man's glare. After a moment, Silas placed the tips of his fingers to his temple and closed his eyes to the night. He could see the man's lips moving, silent language playing on his face, as though receiving word directly from the Host of Hosts on high.

"God speaks to me," Silas called from the bank. "He tells me I've been hasty. That my judgment of you has been unfair."

"I'm sorry!" Nigel said. "I'll do whatever you want."

Silas continued receiving. "God says, have mercy, spare this man who has served ye well."

"I can help," Nigel called. "I can. You need someone to set the explosives, I'm your guy. Honest to God, light the fuse."

Water had filled the front of the cabin, and was now rising past the back seat. There was movement in the waters beyond a jagged tree stump, slippery and unseen. Nigel kept one eye trained on that spot, as he waited for Silas's reply.

After a long, anxious moment, Silas dropped his hand and opened his eyes. "There's a raft inside. Put it forth."

A raft.

Nigel spotted the tightly packed vinyl block that he had mistaken for a tarp, and realized, now, he was looking at an inflatable craft. He didn't waste any time. He dragged it onto the rear bumper, held it there as he found the ripcord and pulled. The vinyl block burst to life, filling with air, and expanded over the sides of the opening. When it had fully inflated, Nigel slipped it into the water, hanging onto the hand rope that was strung through loops about the inflated sides.

"Load the money box," Silas told him. "The explosives, the box of detonators."

Nigel hooked the hand rope to the SUV's trailer hitch, to tie it off. He found the wooden oar that was floating at his feet and tossed it inside the raft. Then found the boxes and loaded them aboard. The weight caused the floor of the vinyl raft to sag. Nigel wondered how much more weight the raft could float. But he climbed inside, happy to be going anywhere away from the sinking vehicle. He picked up the oar and began stroking his way toward the shore.

Silas received him at the waterline, kneeling at the bank's edge to take the hand rope and drag Nigel and the raft ashore. Nigel scrambled quickly to solid ground, looking back across the distance he'd just covered. Out in the swamp the SUV was all but gone. One taillight—that was all—now showed above the surface of the dark water.

"Whew!" Nigel said. "I thought I was a goner."

Silas was staring at him, his eyes narrowed down to mere slits. And now Nigel saw the gun in his hand. The same gun Silas had used to kill Jim Estep.

"Come on," Nigel said. "Don't. There's still work to be done. The Feds, they'll be coming. I can help. I ... I can keep a look out."

Silas continued to glare.

"I don't understand," Nigel begged. "I helped, didn't I? I got the money and the explosives to you. They'd be gone now, see." He directed Silas with his gaze toward the shipwrecked Escalade. "Why would you want to do this now?"

"You ever hear," Silas asked, "the story of the frog and the scorpion?"

Nigel brought his gaze back to the man. He had to think back. Something about the frog giving the scorpion a ride on his back to get him across the river. The scorpion stinging the frog with his deadly tail once they were safely on the opposite bank.

Then remembered the punch line: "*Because I'm a scorpion. That's what scorpions do!*"

Silas said, "Guess which of the two you are?" He squeezed the trigger.

Nigel took the blast square in the chest, felt himself punched back and around to land face-first at the water's edge. Disbelief washed through him, his mind refusing to accept things that were oh-so-clear.

Lying there, he thought strangely enough of a time before Silas. A time shoveling horseshit off the grass at the midway. That time somehow seemed pleasant now. He was having trouble breathing, something gurgling when he did. He heard Silas's footsteps in the gravel and struggled to turn his face that way. Silas was standing over him, the soaked leather of his work boots at eye level.

He wanted to say something—tried to—but heard nothing come out. He wanted to get up, show the man he was still up to the task of helping but couldn't feel the lower half of his body. He wanted to take it all back but couldn't remember exactly what it was he was supposed to retract.

Silas lifted one boot and nudged Nigel in the side with it, testing his lucidity. He could feel the leather toe against his rib, and struggled to look up. Without further comment, Silas pushed with his foot and sent him rolling off the bank and into the water's edge.

Nigel heard the splash of his own body as it hit the water. He felt the cold drive into him. And wondered, oddly, where the smell of hot buttered popcorn came from. Wondered when the last time was he might have tasted some.

Wondered … wondered … wondered …

THIRTY

Lying in darkness, a single cover pulled to her chin against the chill, Ella Shannon heard the bells tolling and the sirens wailing. Her thoughts ran first to the man she knew would be coming soon. Silas. Then to her daughter, Del. They would both be coming. Ella believed this.

Raising herself on one elbow, she could hear the sound of vehicles approaching from far down the gravel road. Pain coursed throughout her body. The effort of rising—just that—had become a monumental task. So unfair, the cancer. With hope arriving in the form of her very own daughter, the curse had seemingly doubled its efforts to speed her end. It took Ella's mind back to a moonlit night long ago. A night hot and humid and filled with anticipation and static sexual tension.

The touch. It had been dirty, clammy, cheap. Silas's words, spoken breathlessly in her ear, had conned her with hope, telling her of God's power. The girl she'd been then was young and naïve and aching desperately to believe. That girl had allowed words, allowed the touch and all that followed, to deceive her. Roy—finding out—it had driven him mad with jealousy. Del had come along nine months later, nearly to the day—though not the result of the biological union with Silas, as Roy insisted on believing.

Roy had taken Del from her as an infant. Stolen her away to someplace. A location she'd never been free to learn.

And Silas?

Silas. *Ha!* He was no man of the cloth. He was the devil—Satan, Lucifer, the Shadow of Shadows, whichever name you preferred. Never satisfied with just one *touch* of anything, he had locked her away, here in this godawful shack. Coveting her away as his prize the way he coveted everything and everyone around him.

If there was one blessing to come of the entire sordid affair—be it fate or divine intervention—it was that she had produced a daughter, and her girl had grown up, beautiful and strong.

Ella drew her feet to the floor. Her legs felt weighted, difficult to move. But she managed her way to her feet and across to the window.

Down the gorge, she could see the glow of the floodlights. Ella went onto the porch, pulling the door closed behind her. Standing close to the railing and secreted in shadow, she watched as the cars appeared on the road. Headlights, two sets of them coming fast. She thought of Silas, and again of Del.

But then the accident.

She refused to imagine it involved her daughter. She couldn't think that.

It had been the Escalade, Silas's vehicle, that had left the road, splashing into the swamp. Her heart leaped at the idea of Silas behind the wheel. God, let it be!

But then, no.

Silas was stepping out of the second car and walking into view in the powerful beams of the headlights.

Ella eased farther into shadow.

Nigel appeared in the rear of the Escalade, which had stuck itself upright in the bog. She watched as Silas brought him ashore. Watched, further, as Silas drew his gun and shot Nigel at point-blank range. She felt nothing at all for the little man as Silas rolled him into the swamp. Next, Silas dragged a red metal box from the rubber raft and loaded it onto the rope ferry. He loaded other wooden crates and tied on the rubber raft. He used the drawropes to pull himself across, letting the rubber raft trail through the water behind.

Now, he was at the landing and stepping ashore, carrying the red metal box. In the light from the vehicle, reflected across the water, she could see the wooden crates below her more clearly now. The word *EXPLOSIVES* was printed in bright red letters across the sides. Ella expected him to come onto the porch and prepared herself for it. But, instead, he halted at the base of the steps, stooped, and deposited the box off to the side, pulling loose brush around to conceal it.

Ella, still hidden in shadow, waited until he had turned away before saying, "There's worry in your face, Silas." It brought him sharply around. "What's the matter, Armageddon not all it's cracked up to be?"

Ella stepped from behind the uprights.

Silas, a silhouette backlit by headlights, glared up at her. "You hear the warning sirens, woman?"

"Yes, but it's not the authorities that have you running scared, is it? It's her. It's Del."

"She's a mere girl. Why should I be worried?"

Ella took time to examine Silas's face, the cragged lines etched by time and deepened by shadow. "Because she won't stop until she finds me. You know it, and it's eating you alive."

"Go back inside, woman. You're not looking well."

Silas turned to go.

"You want a real prophecy, healer?"

The words halted Silas once more.

"My time has come," Ella said. "And God's telling me, soon, yours will, too."

Silas studied her for a moment, his deep-set, black eyes lost in shadow. Then he was off, crossing down to the rope ferry. He loaded the wooden crates back into the rubber raft and unhitched it. Then he withdrew a pocket knife from his trousers and used it to cut the drawropes that reined the ferry to the landing. As they fell away, he used his foot to launch it. Ella watched as the ferry glided off and banged to rest against a rotten tree stump, impotent in the middle of the swamp, cutting off all access to the shack. Silas climbed back into the rubber raft.

Nigel still lay facedown in the water. Off toward the compound, Ella could see the glow of floodlights against the fog. She could still hear the muted wail of the air-raid siren, the distant but imperative toll of the church's bell. Silas rounded the rubber raft and began stroking. He gathered momentum, rowing off up stream toward the dam. Soon, he was no longer in sight.

Ella remained on the porch for a time. The cool night air cut hard beneath her gown. She hugged her arms about her, feeling the weariness in her legs and in her will. Silas was on the run. The bright lights and sirens in the compound and Nigel's dead body in the swamp told her so. And he was taking Nazareth Church down with him. He was heading for the dam, she believed, picturing the bright red warnings on the wooden crates and imagining the cruel, destructive force of whatever they held inside. He'd be there soon, stringing fuse or whatever it took. And then he would return. Del would then be coming, looking for her, for the mother she'd never known. Or for justice, if that's all she could get. She'd be fully equipped for either and totally prepared for both. But walking into an epic disaster that no one could prepare or equip for.

Ella turned back inside. She lit a coal oil lantern, bringing light to the interior. She was weak, her legs threatening to collapse. At the dining table, she paused, leaning against it for support, waiting there for her body to find some last ounce of reserve. About her spun memories of the past, as old as time. All of them preserved in needlepoint in the samplers hanging on the walls. Each sampler had a cradle image stitched somewhere amid the rows of letters and icons; each cradle had the image of a tiny yellow moon above. Reminiscent of the one that had appeared in the sky above the cemetery that hot August night. Appeared as if to bear witness to the miracle that had come.

Twenty-nine years she'd been Silas's prisoner. Much of that time in this cold and hateful shack with her needles, thread, and time. Locked away. And unaware that freedom existed just beneath her feet.

The cave system. *Whiskey runners were a sly lot.* They had built the whiskey shack in the most inaccessible spot in the gorge. Across the swampy bog, on a tiny outcrop of rock against the sheer cliff. But a place, they knew, with its secret passageways and escape routes, running up through the hillside to freedom. *Jesus, the sick irony of*

305

it! Ella realized. She had learned of the passageways only after she'd grown too weak with the cancer to take advantage of them.

Ella wearily straightened herself.

The road out there was dark for now, the fog thickening. But soon the Jeep's headlights would appear, cutting through the haze. On uncertain legs, she crossed to the bed and stripped the pillowcase from her pillow. Then crossed to the wall and began removing the samplers. One by one, she stuffed them inside.

She had precious little life left. Hours? Minutes? It felt like less. And even fewer before Silas returned to make his escape through the cave. Would he leave her to die like the others in the flood? Or would he have pity and put her out of her misery?

She couldn't take the chance on the latter. Not until she'd finished one last task in this world. Something she had decided on ... she would not let Del find her. Because, to do so would further put her daughter's life in jeopardy. It would be too much of a burden getting an ailing mother, as well as herself, out of the gorge alive in time. And she knew that Del would try.

No, there was no time left for heroics.

She had come to the idea, lying there earlier in the dark, that she would provide for her daughter's safety at whatever cost. And she'd decided that she could do this, and maybe, just maybe, at the same time, exact some measure of revenge on the bastard who had caused it all.

Ella had made it right in her mind, before the first sound of the car engines had been heard. Now she reaffirmed her resolve, collected what remaining strength she had, and continued stuffing the pillowcase with samplers.

THIRTY-ONE

DEL PUT THE BABY Eagle on the congregation to keep them at a distance. She drew Julie to a defensible position against the door, retrieved Falconet's service revolver, and now, a gun in each hand, moved the mob back to a respectable distance.

"How you doing, Frank?"

"Hurts like hell," Falconet said. He was sitting flat on the floor, his back to the wall. There was genuine pain in his eyes.

Next to him, Daniel Cole lay in a bloody heap. Five feet eight inches up the wall, the minimum recommended height for a federal agent, was splattered what was left of his brains in a tight, wet pattern.

"We need to get you medical attention," Del said.

There was a conspiratorial rustling among the congregation.

"What we need is to get the hell out of here, before these people decide to tear us apart."

Just then there was a rattling at the door, the sound of chains being unlashed from the door handle, and now the door was swinging open. Mariah stood in the entrance staring at them. "I heard gunshots," she said. Her eyes were already wide, but seeing Daniel Cole on the floor, they grew larger.

"We're okay, sweetie. That's twice I owe you," Del said.

Falconet undid his belt and stripped it free. "Help me with this, will you?"

Del turned to Julie and nodded her forward. The woman, still in a daze, went to her knees and helped Falconet tie off his wound.

"Can you handle this?" Del asked, offering Falconet his service revolver.

"No problem."

She handed it to him, then stooped to slide under his arm and help him to his feet.

Julie moved out first, Mariah holding the door for them. And together, keeping their guns on the mob, Del and Falconet backed their way outside. They put their backs to the wall, and moved off toward the front of the church. Del led, Mariah and Julie followed. Falconet, limping but maintaining on his own now, covered their backs. From the corner, near the front entrance, they could see the men at the gate and others lined along the perimeter wall. There were two dozen of them, some fifty yards out. In the distance, beyond the perimeter, on the gravel road leading into Nazareth Church, were headlights. Five vehicles moving in a slow, steady convoy.

"It's the cavalry," Falconet said. "Darius and the assault team. He's spotted the activity in the compound and he's moving the team up." Falconet turned to Del. "We can't just leave them positioned out there. We need to warn them about the dam."

"I need to get to that shack, Frank."

"You fucking kidding me? I can't let you do that. That thing could go up at any minute."

"I didn't come all this way to stop now."

Falconet seemed to think about it. He said, "We're in position to flank these guys, get this place shakin' and bakin'. Maybe it would be enough to convince Darius to move in."

"Then, I say we bring a little bit of hell to Nazareth Church." Del drew Mariah close. "Listen, sweetie," Del searched her eyes. "Are you listening?"

Mariah nodded.

"You see that cemetery up there?" Del pointed off toward the hillside above the town. "That's high ground and out of the crossfire. I want you to take Mrs. Estep and go there. Can you do that for me? We won't leave you, I promise."

Mariah nodded.

"Go on now. The men with the guns are preoccupied. We'll keep an eye on you. You'll be okay."

Del and Falconet watched and waited as Mariah led Julie up the road past the edge of town and climbed the hill to the cemetery.

When they were safely there, ducked down behind headstones, Falconet said, "If Darius has a spotter on the ridge somewhere, he'll be able to relay information to the team. I believe all we need to do is scatter these guys; the team will do the rest."

Del took a position behind the church's cornerstone. She knelt, drawing her Baby Eagle, and fished spare magazines from her shirt pocket, tucking them into her waistband in front. Falconet took a position above her, standing. And together they scanned the fireline along the perimeter wall.

"Ready?" Falconet said.

"See the guy in the red plaid shirt," Del said. "I whiz one past his ear. You tell me if he craps his pants."

———

DARIUS, leaning against the rear of his Town Car, got the call from his scout on the ridge. The men on the firing line had received flanking fire and were now running for cover, mostly in the direction of the river. The gate was undefended.

"They're giving us flank," Darius called to his men. "Move in!"

The assault team moved down the road toward the entrance, using the vehicles for rolling cover. At the gate, one of the men dropped to a kneeling position in the ditch at the side of the road. He unfolded a handheld rocket, laid it across his shoulder, and lifted the sight. "Fire in the hole," he called, and pulled the trigger. The rocket zipped from its metal tube, streaked on a trail of smoke, and struck the gate just off-center. The blast ripped hinges from the anchored posts and reduced the barrier to a shower of splinters. The tactical team rolled through the smoking hole unimpeded and into Nazareth Church.

———

FALCONET held position, popping off loose rounds in the general direction of the retreating gunmen, keeping the pressure on, not letting them for a moment reconsider the fight. Del had repositioned at the rear of the church, moving with the retreat, chasing the deserters with high gunfire as they fled along the perimeter wall toward the river. He could see her back there, giving them hell and looking good doing it. He couldn't help but want her.

Most of the men had dropped their weapons and fled. Hearing the blast and seeing the front gate disintegrate, others had thrown their weapons to the ground and simply walked into the open, hands raised. These men were now waiting as federal agents fanned out about the grounds, taking up strategic positions, telling them, "Get down on the ground! Do it now!"

Falconet spotted Darius, the man in charge, stepping from his Town Car and coming toward him down the road. It made Falconet think of Patton or some other wartime general maybe, striding onto a beachhead and taking ownership of the scene.

He stepped into the open, smiling, and limped his way to greet him.

"Don't you guys ever knock?" The two men exchanged a handshake as they came together.

"I see, once again, you've picked up some shrapnel. I'm beginning to question your ability to cover your ass, Frank."

"Right?" Falconet said. "Friendly fire this time. It was Daniel. Blew his own brains out in the process. I'm sorry, man, I didn't see it coming."

Darius drew a long breath, a serious look on his face.

"Listen, I'd love to chat, but the C-4 I was telling you about, I believe Silas is on his way to blow the dam. The locals are in the church, refusing to leave, and I can't guarantee we've got much time, *capisce?*"

Darius lifted his radio. Clicking it, he said, "Charlie one, copy?"

When a voice acknowledged, Darius clicked again. "Clear the church and have the men pull back. Get everyone to higher ground, copy."

Darius waited.

"Ten-four," came the response.

Falconet said, "The girl Mariah and the Estep lady are up the hill at the cemetery. It's as good a place as any to move these people."

"What about the husband?" Darius inquired.

Falconet shook his head. "We've got a lot of catching up to do, believe me. But right now isn't a good time."

They watched as the team began executing his orders. Team leaders taking charge and organizing around Darius's command. Falconet liked this man. Would like the opportunity to work with him again someday. He was someone to respect.

"We need to get that leg some attention," Darius said, "but while I'm thinking about it, how'd your girlfriend do?"

"Fucking-A, right? I'd go through a door with her anytime. She's right down…"

Falconet turned toward the last place he'd seen Del, the rear corner of the church, but she was nowhere to be seen.

"The fuck? She was right…" *there*, he was about to say, but was now corrected by the sound of a car's engine starting down in the compound, headlights coming on. He watched as Del's Wrangler pulled away in a hurry and raced off. She made the turn and sped along the river road. Falconet continued to watch as she headed into the gorge. Seconds later she was gone.

"Shit! She's going after her mother. Darius, I need your car." Falconet stepped off, then stumbled, his leg giving way.

"You need medical attention," Darius said. "And I'm not sending *foolish* after *stubborn*."

"You can't just let her go!"

Darius said, "A week with her and you still don't get it, do you? The girl can handle herself!"

312

THIRTY-TWO

Fog now blanketed the gorge, frustrating Del, forcing her to throttle back. She was leaned up across the steering wheel, fighting the glare from the Wrangler's headlights, frantically picking and choosing from the ruts and ridges that pocked the roadway. She was aware of time, hyperconscious of it, picturing minutes and seconds ticking down on some LED counter that, when zeroed, would ignite a blast and unleash a wall of water, sending it rolling her way. Her mother, Ella, in the path of danger also, in a damp, abandoned shack, alone and ill. Del didn't know whether to scream or cry.

There was no time for either.

With a suddenness that almost made her swerve off the road, the taillights of another car came into view. Del hit the brakes and skidded to a stop just inches from the rear of the Esteps' Lexus.

Letting the Jeep idle, she sat there for a time, squinting against the glare. Back at the compound, the siren had ceased its wail, the bell had ceased its toll. Beyond the rumble of the Jeep's engine, the gorge lay silent. Del killed the engine and doused the Wrangler's headlights.

Why was the Esteps' vehicle here in the dark with the headlights on?

Beyond the angled beams, the walls of the gorge rose sharply on both sides. Between them lay the swamp. Cattails and reeds and rotted tree stumps protruded from the still, dark waters.

Del slipped out of the Jeep, pulling the Baby Eagle from her shoulder holster, and made her way along the inside of the road. She used caution approaching the Lexus, inching along its rear quarter panel to peer inside the open driver's door.

The car was empty.

Del paused at the left front fender, letting her eyes and ears adjust to the rhythms of the swamp. It was quiet—dead quiet. Through a thin curtain of fog, she could see the shack sitting on a narrow formation of rock, some thirty-five feet across the black water, the glow of lamplight coming from the window. There was a landing on either side, the murky outline of a raft—likely used as a ferry—floating useless in the middle of the swamp. In the periphery of the headlights, Del could make out another vehicle, a corner of the roofline, black, and a single taillight showing above the water. Silas's Escalade.

Del crossed through the headlights to the water's edge, keeping her eyes and ears alert.

There, in the shallows, lay the midget face down.

Del wondered, had Silas met his end in the Escalade? But from the exit wound in Nigel's back, she realized … no. Silas was still out there somewhere, armed and dangerous.

"Ella?" Del called toward the shack. "Ella May!"

Del waited, her eyes working to penetrate the fog. Silas or no Silas, if her mother was in there, she had to get to her. There wasn't much time.

Del shoved the Baby Eagle back in its holster, crossed quickly back around to the driver's-side door of the Lexus, climbed behind the wheel, and cranked the engine. There was sixty to seventy feet of roadway left, thirty to forty feet of hang time needed to make the opposite landing. How to get back would be a decision she'd have to make later. Del floored the Lexus, feeling the wheels spin, then dig in. The finely engineered vehicle accelerated quickly, gained speed, and hit the landing at nearly forty miles per hour. It went airborne, hung weightless, then hit the water short of the opposite landing, hydroplaned, and come to a jolting halt with its nose dug in at the edge of the bank. Del powered the window down, slipped quickly out and onto the roof. She clambered down across the hood and leaped the remaining distance to solid ground. Now she paused again to listen. Bringing the Baby Eagle once more out of its sleeve, she studied the shack and the swamp leading off toward the dam. There was a rubber raft drawn ashore nearby, its inflatable sides ripped and shredded, flattened and lifeless. Keeping her eyes on the shack and the swamp beyond, Del crossed to it, stooping to inspect the damage.

She imagined Falconet, Darius, and the assault team back at the compound in complete control of Nazareth Church. They would be working efficiently to extract the followers from the church. Would Falconet be coming after her? Not if he had any sense. The full weight of the night was upon her. This was her decision. Her problem to deal with.

Del rose and crossed to the porch. Loose brush lay in the path. Strangely, a trail of water led up the steps and across the porch. Del sidestepped the brush onto the steps, taking them slowly, one creak at a time. Through the window, beyond the end of the porch, only an angled sliver of the inside could be seen. At the entrance, Del put her back to the wall and tried the knob. It turned easily, and she let the door swing wide and away. Dropping to a kneeling position inside the doorway, Del flash-scanned the interior, the Baby Eagle poised and ready for anything.

The shack was empty.

Del stood. And taking one last glance back over her shoulder, she stepped inside.

The trail of water led into the room. Furniture had been pushed aside, an area rug rolled back. And, where the rug had been, a trap door now stood open.

So that was it!

Del thought of the whiskey runners, outlaws who knew better than to box themselves in. This had to lead to another way out of the gorge.

Del followed the trail of water to the opening in the floor. A wooden ladder led down; a coal oil lantern sat on bare rock below, weakly illuminating the darkness. Del listened, hearing nothing but silence.

"Ella?" Del called into the hole. "Ella May!"

Del let her eyes run about the room. The furnishings were sparse. There was an empty, unmade cot. A pillow, lying on the floor and stripped of its pillowcase. There was a single sampler left hanging on the wall, dangling by a corner. The ghost images of others, previously displayed, could be seen as unfaded outlines in the darkly finished pine. One last sampler lay at her feet near the open hatch, as though dropped or abandoned, or ... *left as a bread crumb, a trail to be followed.*

Del slipped the Baby Eagle into its holster, gathered the sampler from the floor and tucked it into her waistband, then climbed down into the hole, retrieved the lantern, and held it to the darkness. A second sampler lay on the rock several feet away. She gathered it and added it to the other one tucked into her belt.

"Mom?" she called into the darkness.

Nothing.

"Ella May?"

Del raised the lantern higher. The basement matched the size of the shack above. She was standing on solid rock, an unusual geological formation that jutted outward from the escarpment, a single piece of solid real estate at one corner of the soupy marsh. Against the back wall was a fissure in the face of the rock, a narrow opening large enough for a person to fit through. She was looking at a cave entrance, Del realized.

Del crossed the basement to the cave and held the light to the opening. At her feet lay another sampler. Extending the light into the opening, she spotted another inside the cave. Beyond that, only more darkness. Del gathered the sampler—another bread crumb—and tucked it in at her waistband. She wasn't sure why she was being led. Or to where. Or by whom. Was it her mother leaving clues to her whereabouts? Was it Silas taunting her to follow?

Del squeezed through the narrow opening to find herself in a small cavern. Off beyond, it narrowed into a tunnel and began what looked to be a steady upward climb through the hillside. Del gathered the sampler and moved farther into the cave. Twenty yards in lay another sampler. There, the cave began to narrow.

Holding the light to the steadily inclining passageway, Del stooped to retrieve this latest sampler. She saw, at the next interval, thirty feet farther, not another single sampler but what appeared to be the missing pillowcase from the pillow upstairs, sitting upright in the middle of the path, stuffed full and overflowing with samplers.

It suddenly occurred to her she could be walking into a trap. What if the cave didn't lead anywhere? What if it dead-ended somewhere just beyond? She was well beneath the level of the dam, the lake, the millions of gallons of water.

Del was standing that way, the thought a whisper in her mind, when she heard the hatch slam shut, and what might have been a deadbolt being jammed solidly into place.

———

ELLA Shannon stood over the closed hatch, the deadbolt securely locked. Her hair was wet, her body soaked and shivering. There were goose bumps on her arms. Her lips were blue. Water dripped from her nightgown, leaving a trail of puddles for a second time from the door to where she now stood. There were tears in her eyes and a hard lump in her throat, more painful to swallow than anything she'd known those long years imprisoned in the shack. It was a longing greater than all those she'd felt during the years she'd spent wondering where her daughter might be, what she might look like.

Ella unrolled the area rug to let it re-cover the hatch. Below, she could hear the muffled calls of Del pleading for release. She fought tears, tried not to listen, as she got her shoulder behind the recliner and began to push. The effort was draining, the chair reluctant to move on the worn surface of the area rug. She doubled her effort, drawing on sheer determination. Gradually the heavy chair began to slide.

Ella poured the last of her strength behind it, until it picked up momentum and was fully back in place above the hatch.

It was a terrible feeling to lock your daughter in a hole. But it was what needed to be done. Tough love, she'd heard someone once call it.

Tough as hell.

The plan had worked. She had waited in the frigid water the first time, for what seemed an eternity, beneath the overhang of the porch, crouched shoulder deep amid the cattails and swamp grass. Praying to God that Silas would come and go before Del would arrive. Praying that she, herself, wouldn't die before she could complete her plan.

Silas returned from the dam, rowing the rubber raft. Ella watched from the water as he dragged the raft ashore, pulled a pocket knife from his pants, and used it to destroy the inflatable craft. He then crossed to the porch, retrieving the red metal box from beneath the brush covering at the foot of the steps, and carried it inside. Next, he would be coming back out to look for her.

And he did.

Coming onto the overhanging porch, he walked the railing and scanned the swamp for signs of her. Ella remained sequestered amid the reeds, feeling her life slowly draining away.

Go! Please! Don't come looking!

The minute it took him to decide seemed to last forever. But at last, checking his watch, Silas returned to the shack. Above her on the flooring that protruded over the water, Ella could hear scrapping and banging, the sound of furniture being pushed aside, the trap door being flung back.

When the shack had once again gone quiet, Ella climbed onto the bank and went inside, leaving the first of two trails of water on the floor. There was little time. She could hear a vehicle in the distance, poking along it seemed, slowed by the deepening fog.

Silas was gone. She was sure of it. Off through the cave, with haste. The healer, being the only man in God's kingdom who knew exactly how much time this small piece of the world had left.

Ella went about laying her trail—the samplers—leaving one on the wall askew, leaving one on the floor near the hatch, then climbing down into darkness, dropping them along the way, spacing them every twenty to thirty feet apart. She finished, leaving the stuffed pillowcase far enough into the cave to give Del the scent of direction, adding a secret of her own among the samplers. Then returned to the swamp, to the frigid water and reeds, and waited for her daughter to come.

Del had come, as Ella knew she would, a daughter to be proud of, a daughter diligent in her pursuit. And she had followed the samplers into the cave as Ella expected.

Ella came out of the swamp for a second time, sapped of strength and operating on nothing more than sheer will. The hardest part— harder than the wait in the cold, vile swamp; harder than the years she'd spent alone—was to slam the hatch and bolt it shut.

There was no time left for regret, no strength left to debate it. With the echoing calls of Del's voice reaching her through the floorboards, Ella crossed in darkness to the tiny cot and laid down. She placed the uncased pillow beneath her head and folded her hands across her chest.

The weight in her heart and lungs was heavy, but there was an airy lightness in her head. What she'd just done was something to smile about.

And she did smile. Then closed her eyes against the night.

THIRTY-THREE

THE EXPLOSION ROCKED THE valley and sent a shockwave racing through the gorge. The sound of it was close and vicious, a rolling wave of thunder. Concrete and steel rained like meteors across the swamp, sending scaly inhabitants slithering for deep cover. The first cracks and groans of dismantlement began as the dam separated and came apart beneath the force and weight of water. The tidal rush that followed ripped free the soggy bottom, churning it into a tsunami that tore through the gorge, gobbling everything in its path.

The shack disintegrated. Its shards and splinters consumed by the churning mass to become part of it and race down the gorge. The Lexus, the Escalade, the Wrangler were all swept away like toys. As was Nigel, his body surfing the crest of the wave for a moment, only to be churned beneath and gone.

The first to witness the destruction was Bender, the lookout, high up on the ridge. Watching through his field glasses, he saw the massive wave gather force and begin racing toward the valley.

He could see the residents of Nazareth Church huddled together in groups along the hillside above the cemetery. The members of the assault team were scattered among them, their rifles slung now across their shoulders, all of them looking off toward the rumbling sound that had finally reached the ridge.

And he could see the black Town Car making the turn from the compound onto the road leading into the gorge, heading directly into the path of the flood. He lifted his radio and clicked it to life.

"Sir, you need to get your ass out of there, now!"

———

FALCONET and Darius didn't need to be told. They had heard the blast and were rocked by the shockwave that followed. Darius slammed the brakes hard and put the sedan into a power slide in the middle of the road. They were going after Del—now that the town was finally secured, and Falconet's bandage was bound tightly against the flow of blood.

"Goddamn it! We can't just leave her up there!" Falconet said. "There's no way out!"

His leg was throbbing, but his mind was on Del.

"You think we don't need to be going just now?" Darius said. "She's a resourceful girl. We'll have to put our faith in her."

Darius backed the vehicle through a quick arc, dropped the shift lever into drive, and planted the accelerator. The wheels spun on the loose gravel, dug in, and the sedan cut a path straight through the compound, across the yard, toward the high ground of the cemetery.

The powerful wave hit the wide mouth of the valley and spread out. The dorms caved against the force of water and collapsed into the flow. Silas's house was decimated, carried away in sections by the tide.

The church offered up the most resistance, standing its ground against the initial force of the blow. Then slowly, as its foundation unearthed, it too crumbled, drifted into the channel of flow, and was rushed away on the swift currents.

Darius pulled the sedan to a halt on the hillside below the cemetery, his eyes fixed in the rearview mirror. Falconet turned in his seat, watching over his shoulder, as the wide flood waters rolled and churned where the compound used to be. Now he turned the other way in his seat, to look out the side window toward the gorge. Del was up there somewhere.

He said, "I think I'm going to be sick."

Darius's eyes came to meet his. This time the man of wisdom had nothing to say.

———

IN the basement of the shack, beneath the hatch, Del had felt the explosion like an earthquake, heard the roar of water like a train heading through the gorge. Instinct drove her away from the hatch and into the cave, as the shack and its flooring above disappeared. Water slammed against the opening and rushed into the cavern. She fled into darkness, the lantern outstretched before her. Snagging the pillowcase of samplers along the way, she raced upward through the cave, scrambling for higher ground. The wall of water, churning in her wake, rebounded off the walls and filled the narrow passage behind her.

It was a race she couldn't win.

The wave hit her from behind, the force of it sweeping her from her feet, first lifting her aloft, then dragging her under. An inrush of water hit her lungs. The lantern was torn from her grip. In darkness now, she fought to find the surface and grabbed a momentary breath of air amid the roil. She coughed water from her windpipe and gasped to pull air in.

The churning swell swept her upward through the cave. Then suddenly, as one might expectorate a seed, it spit her sprawling onto the rocks. The tide now reversed and the surge ebbed back into the hole and was gone as quickly as it came. Del coughed water from her lungs, rolled onto her back, and lay in darkness. The sack of samplers, incredibly, was still gripped tightly in one hand.

Who had locked her inside the cave? And why?

Whoever it was, intended or not, had likely saved her life. Del lay in the darkness, catching her breath. When partially rested, she sat up. It was pitch black without the lantern, no proverbial light at the end of the tunnel to guide her. Del searched the pockets of her shirt and vest ...

Louise, bless your eternal soul! she thought, remembering the woman and the first day they'd met.

... and pulled out the gold-plated lighter, the one Louise had given her that first day they'd met. The one Del had carried with her ever since.

With a flick, the lighter brought life to the cave. Her clothes were soaked, the cave air cold. The pillowcase, stuffed with samplers, was now weighted and heavy. Del sat the sack between her legs and opened the top. In the light of the flame, she removed the top sampler and spread it in her lap, its colorful stitching wet and gleaming, the tiny brownish-yellow moon above the cradle in one of the rows. She removed another, spread it atop the first. She dug more samplers free, handfuls, and piled them atop the previous two.

When the last of the samplers had been removed, Del noticed something else tucked deep inside the pillowcase. Piling the last handful of samplers atop the others, she reached in with her free hand and removed a document. A bearer bond issued by a bank in Atlanta. Value: four million dollars.

Oh my God!

But … Who? How?

There was only one person Del could think of.

There was a swell of pride, followed by a deep and painful longing as realization set in. The image of Ella Shannon, her mother, came into her mind. A frail and sickly woman, placing it inside the bag. She had saved Del's life, then given her own. A mother's sacrifice for her only child.

Closing the lighter to kill the flame, Del lay back in darkness on the cold wet rock. And for the first time in a long, long time, she allowed herself to cry.

THIRTY-FOUR

"You realize this doesn't look good for the Bureau," Racine said.

Falconet was back where he'd started, in the hot seat across the desk from the elder agent-in-charge, in the office overlooking the Ohio River. Darius was in the chair next to him, both men feeling scolded for their role in what the network news and talk shows were now labeling a debacle.

In the days after the flood, four people had been accounted for dead. The bodies had washed up in various places along the river from Biden to Clay City. The surviving residents had been relocated to neighboring towns, to live with relatives or those kind enough to open their hearts to the homeless refugees. Questions were being raised about the community of Nazareth Church, about their rituals, their practices. Dramatic tales of snake worship and sexual perversion filled the media. There were theories offered up about the whereabouts of the sect's leader, the charismatic and now-missing faith healer, Silas Rule. Had he drowned in the flood? Or had he survived? And what about the money, the purported millions? Had it washed away in the current? Or had this messianic evangelist somehow escaped with it? Lots of talk, and everyone had an opinion that they bandied about as fact. The news media was, of course, spinning it all, raising questions as to whether the FBI had perhaps overreacted in their assault on Nazareth Church.

You had to be there, was the way Falconet saw it.

"What part of it don't you understand?" he asked. He was again wearing his leather jacket and T-shirt, kicked back in his chair, legs crossed at the ankles.

Racine sat forward, pressing his palms together, as if ready to pray. He stared across the desk at Falconet, his brow knitted.

"Tell me again who killed the son."

"Is this going to take long?" Falconet said, "I've got a plane to catch."

"You'll catch your plane when I'm satisfied with your answers."

Falconet grimaced. But he repeated the story, emphasizing each fact. "According to Mrs. Estep, it was Nigel Fontaneau who killed Cullen, bludgeoned him in the basement of the church, where Mrs. Estep was tied to the pipes, near the body of her husband, Jim."

"The midget killed the son?"

Falconet nodded.

"And Mrs. Estep was tied to the pipes because?"

"Because she witnessed Silas kill her husband," Falconet said.

"Because she was sleeping with him?"

"There was more to it than that, I figure."

Racine took a moment to think about it. "So, then, who killed the midget?"

"We believe that was Silas. Ballistics show the same gun that killed Jim Estep was used to kill Nigel."

"It's a pretty sordid affair," Darius said. He had been listening quietly, but now came to Falconet's defense. "What we know for sure, George, is that Silas Rule killed at least one person in cold blood, Jim Estep. We have an eyewitness, motive, and opportunity. We have Nigel Fontaneau, tied by ballistics. Based on circumstantial evidence, we think the preacher then blew the dam in an effort to wipe out the community and cover his escape. The result was one more death, that of Ella Shannon, Del's mother. That's three counts of homicide. Add on extortion, theft, not to mention charges of incest with the girl, Mariah, and possibly others if we dig far enough."

Racine shrugged his brow and sat back, shaking his head. "Still the media will question probable cause."

"There's every indication Silas made it out with the money," Falconet added. "Maybe as much as four-and-a-half million dollars. The first four of it the Estep woman claims came from her and her husband. We can figure she'll be willing to go before a grand jury."

"Yes, and we can figure this healer is on a beach somewhere in Brazil. You think he'll ever see justice?"

Racine swiveled in his chair, rose, and crossed to the window. He stood peering out at the river, the rising hills of Kentucky on the other side. Falconet and Darius remained quiet.

After a moment he threw his hands in the air and returned to his seat. "All right," he said. "Make sure it's all in the reports."

Falconet bolted from his chair and headed for the door. His limp was still noticeable but considerably improved.

"Frank," Darius called. "Be back day after tomorrow. I've got another assignment I need you for."

"Come on! You're killing me," Falconet said.

He waited, but when no sympathy came his way, he turned and left the office.

———

FOR the second time in little over a month, Del was back at the Tucson cemetery. This time to bury her mother. Falconet was at her side, limping on one leg, his fingers loosely laced with hers. Randall, her boss, was there, this time with a young Asian woman on his arm, someone Del had never met. Rudy and Willard, her investigative co-workers, were there as well. And Engracia, the former daddy-sitter, who had taken a job turning beds at a senior daycare center. Again the condolences came, each party to the proceedings taking time, in turn, to hug her, pat her, squeeze her hand, and drift away to vehicles parked along the drive.

The sun was low in the desert sky, reflecting off Louise Lassiter's headstone up there on the rise. Louise watching over them, as always. Would she be proud of her?

"That's the thing about the devil, Del. The devil knows how to wait."

She knew her mother would be.

It was only fitting that Del bring her here for burial. To her rightful place among her family. Such as it was. Del could not see her mother spending eternity in a place where she'd spent her life as a prisoner. Could not see it at all.

"You gonna be okay?" Falconet asked, when it was just the two of them left standing by the grave.

"I will be." She gave him a weak smile. "Maybe I'll go fire off a few thousand rounds at the range. That always seems to help."

"I'd like to stay, but Darius wants me back. I have a plane to catch. I'd still love to take that trip to Mexico together."

"It's all right."

And it was.

"Call me," she said.

They hugged, kissed each other on the cheek, let their hands trail apart, as Falconet limped off toward the car. Del remained graveside, watching him go.

Falconet had been a friend for a time. A confidant. And a lover. He had been her backup along the trail to finding her mother. They had come through some things together, and for that she'd remember him fondly. They'd stay in touch for a time. They would recall, in the months and years ahead, their handful of nights together—the lovemaking that had served more as a wellspring of comfort than a starship of passion.

Would it go any further than that?

Frank had an ex-wife somewhere back in New Jersey. And a teenage daughter. He had his work. Besides, he was an East Coast man. Tough and resilient for sure, but in more of a *bumper-to-bumper* sort of way. She couldn't picture him rigged for desert running. Chalk it up to summer romance, Del told herself, it was back-to-school time now.

Del thought of her mother. The casket lowered into the grave. Flowers wilting in the desert heat. Ella had sacrificed herself for her, hadn't she? Shown her the way to safety. Delivered up the money to her. Del believed it both a gift and a message to her, a testament of final retribution. A mother saying, "*I got him, see?*

There's no need for you to pursue any longer, child." Believing . . . *once done, forever finished.*

But it wasn't finished, was it?

Silas would have escaped with the box, believing it to contain both cash—several hundred thousand dollars worth—and the negotiable bearer bond worth four million. But Ella had somehow managed to snatch the bearer bond without Silas realizing.

It was a shortfall Silas would have discovered by now.

Del pictured him opening the box, somewhere along his escape route, to find the four million missing. God! She would have loved to have seen his face then. Had he gotten as far as Mexico first? Or discovered it on some lonely private airstrip halfway there? Whatever. But she pictured—wanted to picture—him finding in place of the bearer bond a sampler. One Ella Shannon might have placed there. A final *gotcha*! To let him know she'd won. And to rub his nose in it.

But, now, it was their little secret—hers and the preacher's. Which led to one other thing only the two of them would know.

Silas would be coming for it soon.

———

FALCONET watched the first-class passengers boarding and wondered why agents of the federal government were forced to fly coach. His wounded leg was hurting a little from the day's exertion, and he was feeling a heavy sense of separation anxiety. Or more than that maybe.

Lying in bed last night, the two of them, she had recounted the events at the shack, including her terrifying race for safety. Del had been propped up on one elbow facing him when she related the trail of samplers. Bread crumbs, she had called them. She told him about being locked below by her mother and how it had been a selfless act of love, the way she'd seen it. A mother showing her the way out but too ill to take the out herself. And she had described the inrush of flood water, how it had spit her onto the rocks, breathless and exhausted.

He had let his eyes run down the curve of her body, up and over the flare of her hip to where the covers were drawn mid-thigh. He could feel himself growing in appreciation for her, felt a need evolving that was more than just a physical attraction. It had come into his head, even before they made love this time, that he could get used to the idea of being with her all the time. He wanted to call Darius and tell him he wasn't coming back, like it or not. They could travel the Southwest, the two of them, maybe drive down to the Sea of Cortez, relax, do the tourist thing, drink a few margaritas together, try on goofy sombreros. That kind of thing. Would she like that?

"*Sure, fine*," she'd said.

But she hadn't put much into it. But then, facing the funeral of her mother, he guessed he could understand.

He told her he thought he could get used to living in Arizona. Was maybe getting tired of his job.

Quitting the Bureau? She had been surprised.

Well, maybe not quitting. Or maybe so. He'd been doing this undercover thing a long time and it'd had its costs. Why not? Maybe take up what she was doing. The two of them a team.

What did she think of that?

"*Sure, fine.*"

See, and that was just it.

What he was feeling was more than anxiety about going back to work. The feeling was more akin to heartbreak. Her eyes had lowered, not come alive with delight, as he had hoped and might have expected.

And when he prodded, "Sounds good, doesn't it?"

There had been silence.

He'd let the idea drop. Maybe it was his male ego that let him tell himself it was simply bad timing ... her mother's funeral planned for the next day ... just coming off a bad shock ... a traumatic experience.

But was that all it was?

Falconet heard his seating section called and rose to join the queue plodding its way toward the jetway. Up ahead, at a podium, a young female gate agent was collecting boarding passes, scanning them, and handing back the stubs. It would be three and a half hours to Atlanta, a two-hour layover, and another two into Newark. Then the drive up to Cliffside Park. There'd be time for a shower and a couple hours of sleep. Tomorrow he'd be back in front of Darius, getting briefed on his next assignment. Shit! And dealing with Jolana, the unofficial, after-settlement settlements that never seemed to get arbitrated in the court of law. Fuck!

Falconet reached the podium, extended his boarding pass, then suddenly withdrew it. He was picturing Del the way she'd been that night in Nazareth Church. The Del that had come to him half-dressed.

That had been her idea, hadn't it?

He remembered the way she'd reached across him—the two of them on the sofa—the way she'd pressed herself into him as she set his beer on the lamp table. The way she had liquefied at his touch.

The way she had drawn his face to hers. There had been passion in her lips. The longing for him genuine. "Your place or mine?" she had said. Not in a cutesie, schoolgirl way, but in the throaty, hungry way a woman says it. Serious in tone. And meaning it.

"Sir?" the gate agent was saying. Boarding passengers were crushing against him from behind, some of them grumbling. "Sir, your boarding pass?"

Faces were looking at him from the seating areas.

"I'm sorry," Falconet said. "I've gotta…"

Fumbling, he removed himself from the boarding queue and turned away. There had been something meaningful there that night. There had.

And he wasn't leaving town until he found out what.

———

FOR more than two days now, Del had felt a presence—returning to work, checking in with Randall, making arrangements for her mother's body: it always seemed to be there. A sense of shadow that would suddenly appear one step off her heel, but just as suddenly disappear when she would turn on it. That kind of thing. Even spending the night with Falconet in her house, she had felt it. Like a specter waiting beyond the door, or outside the window while Falconet slept beside her, snoring softly at three o'clock in the morning. Another person might have chalked it up to the willies. A post-traumatic reaction to her harrowing experience in the cave. Or *Death*, the Grim Reaper with the scythe, hovering near following the loss of a loved one. The feeling of now being alone in the world.

But Del knew it was more than that.

She had remained graveside until the pink and orange, water-colored sunset had turned purple, then faded to charcoal. She drove east from the cemetery in darkness, across town and out Tanque Verde Road, listening to the purr of the engine of the rented pickup. She was feeling the presence now, even stronger than before. And seeing a vehicle's headlights in her rearview mirror—back there in the distance, present, always present, and tacking with her every turn—reaffirmed her belief.

She continued on toward Reddington Pass, past the point where the highway narrowed to two lanes. Two miles farther, she took a left onto a gravel road, crossed down into the sandy wash, and came out the other side. In her mirror, the omnipresent headlights pulled to a stop on the paved road. The vehicle sat waiting, watching, then quickly moved off along the paved road and disappeared.

Del ground the gearshift into four-wheel drive and continued on toward the foothills, the rented pickup bouncing through ruts in the road. A quarter mile farther, she turned into a drive that led down a slight decline and into the dirt-packed parking lot of Scotty's Indoor Shooting Range.

The range was nothing fancy. Just a long, narrow cinder-block building with a high, corrugated metal roofline. Its down-range end was backed against the mountain. The parking lot was empty, and the building was dark but for a security light above the entrance.

Del waited with the motor running, watching for headlights to appear on the gravel road.

None did.

"You know just how to play this game, don't you?" Del said aloud. "Well, so do I."

There was a stillness to the canyon. A full moon had risen on the horizon. It bathed the road leading up to the range in a soft, clean light.

Del stepped out, retrieving her shoulder rig as she did. She slipped it on and adjusted it until she felt the weight of the little gun snug against her side, then rocked the seatback forward to collect her work duffle and the pillowcase full of samplers from behind the seat.

There were still no headlights on the road leading up. Del closed around the back of the truck and let herself inside the range, using the passkey that Scotty had given her.

The interior was like an elongated basketball court, narrow but fifty yards deep, well constructed. It had powerful halogen beams that could be directed toward the target area to flood it with light. The firing line was partitioned into a dozen sound-baffled stalls. Motorized cable systems ferried half-silhouette paper targets out to a chosen shooting distance, and shuttled them back—blasted full of holes—when the firing round was complete. There was a PA system, used for competitions—the line marshal's tool to call shooters to the line, instruct and command.

In front of all this were several seating arrangements. Sofa chairs and side tables were placed in comfortable groupings, where shooters could gather behind the line to chat and watch others drill holes in make-believe villains. Here the lighting was subdued, giving it something of a smoking-lounge atmosphere.

Tonight, the lounge and the range were dark. The PA silent.

Del dropped her work duffle next to one of the sofa chairs and opened the pillowcase full of samplers. Images of her mother, a frail and lonely woman in a shack, came to mind. She pictured her there with needle and thread, and felt the weight of time and heartbreak her mother had suffered, as though it were here, surrounding her now. One by one, she removed the samplers, and using a flashlight, began hanging them about the space. She found the breaker panel, let the flashlight beam run down the rows of breakers until she found the one for the entry lights and flipped it off. She adjusted chairs, positioned tools in her bag, got ready. And when she heard the first sounds of a vehicle on the road leading up, she killed the flashlight and waited.

———

FALCONET found Del's house empty, the lights out. The Tundra pickup she'd rented to temporarily replace her Wrangler was not in the driveway.

Fuck! Falconet thought.

He tried the front door, then crossed around the house to the back. Somewhere in the neighborhood a dog barked and continued barking. He let himself in through the unlocked patio door, found the light switch and flipped it on.

The place was as it had been when he left earlier. Dishes in the sink, bed unmade. The smell of her—a good smell—still present on the rumpled sheets. Back into the living room, clenching his jaw, he realized he had no knowledge of Del's life outside of Nazareth Church. Did she have friends? What places did she frequent?

There was one thing missing, he realized—Ella Shannon's samplers. They had been laid out this morning on the dining room table, the pillowcase draped across the back of a chair. Now they were gone. Could she have taken them to the cleaners? Del, alone after the funeral, looking for mindless things to do to keep her thoughts off grief?

It was going on eight o'clock. Outside the dog had ceased its barking. Falconet searched the house, peeking in drawers and closets, looking for anything that might be a clue. He realized Del's work duffle was also missing. Maybe it was in the truck.

Falconet returned to the front room, wondering about the samplers and the duffle. He was left only to speculate where Del might be. Then he recalled the scene earlier at the gravesite. Del saying, "*Maybe I'll go fire off a few thousand rounds at the range. That always seems to help.*"

Falconet moved quickly to the phone on the kitchen wall. He pictured Del taking her grief out on cardboard cutouts, maybe one with the name *Silas* written above the silhouette. He found a phone book and searched the yellow pages for firing ranges. The half-page ad for Scotty's—a name he remembered from their earlier conversations—showed the location in a small map. *Beyond the wash, off Tanque Verde*, the directions read.

With the dog barking once again, he was back in the rental car, gunning the engine, and backing out. Maybe he would look like a fool, giving up his flight, racing off to the range to find her. The climactic scene from *The Graduate* came to mind.

But, hell!

If she blew him off, he would have the entire flight back to Newark to lick his wounds. Until that time came, he was going for it.

SILAS came in the way Del imagined, eyes searching the darkness, ears cocked to the silence. She saw his outline framed in the doorway, a dark silhouette against the moonlight outside. Saw, in one hand, the outline of a gun. Saw him reach for the light switch with the other hand, toggle it and get nothing.

Del waited until he was fully into the room, and the door had closed softly behind him, before saying, "Silas!"

In the darkness, Silas swung the gun toward the sound of her voice.

Del moved stealthily along the firing line, keeping the partitions between her and the healer, letting the sound-deadening panels and the echoes downrange confuse the sound of her voice and her steps. When she'd crossed down the full length of the line, she waited, then said, "I've been waiting for you, Silas."

Once again, Silas spun toward the sound of her voice, searching the shadowy darkness with the muzzle of his weapon.

"You're not going to shoot me, are you, healer?" Her voice held a seductive quality. "How will you know what I've done with the money?"

"So, you do have it," Silas said.

"Of course." Del moved in darkness.

"You have once more defied God's will!" Silas said. "And you have once more defied me!"

She could feel his eyes searching for her in the dark. "You can cut the Bible-babble, preacher. It doesn't work with me." Once more she moved.

"What is it you want, girl? Money?"

"I've already got the money, Silas. Four million dollars."

"What then?" Silas's voice rose to echo off the walls.

"That's simple. I want to see you spend the rest of your life locked away in prison, the way you imprisoned my mother."

"How is your mother, by the way?" Silas said, a sneer in his voice. "I hear the adulterous whore sucks cocks in hell now."

He was moving, inching toward the last known sound of her voice, crossing up to the firing line, searching the darkness down-range, his eyes beginning to adjust.

Del slipped to the last stall at the end of the line. When she felt his presence beyond the partitions, she hit the wall switch and the powerful halogen floodlights filled the range. White-hot brightness struck Silas in the eyes, causing him to cry out and turn away.

Del moved quickly.

"God strike you!" Silas cried. He was searching into the brightness for her.

She said, "I'm here, healer."

Silas spun to meet the sound of her voice—behind him now—and stumbled backwards at the sight of her sitting in one of the sofa chairs, her eyes observing him through aviator sunglasses. Her legs were crossed at the knee, the Baby Eagle was leveled at his middle.

Del watched Silas's eyes move from her to take in the lounge. From every wall, nook, cranny, and post, Ella Shannon's samplers peered back at him.

"Do you like it?" she said.

"They're a dalliance. The work of idle hands."

"They're evidence, preacher. They tell the whole story. The story of how you held her against her will and used her. They tell of others you've destroyed."

Silas's eyes came back to her. When he spoke, his words were slow and deliberate.

"Where's my money?"

Del gestured downrange with the muzzle of the gun.

Out there, on the cable shuttles, twenty-five feet from the firing line, hung a row of twelve half-silhouette targets. The targets, eleven of them of them, had been used—bullet-punched, until there were softball-size holes where the hearts should have been. The twelfth silhouette, hanging just right of middle, had not been shot. On it, above the heart, was taped the bearer bond—Silas's money.

Silas's black eyes seemed to tighten down.

"Who are you? Who really?"

Del reached for her bag beside the chair and came out with a string of shackles. She tossed them toward him. The chains hit the floor and skidded to a stop at his feet.

"I'm my mother's child, healer. That's all, and I've come to see she gets justice."

Silas looked at the chains at his feet.

"What do you expect me to do with those?"

"I expect you to put them on."

Silas swept the shackles aside with one foot, sending them skidding along the firing line to gather in a heap against the wall.

"Get them," Del said, the Baby Eagle leveled on him.

"And if I don't?"

Del pointed the muzzle of the Baby Eagle downrange and squeezed the trigger.

Pop-pop-pop-pop-pop-pop-pop-pop-pop-pop.

The rounds struck the unshot target to the left of the bearer bond in a clean tight pattern and ate a large jagged hole in the chest. Before Silas could blink, Del expelled the empty magazine and jammed another in its place.

"Put them on, or I'll shred your lousy bond like so much confetti."

"That's four million dollars, girl."

"It belongs to Julie Estep, but I'll spend it to bury you."

"You're bluffing."

Del said, "Silas, before you misjudge my commitment, there's something you should know about me."

"What's that?" His eyes were ablaze with hatred; his voice, sharpened to a razor's edge.

She said, "I never bluff."

Silas hesitated and Del fired off a quick round taking the upper right-hand corner off the bond.

"All right!" Silas cried.

He hesitated. Then slowly, reluctantly, crossed down the firing line.

Del let the muzzle of the Baby Eagle follow him.

When he'd reached the wall where the shackles lay heaped, he turned to look at her. A hard-sly grin formed at the corner of his mouth. At once, his hand shot out and hit the light switch, and the range fell to darkness.

Del rolled quickly from the chair, taking a new position behind the sofa. She could hear the same, sound-confused footsteps that

Silas had heard earlier—seeming to come first from her left, then echoing off to her right. She caught fleeting motion in darkness and knew that Silas had gone for his gun. She heard more soft movement and turned her eyes toward the far end of the firing line.

"Whore-child!" Silas called, his voice coming from the right of where she had calculated.

Silas fired.

Del saw the muzzle flash, and in the same instant, heard and felt the bullet rip through the sofa next to her. She rolled to come up at the opposite end. Footsteps scrambled in the darkness.

"You defy me no more!" he called out, his voice coming from somewhere up the line.

Again Silas fired and again a bullet tore through the sofa, sending a puff of stuffing into the air.

Del slipped behind a chair.

"What's the matter, girl, you afraid to fire? You afraid you might accidentally kill me? Be robbed of the joy of seeing me wither away in a prison cell?"

Another shot hit an ashtray on the table, sent glass flying. Another came all too close, shattering the leg of a wooden chair. Now, there was no movement at all, no soft scuffling.

Del waited and listened. "You're not getting out of here," she told him.

"I'll be leaving over your dead body," Silas said. He was somewhere downrange.

Just then, the door at the entrance opened, and a silhouette appeared, framed by moonlight.

"Del?" she heard someone say. It was Frank's voice.

"Frank!" Del called, too late.

Silas's gun blazed, the burst cutting off the sound of her voice. Del heard Frank cry out and saw him stumble into the space, the door closing behind him.

"Get down!"

Silas blasted away, unleashing his rage in one long, shrill cry.

Pop-pop-pop-pop-pop-pop-pop.

He held the trigger down and emptied the magazine toward the door.

Del came up, leveled the Baby Eagle across the back of the chair, and fired three quick rounds ... *pop-pop-pop* ... into the muzzle flash of Silas's gun.

THIRTY-FIVE

It was three weeks after the incident at Scotty's firing range, Del and Falconet back together again for the first time since Falconet had been wheeled off to surgery.

Falconet said, "Do you feel robbed?"

"What, because I didn't get to send Silas to prison?"

"Just asking."

"It's over, Frank. It is what it is. At least he won't be around to hurt anyone else, ever."

"Well, I really am sorry about your mother. I mean, well, it just seems, like, unfair, you know?"

Del nodded.

They were under a straw-covered cabana—the beach at Cabo San Lucas—looking out from lounge chairs onto white sand beaches that snaked along the shore, to azure waters where the Gulf of California met the Pacific Ocean.

Del was in shorts and a halter top, the nails of her bare toes painted red. She had a visor pulled low over her aviators.

Falconet—God save Cabo—was wearing a Hawaiian shirt over a Speedo swimsuit, already looking tanned above the bandage on one leg, the cast on the other. There was a half-empty pitcher and stemmed glasses of margaritas on the low table between them, a soft breeze coming in off the water. Falconet was scanning a Mexican newspaper as if he could read it.

"You made the news, right, all the way down here," Falconet said. "Your picture's all over the front page, *La Jornada*. I can't read a word it says. 'La investigadora … something, something, something …'"

Del said, "The call I took on the hotel house phone this morning … Diane Sawyer wants me to do an to interview, share dirty laundry about the people of Nazareth Church. And Barbara Walters … wants to have me on *The View*. 'Women in nontraditional roles.'"

"You shittin' me?"

Del shook her head.

"And?"

"I told them both no."

"You gotta be fucking kidding?"

"Huh-uh," Del said with a shake of her head.

Del turned her gaze off across the waters, the ocean breeze stirring her hair beneath the visor. The death of her father, nearly two months ago now, seemed like decades in the past. The place back there, Nazareth Church, seemed more like something out of a dream.

There were things to be resolved in her mind: the loss of her mother, the incredible bittersweet memory of her in the laundromat. There was the overwhelming unfairness of the whole idea, coming so close to finding and meeting her mother after years of searching, only to come within feet of her before having the dream snatched cruelly away.

And there was anger.

Falconet was right: she did feel robbed. The woman outside could be pragmatic about it, but the woman inside was filled with rage. That woman wanted to see Silas strung up and tortured for years to come. If there was any saving grace, it would have to come out of religion, the idea of heaven and hell and the belief that Silas Rule was now burning in fires that never consumed and never ceased.

Breaking into her thoughts, Falconet said, "I've been meaning to ask. Were you able to collect the reward? Did they pay it out?"

Del nodded, "I signed it into trust for Mariah."

"Seventy-five-thousand dollars—the hell?"

"She has nothing, Frank. I keep thinking about her and wishing I had brought her back to Arizona with me. They moved her grandmother to a nursing home. Mariah's living with her aunt in Clay City. Which, I guess, is an improvement for both of them. Still … I worry what's to become of her."

"Mother Del," Falconet said. "I mean … I know you like the kid and all … but fuck. Seventy-five-thousand dollars."

Del shrugged. "I look at her, I see me, Frank. It's like looking in a mirror at who, and what, I might have been if Dad hadn't taken me away from Nazareth Church."

"You realize you just called your father 'Dad.' I don't think I've ever heard you call him anything but Roy."

Del nodded. "I guess it all seems different somehow."

There was a lull, then Falconet said, "What about Julie Estep?"

Del retrieved her margarita, sipped it, then wiped salt from her lips. "She got her money back. The bearer bond was clutched in Silas's hand. He was in the process of grabbing it from the silhouette when you blundered through the door."

"I didn't blunder," Falconet said, a pout in his voice. "I was looking for you."

"Shots being fired, and you step broadside through the door."

"It was a firing range, there's supposed to be gunfire."

"All right, I'll give you that one…Oh, and while you were down here on the beach, ogling the girls in the bikinis, the desk delivered flowers to the room."

"From Darius?"

Del nodded, taking another sip from her drink and setting the glass back on the table between them. "He included separate cards for each of us. Mine says, 'For a job well done!' Yours says, 'Get your ass back to work!'"

"That's my man Darius. They've already got another gig they want to send me on."

Del took time to look Frank over.

"How's the leg?"

"Which one?"

"Take your pick. They both look painful to me."

"You know, when I went down," Falconet said, "all I could think was, every assignment I get shot. This time—fuck!—I get shot twice."

"Maybe it's a message, Frank. Someone up above working overtime to tell you something."

"Like get another line of work?"

"Uh-oh, here we go." Del sat up, pulling her feet up under her.

"What? We could move in together. Start our own bail-bonds company, do private investigation on the side, why not?"

Del gave him a sideways glance.

"Come on! We'd be good together."

"Yeah, except that you draw gunfire like wool draws lint. What kind of good-luck charm would you be to have around? You're a lightning rod for bullets. Besides, Frank, can you see yourself working for anyone but the Feds? I can't."

Falconet seemed to think about it. Then shook his head. "I guess not."

Del took a moment to study him. Then picked up the margarita glasses and handed one to him. "Don't look so glum, Frank, it'll all work out. Maybe we'll get the chance to work together again sometime."

Frank brightened. "Really? You think so?"

Del lifted her glass to his. She said, "A girl with a gun … a guy with a badge … I don't see why not."

Del turned her eyes to the waters of the Sea of Cortez. She realized it was possible. And realized one thing more …

The moon tattoo had stopped itching.

THE END

ACKNOWLEDGMENTS

I wish to thank Terri Bischoff, acquiring editor at Midnight Ink. Thanks also to Sue Ann Jaffarian for her friendship and gracious support. And to Bobby Heege, the imaginative spark behind our Wednesday-night writing sessions.

© Lesley Bohm

ABOUT THE AUTHOR

Darrell James lives in Arizona. He is the author of *Body Count: A Killer Collection*, an anthology of fifteen of his short stories. His work has also appeared in the *Deadly Ink 2007 Short Story Collection*, as well as in the anthologies *Landmarked for Murder* and *Politics Noir*.

James won the 2004 *Futures Mysterious Anthology Magazine* Fire to Fly competition and was a finalist for the 2008 Eric Hoffer Award.

Please visit him online, at www.darrelljames.com.